Ruth Prawer Jhabvala divides her time between New York and New Delhi, where she lived for more than twenty years. She has published twelve novels including the Booker Prize-winning *Heat and Dust*, for which she also wrote the screenplay of the Merchant–Ivory film, and five volumes of short stories. She has written over a dozen screenplays for Merchant–Ivory, including *Howards End* and *A Room with a View*, for both of which she received an Academy Award, and she has just finished a screen adaptation of Henry James's *The Golden Bowl*. She was awarded the CBE for her writing in the 1998 New Year's Honours List.

*By the same author*

RUTH PRAWER JHABVALA

# EAST INTO UPPER EAST

## PLAIN TALES FROM NEW YORK AND NEW DELHI

ABACUS

An *Abacus* Book

First published in Great Britain by John Murray (Publishers) 1998
First published by Abacus 2000
Reprinted 2000 (twice)

A CIP catalogue record for this book
is available from the British Library.

ISBN 0 349 11249 5

The following stories originally appeared in *The New Yorker*:
'Expiation', 'Farid and Farida', 'Husband and Son',
'A Summer by the Sea' and 'Parasites'. 'A New Delhi
Romance' first appeared in *Tri-Quarterly*, and
'Independence' in *London Magazine*

Illustration on page 2 and page 146 by C.S.H. Jhabvala

Typeset in Electra by
Palimpsest Book Production Limited,
Polmont, Stirlingshire
Printed and bound in Great Britain by
Clays Ltd, St Ives plc

Abacus
A Division of
Little, Brown and Company (UK)
Brettenham House
Lancaster Place
London WC2E 7EN

# CONTENTS

# EAST

*Temple, off Chandni Chowk, Delhi*

# EXPIATION

I was thirteen when he was born. He was the youngest of seven of us, of whom only I, my brother Sohan Lal, and one sister (who is married, in Kanpur) are still living. Even after he had learned to walk, I used to carry him around in my arms, because he liked it. The one thing I couldn't bear was to see him cry. If he wanted something – and he often had strong desires, as for some other child's toy or a pink sweet – I did my best to get it for him. Perhaps I would have stolen for him; I never did, but if called upon I might have done it.

Our father had a small cloth shop in the town of P – in Haryana, India. Today this town is known all over the world for its hand-spun cotton cloth, which is made here, but when my father was alive he could barely make a living from his shop. Now we take orders from all the rich Western countries, and our own warehouse is stocked so full of bolts of cloth that soon we shall need another one. I have built a house on the outskirts of the town, and when we have to go any distance we drive there in our white Ambassador car.

On that day – a cold Friday in January – I stood outside the prison gates. I wore a warm grey coat. There was a crowd there waiting, and everyone looked at me. I had got used to that. For more than two years, wherever I went people had pointed and whispered, 'Look. It is the eldest brother.' My photograph was often in the newspapers; whenever I went in and out of the court, I had to walk past all these people with cameras, from the newspapers and from the television station. So when they took my photograph outside the prison that day, I didn't mind it. I stood and waited. My brother Sohan Lal was with me, along with some cousins and one elderly uncle. We waited and shivered in the cold. Our thoughts were only on what was going on inside. I kept reading the words that are carved over the prison entrance: 'Hate the Sin but Not the Sinner.'

When they opened the gates at last, everyone rushed forward, but they would permit only me to enter. The old uncle tried to squeeze in behind me, but he was pushed back. I felt angry with him; even at that moment I had this anger against the old man, because I knew he was trying to come in not out of a feeling of love but to put himself forward and be important. They led me through the prison, which I had come to know very well, to where the body was. Everything was different that day. The courtyard and passages were empty, for whenever there is an execution they lock all the prisoners inside their cells. The officials and the doctor spoke to me in a very nice way. They stood with me while we waited for the municipal hearse, which I had ordered the night before. They had put a sheet over the face. I uncovered it to see him once more, though I knew it would not be the same face. Then I covered it again. I stood very straight and looked ahead of me. They offered me a place to sit, and I thanked them and declined. They spoke among themselves about the other body, which no one had come to claim. They would have to cremate it themselves, and they were discussing which warders should be assigned to this duty. They had neglected to place an advance order for a hearse, so they would have to wait. I didn't know where the other body was; it was not with his. They must have put it aside somewhere else.

His name was Ram Lal, but we always called him by his pet name, Bablu. Besides being much younger than I, he was also much smaller in build. All our family, including the girls, are big; only he stayed small. I could lift him even when he was grown up. I used to do it for a joke. When I put him down again I would hug him. I often hugged him and kissed him. He knew I loved him. Before my marriage we shared a bed, and when he cried out in his sleep – he often had bad dreams –

I pressed him against my chest. He was six years old when I was married. A little satin coat was stitched for him, and he sat behind me on the mare on which I rode to the bride's house, with a band playing in front and cousins and friends (they had taken opium) dancing in the street. My wife's family made a good wedding for us, and he enjoyed it all. But he never liked my wife and she never liked him. From the beginning there was this between her and me. She tried to change my feelings for him and could not succeed.

It was not just weddings he was fond of but all festivals where special food is cooked and good clothes are worn. He didn't like anything that was old or ugly. He didn't like our home – two rooms in an old house in Kabir Galli, where we had to share a bathroom with eight other families. He was also unhappy sitting in the shop with me, because the bazaar is so crowded and smelly. At that time, the whole town was in a bad state, with all the old houses falling down and with dirty water from the gutters overflowing in the streets. In the old parts, it is still like that – in Kabir Galli, for instance, and in the bazaar where my father's shop used to be – but now there are also completely new areas, with bungalows and the temples that people have donated out of their black-market money. When we were children, all these areas were fields and open ground where we could play. He spent many hours there alone in those days. He sat by the canal or lay under a tree – whole days sometimes.

I expected him to be a good student when he grew older, because although he was so quiet, his mind was always busy. Even at night he was alive with those bad dreams he had, while the rest of us, heavy with food and the day's work, lay asleep like stones. But it turned out he wasn't fond of studying, and whenever possible he stayed away from school. By this time, with the growing market for our cloth, I began to get free of the debts by which our family had been bound hand and foot since my grandfather's time. There was nothing to spare yet, but when he wanted some little sum he could ask me and I was in a position to give it. He was fond of going to the cinema, and if it was a good film he would see it six or seven

times. Like everyone else, he knew all the film songs, though
he didn't sing them out loud. He never sang and he didn't
speak much, either; he was always very shy and alone, even
when he was enjoying himself in the cinema or at a wedding.
His face was always serious. It was unusual, almost strange, to
see him smile. That may have been because his teeth were so
odd – very small and pointed with spaces in between. When
he did smile, his gums showed, like a girl's, and when he grew
up and became very fond of chewing betel they were always
red and so were his lips and tongue.

Now I must record a small incident that I have never liked
to remember. It was not just one incident, in fact, but several.
The first time it happened, he was about nine years old. One
day when I came home, my wife told me that she had seen
Bablu taking money out of the metal box that I used to keep
under my bed. Her eyes shone as she told me this, as if she
were happy that it had happened, so I frowned and told her
he had taken this money at my instruction. She didn't believe
me. 'Then why did he say he was looking for his slippers under
the bed?' she said, challenging me. She said that he had tried
to run away but that she had caught him and given him one
or two slaps. When she told me that, I became angry, and
said, 'How many times have I told you never to raise your
hand to this boy?' For she had done it before – she is a strong
woman, with a strong temper – and he had come to me crying
bitterly and didn't stop until I had rebuked her. But when she
slapped him because of the metal box he never mentioned the
incident to me.

From then on, she was like a spy with him. She would
watch his movements, and more than once she reported to
me that she had awakened at night and seen him searching
through our clothes. I wouldn't believe her; I told her to
keep her mouth shut. She became cunning, and one night
she whispered in my ear, 'Wake up and see.' I didn't open
my eyes. I didn't want to see what she wanted me to, so I
turned around on my other side and pretended to be angry
with her for waking me. Next day, when he came to bring me
my food in the shop, I said, 'Bablu, do you want money?' He

said yes, so I gave him three rupees and said, 'Whenever you need money, I'm always here.' He was silent, but he looked at me as if he were saying 'Why are you telling me this? I know all that very well.' His eyes had remained as I remembered them when he was a baby. All small children have this very serious look – as if they know things their elders have forgotten – but with him it remained till the end.

People say that you can learn a lot from a person's eyes. The moment I saw that one – the other one, the one whose body no one wanted to claim – I noticed his eyes. Although he was dark-complexioned, his eyes were very light – like a Kashmiri's or a European's, or even lighter, for they had no color at all, so that at first it looked as if he had no vision but had lost it because of disease. I hated and feared him from the beginning. We all did, yet we had to tolerate his presence in our house. I even had to be grateful to him, because it was he who had brought Bablu back after he was lost to us for over two years.

When Bablu was sixteen, he wasn't like other boys – nothing like the way Sohan Lal had been at that age, when we had to find a bride and marry him off before he became too troublesome. Bablu was no trouble at all in that way – or in any other way. He never even smoked or drank anything. He was fond of nice clothes made of terylene, and modern shoes with pointed toes. He also grew his hair long, and to keep it in place used a costly brand of oil, with a very sweet smell. But it is common for young boys to be careful of their appearance. Sohan Lal also dressed up and sat with his friends outside the Peshawar Café, and they talked among themselves the way boys do, and when girls walked past they shouted. This behavior is to be expected before natural satisfaction is obtained in marriage.

Bablu, though he dressed so nicely, never sat with friends in the Peshawar Café. He was always by himself. Never once did I see him with a friend. He didn't care to come and help us in the shop or with the rest of the business, which was just starting to do well. Most of the time he stayed at home. We were still in our house in Kabir Galli, it was a very small place, but during the day the children were at school and Sohan Lal's wife liked to go to neighbors' homes to talk. So usually there was only my wife at home with Bablu. She didn't like it; she kept asking me to send him to the shop or find some other work for him, but I said let him be. Although he never did anything or had anything to read except some film magazines, I could see that he was thinking all the time. I had respect for him for being such a thoughtful person and not at all like Sohan Lal and me, who were always busy and had no inclination for thinking at all.

One night when I came home, my wife called to me from the other room – the one where our beds were put out at night, and also where I kept a metal safe I had bought when the business began to progress. When I went in, she wouldn't let me put on the light, but I saw at once that the safe was open; the bundles of money I'd had in it were gone, though the jewelry was intact. My wife was sitting on the floor. 'Quickly,' she said. 'Help me.' I squatted down beside her, and she put one hand over my mouth to stifle my cry. I saw that she had tied up her arm with a bundle of cloth, but already this cloth was soaked in blood. Neither of us spoke. I threw a shawl round her and, hurrying through the other room where the family were all sitting, I took her out into the street and put her in a cycle rickshaw, and we went to the hospital. There she explained that the knife had slipped while she was cutting up a chicken that she was preparing for a feast.

We didn't see him again for two years. At first I was glad he was gone, and I told a lie to everyone about how I had sent him to Ludhiana to look after a new business I was starting there. I even told this lie to Sohan Lal, and he kept quiet, knowing there was something it was better for him not to know. If only I, too, could have remained as ignorant! But my peace was gone, even my sleep was gone. Every night my wife lay beside me, and she too was awake, and I knew she was seeing again what she had described to me – the expression on his face when he turned round to her from the safe. He had raised his hand, and though she didn't see the knife in it she quickly put her arm over her chest – and what if she

had not done so! Even in the dark, I covered my eyes so as
not to see such a thing. I thought also of how he had taken
the key of the safe out of my pocket and had had it copied
in a shop, and of how he had thought all this out while he
sat with me at meals, so quiet and sweet-natured, and while
he had stood before the mirror and combed his hair up into
a wave, his eyes serious and pure like a child's.

So at first I was glad he was gone. Then I began to miss
him. I thought of the bundles of money he had taken with
him and of how unsafe it was for anyone, let alone a young
boy, to travel with so much cash. Secretly, I arranged to put
out a search for him. I changed my story and I told everyone,
even relatives, that he had run away – probably to be in films
in Bombay, like so many other boys. I inserted advertisements
in many newspapers all over India, in English and in Hindi,
with his photograph and, printed underneath, 'Bablu, come
home. All is forgiven.' The advertisements offered a reward of
two thousand rupees. There was no result.

During all this time only my wife knew the true story. She
kept quiet – even with her own family, her own brothers. She
told them only what I had instructed her to say: first, that he
had gone to Ludhiana, then that he had probably run away to
Bombay, where the film studios are. Her arm healed slowly;
she was often in pain, but no one knew what had happened
except me. Up to this time we had enjoyed frequent marital
intercourse; now we only lay silently side by side. I thought not
of her but of him – not of his turning around from the safe with
his arm raised but of his traveling alone with the money and
of what could have happened to him. She knew what I was
thinking, and to calm me she made those sweet noises at me
she makes at our children when they are sick or crying.

So two years passed, and in that time our new house was built.
The house was also intended for Sohan Lal and his family, but
because his wife does not get on with mine – it is the usual
story with sisters-in-law – they all stayed behind in Kabir Galli.
Of course, I was sad to see our joint family split in this way,
but secretly I hoped that Bablu would come back one day and

then I would find a wife for him and they would live with us in our precious new home. And then he did come back, and he did live with us – not with a wife but with that one, the other one, Sachu, he called himself.

Although the things Sachu had done and the way he lived only came out afterward in court, he seemed to carry them around with him, so that wherever he was the air became foul. He was small and thin, like Bablu, and except for his colorless eyes there was nothing to notice. He wore a dirty, torn pajama, and a dirty, torn shirt over it. Bablu, too, was in rags. All the money must have gone long ago and they were destitute. They were hungry, too. When I saw my brother fall like a starving dog on the food we gave him, I said, 'If you had written one word, I would have sent whatever you needed.' Sachu said, 'Don't worry, I've brought him home now.' Neither of them ever said much, but when there was an answer to be given it was Sachu who spoke. And it was he who said, 'Don't forget the reward – two thousand rupees.' He laughed, so I thought he was joking. It was always difficult to know what he meant, because his eyes were always blank like glass.

Our new house was built in such a way that the room where visitors are received is separate from where the family lives. This room is at the front of the house and is much larger than the rooms crowded together at the back, where we keep our cots and cooking vessels and other very simple furniture. For the front room we have bought a sofa and matching chairs and a table with a glass top, and there is a glass cabinet in which my wife keeps pretty dolls and other ornaments. Here we also have a television set and a radio. This room was now given over to Bablu and his friend, and they made themselves comfortable there. It was hard to see Sachu putting his dirty feet on the blue velvet sofa, but it was better than to have him in the back of the house with the family. So I kept quiet, and my wife also kept quiet. She had to – the same way she had to about the wound in her arm. We didn't even speak out our fear to each other.

When Sachu asked me again for the two-thousand-rupee reward, I gave it to him. After all, it was his right. And when he asked me, 'Aren't you grateful I brought him home to you?' I said yes. It was true. Now at least I knew where Bablu was – in the front of my own house – and I did not have to imagine what his fate might be. He was alive and well! – and now that he ate good food and slept comfortably he was very well! I had never seen him so happy before. I have mentioned how rarely he smiled and looked glad, but now he did it all the time, showing his little pointed teeth and his gums stained red with betel. For the first time, he had a friend whom he loved. They were together all the time. They sat side by side on the low wall around our house, swinging their feet and holding hands, the way friends do. They both liked playing the radio and watching television. Once I saw them dancing together, holding each other the way English people dance. I had to smile then, because it was a strange sight and also nice for me to see Bablu enjoying himself. I began to think that my fears were foolish and that it was good for him to have Sachu as a friend. I can't say they were any trouble to us. My wife also had no complaints on that score. They were never disrespectful, and they behaved decently. They didn't mix very much with us but kept themselves apart in the front room. They even ate their meals there, brought to them by the servant boy we kept in the house.

Although he has nothing to do with what happened later, I must say something about this servant boy. Before he came to us he was working in a tea stall, serving customers and washing cups and plates in a bucket in the back. He also slept there at night. He had no other home and no family; no one knew where he came from. He was about twelve or thirteen years old. He couldn't read or write, but he was a willing worker. When Sachu and Bablu came, this boy changed completely. Now all he wanted was to be near them. He would sit in the doorway of the front room, waiting for them to send him out for betel or cool drinks, or to take their clothes to the washerman. They had good clothes now and were very careful to have them always nicely washed and pressed. I have seen this boy arranging their clothes and touching the fine cloth as if he were touching a woman. When my wife called him he pretended not to hear; perhaps he really didn't hear her, because all his attention was focused on those two. He tried to comb his hair up in a wave like theirs, and he begged my wife to buy him bell-bottom pants instead of the khaki shorts she had given him. Later, after the two were no longer with us, this boy became worse and worse. He mixed with bad characters and hung around the bazaar and cinema with them. He stayed out all night and could never be found for work, until at last my wife dismissed him. He got a job as a servant in another house but soon disappeared from there with money and valuables. A report was lodged with the police, but he never was found. Probably he got on a train and went to some other town. There are millions like him, and no one can tell one from the other. They eat where they can, sleep where they can, and if they get into trouble in one place they move on to another. They may end up in jail on some case that never comes up for trial, they may die of some disease, or they may live a few years longer. No one cares where they are or what happens to them. There are too many of them.

That was Sachu's defense for his crime: no one cared for him, so he cared for no one. The time of the trial and afterward, after the sentence, was Sachu's great hour. He became a big man and gave interviews to journalists and made them listen to his philosophy. He boasted of all the crimes he committed before he came to our town. He had been in jail many times, he said, but he had never been convicted of any of the other murders to which he now admitted. He said he would kill anyone if he wanted something they had, even if it was only a ring that he liked. He said that human beings were not born to be poor, otherwise why should the earth be so full of riches, with mines full of gold and precious gems, and with pearls scattered in the ocean? His father had pulled a handcart for a living and had had nine children. Probably those who had survived were all pulling handcarts now – all except him, Sachu. He had wanted something else, and if it had brought him death on the gallows, all right, he was ready. He had always been different from his family; he had run away from them at the age of ten, when he had overheard his father and elder brothers planning to break his leg in order to make him change his bad ways. Since that day he had been on his own.

My prayer to be relieved of their crime has been answered, so that it is no longer before my eyes day and night. Now it is as if it were locked away in a heavy steel trunk; this weight may be taken from me at my last hour, but until then I carry it inside myself, where only God and I know of its constant presence. After a while there is nothing more you can do or suffer. I have also prayed on behalf of the father of the victim – that the man's suffering may be made bearable for him, if such a thing were possible. Day after day I was with this man in the courtroom, but I can say nothing of his appearance, because not once in all that time did I dare to raise my eyes and look at him.

The famous Parsi lawyer I engaged for Bablu's defense believed that they never intended to kill the boy but meant to release him, after collecting the ransom money. Very likely this is true. It is certainly true that while they were living in my house they made their plan to kidnap him. At that time there was a popular film playing about a dacoit who kidnapped a high-born girl for money, but then he fell in love with her and she reformed his ways. It was one of those stupid Bombay films that people like, including my wife, who made me take her to see it because her favorite actor was in it. A mother with three children, but still she has a favorite actor! Sachu and Bablu went four or five times, and they knew all the songs and dialogue by heart. So the idea of kidnap must have gotten into their heads. There were enough rich people in our town – many of them like myself, who a few years ago were only humble shopkeepers and were caught up in the big boom in cotton cloth. Such people spent a lot of money on themselves and their children and lived like millionaires; some of them already *were* millionaires. However, it was not one of their children who was chosen.

P – is a cantonment town, and we have always had a

regiment stationed here. The cantonment area is quite separate. It has wide roads and brick barracks, and the officers
live in bungalows with gardens. Everything is very clean
and very well kept up. The soldiers are healthy and sturdy
and look quite different from the townspeople. The officers
and their families are like higher beings; they are well-built,
with light complexions, and they are educated gentry, speaking
English with each other. Some of them even speak Hindi with
an English accent, like foreigners – like sahibs. They also live
like sahibs in their big bungalows, and drink whisky-and-soda,
and their cooks prepare English-style food for them, with roast
meat. The boy's father was the commanding officer – he had
the rank of colonel – and his memsahib, the boy's mother,
was from one of the princely families who have lost their title
but still have houses and land. (She has since passed away.)
The boy was their only child, and they had sent him to a
boarding school in the hills to get a good education. The
reason he was in the cantonment at that time was that there
had been a measles epidemic in the school; all the unaffected
children had been sent home as a precaution, to safeguard
their health.

Everyone knows what the boy looked like. His photograph
has been in the newspapers as often as Bablu's and Sachu's.
Sometimes all three photos were on the same page, and even
though they were not clear in the newsprint it was evident that
the boy was of a different type from the other two – as if he
came from some different stock or species of human being. In
Sachu's interviews with the newspaper reporters, he sounded
as if he hated the boy, because the boy was plump, with big
eyes and a light complexion, and wore a very good blue coat,
with the badge of his school on the pocket. And because he
had roller skates. No one had heard of roller skates in our town
till the boy was seen with them. His parents had brought them
as a present for him from abroad, and the boy loved them so
much that he went on them everywhere, as with wings under
his feet.

It was because of these roller skates that Bablu and Sachu
were discovered very quickly. It was also all they got from

their crime, for although the father had put the ransom money in the place they had indicated, they did not dare collect it after killing the boy. They had so little cash that they had to sneak on to a train as ticketless travelers. When an inspector came, they had to jump off. This was in a town less than two hundred miles from ours. They took a room in a hotel in a bad part of town, and they never came out except at night, when one of them went to buy gram, which was all the food they could afford. Their room was very small, with only one bed and an old fan, but here Sachu tried to learn to roller-skate. This made the whole house shake, as if it were in an earthquake, and everyone in the hotel wondered what was happening. They also heard the noise of someone falling, and then the two young men laughing in enjoyment, so they tapped on the door of their room to inquire. Sachu let them come in and look, because he was so proud of learning to roller-skate. Everyone smiled and enjoyed his feat, but when there was news everywhere of a boy killed and of his missing roller skates the police were informed at once.

Up to that time, the two of them had been lucky, even though their crime had not been well-planned. They had stolen a car from outside the interstate bus depot, and had waited near the cantonment for the boy to pass on his roller skates. They had no difficulty getting into conversation with him; he was frank and open in his manner – everyone said so later – and was always glad to talk to people and to make friends. They got him into the car and drove him to the place they had chosen for their hideout. Here they tied him up with chains, and Sachu – Bablu couldn't drive – took the car to the other side of town and abandoned it there. It was found by the police the same day, though they found the boy only when he was dead.

There are many places where a person can hide around our town. Important battles have been fought here, and it has been destroyed and built up again many times. Ruins are all around – the foundation of beautiful cities, with the remains of tombs, mosques, and bathing tanks. Since it is a very dry area, very little vegetation has grown, and there are only mounds of rubble and dust, where jackals live and can be heard howling at night. The two took the boy down into a bathing tank, which had been dug so deep into the earth that there were forty steps descending into it. All round the tank were arched niches like rooms. In olden days, it must have been a beautiful, cool place for royal people to bathe and rest and take enjoyment. Now the tank is empty and dry. They kept the boy in one of the niches and stayed with him there for four days, all of them living on milk sweets.

After they were arrested, Sachu talked freely. It was as if he had waited all his life for people to listen to what he had to say. He was a person of no education, and could not express himself, yet words and thoughts always seemed to boil up in him and come gushing out freely. One thing he could never bear was to be contradicted or interrupted; he wanted to be the only one to talk, and others were there to listen. After his arrest, if any journalist challenged him or talked back to him, he went into a rage. Sometimes he seemed to fly into the same rage when talking about the boy; he spoke as if the boy were still alive and challenging what he was saying. Then anger filled his empty eyes.

The Parsi lawyer wanted to present the case in such a way as to show that Sachu had stabbed the boy with his knife during an argument between them. It was soon established that the boy didn't sit quietly and whine for mercy while he was being kept prisoner. He was a fearless boy and also a first-class debater who had competed for an inter-school trophy. He liked talking and arguing as much as Sachu did, and although he was seven years younger (he was thirteen), he was much better educated. When Sachu spoke to the boy about society and astrology and what is man's fate – the same way he later talked to the reporters – the boy could answer him and argue with him, and he could even quote from books he had read at school. The Parsi lawyer said that when Sachu was defeated by the boy over and over again in argument he became so enraged that he killed him. Sachu alone did it, and Bablu was innocent. And Sachu said yes, that was the way it happened, and then he boasted of the other murders he had committed, which no one had ever discovered.

But Bablu said no to the Parsi lawyer, that was not the way it happened. Bablu said, 'I did it – not Sachu.' Then the lawyer appointed to defend Sachu wanted to make a case that Bablu had killed the boy out of jealousy, because he saw that his friend was paying a lot of attention to the boy and spent many hours talking and arguing with him. The lawyer said that the boy was not only educated and cultured but also very handsome – soft-skinned and wheat-complexioned. (The medical report had established the fact that sodomy had taken place.) Bablu was ready to confirm what the lawyer said and to admit that he had killed the boy because he could not bear to watch what Sachu did with him. He confessed this in a very quiet voice and without raising his eyes – not out of shame, it seemed, but because he felt shy about talking of this matter.

All this time, Bablu never changed. Unlike Sachu, he hardly spoke to anyone but appeared so sunk in his own thoughts that one didn't like to disturb him. As before, his face was very serious, and his expression altered only when he read the newspaper reports of the interviews that Sachu had given. Bablu eagerly waited for me to bring him these newspapers, and when he read them he smiled – that smile, with his little pointed teeth and betel-red gums, which always gave me a shock to see. It didn't seem to belong on his face – any more than that other expression my wife had once described to me, when he had turned from the safe and raised his hand with the knife.

Since each of them was ready to plead guilty to save the other, their lawyers got together and tried to prove that they had never met the boy – that someone else had killed him and they had only stolen the roller skates. It was a very weak case, and no one believed it. In the end, both were found guilty, and both were hanged. The burden of what was done has remained with us who are living. My brother Sohan Lal and his family have emigrated to Canada, and at first I, too, intended to leave this place where our name is known. But in the end I stayed. We are still living in the same house, though at first I had intended to sell it. For a long time we kept the front room locked and lived only in the back – no one even went in there to clean – but slowly we have got used to going in there again. At first, only the children went, to look at TV if there was a good program on, but now my wife and I also sit there sometimes, and it is becoming like an ordinary room where nothing has happened.

After the final appeal was dismissed and there was only one week left, they allowed me to visit the prison every day. I always brought his food with me. All this time, I had been providing his meals at the jail. At first, I brought his food from a cooking stall and sent it to him in the little mud pots covered with a leaf that they give you in the bazaar. But after a time, and without anything being said, my wife cooked his food herself, and it was carried to him in dishes from our house. I was glad to be able to provide this home-cooked food, which he liked and was used to. But soon I discovered that he ate only a part of it, and had the rest taken away to Sachu, for whom no one sent anything, of course. When I mentioned this to my wife, she began to send more food, and after a time there were always two dishes of everything.

On the last day, when he asked me to see Sachu and say goodbye to him, I said I would but I didn't do it. So it was that my last word to him was a lie. He asked, 'Did you see him?' and I said, 'Yes.' But next day I did something I hadn't expected. When the hearse arrived to take Bablu, I told the prison officials that I would take the other one, too. They agreed and were glad to be relieved of this charge. So I took both of them to the electric crematorium, and there I performed for both the ceremonies and prayers due to a brother. Sohan Lal and the rest of my family blamed me for this and said I had polluted the last rites. They were all angry and refused to participate in the final ceremony, when the ashes are committed to the river. I didn't care and prepared to do it on my own.

I bought two silver urns and returned to the crematorium to collect the ashes. I had determined to go to Allahabad, to the most holy and purifying place of all, where the three great

rivers meet and mingle, but a lot of business came up during
the next few days and I could not leave at once. I placed the
two urns in the front room, and when I was ready to leave
I packed them in a cardboard box I had brought from the
warehouse for this purpose. The night before, I told my wife
to wake me early so that I could be in time for the plane. She
said, 'I will come with you,' and in the morning she was ready
in new white clothes. We drove to Delhi to go to the airport
there. They allowed us to take the box on board with us. My
wife had never been on a plane before and was very excited,
though she pretended not to be. She kept looking out of the
window to see the clouds and whatever else you see. Once,
she turned to me and said, 'Bablu has never been on a plane
before.' I didn't answer her but I thought, Yes, it is true; it is
the first time for all three of them. The two others would have
enjoyed it too and would have been as excited as she was. In
Allahabad we took a boat, and a priest went with us, and there
was a beautiful ceremony as the ashes were committed at the
confluence of those very holy rivers – the Ganges, the Jumna,
and the Saraswati.

# FARID AND FARIDA

Farid couldn't believe what he heard about Farida. She was his wife, and he would have thought that no one had known her more deeply, in every way, than he had. But now, they said, she was a holy woman sitting under a tree in some holy place in the Himalayas, and people came from all over India to take blessings and good vibrations from her. Ludicrous, he thought. She might fool all the world, but she couldn't fool him. Or could she? He hadn't seen her for twenty years.

He still lived in London, in the flat they had rented long ago when they had first come to England as newlyweds. It was just one room, badly partitioned into two, with a makeshift kitchen and bathroom wedged in between, but the address was good, behind Harrods, so Farid hung on. The place was falling into decay. The landlord had been trying to get him out for years and refused to make any repairs. Farid couldn't afford to go anywhere else. He had not got on and now never would, and no longer cared. He was in his fifties and slovenly, fat from drinking too much.

In his youth, in India, he had been exquisite, and so had Farida – both of them small-boned, elegant, and quick in mind and body. Much had been expected of them, and they were confident of living up to these expectations. Their families were not rich but were very old; the overgrown gardens of their decaying mansions in Delhi abutted on each other, and from their earliest childhood Farid and Farida had gone back and forth through a gap in the boundary wall. They grew up and of course fell in love; now they met not only among the flowering jasmine bushes of their own gardens but also at the university, with its stone-flagged corridors and courtyards. They graduated, they married, they went to live in London. They felt they needed a wider horizon for their talent, which lay mainly in their own personalities – in their intense Indianness, which at that time was regarded, in the self-deprecating countries of the West, as synonymous with every kind of natural and spiritual superiority.

Using their charm and their contacts, Farid and Farida had attempted to set up a business importing hand-loomed Indian textiles. It failed to prosper, and they became impresarios for visiting Indian musicians and dancers, and when these turned out to be unreliable and ungrateful they tried, in succession, ready-made Indian garments, hand-crafted Indian jewelry, Indian lampshades, Indian bedcovers, and Indian table linen – all those indigenous handicrafts by which others of their countrymen, far less gifted than Farid and Farida, made their fortunes in London, Paris, and New York. Ten years passed, then fifteen. They were still living in the temporary flat they had rented, and the landlord began trying to get them out. Farid was drinking. Farida stayed out late and went away for weekends; their erotic quarrels had turned into bitter fights. They had no money, they hated each other. One night, she packed up and returned to India. He stayed on, drank on – and survived, but only just.

After he had heard that she had become a holy woman, he kept muttering, 'We'll see about that.' He didn't know what he meant; he was a person impelled by instinct rather than thought. This impelled him one day to go to Sunil's elegant offices, where he had to wait in the outer reception area before finally being admitted, as a special favor to an old friend. Sunil sat behind his desk and looked at the watch on his hairy wrist and said, 'Ten minutes, Farid.' Although he was without charm or contacts or aesthetic sensibility, Sunil had become rich from the very handlooms and handicrafts that had broken Farid's back and spirit. When they had all been students together in Delhi, Farid and Farida had laughed at Sunil, who was ridiculously in love with Farida. At that time, when Farid was slim and beautiful, Sunil was fat and ungainly. He hadn't changed, but now he had the best tailors and shirtmakers to help him, and he exuded confidence and eau de cologne. Farid still addressed him in the condescending tone that he and Farida had always used toward him. Sunil was too busy to notice. He got rid of Farid within the scheduled ten minutes, though not without handing over the check to cover the air fare to India and expenses. Sunil had also heard about Farida, but he didn't laugh at the news. As was his habit, he would wait and see.

When Farid found her, Farida really was sitting under a tree. She was in a pure white sari, and she looked the way she always did: supremely elegant. Trust her, Farid thought bitterly. Apart from her astonishing situation, she really was the same Farida – God knew how she did it. She was now in her fifties, but sitting there in the lotus position she looked as slim, lithe, and upright as ever. Her hair – dyed, no doubt – was black; her skin was clear and shone with a radiance that could only be the result of the best cosmetics, applied, he knew, with consummate skill. She was surrounded by four or five handmaidens, as exquisitely draped in orange as she was in white, and pilgrims came and went, touching her feet in reverence. She sat on the deerskin traditional to holy people, and someone stood behind her waving a fly whisk. If a fly happened to land on her, Farida waited for it to be flicked off. Her hands were folded in her lap, and she fingered a string of prayer beads in the same way, it occurred to Farid, that she had once fingered her pieces of jewelry, before they were sold off, one by one, to cover her expenses in London.

Farid regarded the scene from a distance. The tree – a huge banyan – spread its foliage over Farida and her handmaidens, but the people lining up to see her had to stand outside in the sun until it was their turn to be admitted into the shade of the tree. Farid watched her as she dealt with the pilgrims. To some she spoke at length, while others she only lightly touched as they bowed down to her; a few favored ones were handed some holy talisman by a handmaiden. But everyone appeared

to come away fully satisfied, for Farida radiated blessing. Farid
couldn't help admiring her; he had often told her that she
would have made a first-rate actress. At last he approached the
tree and lined up with the other pilgrims. When it was his turn
to be led up to her, he didn't bow, like the others, but stood and
looked down at her, one hand on his hip. She looked up at him
and met his cynical smile with an ambiguous one of her own.
She made it seem as if she had been expecting him, even after
twenty years. They kept on looking at each other, and he felt
the challenge that had always lain between them.

She looked away first, turning around to a handmaiden to
murmur some command. Straightaway, he was led off and
installed in a whitewashed little cell in one of a chain of plain
brick structures that rambled all over the mountainside. These
constituted an ashram, and of course the accommodations
were of the simplest, but everything was clean, pleasant, and
orderly. He decided to stay on, at least for a while. There
was little expense to him, he discovered – in fact, none at
all – which was just as well, because Sunil's money wasn't
going to last forever. He couldn't say he was uncomfortable.
Within a day or two, he realized that he was being treated
as an honored guest. Regular meals were brought to him
on a tray, and there was always someone hovering around
to see if he needed anything; someone even brought him
his cigarettes from the bazaar. He decided to treat the whole
thing as a holiday – a well-deserved one, at that, for God knew
he'd had a pretty rough struggle to keep himself going, while
Farida apparently had experienced no difficulty landing on
her feet. She was his wife, after all, and if good fortune had
come her way it was no more than right that he should have
some modest share of it.

The days passed as evenly for him as they did for everyone
else. The place had its own rhythm. It was a traditional sacred
spot – almost as sacred as Banaras – and there were other holy
people like Farida living there. They were Hindus and she was
a Muslim, but that didn't matter. Allah and Ishwar were equal
here, and no one questioned which of them was responsible
for the mountain peaks rising against the immaculate sky, or

the sun that set in orange glory on one side and rose in pink effulgence on the other. Cymbals and temple bells rang out at regular intervals, and everyone hurried smiling to a variety of little white shrines and temples adorned with flags and garlands. Not Farid, of course – he didn't go in for anything like that. Instead, he took little walks in the mornings and the late afternoons, climbing up a green path till he got tired and began panting, which was quite soon. At night, he slept on a string cot in his whitewashed cell. They had given him an old electric table fan, which kept him moderately cool, though he could have wished it made less clatter. When he got tired of the vegetarian meals they brought him, he wandered down into the little bazaar at the foot of the hill and ate a meat curry at one of the stalls there and had some worldly conversation with the shopkeepers and customers. Once, he went into the town cinema, together with the other town loafers, and saw one of those long, loud Hindi films, which he enjoyed more than a sophisticated person like himself should have. Once a day, he visited Farida under her tree. When she asked him whether everything was to his satisfaction, he replied with a shrug that suggested he neither asked for nor got much. Altogether, he conveyed the impression that he was doing her a favor by being there at all.

He was waiting for a showdown with her. He expected it. They had always had showdowns – explosions ignited by the fuel of their fiery temperaments. In their youth these upheavals had ended in excited lovemaking, but later, during the years in London, the showdowns had become a release from the tensions not of love but of failure and frustration. They lived in misery. Their flat was horribly cramped and always smelled of cabbage and mutton from their English neighbors' cooking. (They themselves had given up on cooking and only opened cans and frozen packets.) The flat also held the odors of Farida's scents and lotions and of the dregs of Farid's drinks.

It was no wonder that, in their last years together, Farida had gone away as often as possible. She told him she went to follow up useful contacts – though these were vague by now, for they no longer had definite plans but just lived on in the hope of something turning up. It was when she came back from one of those expeditions that they had had their final quarrel. He had been alone in the flat all weekend, drinking. His eyes hurt, his head felt huge, and now he lay on the bed watching her brush her hair in front of the mirror. He could see her smiling to herself in a secret, sensuous way. He began to taunt her, asking her questions about where she had spent the weekend and taking pleasure in trapping her in discrepancies. Actually, she wasn't very careful about her excuses any more and presented them to him with a take-it-or-leave-it indifference. But that day he persisted and she became angry, which was what he had wanted, for why should she be smiling that way when he was feeling so rotten?

In the past, in their years of happiness, he had known just how to wind her up so that she flashed and blazed in a pleasurable way. Later, he began to miss his mark, and that was what happened that day. Before he knew where he was, with his sick eyes and head, she had jumped up from the mirror, crashed her hairbrush against the wall behind him, and stood above him in an attitude of menace. He squinted up at her, mocking and malevolent. Her silk robe, cut down from a sari, swung wide open, and her full breasts, unconfined by a brassiere, were before him. Her breasts had always been an exciting contrast to her small waist and slender arms, though not to her hips, which also swelled voluptuously. He reached up his hand to squeeze one breast, and remarked with a sneer that these fruits must have been damaged by being handled too often on too many weekends. All at once she was on top of him. She sat astride his chest and seized his hair and banged his head up and down. Even without a hangover, there would have been no way he could defend himself against her. At that moment, she was as irresistible, as inexorable, as the goddess Kali, who, with bared and dripping fangs, rides her victims to destruction.

The next moment – well, it came twenty years later, but he had no intervening image – there she was, holy under a tree. It was only natural that on his daily visits he should continue to look at her with the same cynical, not-to-be-fooled expression – with his legs apart and his hands on his hips, in a most unreverential posture. She didn't seem to mind. The eyes she raised to him were absolutely clear, inviting him to read what he would in them. Meanwhile, her other visitors, the pilgrims, came and went, touching her feet and taking her blessings. As they drew near, their faces became radiant, and they appeared to retain this glow as they departed. Farida's handmaidens glided about, and now and then one of them sang a song of spiritual love while another accompanied her, plucking a slow, droning sound out of a lutelike instrument. If Farida felt the song was too low-spirited – and her handmaidens, so gentle and good, did have a tendency to droop – then she herself would chime in, giving more of a swing and lift to it, and snapping her fingers as if to say, 'Come on, let's get going!' Then everybody responded; voices rose, the drone hastened and took on melody, gentle smiles shook off melancholy, and at the end, when the women had finished in unison on their top notes, Farida said, 'That's better,' so that everyone laughed out loud, and this sound mingled with the last joyful notes still vibrating in the air.

At home, in her youth and heyday, Farida had always had this ability to make a party go. When things got too slow for her, she would turn up the record-player or replace the LP on it with a faster one to dance to. If her partner couldn't keep up with her, she would discard him and try another and another, and if none of them could come up to the mark – 'What a bunch of dummies!' – she simply danced by herself, with her slippers kicked off and her hair and gossamer veil flying, while everyone stood around her and applauded. In London, too, at the beginning of their life there, she and Farid had given terrific parties, cramming the flat with more people than it could hold, so that the guests spilled into the kitchen, where Farida was boldly throwing spices together. She was always experimenting with curries she remembered from her grandmother's cuisine, and these usually turned out extremely well, filling the flat with their rich aromas. Everyone sat on the floor, eating with their fingers Indian style, while Farida picked her way among her friends, putting more delicious things on their already overflowing plates while Farid refilled their glasses, and both of them – Farid and Farida – talking in their high, excited voices, which could always be heard above the hubbub of their guests.

At that time it had been easy for them to enjoy themselves and make everyone else happy too. It was all done with no more effort than the way Farida made herself look beautiful; he never saw her do more than glance over her shoulder in the mirror, twisting her hair quickly into a coil on top of her head, or else deciding to leave it loose down her back, with a rose stuck in it. Later, however, this changed. It irritated him to watch the painstaking way she got herself ready to go to other people's parties – by then, they could no longer afford to give them – painting larger lips and darker eyelids over her own; she had begun to wear curlers at night, and she got up with them in the morning, looking cross and ugly. And, just as she had to take pains over her appearance, she had to work harder to be successful at these parties. Now when she cried, 'Come on, let's get going!' no one seemed to hear her or pay attention. Her voice had become shrill, her laugh harsher and louder. When she had decided who was worth her attention at a party, she would hang on to his arm with her skinny hands. Often it was Sunil on whom she concentrated at parties. He was getting to be the richest and most successful of their circle. Once he had mooned after Farida in a dogged, hopeless way, but now he liked plump Scandinavian blondes, who sometimes perched on his lap. Farida, ignoring them, would bring some tidbit for him from the buffet table and dangle it above him until he opened his mouth to receive it; she cried, 'Good boy!' and clapped her hands, while he chewed with indifferent relish. It sickened Farid to watch this, and perhaps it sickened Farida too, because when they got home she was in a rotten mood and turned her back on him and went to sleep as if she never wanted to get up again.

Somehow she did get up, every morning, and although all their projects failed, one after the other, she was always starting new ones. Elegantly dressed, meticulously made up, her jaw somewhat set, she went out each day in pursuit of some business she had just thought up that was certain to pull them out of their predicament. When they had been in London for about ten years (she was well into her thirties by this time), she decided to organize a line of Indian cocktail delicacies – samosas, pakoras, kebabs – to be sold in the delicatessen departments of leading London stores. She dealt with the very fanciest places, and only with their top directors; it was taken for granted that no secretary or any other underling could stand in her way when she presented herself, without an appointment but emanating an almost royal authority, and quickly sailed right into the innermost sanctum of these offices. And when she came out again she was invariably escorted by the director himself, smiling and flattered by her direct approach to him. She gave the impression that she was conducting the affairs of her own exclusive catering firm – which was true, in a way. What the directors did not realize was that she made all the delicacies herself, working alone in the makeshift kitchen of their flat, while Farid lay in bed and complained about the smell of her deep-fat frying.

She had bought a wholesale supply of cardboard boxes, which stood piled in their living room. She packed them with delicacies she had fried, and spent the rest of the day delivering them to the stores, going from one to the other in a taxi. By the third week of this, she was exhausted from her hours of cooking, from her slow and expensive delivery rounds, and from the complaints that were beginning to come in. Also, it was becoming evident that the cost of the ingredients, the packaging, and the taxi were destroying the profit she had expected, and one night when Farid again complained about the smell she marched into the bedroom with a pan of hot oil and threatened to pour it on him. He locked himself in the bathroom, and when at last he emerged he found her sitting on the floor with the deep-fry pan beside her. Her knees were hunched up and her head was laid on them; her hair was half uncoiled, and she was wearing an old cotton sari spattered with grease. He grew angry at the sight of her. 'What are you – a cook or something?' he shouted, and when she didn't answer or stir he worked himself up further. 'No one asked you to do this kind of work. Tcha – what would your parents say, what would my parents say, if they knew?'

Still with her head on her knees, she murmured, 'Then what are we going to do?'

'We'll find something,' he said, her defeat making him strong. 'We don't have to put up with this nonsense. Get rid of all that filthy stuff.' He seized her pan, carried it into the bathroom and emptied it into the toilet. When she heard the firm way in which he flushed it away, she raised her head and wiped her eyes with the end of her sari and felt better.

But then it was his responsibility to raise some money to keep them going, and the only way he knew was to borrow from Sunil, as he had done so often over the years. Sunil received him in his Mayfair flat, and Farid looked severely around the place, which was sumptuously furnished with everything that money and bad taste could buy. 'What's *that* picture?' he said. 'Is it new? Oh, my God.'

'Listen, Farid, it's from a very ritzy gallery in Brook Street,' Sunil said calmly. 'It cost me a packet, I can tell you.'

'A fool and his money are soon parted. Except of course when it comes to his friends – then it's a different story.'

'When have I ever said no?' Sunil said in dull resignation.

It was true, he didn't often turn down his old friends, but that did not improve Farid's feelings toward him.

Matters grew worse as the years passed and Sunil went up and Farid down. Farida began to go away for weekends. Farid suspected that she went to meet Sunil, but when he accused her of this she just laughed. What made him think that she would go to Sunil for anything but money, she said. And what made him think Sunil had any time left for her, now that Sunil was what he was and she was – well, she said with a shrug, anyone could see what she was now. Farid stared at her. She was now in her late thirties – they had been struggling along in London for a good fifteen years – and she had grown very thin. Her face, under her lacquered hair, was heavily made up. But beneath it all she was still Farida – just as, he realized, beneath all his bad feeling, and all his anger against her, there remained still the heart, the flower, of love. He kissed her hand and then her wrist, and then the soft skin of her inner arm.

She took advantage of his good mood to murmur that they would have to sell some more jewelry. 'I need the money,' she urged. 'For a new business – no, no, this one's going to make it for sure, you'll see. It's in taxis for tourists.'

'What's left to sell?' he asked.

She got out her jewel box, which was empty except for the one piece they had agreed never to sell. This was a single large and lustrous pearl in a gold setting. It was said to have been given by the last of the great Mogul emperors to Farida's great-great-great-grandfather, who had been a nobleman at his court, and it had always been coveted by Sunil, whose own great-great-great-grandfather had been a moneylender's clerk at the same court. Farida had worn the pearl on her forehead at her wedding, but that time only the bridegroom, Farid, had seen it, for only he was allowed to look under her veil. It was years later, in London, when Sunil caught his first sight of it. This was at a reception he was giving for an American buyer of table linen, to which Farida had come all dressed up. She was trying to start a business in batik table mats with matching napkins, and so was out to make an impression. Sunil had eyed the ornament, which was on a chain around her neck. When he tried to touch it, she put her hand over it and said, 'Not for sale.'

'Let me know when it is,' he said in his phlegmatic voice, which he made even more phlegmatic when he was eager to acquire something at a bargain price.

Farid never knew at what price Sunil finally did acquire this ornament – the money soon vanished anyway in the tourist taxi business. He often wondered what Sunil had done with it. Had he sold it? Kept it? Hung it around the neck of a girl? Sometimes he asked him, but Sunil never let on. Actually, Farid was almost sure that Sunil had locked it away in the deepest and most secret of all his safe-deposit vaults, for Sunil – one had to admit it – recognized a thing of value when he saw it. It was greed, of course, but Farid knew that when it was a question of making money Sunil's

greed could be as subtle and unerring as anyone else's taste
and wisdom.

After several weeks at the holy place, during which he faced her
every day, Farid had still not arrived at the expected showdown
with Farida. He was even beginning to enjoy his visits to her
for their own sake. They became the high point of his day. At
first he had stood in line with all the other pilgrims awaiting
their turn, but then he noticed that there was a time, just after
the midday meal, when no one else was there and even the
handmaidens had lain themselves to sleep. Although Farid
enjoyed a siesta as much as anyone, one day he spruced
himself up a bit, making the most of the strands of hair
that lay across the top of his head and smoothing his bush
shirt over his stomach. He looked down at his stomach and
decided he had seen worse on men his age. Then he hurried
– yes, hurried – across the empty compound that separated
his quarters from her tree. The sun beat down on him from a
fierce white sky, the paving stones burned underfoot, and a hot
glare as tangible as glass permeated the air, but Farid hardly
noticed. Once he reached his destination, the air felt absolutely
different. The shade spread by the tree was as wide and cool as
the interior of a shuttered house. The handmaidens lay asleep
off to one side of the thick tree trunk, on the other Farida sat
reading some ancient text. She was wearing big spectacles to
read with but took them off quickly when he arrived. They
had begun to have little conversations now.

'Look at you, how hot you are,' she said now, watching him
wipe the perspiration from his face and neck.

'Naturally, a person gets hot,' he answered irritably. 'Not
everyone has the opportunity to sit under a tree all day.'

'At least you should wear a hat.'

'You know I never wear a hat,' he said still impatiently,
though he didn't feel that way at all. It was cool and peaceful
under her roof of foliage.

The next day, he set out to find a hat in the little bazaar at
the foot of the mountain. He was a well-known figure there
by now – he always made friends quickly – and his quest

for a solar hat made the shopkeepers smile. They said that only English-style sahibs like himself needed to protect their brains from the good Indian sun. It was not until he came to the end of the row of narrow booths that he discovered what he was looking for among a stock of cotton undervests, bottles of hair oil, and oleographs of gods and saints. As he put on the hat and looked at himself in a little metal mirror, his attention was caught by one of the highly colored pictures – a portrait of a saint that featured its subject against a traditional background of shrines, forests, rivers, and mountain caves. Farid would not have noticed this one except that it bore some resemblance to Farida. He looked closer and then realized that the saint in the picture actually *was* Farida. He stared at her, and it seemed to him that out of her painted background she stared back at him in the same way she did every day under the tree.

Suddenly he remembered that it was past the hour of his usual visit to her. He paid for his purchase and hurried back through the bazaar and up the path toward her tree. He didn't even notice the stiff climb, which usually made him pant and stop several times. But when he came within sight of the tree he slowed down. He was approaching from the bazaar instead of from the ashram, and so it happened that he caught sight of Farida half rising from her place to peer anxiously along his usual path. He tiptoed up from behind her. 'Were you expecting someone, Madam?' he said suddenly, and when she turned around he swept off his new hat and made a deep bow, at the same time tilting up his face to look into hers. Although she tried to hide her feelings with a frown, he knew that he had caught her out, and that was as satisfying as the showdown he had been hoping for.

For the next few weeks, Farid felt particularly light-hearted and happy. With his solar hat, bush shirt, and an alpenstock he had acquired, he looked every inch a Westernized Oriental Gentleman, but he didn't feel that way. It seemed to him that he had shaken off that part of his life and was now as much at home with his surroundings as Farida, that he was at one with the little ashram, and with the other pilgrims, the shrines, the trees, the mountain paths, the water springs. He climbed up and down the hillside – a bit out of breath because of his smoking and because of not being very slim (as he politely put it to himself) but nevertheless feeling nimble and agile and certain he could go up as high as he wanted. He never did climb very high but found a small incline a little way up the mountain that flattened out almost into an overlook. He liked to stand there and lean on his alpenstock, surveying the scene and feeling himself part of it. His visits with Farida in the afternoon became longer and more intimate. He sat beside her on the deerskin, and they talked like two people who have always been close to each other. They caught up on the last twenty years – or, rather, he caught up with her; there was nothing he needed to tell her about his years in London. She told him how, after that last scene with him, she had borrowed the fare from Sunil and gone straight back to her parents' house in Delhi.

'The moment I got there,' she said, 'it was as if I'd never been away, never got married, never been to London, never been broke. I did what everyone else did, all the sisters and cousins – went to the club in the evening, played tennis, played bridge, sat on committees to help the poor. Oh, you know your family's old house next door that was sold? They'd pulled it down and built a block of flats on it. It was sad. Well, everything was sad. Papa got sick and then he died, and just six weeks later Mama died, too. Yes, you know about that. We had to start dividing everything – the furniture and carpets and silver and Mama's jewelry – and there were such quarrels, you can't imagine. How can such things happen between brothers and sisters! One day, Roxy and I got into this really awful fight about Mama's diamond necklace. You remember how fat my sister Roxy always was? Well, she's ten times fatter now – *huge* – with a huge face all painted with lipstick and mascara. And when we were tugging at the necklace – she at one end, me at the other, and both of us screaming – I looked into this face of hers and suddenly I thought, my God, that's me, I'm looking in a mirror. And at the same moment I won the battle and had the necklace in my hand, only now I couldn't bear even to hold it. I flung it away from me as far as I could, and then I rushed out of the room and out of the house and got into Papa's old Fiat and drove without stopping – all the way up to Kasauli, you know, to the summer house there. No one had been there for ages, because of the lawsuit about it between Papa and his nephews. Everything inside had been taken away, completely stripped, and in what used to be the dining room there was a dead squirrel, with water dripping on it from a burst pipe. I got back in the Fiat and drove further up, as far as I could go, till I got to the first snow. It was completely silent there and completely bare; there were no birds and nothing growing, nothing at all. The snow sparkled white and the sky sparkled icy blue. The air was so sharp that it was like being inside a crystal. I found a cave in the side of the mountain, and it had icicles festooned around its entrance, as if someone had hung up decorations to welcome me. So I went in.'

That was as far as Farida got in telling her story to Farid. There was a silence, and when he asked, 'And then?' she said, 'And then I came here.' He never could find the connecting link between the entrance to the cave and this tree where she sat as a saint, with people lining up to see her. Whenever he pressed her for more information, she blushed and glanced down and smiled; she looked exactly the way she had when they were passing from childhood into adolescence and were awakening into new secrets that made him tremble with boldness and her with shyness and shame.

One day, Sunil turned up on the mountain. He came in an air-conditioned limousine driven by a chauffeur. Sunil was wearing a suit of the lightest tropical weight, but this did not prevent him from sweating most disagreeably. Farid felt at a tremendous advantage over him – a feeling that grew as the days passed and Sunil stayed on. For one thing, Sunil never had a private audience with Farida but had to line up with the other pilgrims. Also, the living conditions were not at all what he was used to; instead of occupying a suite in some five-star hotel, he was forced to sleep on a string cot placed beside Farid's in the whitewashed cell. He could not get used to the plain meals prepared in the ashram kitchens, and when Farid took him to one of the eating stalls in the bazaar he got sick from the kebabs served there. At night he sweated and groaned and suffered tortures from the mosquitoes whining around him, though they never seemed to bother Farid. His air-conditioned limousine stood waiting to take him back down, and the chauffeur grumbled and had to be bribed to stay, but Sunil did not leave. It was almost the way it used to be when they were children and Sunil came to Farida's birthday parties and stuck on stubbornly even though the other children pricked his balloons and hid his shoes and ate up his chocolate cake.

Of course, it was all for a purpose, a plan, and one night when he couldn't sleep because of the mosquitoes he woke up Farid and broached it to him.

'She's wasted up here,' he said.

Farid sat up. 'What's on your mind?' he said.

'It's ridiculous,' Sunil grumbled. 'Instead of sitting under that tree of hers, she could be making a fortune in London. Not to speak of New York.'

'You must be crazy,' Farid said in a shaky voice.

'*You're* crazy,' Sunil said. 'You and she both. But it's always the same story with you two. You have absolutely no business sense.'

'Business!' Farid shouted. 'What's she got to do with business! She's beyond all that now.'

'All right, call it something else then, call it whatever you like. But I'm telling you, she'll go over big. They've never seen anything like her before. There's money in what she does – *money*,' he repeated, irritably rubbing his thumb and middle finger together to make his meaning clear.

Sunil settled in. Each day, his car could be seen driving up and down the mountain roads, with Sunil sitting in the back, phlegmatic but confident, picking his teeth. He was setting up everything for Farida's first public appearances in London; it meant getting a whole organization going, but of course that was the sort of thing he excelled at. He had made an arrangement with the post office in the bazaar to get his international calls through several times a day, and soon a contingent of publicity people arrived – very incongruous Englishmen in Daks slacks and Hush Puppies shoes who moved in on the group under the tree. They shot photographs, made sketches, took the measurements of Farida and the handmaidens, and called everyone 'darling' and 'angel' in cold, indifferent voices. They did their job and went away. But Sunil stayed on.

Farid sneered at all this, but he was frightened. He knew that Sunil was stupid, but he also knew that the man was capable of pushing and lumbering ahead like an army tank unencumbered by human intelligence. The worst of it was that he seemed to have sold his idea to Farida herself. She was fully persuaded that it was time for a wider, more international audience to be given the benefit of her spirituality, and that Sunil was the man to arrange it. One day when Farid arrived for his own session with her, he found Sunil there before him, sitting on the edge of her deerskin as though he had every right to be there. From then on, he was there every afternoon, and Farid's blissful tête-à-têtes with Farida were finished. Now the handmaidens no longer slept quietly on the other side of the tree but tripped up and down, primping and preening, studiedly graceful. Farida was different, too. She didn't lose the serenity that was now an integral part of her personality, like a shawl on a mature and beautiful woman, but she had that small half smile of satisfaction she had always worn when things were going well for her. It made Farid want to slap her. Doesn't she see, he thought. Doesn't she know? His anger turned on Sunil, who took no notice of it at all.

Farid stopped going to the tree in the afternoons, and instead began to nap on the cot in his cell. No one seemed to miss him; no message came from Farida to ask where he was. He slept as much as he could. It was the same thing that had happened to him in London, when he didn't want to get up any more, and day turned into night for him, except that now he was dulled only by despair. He didn't drink here; he didn't need to. Now he took walks by moonlight, as he used to walk in the daytime. He climbed up to the same incline as before, from where he could look down on Farida's tree and the bazaar on one side and a steep slope descending into a ravine on another. He wished it would never be day again.

One night, he went to Farida's tree, descending very carefully, so that no stone might clatter down and make a noise. Everyone was sleeping – Farida on one side of the tree, the handmaidens on the other, on moss. The tree shaded them from the moon except for some silver streaks that spilled through the foliage and covered them as with a veil of finely patterned lace. Farid stood looking down at Farida. It seemed a pity to wake her, and when he did she wasn't at all pleased. 'Is this a time to come visiting?' she said irritably.

'Then when should I come?' Farid said. 'With that slob sitting here all afternoon.'

She continued to lie there under her veil of moonlight. Her eyes were open and looking at him. It wasn't so different from when she used to wake up at night in the other half of their double bed in London and regard him silently and speculatively in the dark. 'Move over,' he said suddenly now. Didn't he have the right? Wasn't he still her husband? She didn't argue but made room for him, so that he could nestle beside her. She no longer used the scent, *Jolie Madame*, she had in London but smelled of something else. Maybe it wasn't a scent at all but only a fragrance rising from within her. It was somehow strengthened and given body by the racy smell of the deerskin.

'Let's go away,' he whispered to her.

'We *are* going away,' she pointed out. 'We're going to London. I'm booked in the Royal Albert Hall in October.'

'Not like that. Not with all these people. Just you and me.' Chastely he kissed her cool neck.

'Where were you thinking of going?' she murmured.

'Away. Up there,' he said, gesturing toward a mountain peak glimmering with moon and snow.

'There's nothing up there.'

'Yes there is. You said so. You've been there. You said there's a cave.'

'Oh, my goodness,' she said. 'That old story. You'd better go to bed and get some sleep. You're dreaming with your eyes open.'

His reply was to move closer to her; he put his arm across her. After a long silence, during which both of them lay quite still, she said, 'I don't want to go up. I want to go down – go back. This time, it'll work out. You'll see.'

How often he had heard that from her – each time she had started some new scheme. She seemed to remember this herself, for she went on: 'Sunil will help us. He'll look after all that – you know, the business side you and I could never manage.'

'Sunil!' he said scornfully. 'All he knows is buying and selling.'

'No one can live without buying and selling,' she said.

He was shocked. He sat up and stared at her in the moonlight. She looked back at him defiantly; and again he was reminded of how it had been between them all the years in London. Was she still the same? Hadn't she changed after all?

She knew at once what he was thinking, of course. 'It's you who haven't changed!' she cried. 'You still think you can lie around with your mouth open, waiting for sweets to drop in. Well, that's not my style at all, and this time you're not going to drag me down with you.'

'But I told you, I don't want to go down,' he said. 'I want to go up – up to where that cave is.'

She snorted loudly – a sound of impatient anger that he knew very well. 'And go away now,' she said, and when he didn't move she gave him a little push. 'Go on, before anyone sees us.'

'So what?' he said. 'We're married, aren't we?'

A shipment of boxes arrived from London – the men in Daks slacks had arranged it all. The boxes contained new uniforms for the handmaidens and a white robe of Italian silk for Farida, along with a string of prayer beads set by a famous Italian designer, and a new deerskin, which must have been synthetic, for it had no smell at all. Everyone had gathered around for the unpacking – everyone, that is, except for Farid, who kept himself completely aloof from the

excitement. By the time he next came to visit the tree, the
handmaidens had changed into their new permanent-press
robes and were gliding up and down in them like ethereal
airline stewardesses. Farida appeared tremendously pleased
with herself in her new white robe and Italian beads. She
looked at Farid as if she expected a compliment, which he
refused to pay. Sunil was there, surveying the scene with the
satisfaction of an impresario. He stared at Farid, and Farida
said at once, 'Yes, he'll need a new outfit, too.'

Farid shrugged contemptuously and went away. But when
night came and everyone was asleep he got up and went to
her again. She was awake and seemed to be expecting him.
When he lay down next to her, she ran her finger over his
frayed collar and said, 'We'll get you a new shirt and new
shoes and ties and everything. We'll start again.' She stroked
what was left of his hair. 'It'll all be different this time,' she
said. But when he groaned and said, 'Oh, no,' she pulled back
from him. 'That's all I've ever heard from you!' she shouted.
'Whatever I wanted you to do, your only contribution was "Oh,
no." I'm sick of it! I'm tired of it and I'm tired of you.'

Though she spoke in anger, Farid saw the tears trickling
from her eyes.

'Who did I ever do anything for but you?' she said. 'All those
businesses I started – who was all that for? And even now, who
is it all for?' Her voice broke. Her tears fell in perfect drops
like pearls.

'Never mind,' he said. 'Don't say any more.' He lay beside
her and held her hand, and remembered the time when he
had had to rescue her and flushed her cooking oil away.

The next day, he invited Sunil to go for a walk with him.
Sunil, who was in no condition to walk uphill, didn't want
to go, but Farid used his old tactics – taunting him about his
ungainly figure, his breathlessness, his age – until Sunil gave in.
Farid walked ahead, jaunty with his hat and stick, sometimes
stopping on the steep path to look back at his friend panting
behind him. When he reached his destination, which was his
usual overlook, he sat comfortably on a stone and watched

Sunil slowly coming up and, beyond him, the mountainside that spiraled away below.

Sunil arrived flushed and angry. 'You want to kill me, making me climb up here?' he said.

'Clam down,' Farid said. 'Take it easy. I only want to tell you something. Farida and I are leaving.'

'Oh, my God, is that all?' Sunil said, standing above him. 'I know you're leaving. So am I. Everyone is. Is that all you have to tell me?'

'We're not going with you,' Farid said calmly. 'We're going up, not down. I just wanted you to know there's been a change of plan.'

'Oh, sure, sure. A change of plan. I make the arrangements, spend a few hundred thousand, and he changes the plan.'

Farid remained serene. He pointed toward the mountaintop far above them, where its peak disappeared into mist. 'That's where we're going, Farida and I,' he said.

'Listen, Farid,' Sunil said. He took a deep breath to keep his patience. 'I don't know what's on your mind, but please try to get this straight. We're going to London. Everything's booked. Everything's arranged. There's a whole public waiting for us out there. There's money to be made, and we're going to make it.'

Farid, still seated on his stone, looked up at his friend. It was so easy. One push in the right direction and Sunil would go rolling off the path and down the steep ravine. He would not be heard from again. Farid stood up. He gave Sunil a sharp little push in the chest – he could have laughed at the expression on Sunil's face as he lost his balance and began to tumble backward. The next moment, he didn't feel like laughing at all but went running after him down the path. Sunil didn't roll far. His bush shirt caught in the lower branches of a little pine tree, which stood a foot or two above a mountain ledge, and Sunil stuck there, while a few stones he had dislodged went bouncing down the path and sailed off into empty air. Farid jumped after him. He pulled and tugged at him, while Sunil awkwardly tried to heave himself back onto the path. It was not easy for either of them, for they were both overweight, out of breath, and terribly upset. When at last they managed it, Sunil slowly arose and stood there with his eyes shut in fright, while Farid felt him all over, pressing his limbs to see if anything was broken, and trembling as much as Sunil himself. Without opening his eyes, Sunil said at last, 'Let me go. Take me down.'

Farid carefully led him down, his arm around Sunil's stout waist, stopping solicitously every few steps to see if he was all right. Then he took his hat off and put it on Sunil, to guard him from the sun.

Later that day they presented themselves before Farida. 'We're all leaving tomorrow,' Sunil said.

'Certainly,' Farid said. 'He can go down and we'll go up.'

There was a pause. When Farida spoke, it was to Farid. 'There's nothing up there,' she said coldly. 'Can't you get that into your head? Absolutely nothing.' She looked at him with a face of stone.

What could he say to convince her? What could he do? He knelt beside her on the new deerskin; seen through his tears, she swam in a halo of light. He called her name out loud – 'Farida! Farida!' – as if she were far away, instead of right next to him. He seized her hands and began to talk and cry desperately. He told her how he had tried to kill Sunil, so that the two of them, Farid and Farida, could go away together and everything could be again as it was. Yes, for that he had been prepared to murder their childhood friend. He said this twice, to impress it on her, but she only extracted her cool hands from between his and said, 'You're neurotic.'

'Neurotic!' Sunil exclaimed. 'He's completely psychotic. We have to get him to London for treatment.'

The next day, two other air-conditioned limousines arrived, and Sunil and Farida and the handmaidens and their luggage prepared for a stately departure. Pilgrims gathered while the cars were being loaded; they joined their hands in respectful salutation and shouted '*Jai Mataji!*' Some of them waved little orange flags with Farida's picture imprinted in black. Sunil and Farida were sitting in the back of the third car, waiting for Farid to join the chauffeur on the front seat. But Farid could not be found. Sunil tapped his foot and said, 'We'll miss our plane.'

'Give him a few more minutes,' Farida said. Under her breath she muttered, 'Isn't that just like him!' A signal was given, and the two cars in front moved off. 'We can't just leave him behind!' Farida cried, as the procession began to wind downhill.

'Please smile, Farida,' Sunil said. 'Please wave.' She waved at the pilgrims by the roadside as the car slowly descended, but kept turning in her seat and craning to peer behind her. For the first time in many years she looked discontented, disappointed.

Farid was standing above them at his overlook, at the terminal point of his daily walk. He looked down at the cars leaving. They seemed to go very slowly and reluctantly, and he knew it would be easy, if he wanted to, to run after them and catch them up. He felt a sensation in his heart as if someone – some other heart attached to his – were tugging him down. But he planted himself a bit more sturdily, with his legs apart, and stood his ground. The cars grew smaller, creeping down the mountain into the bazaar, into the town, into the plains below. When they were completely out of sight, he descended the path and returned to her tree. The place was deserted now, and there was nothing to be seen except her old deerskin, which someone had rolled up and stuffed under a root. Farid spread it out again and smoothed it and sat on it. He thought he would just wait here until she came back for him. Of course, this might take a long time – many years, even – but when she came at last he would say, 'Let's go up, Farida,' and after the inevitable argument she would agree.

# INDEPENDENCE

Kuku Malhotra was a modern Indian girl who lived with her boy friend in a roof-top studio in New Delhi. Kuku was a documentary film-maker and had lately obtained a grant from the Ministry of Information and Broadcasting to make a documentary about her grandmother Sumitra. It may already have been too late. Nowadays the old lady sat mostly on her lawn or her verandah, bundled in shawls in the winter, fanned by a woman servant in the summer. Her name was still known, though she herself forgotten. Most people thought she was dead, along with all the others of her generation, who had been pioneers in the early years of Independence, the first truly modern Indians. When Kuku tried to interview her about those days, she remained silent, sunk into apathy. Only her lips chewed and mumbled; she rarely wore her teeth nowadays, except when it was time to eat. She still relished her food and got very excited over it, making frantic signs to her servant to hand her more hot bread and refill her little bowls with rice and fish. It seemed to Kuku that it was only in those moments that there was any trace left of the former Sumitra – of her boundless energy and her uninhibited enjoyment of life (and, Kuku thought, of lovers) that had broken down so many barriers for Kuku's own generation.

Born between two European world wars, Kuku's grand-mother had come of age at the right time – just as Indians were reclaiming their country from British rule. She had grown up in Bombay where her father was a very rich businessman. She had lived in a big house on a hill overlooking the Arabian

Sea and surrounded by a garden thick with palm trees. Her father's money was at her disposal and she used it freely on herself and her friends. They had parties for every occasion, birthdays and the New Year and even Christmas, besides all the Hindu holidays. There were plenty of servants, and her father employed two cooks, one for Indian and the other for European cuisine. The parents and the servants enjoyed the parties almost as much as the young guests, who had names like Bunny, Bunti and Dickoo, carried over from their pampered childhood. The parties too were carried over from their childhood, together with the balloons and the jokes and the nicknames they shared. They were attractive, high-spirited young people, and it would have been impossible to predict how serious and important and even pompous they would become within a few years. Those who stayed in Bombay entered their fathers' businesses and expanded them beyond all previous limits; those who went to New Delhi took over the highest posts of government and became rulers, kings of their country, crowned with offices.

It may have been the pull of New Delhi with all its might and power that influenced Sumitra to marry a boy from an old Delhi family. She could have married anyone she wanted. Many offers came for her, from all the leading families of their caste. Her father laid them before her for her consideration, always emphasizing that she was entirely free to choose or reject. She rejected them all, for of course she was going to make a modern love marriage; but she refused other young men too, those with whom she had grown up and partied in their father's mansions. Many of them were in love with her, and she in love with some of them. She met Hari Prasad – known as Harry – on a visit she made to a cousin in Delhi. Here too the young people were throwing parties, and though these were not as lavish as the ones in Bombay, they held another kind of attraction. A transfer of power was taking place, and while the young people were dancing to gramophone records in the drawing room, their fathers and uncles were closeted in the study distributing cabinet posts among themselves. This was intoxicating.

Even without all that, Harry was attractive enough in himself, and different from the boys she had grown up with. He liked painting and literature; he had been to Oxford where he had developed his taste for oriental poetry and French wine. Somewhat languid and passive, he let Sumitra woo him; that suited her too, for it was in her nature to initiate and take the leading part. It made him laugh and pleased him – at that time – the way Sumitra took charge of things. It pleased his father too and was useful to him, for she became his hostess – a part few women at that time were qualified to play, for most of them were like Sumitra's mother, and Harry's, who spoke little English and spent their time in their prayer rooms or closeted with their spiritual advisers to ward off evil influences. But Harry's father was entering a new, a wider world than any known to them before. He was a brilliant lawyer who had defended Indian leaders and kept or sprung them out of jail. He lived with his family in his own large New Delhi residence built many years before Independence with his own wealth and in the style of the surrounding residences of high-ranking British administrators.

Before moving in with her boy friend, Kuku Malhotra had lived in this house, with her grandmother Sumitra and her mother Monica, who was Sumitra and Harry's only child. By that time the other grand British-style villas around them had been requisitioned for ministerial residences or torn down for modern blocks of flats. Monica too would have liked to sell the house and land at huge profit, but this was impossible while her mother was still alive. Monica took over a plot of land at the rear – part of what had been extensive servants' quarters – and here, under her supervision, a group of flats was built as rental units. Her mother Sumitra did not like this activity on her estate, and she squinted malevolently at the workmen trampling over her lawn. Monica, busy fighting with the contractor, ignored Sumitra's resentment: now, at fifty, she felt free for the first time to do what she and not what her mother wanted.

Monica had always been eclipsed by her mother, in looks and personality. Yet Sumitra herself had not been beautiful, not even in her youth – she was short and had always tended to be plump and her facial features too were rounded. But her gestures were as graceful as an Indian dancer's, and like a dancer, she jingled with golden bangles and with the anklets that it had become fashionable to wear along with other traditional Indian jewelry (Sumitra also tried a diamond nose stud but it didn't suit her). The blouses she wore under her saris were copied from Indian miniatures – it was all part of the cultural renaissance – and they were very short, just sufficient to support her breasts, leaving bare a large expanse of her midriff, as smooth as beige satin.

As her father-in-law's hostess, Sumitra had introduced an original style of entertaining, which was partly modern and partly derived from the traditional refinements of an Indian royal court. Later, after he died, she was greatly in demand at the official parties to which foreign dignitaries were invited. At that time, many of the cabinet ministers and even the President in his palace were peasant politicians with village wives and no idea how to function in society. Sumitra became New Delhi's semi-official hostess. The food she ordered to be prepared was mostly Indian but with the spices so cunningly blended that only their exquisite fragrance and none of their sharpness remained. Often a classical musician or dancer was brought in to entertain, their art also toned down to appeal to blander tastes; and though the guests were encouraged to immerse themselves in this cultured Indian ambience, they did not have to sit on the floor reclining against bolsters but were provided with chairs and sofas to support their stiff European spines.

At first her husband Harry accompanied her to all these grand receptions. Tall and slim, handsome and educated, he was an asset to her, though all he did was talk to the second secretary of some embassy or a cultural attaché's wife. This became very boring for him, and after a while he began to refuse to go with her; he said he couldn't stand another set of speeches extolling the amity and friendship between two great nations. At first she coaxed him – laughingly agreed with him that yes, wasn't it horrible, but if she could suffer why couldn't he, and anyway please for her sake – till he said, oh all right, and put on his high-collared coat with the jeweled buttons. But more and more he preferred to stay at home and cultivate his own interests. He tried his hand at translating couplets of Urdu poetry – purely as an amateur of course, he wasn't a poet, he wasn't a scholar; and when collections of these verses were published by real poets and scholars, he was content to admire and retreat, claiming nothing more for himself than the pursuit of a hobby. And as with all hobbies, this one could be taken up and put down at will, which suited him for he liked to spend his time in his own way. He lay under the ceiling fan, thinking about translating Urdu poetry and reading English detective stories. With the cessation of imports, he could no longer cultivate his taste for fine wines so he took to stronger drink – whisky and vodka.

His daughter Monica became his most constant companion. By this time she was old enough to be aware of the increasing tension between her parents. There was a quarrel now every time Sumitra wanted Harry to accompany her to one of her important functions. She no longer coaxed, she begged, and then she commanded, and then she remonstrated: didn't he realize that this was her *work*, her contribution to her country? That made him laugh: oh yes, wonderful contribution, to flirt around in her sari and jewels, like a professional – if he didn't come out with the word, she challenged him: professional what? What? And she stood demanding an answer, and he said, Courtesan. It amused him the way she went wild. They no longer shared a bedroom but they had a connecting dressing room, and with her gorgeous brocade sari half tucked in and half trailing on the floor behind her, she stamped up and down between their two bedrooms, reproaching him with the difference between her sense of duty and his utter lack of responsibility. He hummed to himself, and the more she worked herself up the calmer he became. Once he playfully trod on the sari trailing behind her so that she tugged it furiously from under his foot and it tore, and she sat down on the bed and burst into tears and he did not comfort her.

She accepted her fate and went everywhere by herself and he accepted his and stayed home and drank and read and played snakes and ladders with Monica. Later he taught Monica whist and contract bridge; by this time she was at college – she read history and international affairs – but she spent all her evenings with her father and they ate their dinner together, usually the two of them alone while Sumitra was needed elsewhere. And she was really *needed* – even Harry admitted it, that she was there to lay down the social and cultural guidelines of her newly independent country. An official car and chauffeur were at her disposal and stood parked in their driveway. Sometimes she had to go at dawn to the airport to receive and be photographed with some foreign cabinet minister and his wife; later in the day she took the wife shopping for Indian handicrafts. She had become an arbiter of taste, an expert on all aspects of Indian culture. Almost singlehandedly she revived cottage industries to export the best in Indian textiles and craftsmanship. She was the chairwoman of a committee to rename New Delhi streets, which had once commemorated English statesmen and soldiers such as Lord Kitchener, in honor of Indian freedom fighters; also of another committee appointed to take down statues of Queen Victoria and arrange design competitions for sculptures of Mahatma Gandhi.

She and Harry had settled down to a sort of brother and sister relationship. He mocked her work – of which however he was also quite proud – and the busier she was the more languid he became. He drank steadily – only vodka now – and this wrapped him in a pleasant haze, which made him very tolerant. She saw to it that he always had clean linen; he had taken to wearing only Indian clothes, fine white shirts with embroidery at the shoulders and neckline. Before leaving for her many duties, she arranged her household and ordered the day's meals for her husband and daughter. These two remained very close, and Sumitra was aware that this was partly the result of an alliance against herself. When Harry mocked Sumitra – he imitated the way she posed for the photographers while garlanding a VIP – Monica laughed loudly in her mother's face; and she too mocked her, not in the good-natured way that Harry did but bitterly. She blamed her mother for many things. Later, whenever

Kuku spoke admiringly of her grandmother's achievements, Monica would pull a face: 'She did it for herself,' she told Kuku. 'To show off and be admired by people; by *men*,' she said.

In her mid-thirties, when she met Lieutenant-General Har Dayal, Sumitra was even more attractive than in her youth. She had become elegant and worldly, befitting the part she played on the national stage. She rustled around in her brocades with masculine purpose and feminine grace; there was a somewhat set expression about her mouth now, which may have been the determination of a busy woman, an almost public personage, but also an indication of some disappointment. There was no one really she could open herself to fully: husband and daughter had ganged up against her, at best indifferent if not contemptuous of the great role she played. As for those among whom she played it – the politicians and higher bureaucrats – they were not of her background, not of her education, not of her class. There was no one, she felt, who understood her: except her husband, and he wilfully misinterpreted her. So she was ready for Lieutenant-General Har Dayal when he entered: for not only was he, like her husband, a man of education and refinement, he was also, unlike her husband, an important person – in fact, a sort of national hero. He was a career officer, among the last batch of Indians to be trained at Sandhurst where he had acquired the manners of a British gentleman. At the same time he was an Indian aristocrat, a minor raja in a minor state, not more than a large landowner but with an ancestral habit of command. He was of the traditional warrior caste and looked like a warrior: tall, broad, upright, manly and shining in his uniform. And he had just won a border war against a neighboring enemy country and had been decorated with the highest award for gallantry. Now he had been brought to army headquarters in New Delhi with a view to succeeding the present commander-in-chief.

Meanwhile he was an honored guest – an indispensable ornament like Sumitra herself – at all receptions and banquets for foreign dignitaries. He knew how to behave: to make conversation in English, to use the right cutlery, to let ladies precede him through a door. The Indian politicians still tended to rush in first and even to jostle and push their way to the front at the buffet table, so that Sumitra had to be on constant guard: it was mortifying to see a plate being snatched from the French ambassador's wife by the Minister for Trade and Commerce. Sumitra and Lieutenant-General Har Dayal became allies, each signaling to the other to prevent or make up for some breach of manners; sometimes both rolled their eyes in mock despair.

Lieutenant-General Har Dayal – or Too, as he came to be known to Sumitra and her family – had been married for many years and had teenage children at boarding schools. After the first few months in New Delhi, his wife, unable to stand the sort of official life they led, had gone back to their estate. Theirs had been an arranged marriage and, like him, she was of a minor royal house of the warrior caste; she rode horses and hunted tigers and was more at home in deserts and jungles than in political drawing rooms. So Too was mostly alone, and lonely; and Sumitra was also lonely. It was easy for them to come to an understanding, not so easy to become lovers. At the conclusion of the social events at which they met, they were driven home in their respective official cars; and although no family members lived with him, he was surrounded by his family retainers. However late it was, his batman waited up for him, to take off his boots and help him change for bed; and in case Too wanted anything at night, he slept outside his door on a little string cot, the way he had done throughout their army years together.

By the time Sumitra came home, her husband Harry was asleep. His drinking made him breathe heavily, even snore, which disgusted her so much that she tried to wake him; but he only grunted and turned over onto his other side, his long nerveless arm flung out on the sheet. She shut the two doors of their connecting dressing room, and lay in bed thinking of Too. In the course of their evening together, they had managed not only to exchange glances but also surreptitiously to brush up against each other, the lightest of contact – of arms or hands

– setting up a conflagration of nerves. It was fearful, painful, but also so exquisite that they kept finding opportunities to do it again. It was strange how they managed to contrive their understanding; neither of them had experience of secret affairs, they were innocent except in marriage. But it may have been that both had an ingrained habit of secrecy – of snatching moments of privacy out of communal living among family members, and the ever present family retainers, wakeful in service.

Night after night she lay in bed, longing for and plotting the next step beyond the secret touch of arm against arm. She liked to think that Too was lying in his house, in his bed, plotting in the same way. It was only later that she discovered how deep was his sleep, deeper than Harry's and in his case not induced by drink but by an untroubled mind and a robust constitution. But at that time, at the beginning, she lay awake straining her ears for the sound of his arrival, certain that he was as tormented as she was and had contrived a way to come to her. But all she heard was dogs barking to each other across the dusty night, and sometimes the howl of jackals that still infested the unbuilt areas around the capital; and worst, though faint through two closed doors, her husband's troubled alcoholic snores.

One night she could bear it no longer – she got up and let herself out and started up the little sports car she kept for her private use. She woke the watchman and put on such a stern preoccupied face that he unlocked the gate fast and without question. She drove through the wide and silent tree-lined streets. Too lived in an area of mansions requisitioned by the government of India for their own high-ranking officers; in the evening there were always many cars parked outside under the trees, for in almost every house there was some official function to which important guests came. But now all the parties were over and the houses shut up behind their high wrought-iron gates.

She reduced speed when she approached his house. She had vaguely planned to rouse his watchman in the same domineering manner as her own: but his watchman was not the usual sleepy old retainer with a blanket thrown over his shivering shoulders but a brisk little Gurkha soldier with a rifle that sprang alive in his hands as he shouted, 'Who's there!' At once the dogs started up – Too's Alsatians, brought from his estate – and, frightened as any miscreant, Sumitra stepped on the accelerator and drove off. Tears of fury and frustration splashed on her wheel, and when she got home, she was so careless in her anger that she sounded the horn repeatedly to have the gates opened. As she parked the car, she saw that a light had come on in the house; she bit her lip, angry now with herself but also determined to face down anyone who dared to challenge her.

Monica stood at the top of the stairs, watching her mother walk up them. Sumitra was calm; she said, 'What, aren't you asleep yet, Moni?'

'Where have you been?' Monica said in the imperious way in which she often addressed her mother. It was to assert herself against Sumitra's dominant personality, and also to counter the look of disappointment that was always in her mother's eyes when they looked at her. It was there now – Sumitra couldn't help it. Monica was lanky like her father, and her hair, her eyes, her complexion were dull: as if Sumitra had taken all the sparkle and warmth there was to be had and left none for her daughter.

'Goodness, I'm tired,' yawned Sumitra. 'I thought no one was ever going home – why, Moni, you know there was that banquet for the King of Nepal, I told you—'

'You went to a banquet for the King of Nepal – in this?' Monica scornfully indicated the lilac robe Sumitra had thrown over her nightdress on her way to Too.

Sumitra had become skilled enough in the ways of diplomacy to know how to handle a mistake that could not be redeemed. One simply swept over it – the way Sumitra now swept past Monica and into her bedroom where she stood at the mirror applying the night cream she had already applied some hours ago before retiring to her restless bed. Monica had come up behind her; she had no diplomacy at all: 'I'll tell Papa,' she said.

Sumitra went on smoothing cream into her smooth skin.

They could see each other in the mirror. After a while she replied, 'What will you tell him? That Mummy couldn't sleep and went for a drive? Yes, that's a stupid thing to do but it's not a crime, I hope.' She could see the grim expression on Monica's face falter into doubt. She went on, 'I get so exhausted with these interminable dinners that afterwards I can't sleep; I toss and turn half the night and don't know what to do with myself.' She unfastened her robe and, in a gesture of weariness, let it drop to the carpet. 'Sometimes I go down to make myself a cup of tea, and if that doesn't work, I take the car for a spin.' In the mirror she probed her daughter's indecisive face, then turned around to her: 'I try to be very quiet and not wake you or Papa – but tonight I'm sorry I was so upset—'

'Why were you upset?'

'I told you! The strain! You don't know, nobody knows what hard work it all is. They're so stupid. No one has the faintest idea how to do anything – tonight, you won't believe this, they were serving the fish *with* the soup – oh, I don't want to think about it! Every time I ask myself, why am I doing this, why can't I just stay home and eat my dinner in peace with you and Papa.' She laid her head on Monica's shoulder. Monica put her arm around her – but cautiously, as if not quite trusting her mother and ready to retrieve her affectionate gesture. Before this could happen, Sumitra kissed her: 'You must go to sleep now. It doesn't matter about me, but you shouldn't be missing out on your beauty sleep.' And when Monica hesitated – 'I think I'm getting there too – at last. That drive must have done me good.' And she yawned to prove it and was altogether so tired, so needful of sleep that Monica had to leave her and go back to her own room. It was some time before either of them was really asleep, for Monica too was restless now, not knowing what to believe, or even to feel about her mother.

Sumitra never told Too about her nocturnal expedition, nor did she repeat it. She still waited for him to plot the right maneuver, but finally her desire was fulfilled without any plotting at all. A Chinese military delegation was on a visit to New Delhi, and Too was among those appointed to entertain them. He had the large establishment and many servants for handsome entertainment; but he had no hostess, and it was natural for him to turn to Sumitra for help. She came to his house on the day before to check up on the glasses, the china, the silver; everything was there in plenty, but arranging it for the following day took many hours, so that Sumitra had to stay in the house till late at night. Too, always a considerate master, sent the servants away to rest in their quarters; he told his batman that he would not be needing him, even slipping him some money with a wink that meant he could have his evening of enjoyment with the dancing girls of GB Road the way he liked to do once in a while. Too himself was very tired – he undid his regimental tie and opened his shirt and fell down on his bed, saying 'Phoo' in exhaustion. Sumitra stood above him: 'Come on, what do you think you're doing, I still haven't been through the dessert plates or the coffee cups!'

'Golly, I can't keep up with you,' he said, letting himself sink into his satin bedcover. She tried to tug him up, but he only sank in deeper and half shut his eyes as if about to fall asleep. But his pupils glinted at her, and when she tugged at him again, he let his limbs go limp like those of a dead man. Laughing and scolding, she tried to pull him up – till suddenly his limp arms tautened and he grabbed her and brought her down, and at last they were where they wanted to be with each other.

The next day was brilliant – it was a garden party and all Too's roses were in bloom and pigeons and parrots flew about between the deep green trees and the deep blue sky. There were also some kites, but these were kept away by serv-ants vigorously flapping starched dinner napkins at them. All Sumitra's arrangements worked splendidly, so that the guests of honor relaxed enough to let down their stoic silent guard (but a few months later they attacked several border posts and penetrated into Indian territory). Monica was studying Chinese history and current affairs – it was her optional subject in her college course – so she had come along, escorted by her father. Of course they were entirely on the periphery of the party while Sumitra held the centre. She summoned the servants to bring platters of oven-baked chickens and fish kebabs and then instructed the Chinese guests to eat them Indian style with their fingers. She did this so charmingly that they all tried it and laughed at each other in Chinese while she laughed at them in English and the interpreter interpreted and all were comrades together.

Too was pleased with the success of his party but couldn't quite keep pace – no one could, when Sumitra was making a party go – so he wandered away from the buffet tables and found himself next to Harry, who stood admiring the roses with a glass in his hand. 'I'm Harry,' Harry introduced himself, and Too said, 'I'm Harry too.' They both laughed and it was from this time, that is from the first moment of their acquaintance, that Harry Too became Too.

'I belong to her,' Harry said, pointing to Sumitra in the distance. For a moment they both glanced at her – mature and fully ripened like Too's roses – then Harry turned back to these latter in their beds, and pointing to a particularly large and luscious specimen, 'What's that one?' he asked. Too wasn't sure, he had to get down to read the label. But Harry was no longer interested. 'Rose,' he said, 'it's called rose; eternal rose,' and he quoted: '"The nightingale has heard good news: the rose has come."'

'Ah,' said Too, getting up and dusting the earth from his knees; he didn't know much poetry but he loved hearing it.

This was the beginning of the friendship between the two Harrys (Hari Prasad and Har Dayal). Too often dropped in at the house between his various duties and engagements to spend time with Harry. He really enjoyed his company. Mostly Sumitra wasn't home, there were so many places where she was needed, but her husband had nothing whatsoever to do and was always available for a drink and a chat. Too matched him drink for drink, but whereas Harry was soon wrapped in the haze that alone enabled him to carry on his existence, Too gave no sign of diminution of energy – on the contrary, he became more alert, more vigorous, and more loudly appreciative of the poetry Harry recited to him. Monica often joined them; she also enjoyed Too's company and he loved having her with them, treating her as if she were a child, his child, and indeed he called her 'Beti,' daughter. At the same time he regarded her as his intellectual superior – not out of flattery, but admiring her because she went to college and could answer his questions, such as whether nineteenth-century Turkestan was part of Russia or China. And if she didn't know the answer, she looked it up next day in one of her textbooks, so in the evening she was ready for him and all three had a discussion about the Afghan wars or the three battles of Panipat. Too told them about his own military adventures, which were often of a secret nature such as smuggling sentry posts into enemy territory, or taking a detachment of troops to help quell a palace revolution in a neighboring kingdom.

These evenings were so enjoyable that Too sometimes forgot about an official function where he was expected; and once, when he did remember, it was already too late and he said, To hell with it, and stayed to dine with Harry and Monica. So it happened that when Sumitra returned from *her* official function, she found Too still in her house, with her husband and daughter. 'Oh my goodness,' she said, 'aren't you supposed to be at the Admiral's dinner?'

In one way, she was put out by his dereliction of duty, for in order to succeed to the post she wanted for him, he had to keep up his connections. But it also suited her to have him at home when she arrived. There was, as always, something she had to discuss with him – the war widows' fund, of which she wanted him to be the patron-in-chief. Harry was tired, he yawned, excused himself and went to bed. She sent Monica upstairs too – 'Don't you have an early class tomorrow, Moni?' But as soon as they were alone, Too got up and said he had to leave.

'Why?' she said – reproachfully, for it seemed so unfair to her when she and Harry hadn't slept together in years and were in separate bedrooms, with the doors of their connecting dressing room shut and, if she wanted, locked.

But Too would not stay – he wouldn't even kiss her goodnight. 'Not here,' he said when she clung to him.

'Who's there to see?' she whispered, but he disengaged himself and went out to where his car and driver were waiting.

When she went upstairs, pulling hairpins out of her hair so that it tumbled angrily around her shoulders, she found Monica standing at the top of the stairs. 'Go to bed,' Sumitra told her, but Monica would not relinquish her post until her mother was inside her bedroom with the door closed behind her.

But Sumitra was aware of Too's frustration and that he yearned for her as she did for him. It took her some time to realize that, in spite of his training in military maneuvers, in everyday affairs he was straightforward to the point of being simple, and it was up to her to devise a way. Now, whenever there was a function they had to attend together, she drove herself there in her little sports car; and when he arrived, he sent his car home, so that it was left to her to drive him back to his house. Only it was not there that they drove but beyond the confines of the city – this was before it had crept up with rows of government housing, and also before pollution from industrial plants and noxious fumes from decrepit buses had cast a pall over the Delhi sky. The stars were still visible and pure, and moonlight washed like ice water over the tombs and palaces and the desert into which they had been sinking for undisturbed centuries. Sumitra parked the car, and they crept up the stairwell of a deserted pleasure pavilion (only the bats stirred and squeaked). They carried a mat and cushions that she had brought, and spread them on a balcony with a railing of stone arabesques. Music was missing, but the air was laden with the scent of plants mysteriously flowering in the desert dust. Their lovemaking – undisturbed now, unbridled – was charged with the energy of those male and female divinities who between them are responsible for creating and upholding the world.

But when the schools were closed and his children on holiday, nothing could keep Too in New Delhi. Sumitra argued with him, pleaded the importance of his being in the capital at this time, when only a few months were left before the retirement of the current commander-in-chief. She pointed out that Too had to be constantly seen in the right circles to remind those who mattered of the superiority of his claim. But Too wouldn't listen to Sumitra. He took all his accumulated leave and returned to his home state for several of the crucial weeks when he should have been in the capital advancing his career.

It was left to Sumitra to keep his interests alive, and at this time she made herself particularly indispensable to the Minister of Defense, who was in overall charge of the top military appointments. This portfolio had been assigned to him not because he was in any way qualified for it but because some such cabinet post was due to his political standing. He however coveted another Ministry – that of Foreign Affairs – for which he was even less suitable. He was a peasant who had worked his way up from his village council through the political machinery of his native state, and from there, by shrewdness and cunning and the majority of votes he commanded, to a position at the national centre. In New Delhi he had been allotted one of the stately requisitioned mansions, but he had no idea how to live in it. His family were left behind in the village to look after their fields and their herd of buffalo (he had been, and still was, the local milk supplier). Like others, he turned to Sumitra to help him furnish his ministerial residence and, on diplomatic occasions, to act as his hostess. He made use of all her skills; and of her time too – she had hardly arrived home at night when there was a note from him to accompany him in the morning to the airport where some VIP had to be received with garlands. Or he telephoned – here he never made use of an intermediary but his own voice oozed down the line in the unctuous tone he had adopted with her, suggesting a wealth of understanding between them. And there was such understanding – when she urged Too's claim to him, he nodded to reassure her that he was ready to fulfill his part of whatever bargain it was they had made with each other.

Harry scorned him – he called him the Milkman, and whenever his peon arrived with a note, Harry told Sumitra, 'Here's another love letter from your Milkman.' She retorted angrily that he knew very well how all her efforts were to help their friend Too; and Harry shrugged and said yes, Too was a decent chap, one of their own sort, but the Minister was not. Sumitra defended the Minister, holding him up to Harry as an example of that manly ambition that was so lacking in Harry himself.

'What a pity he's so ugly,' Harry said.

She shouted, 'How does that matter? I'm not going to bed with him!'

'You're not?' Harry taunted her – aware that this would make her more furious than anything, the suggestion that anyone so squat and ugly and stinking of peasant fodder might be thought to aspire to her bed.

Yet later – many years later – that was what her daughter Monica alleged. With outsiders, Monica always spoke in glowing terms of her mother's contribution to her country and boasted of the honors she had received. But to her daughter Kuku she said, 'How do you think she did it! By sleeping with people of course . . . Well, what else!' she added, as though Kuku had contradicted her. 'How do you think she got her appointment to the UN – or her Padma Bhushan or whatever medal it was they gave her.'

Kuku protested, 'It was on merit; because she was so extraordinary for her time, so absolutely modern.'

'Oh yes, so absolutely modern that she'd sleep with anyone – even the Milkman,' Monica sneered. She still called him that, as her father had done, although he had filled some of the highest offices, and when he died, schools and government departments had been closed for two days as a mark of respect.

Kuku asked, 'What about Too? Did she—'

'Oh, I'm sure she'd have liked to, but he wouldn't look at her. He was *our* friend – Papa's and mine.'

Certainly, when Too returned to Delhi, his first visit was to Harry and Monica. It was the day of his arrival and he showed up unexpectedly and stood in the doorway, declaiming, '"The nightingale has heard good news: the rose has come."'

All three laughed with the pleasure of being reunited. It was teatime, but when the tray was brought, Harry said, 'Do we really want this?' so only Monica drank tea while the other two recalled the servant to bring out the drinks of their preference. 'Much too early of course,' Harry admitted, 'so it's lucky for us that she's at the All India WC' – this being his facetious name for the All India Women's Conference, of which Sumitra was the president.

Too had a lot to tell them – about his children, especially his eldest daughter who was already such a good shot that he was thinking of entering her for the Ladies Olympic team. Oh yes, and he himself had shot another tiger: not a man-eater this time, but the villagers had complained of some goats being killed, so he had gone out with his gun-bearer. He knew of its whereabouts because of the monkeys.

'The monkeys?'

'Yes, the monkeys. When they know a tiger's near, they run up to hide in the trees, shivering and chattering, and all the tiger has to do is walk around and around the tree. Around and around – around and around – and they become so completely paralyzed with fright, they drop off the branches like apples, one by one they come down: *plop*,' and Too raised his arms and let himself drop out of the chair onto the carpet.

At that moment Sumitra entered, and he quickly got up, laughing uproariously to hide his confusion. Whatever *her* feelings at the unexpected sight of him, she showed nothing but the pleasure of greeting an old friend and became at once the gracious hostess: 'Have you had tea – ah good, they brought the tray.'

Harry raised his vodka glass to her: 'Yes, have some . . . Too was telling us about the monkeys and the tiger. And how to shoot a croc. Do you know how to shoot a croc?' he asked Sumitra.

'In the eye,' Too said, raising an imaginary rifle. 'Straight in the eye.'

Harry said, 'Bang bang,' then turned to Sumitra, 'How dull it's been without him – we told him it was really high time he came back.'

'Yes, high time,' Sumitra confirmed with her hostess' courteous smile.

Only two days later an important reception was given by the Minister of Defense (the Milkman) to honor the visiting president of a neighboring country. This man had seized power after a *coup d'état*, and executing friends and enemies alike, had made himself dictator. He had been a general in the army – he was still known as the General – and, on his visit to India, was particularly interested in meeting members of the military establishment. This of course included Too, and Sumitra anticipated that his presence at this reception would clinch his triumph over his rival for the post of commander-in-chief. Her heart leaped with pride as soon as he entered – Too eclipsed not only his rival but everyone there except the visiting General, who was even taller than Too and had more medals on his chest.

Sumitra worked very hard for this party. She knew that the Minister as well as Too had to prove himself on this occasion, when the Prime Minister, the Vice-President, and members of the cabinet were guests in his house. She had had the place polished in every corner, changed the curtains, brought in additional carpets, lent her own silver and china and crystal and raided Too's house for more. The result made it clear to all present that the Minister's establishment and his style of entertaining were of a standard to do honor to his country, if he were to represent it as its Minister of Foreign Affairs. He himself unfortunately fell short – literally, for though strong and fat, he was of stunted growth. With his muscular build, like that of a wrestler, Sumitra had suggested to him a different mode of dress from the usual farmer's dhoti that left his stout calves bare. There was not much she could do about his manners – he ate with noisy relish and had not yet quite mastered the use of cutlery; but he was determined to please his guests and showed the intelligent concern of a practised host, sharp-eyed for every detail. He and Sumitra worked different parts of the reception area, both of them charging around with tremendous energy and sometimes signaling to each other across a room. It was always the Minister's eye she caught, wanting her to do something or seeking her advice, even when she was looking around for Too.

And she was often obliged to look around for him. Although this was the occasion for him to outshine his rival, it was the latter who was everywhere visible. Searching out Too, she at last found him sitting alone and morose on a back verandah. 'Why are you here? The PM is asking for you, he wants to talk to you, you know about what.'

'I don't know about what. I don't have anything to say to him. Or any of them. Not a blasted thing,' he said and took a long draught from his glass, as though it alone contained what was healthy and clean.

She wanted to remind him how hard she was working for him, how much she was doing on his behalf; but there was something else that took precedence. She stepped closer to him: 'Did you send your car away? . . . Why not? I've brought the MG for us.'

'Where did you want us to go – in this?' He was right: it was the monsoon season and rain fell in torrents over the Minister's garden, as it would be falling in torrents over the ruins of the pleasure pavilion and its latticed balcony on which they had spent their fragrant summer nights.

'There's that guest house out there.'

'With a hundred spies inside it.' Again he was right: this guest house – the converted mausoleum of a medieval prince – served as a secret rendezvous for so many important officials that the staff were all in the pay of foreign embassies needing incriminating information.

'We could drive to Gurgaon,' she pleaded. 'There are any number of little hotels where no one would guess or care who we were.'

'To Gurgaon: and arrive there tomorrow morning if we're lucky and don't get stuck in the mud. Do you have any idea what the roads are like with these rains?'

'And do you have any idea how I've missed you?'

She had stepped even closer to him but now quickly drew back: for the Minister had appeared in the doorway to the verandah, beckoning to her. His intelligent eyes darted from her to Too, taking in whatever there was to take in; it did not in the least divert him from his business with her.

'The General is leaving,' he informed her, causing her to hurry inside where a bustle of aides-de-camp and security men were clearing a path for this departure. Sumitra saw that Too's rival had made himself very prominent and had the General's attention. She did not hesitate to cut in on them: it was her privilege, as hostess, to have the last word of gratitude and farewell with the guest of honor and to accompany him to the front door. She mustered all her grace and her little courtly ways for this ceremony and was rewarded by a swift glance of appreciation from those vulture eyes (the General preferred blondes but was known to have a weakness for all feminine charm). She was also rewarded by the Minister: he patted her arm in a gesture that was not in the least disrespectful but expressed his gratitude, and also perhaps his promise of return for the service she had rendered him.

It was only a week later that Too was offered, over the head of his rival, the appointment of commander-in-chief. He turned it down, saying nothing about it to anyone. He spent most of that day with Harry and Monica, drinking, discussing their usual variety of interesting topics, and appreciating Harry's poetry recital over their glasses of vodka: '"Respect the cup you hold – the clay it's made from was the skulls of buried kings."'

'Ah-ha-ha-ha-ha,' said Too in applause.

He stayed for dinner but left early and went home and to bed, sinking immediately into his usual deep sleep from which nothing could wake him.

It was the servants who were roused by Sumitra – first the armed Gurkha, whose rifle she contemptuously pushed aside, then the bearer, and finally the batman, whom she stepped over where he lay at the door of Too's bedroom. She made a lot of noise and so did the dogs and the servants trying to stop her, but Too did not wake till she shook him hard by the shoulder: 'What have you done!' she cried.

He started up at once, like a soldier in ambush ready to face the enemy who has taken him by surprise; but the enemy was Sumitra.

He sent the servants back to their posts, calming them with his own unruffled manner. It was more difficult to calm Sumitra, but he managed to persuade her to wait for him in the drawing room. He wore his robe over his pajamas and brushed his hair with his silver brushes, planning his strategy. By the time he joined her, he was ready with his defense but she launched out immediately: 'I couldn't believe my ears when he told me! After all I did, after all he did, pulling all those strings for you—'

His face darkened: 'I want no strings pulled for me by a person like him.'

'Why? Because he's not a raja – because he hasn't been to Sandhurst and can't speak your kind of English – all right, our kind—'

'No. Because he's not a decent chap.'

Although he said nothing more, she knew what he was referring to. There was some scandal involving the Minister about contracts for army equipment, rumors of bribes taken – but good heavens, there were always rumors, always scandals, that was what political life was like: accusations and counter-accusations, intrigues and counter-intrigues.

It was useless to expect Too to have any understanding of these realities. She dropped the subject of the Minister and took up her own – and his: 'As commander-in-chief you would be in Delhi all the time – we would see each other whenever we want . . .' But his face remained closed, his eyes fixed on some distant place above her head. She broke down: 'What's the matter? Ever since you've come back, it's been like this – as if you don't want to be back; as if you don't want to be with me.'

He did not reply but began to pace the room in thought. It was a large room, with sofa-sets imported from England, hunting trophies on the walls, and family photographs in silver frames scattered over occasional tables. He circled it several times, but his pacing brought him nothing – he still had no idea how to deal with the situation.

Again it was she who had to take the initiative: 'All that matters is that you should be here; near me; that we should be together. All right, refuse, if you don't want to be the army chief, if you feel it's not for you—'

'That's right!' he exclaimed and stopped pacing, relieved to have this thought expressed for him. 'It's not for me!'

'Then what's for you?' she said softly; she laid her face against his chest and stroked it with both hands. But she felt him stiffen. She stepped back to gaze up into his face, which remained closed against her. Her heart beat in anguish; her eyes swept around the room as though seeking some other help. She took in the photographs – most of them were of his children, his handsome young family of two girls and a boy, also some of his wife, who was very beautiful but had always remained cold to him, caring more for her own family, her sister and brothers, than for him.

Sumitra became desperate: 'If you resign your commission, we could go away somewhere, you and I. Why not – look at me! I'm willing to do it, why not you? I'd arrange it, everything – we'd go abroad to some place where not a soul knows us and we need never come back here ever again—'

He groaned aloud. If she was desperate, so was he, and now he dared to say this much: 'I need to be at home – no, not here but *my* home – yes, with my family and in my house and on my land and with my people – what shall I tell you!' He broke off, unable to continue and tell her what it was he intended to do.

He told Harry and Monica – but only just before he left. By that time Sumitra was away on one of her cultural relations tours – she had taken a group of potters and weavers to a symposium on handicrafts in Bangkok – so he was relieved of the necessity of telling her at all. She was only away for ten days, but by the time she returned, he was dead. He had been shot in the back of the head, ambushed by the outlaws he had gone to suppress. Harry read the news on the front page of the newspaper, which also carried a photograph of Too's corpse. Harry hid it from Monica and broke the news to her himself as gently as he could. Both of them were devastated. They could not believe it: Too had left in such tremendous high spirits! He had himself asked to be sent on this expedition and had been looking forward to it as to a tiger shoot. And in a way it had been like a tiger shoot for him: this band of outlaws had for years been harrying the countryside – *his* countryside! *his* people! – pillaging, burning, raping, kidnapping, killing, worse than wild beasts. Worse, much worse than wild beasts! cried Too; and if he caught them – and he would catch them, he promised – he would shoot them in cold blood. 'Killed while attempting to escape,' was the usual formula, Too told Harry and Monica with a chuckle. He would have them shackled together in a row and them one by one – bang! bang!

It was about this time that Monica had her nervous breakdown, which her daughter Kuku later diagnosed as due to a lack of sex life. Kuku, who had plenty of sex herself, ascribed most malfunctions to this cause; but at the time Sumitra must have come to the same conclusion, for it was around then that she had arranged a marriage for Monica with the ambitious young under-secretary Malhotra. This marriage had only lasted long enough to produce Kuku, and then Monica and her baby had moved in with Sumitra, who was by that time a widow. So Kuku, growing up with these two women, had from childhood been a witness to the fights between them. Monica, who continued to blame her mother for everything, was always on the attack, forcing Sumitra to defend herself. For instance, Monica blamed her for letting Too go on the expedition that had led to his death: 'You could have stopped it,' Monica said.

'How? How? I was in Bangkok, I didn't even know about it.'

'You could have got him some appointment to keep him in Delhi. You could easily have done it, you were in so thick with the Milkman. You certainly got everything out of him for yourself, though goodness only knows what you had to do in return.'

Once, when Kuku was about twelve, her grandmother told her about the Minister, 'He was very kind to me.'

'But what did you have to do for him?' Kuku innocently inquired.

Sumitra shrugged: 'I suppose I helped him to become the Foreign Minister.'

*    *    *

She always considered that he had done more for her than she had for him, and at a time when she needed it. After Too's death, she had to contend not only with Monica's nervous breakdown but with Harry's increasing alcoholism. He began to drink the moment he got up and continued steadily until his servant helped him to bed at night. He and Monica no longer had their pleasant times together – it was as though, without Too, they had broken apart and each was locked up in solitary misery. Sumitra meanwhile was kept busier than ever, for it was the winter season and many important foreign visitors had to be entertained and taken to see the Red Fort and the Qutb Minar. It was always very late when she was at last driven home; but however late it was. Monica would be waiting up for her. She seemed to have spent the day brooding about her mother, whom she held responsible for Too's death, Harry's drinking, and Monica's own inferiority complex and generally unhappy life. Sumitra, although exhausted after her long day, tried to calm her, and it always ended in the same way, with Monica's rage melting into tears and Sumitra tucking her into bed and tenderly kissing her goodnight. It was only then that Sumitra could go to bed herself and give way to her own grief, which she shared with no one.

After Too had refused the high command, the Minister and Sumitra did not mention him again between them; except on his death, when the Minister spoke some conventional words of condolence to her, on the loss of her family friend. At this time the Minister was even more occupied than Sumitra, for besides all the social activities and the official meetings, he was involved in the many secret comings and goings preceding a major cabinet reshuffle. When, at the end of that busy season, he was offered the post he had coveted, Sumitra was the first person he informed of his success. She almost admired him at that moment: he was not a handsome figure – the very opposite, even now after she had done all she could to improve his appearance. But there was something about him in his triumph – an energy, a manliness – that she had known in no other man, not even in Too with all his shining looks and chest full of medals. And where had it all led to, with

Too, she thought, shot like a dog by thieves and murderers: and for the first time the tears she shed by herself every night sprang to her eyes in broad daylight and in the presence of another person.

It could not have been the reaction the Minister had expected to his announcement; but it was his life's business to deal with the vagaries of human psychology and conduct. He scrutinized her face with his eyes that were set too deeply in fat to reveal their penetrating intelligence. Then he joined his palms together like a supplicant and said that there was something she must do for him; that she could not refuse him, must not. He offered her three choices: the high commission in London, the embassy in Washington, and the Indian mission to the UN in New York. He knew it was much too much to ask of her who had already done everything for him, but he needed her more than ever in his new responsibilities, and without her he was helpless as a little child and could proceed no further.

During the following years, Sumitra lived mostly abroad. Although she was already middle-aged during her great years as India's ambassador to the UN, she had retained her smooth olive skin and her pitch-black hair and sparkling eyes; and she wrapped herself so skillfully in her sari that she appeared merely plump, as she had been, and not fat, as she had become. She had always loved jewelry and now was so laden with it that she resembled a barbaric queen – an impression enhanced by the bolder colors and patterns of her saris, which were of traditional designs adapted to modern tastes. The expression on her face was that of a person used to giving orders to people – in contrast to her manner, her exquisite gestures of courtesy and submission to the point of immolation which were a mark of royal breeding as well as of the courtesan and temple dancer. Her parties were, like herself, an enchanting mixture of east and west. There was always plenty of liquor, but also pomegranate and mango juices and spiced yoghurt drinks; the servants glided around with silver trays of delicacies that were to be found only in the finest Indian homes where they were made from recipes handed down by a grandmother.

A visiting Indian musician – always a maestro of the first rank – would entertain after dinner; but for those who had business with each other there were brandy and cigars in the study and doors that could be closed. Sumitra herself closed them, smiling for a moment as she did so with perfect understanding and a promise of privacy for whatever matters of high state had to be discussed.

Now in charge of foreign affairs, the Minister frequently traveled abroad, stopping off in New York whenever he could. She looked forward to his visits. He consulted her about policy and discussed the personalities of the world and national leaders they both had to deal with. She continued to monitor his personal habits, and here too he followed her advice – for instance, he left off using a certain pungent body oil prescribed as beneficial to the flow of blood to the brain and other important organs.

Monica quarreled with her about the Minister, as she quarreled with her on all subjects. Monica traveled between her mother in New York and her father in New Delhi, and it would be difficult to say in which place she was more unhappy. She was undergoing treatment with a New York analyst and was learning far more about herself and her relationship with her mother than was good for either of them. She also learned not to suppress her natural feelings, and whenever the Minister visited, she made no secret of her contempt for him. But even though she tossed her head and flung out of the room without returning his courteous greeting, he smiled tolerantly and reassured Sumitra that the girl was young, a child only. Nevertheless, it was he who suggested matrimony in place of psychiatry (he had just married off his own sixteen-year-old daughter, with two thousand guests consuming five hundred pounds of clarified butter). And it was he who found Monica's bridgeroom: on his return to New Delhi, he made discreet inquiries in his own Ministry, and after personally interviewing several likely candidates, he finally selected Under-Secretary Malhotra. However, Monica always denied that her marriage had been arranged. She claimed she had met Malhotra at a diplomatic party, and had been fool enough to be taken in

by him. 'It was because I was so unhappy,' she explained to
her daughter Kuku. 'Because of Mummy and what she had
done to me.'

During her years at the UN, Sumitra's husband Harry also
sometimes came to stay with her. Unlike the Minister, he fitted
well into her diplomatic salon. Harry had elegant manners and
conversed easily in English and with charm. Unfortunately he
also got drunk very quickly – and now it only took a drink or two
to get him into that state. He was never rowdy or ill-behaved
but continued to stand holding his glass with a smile frozen on
his face. If anyone spoke to him, he tried sincerely to respond,
but so unsuccessfully that people tended to back away and he
was left standing by himself, still smiling and still on his feet,
though by now supporting one shoulder against a wall. He
was very apologetic about his condition, and readily agreed
to enter a clinic in Virginia that Sumitra had arranged for
him. But he returned after less than a week – 'Leave it,'
was all he said in answer to Sumitra's reproaches. That same
night he was for the first time noisily drunk and she had to
make signs to the servants, while her guests pretended not to
notice him being hustled away, loudly declaiming poetry as
he went.

Nevertheless, she liked having him there, at least during
the few hours of the day when he was sober. He was the one
person with whom she could be as she had been. They spoke
of old friends – about these also as they had been and not
as they were now: some of them were bureaucrats or judges,
some were alcoholics like Harry, some dead like Too. They
both spoke of Too with loving nostalgia, and it didn't matter
that she was nostalgic for the moonlit nights in the ruined
pleasure palace and Harry for the poetry and vodka and chit-
chat in his New Delhi garden. It all appeared as remote now
as those scenes of royal indulgence depicted in the miniature
paintings that hung on Sumitra's walls. These pictures were
just beginning to be recognized at their true value, and she had
been among the first to acquire, for a few rupees, a collection
that was later auctioned at Christie's. Harry himself seemed to
belong in those paintings, to be one of the long dead princes,

from Kulu or Kashmir, shown reclining among little golden drinking vessels and flowers that scintillated like the jewels in their turbans.

Harry's last visit to New York – he died shortly after his return to India – coincided with one of the Minister's foreign tours. Both of them were present at a cocktail party given by Sumitra in honor of the Minister, preceding a dinner at the Iraqi embassy, also in his honor. Sumitra had been nervous all day, for Harry was very irritated by the presence of the Milkman (as he still called him), who was living in the house with them. 'Well, what should I do?' Sumitra defended herself. 'It's not my house, it's an official residence belonging to the government of India.'

'Oh yes,' sneered Harry, 'he *is* the government of India. He's certainly got his dirty hands in the treasury up to the elbows.' He was referring to a major financial scandal that again involved the Minister: this was nothing unusual – rumor as pungent as his body oil clung to him throughout his career.

Sumitra did not try to argue with Harry. Like Too before him, he would never understand. He had no conception of the shifts and makeshifts necessary to hold on to a position of power, and that what appeared to him as bribery and corruption was nothing but a judicious balancing of funds to keep the machinery of government oiled and functioning.

That evening, though performing with her usual accomplishment the role of diplomatic hostess, she glanced more often than ever toward Harry in his corner. It was also second nature for her to keep an eye on the Minister; but this was really no longer necessary, for by now his very defects had turned into assets. His English had remained rudimentary, but that only made people listen to him more attentively, as if fearful of missing something important he was saying. And there was a sort of power in his earthiness – the smell of cow dung still seemed to cling to him, if no longer physically – a suggestion of roots and soil that was exciting to Sumitra's cosmopolitan guests. Elegant women clustered around him and he made no secret of his liking for them, though of course in a very respectful way. He knew perfectly where to draw the line, and also where it was permissible to go beyond it – there were rumors about him in this area as well, and whenever he arrived in some backwater of his electoral district, the local bosses knew what sort of girls to bring for him from the bazaar.

Now, at Sumitra's cocktail party, he was playful with a kind of crude gallantry that charmed his listeners. Although at home he was a strong advocate of the national program of total prohibition, here he indulged his liking for strong liquor, at the same time retaining the full use of his perfectly honed faculties. His eyes darted around as swiftly as his mind to pinpoint those guests who were the most important to him on his present visit. At that particular party it was the head of an international monetary found, and he had already taken care to establish a friendly rapport with him prior to their official meeting scheduled for the following day. Now he felt at liberty to relax and to amuse his sophisticated audience with his own brand of rustic humor. Stretching out his hand to a servant for another glass, he burst into a snatch of song – a simple folk melody that suited his remarkably pleasant singing voice. There was applause and delighted laughter, so that Sumitra – now herself occupied in exerting her charm on the head of the monetary fund – glanced over to the little circle of which he was the admired centre. She smiled to see this strong and wily politician, who held power over millions of souls and vast stretches of land, turn back into the lusty village youth he had once been. He sang of the dust swirled up at dusk by the homecoming cows, and the jingle of the ornaments adorning the village bride. He also shared his taste for Bombay talkies and switched from folk song to popular film song – the rose and the nightingale at their last gasp but now shrill and sweet enough to delight his sturdy peasant soul. 'When you dip in the lake, O bathing Beauty, beware of driving us mad!' he sang and even broke into a little shuffle of a dance. Although squat as a toad in his politician's homespun garb, he transformed himself into a screen heroine with a wet garment clinging to her body, combing the long tresses that cascaded down to her hips.

Along with everyone else, Sumitra was so intent on this

performance that for a moment she relaxed her vigilance over Harry in his corner. It was only when she saw the Minister – seemingly engrossed in his little song and dance act – glance in that direction that she too looked at her husband. Harry had climbed on to a chair and was declaiming something – but already, at a sign from the Minister, the servants had closed around him and were half coaxing, half lifting him down. The Minister was giving another sample of a film song – 'I'm a vagabond, wandering in the woods of the heart' – so that everyone's attention continued to be fixed on him. Only Sumitra was with Harry, along with several servants – some of them brought from his childhood home in Delhi – who had got him down from his chair and were edging him toward the door. He was trying to tell them something with all the earnestness of someone completely drunk, and when they didn't understand, he appealed in frustration to Sumitra: 'Dragging our poets in the mire – Ghalib and Faiz!' Then he shouted, 'Degradation!' and tried to point at the Minister, who was still giving his audience a taste of Bombay film lyrics; but the servants quickly lowered Harry's arm and kept it pinned to his side. Sumitra followed them through the door and stood at the foot of the stairs, watching them lead Harry up to his room. He was looking back at her and quoting something but slurring his words, so that she wasn't sure whether it was about the rose and the nightingale, or Jamshed's throne gone on a puff of wind.

When she returned to her party, it was still going splendidly. The Minister had finished his act and, pleased to have given pleasure, was laughing together with his audience. He had taken off his little boat-like cotton cap and was wiping the perspiration from his head. As he did so, for a brief second his eyes slid toward Sumitra, and she gave him the briefest nod to reassure him that Harry was being taken care of. From here on – according to the official report to New Delhi – the evening's program proceeded as per schedule.

# DEVELOPMENT AND PROGRESS

I

We were all young then and in our beginnings: Sanjay and I, Gita and Ratna – the country itself, for it was only a few years after Independence. I was in New Delhi on my first diplomatic posting, and along with everyone else at the British High Commission, I had come in a spirit of atonement. We felt it to be our mission to make up for two hundred years of colonial rule and, in contrast to our predecessors, to show our full appreciation of India and Indian culture. I had no difficulty with that; like some before and many, many after, I fell in love with the country. There is no need for me to go into detail. Others have done so, describing the overwhelming sensual and emotional effect India has had on them; and, in some cases, how this was enhanced by their feeling for a particular person, or persons.

I lived in a flat in what was then becoming known as new New Delhi, extending beyond old New Delhi, which had been built as the imperial capital. Now it was the national capital and everyone who could, including all the foreign missions, was buying up land and building on it. While waiting for the British High Commission complex to be completed, we staff members rented accommodation in private houses, most of them newly built by newly rich Indians. My flat was in an area known as Golf Links because one of the sites had been earmarked for a golf club. Only a few years ago it had all been desert land, nothing but dust and jackals, but now, besides the potential golf club, there were rows of expensive villas, all of them ultra-modern, pastel-colored, air-conditioned. Spindly trees had been planted along what were not yet streets; a market was coming up, not bazaar stalls but proper shops, with doors and plate-glass windows, selling things required by Westerners and Westernized Indians, such as pastries and ham.

Although Sanjay was entitled to government quarters – he was among the very bright young men at the very new Ministry of External Affairs – he chose to remain with his sisters, Gita and Ratna, in their house in the Civil Lines of Old Delhi. The house had been built by their grandfather in a vaguely Gothic style with a turret on the roof and pointed arches enclosing the surrounding verandah. It was in an enclave of houses belonging to members of their family, for several brothers had bought up the land together. When Sanjay was sixteen, Gita twelve, and Ratna nine, their parents were killed in a car accident. Instead of moving in with their neighboring relatives, the three young orphans elected to remain on their own; so by the time I got to know them ten years later, they were used to being entirely free and independent. This somehow enhanced their glamor – already considerable, for all three were extremely good-looking. They had two cars which they loved to drive, one hand lightly on the steering wheel, the other, holding a cigarette, on the open window. Sanjay took the Chevrolet every morning to the External Affairs Ministry, while Gita and Ratna disputed – they never quarreled – the use of the other car, a dashing MG. Gita usually took it, for she often had to drive to New Delhi, to help one of her artist friends set up an exhibition. Ratna only had to go to her nearby college, where she studied English literature; she also wrote poetry and stories, which she was too shy to let anyone see.

All of us at the High Commission were very conscientious about mixing with Indians: mostly higher-ranking civil servants and people in culture and the arts. But these social efforts tended to break down, and our parties often ended up with the Indian guests on one side talking shop with one another and foreigners doing the same on the other. I attended enough

High Commission parties to learn that there was always an unheard – and later, when everyone was more outspoken – a positively audible sigh of relief when the Indians left and the rest of us could draw together into our own cosy circle. Still, we continued these 'bridge parties' – we had even ironically adopted the old Anglo-Indian term – for they were so much part of our job that we were paid per head for each local guest we entertained. But for most people, on either side, it became more and more just part of one's official duties, and finally there were only a few of us left who genuinely enjoyed the company of Indians. And then sometimes it happened – as it did to me – that we preferred it to that of our compatriots whose social occasions we got through as quickly as possible, to rush off to our Indian friends.

I spent every moment I could with Sanjay and his sisters in their Gothic house in the Civil Lines. Friends were always welcome there, for any meal, at any hour. There were plenty of servants, some of them descended from several generations of retainers, who considered themselves part of the family and even as guardians of the three young orphans. The house had not been changed since the time of the parents and grandparents. The long drawing room, which formed the center of the house, was still basically Indo-Victorian, with carved sofas and armchairs and many occasional tables, and weighty silver pieces like a rose-water sprinkler and an ornate tea-set on a tray with scalloped edges. There were no windows but skylights set high up under the ceiling so that it was always dark in there – dark and cool in the summer but freezing in the winter months, since no ray of sunlight could penetrate the thick masonry of the outer and inner walls. So during the cold season there was always a fire lit and the friends gathered around it and drank mulled red wine. They talked incessantly on the many topics that burned inside them like the hot wine they were drinking. This whole country was theirs now at last, in all its breadth and multitudes, with all its history and relics left behind by its defeated conquerors (including us, the last of them). Many of these young people already held positions of great authority, like Sanjay in the Ministry of External Affairs;

others, like Gita's painter friends, were developing a whole new line of indigenous culture, exploring the depths of their Indian souls. Of course everyone had a different agenda – everything was so wide open – and they argued loudly in their rather high-pitched voices that were such a pleasure to listen to that sometimes I simply enjoyed the sound of them without following their arguments. They spoke in an English that was perfect but more softly accentuated, more mellifluous, more feminine even than is characteristic of our language.

Naturally, there were romances – but mostly with no cost attached because serious arrangements were left to their elders. There were however a few love matches, and I'm sorry to say that these did not always work out. It is a pity to turn from those days of hope and romance to the grimmer future that awaited some among us. Let me get it over with: both Gita and Ratna married for love, both marriages ended badly. Gita married one of her artist protégés – she went so far as to elope with him, for a civil service in Meerut where his family lived in poor circumstances. He did not turn out to be the genius she had expected and she soon left him and had other affairs, some with foreigners, none of them happy. Ratna made a more suitable choice: she married a young diplomat, a colleague of her brother's, who started off with the same chances of high promotion as Sanjay but ended them through his heavy drinking and his ugly, dishonest character. He was finally suspended from the service but that was after Ratna had committed suicide during a posting in Kampala. It was a great scandal at the time, but what is the point of talking about the dismal future that followed those early radiant days.

Whenever I was with them, our Indo-British relationship was a frequent and favorite topic. They warned me that it would all go out of the window, everything we had tried to foist on them: our mode of dress, our method of government and of education. The English language itself, they said, would end up on the dust-heap, for it had no potential to express the Indian soul – all this delivered in their very pure English sprinkled with some rather old-fashioned slang like 'what the

heck' and 'putting on side.' They teased me for being so English
– but how could I help it? I was tall, thin and pale and had
inherited my mother's blue eyes and rather long chin; before
joining the foreign service, I had studied PPE (Philosophy,
Politics and Economics) at Oxford. In my Oxford accent I
would pretend to contradict them – 'Yes, but we gave you
the railways, the telegraph and the telephone and all the rest
of it: where would you be if we hadn't dragged you with us
into the twentieth century?'

'Where would we be? Listen to her – you gave us Macaulay
and denigrated our Indian culture—'

'Hey wait a minute! Who was it translated Kalidasa and the
Upanishads?'

'A German! It was Germans, not you people, all you gave
us was your steamed pudding and custard!'

So we went on, mostly in good fun; I remember only one
person who was seriously angry with me for our two hundred
years of colonial oppression, and that was Pushpa. But she, I
suppose, was angry for other reasons as well.

I have spoken of our winter evenings, but there were also the
summer ones. After the scorching day, we gathered on the lawn
that had been deeply watered by the gardener and his assistant.
The flowerbeds were empty – the roses and chrysanthemums
bloomed in winter – but there were jasmine bushes and
Queen of the Night emitting scents that were so pungent
that the first wave deadened the olfactory nerves and it was
some time before they revived enough to receive the next
onslaught; and the hotter the day the more lusciously sweet
the perfumes drenching the night air. We sat in white wicker
armchairs and drank iced sherbet, while fans, plugged in from
the verandah, whirled around to keep us cool. The only sound
came from the excited voices of the very new and very young
administrators of India, raised in debate. Sometimes we went
up on the terrace where the turret held more armchairs and
fans. We leaned on the parapet and gazed over the tops of the
trees to the open land surrounding Delhi where jackals and
peacocks lived, emitting untamed cries.

It was here one night that Sanjay joined me. We leaned

side by side, breathing in the air of jasmine and desert dust, spanned by the sky with its crowd of diamond stars scintillating like wedding guests.

'Ah Kitty,' he said, 'here you are – getting away from us all, I suppose. Escaping our endless talk, talk, talk.'

I said, 'I could listen to you for ever.'

'No, don't encourage us. We talk too much. Far too much.'

We gazed down at the group on the lawn. The girls in their pastel saris were only a soft glimmer but the young men shone in their starched white Indian clothes. We couldn't hear what they were saying, just their voices drifting up to the terrace, melodious and indistinct.

Sanjay said, 'But it's not *just* talk. We really mean it.'

'I know you do.' I wanted to keep it vague and not have him explain what it was they really meant. All winter I had heard about their concern for the future of India, and I believed in it and was on their side; now I wanted him to say other things to me.

'You must understand our dilemma,' he said. 'Nehru's steel plants versus Gandhi's spinning wheel. Of course, the spinning wheel has to go, there's no question.'

'But how to preserve its spirit.'

'Exactly. You understand us exactly, Kitty.' He had a caressing way of saying my name. He said it again: 'Kitty ... It's a nice name, I like it, but it doesn't really suit you. It's not serious enough. And I think you're basically a very serious person. Of course you are: I mean, my goodness, not everyone can get a First in PPE and pass the foreign service exam.'

'You've passed yours so you must be a basically serious person too.' I was teasing him: a lot of teasing went on among us, I suppose it was a form of flirtation.

But he remained grave: 'I try to be, but sometimes I feel I'm too playful.'

Playful! I loved the word, it expressed the light-hearted spirit that bubbled like a spring under all their high ideals and ambitions and kept these fresh.

'We have terrible problems, Kitty. Poverty – backwardness

– diseases, medieval diseases that have long been wiped out in the developed world—'

'My real name isn't Kitty, if that's any help. I mean to your conception of me. It's really Katharine.'

'Katharine.' He considered it. 'Yes, Katharine is seriously English.'

He stood close beside me; his breath was very sweet. Waves of deliciousness welled up inside me: so this was love, falling in love, the real thing.

'But you know what?' he said. 'I prefer Kitty. Because I don't believe you're so very English. You're sensitive, understanding – in a way the others aren't. You know what I think? I think you're more like us. You're really Indian.'

'I wish I were.'

'Really? You wish that? Why, Kitty? Please tell me.'

His eyes, dark pools melting in moonlight, were fixed on me. Perhaps from that moment a new intimacy might have arisen between us. But we were interrupted.

'Sanjay? Are you here?'

It was Pushpa, the fat girl whom no one liked very much. She stepped closer and peered to make us out: 'Oh, it *is* you. What are you doing up here? Listen, I have to go and my car hasn't shown up. That new driver is completely unreliable, I've told Daddy again and again, but of course it's me who'll get the scolding if I'm home late.'

'I'll drop you,' Sanjay said at once.

'Sorry to break up the tête-à-tête,' she said with an unapologetic laugh.

'Oh yes, you should be sorry. Kitty and I were on the verge of solving all the problems of the world, weren't we, Kitty? Wait a sec while I get my car keys.'

We trooped down the stairs. I left shortly after they did, driving my little Morris Minor through the ancient city gates of crumbling masonry that led from Old to New Delhi. I wasn't disappointed but very excited. The city was asleep, people were stretched out on the sidewalks, some on string cots, others on tattered cloths spread on the ground or on handcarts from which in the day they sold peanuts and bananas. On one side the turrets and bastions of the Red Fort stood massed in shadow, on the other the dome of the great mosque was veiled in a reflected light, dimly white but with the moon in its first quarter glittering beside it, a diamond-hard scimitar.

Pushpa was different from the other girls. They were all bright and intelligent, but she was brilliant. She was among the first women to pass the Indian Administrative Service exam and was at present with the Ministry of Health and Family Welfare. Before that, she had been sent out to a district in central India, where she had been responsible for administering vast areas of land and a rural population of several hundred thousand. This had given her a very authoritative manner and a loud voice that drowned out every argument. She was respected for her brains, but she was not popular. Sanjay's sister Gita was positively hostile to her. She warned Sanjay that Pushpa was 'out to catch him' (this was the phrase she used). Sanjay just laughed in his easy charming way and said, Don't worry, he had no intention of getting caught before his time. As a member of the élite foreign service, he was of course a highly desirable match; very good offers kept coming for him, from landowning and even royal families of their own caste. These offers were rejected out of hand by his two sisters. They were none of them in a hurry to give up their carefree life in their own house. And besides, they were radically opposed to the concept of arranged marriages – at least, the two girls were: both of them were determined to marry only for love. Sanjay's attitude was more ambivalent.

The subject of arranged marriage was among those often discussed by these friends. It came under the category of tradition versus modernity (spinning wheel v. steel plant), though with a more personal edge to it. Some agreed with Gita and Ratna that only the free choice of a love match was acceptable to a modern educated Indian; others urged the wisdom that their elders would bring to the selection of a suitable mate. Pushpa was among those advocating a middle course. By all means, she shouted, meet each other, get to know each other, make your own decision, but for goodness sake, nothing rash, no elopement! Let parents have the say to which they were entitled. Since her argument was delivered more cogently and more loudly than anyone else's, it prevailed with some who wavered in their opinion. These included Sanjay. Much annoyed, his sister Gita tossed her shoulder-length dark auburn hair and said that *he* could do what he liked but *she* wasn't going to let herself be led like a lamb to slaughter. This caused laughing protests that they were talking about marriage not slaughter. The wit among them – it was Ratna's future husband – called out: 'Isn't it the same thing?' Amid more laughter, Gita stamped her foot: 'I thought we were having a serious discussion!' Then she turned to me: 'What do you think?'

They often did that – asked for my opinion as that of an impartial outsider. Now too they all turned toward me and Sanjay said, 'Yes, let's hear your side of this highly interesting question.'

Although I felt myself stupidly blushing, I spoke up bravely: 'Well of course, I could only marry if I were in love.'

'But how would you *know*?' Sanjay said, frowning the way he did when he wanted to get to the root of a problem.

'Oh, I would know all right. That's easy.'

'Too easy,' put in another brilliant young man (later India's ambassador to France). 'Who was it said, "Many people would never have been in love if they hadn't heard others talk about it"?'

'That's utter and complete rubbish,' Gita said, and Ratna felt even more strongly: 'It's horrible. I hate cynicism.'

Pushpa's voice was firmly raised again: 'And supposing you were what you call in love with the wrong person – someone completely unsuitable? Like an uneducated person, or someone from a different class or caste or a different race?'

Gita challenged her: 'If Kitty fell in love with an Indian – is that what you're asking?'

Then Pushpa challenged me: 'Would you marry him?'

'Of course I would. If he asked me.' I laughed away my own embarrassment: 'This is purely theoretical – probably I'll never marry. I'm supposed to be a career woman.'

'So am I,' said Pushpa. 'But I hope and trust I shall also be a good wife and mother.'

And Gita murmured, 'Keep on hoping and trusting till you find some blind fool to ask for you.' Only one or two girls heard her, and it made them titter. Secure in their own beauty, they could afford to be patronizing about Pushpa. She was squat and overweight, and her arduous studying – it was not easy to pass the IAS exam – had weakened her eyesight, so that she was the only one of the girls who had to wear glasses.

After that one almost romantic moment on the roof of his house, I never again found myself alone with Sanjay. Yet others in our group were not shy about being alone with each other. They even managed to sleep together – making secret sexual arrangements seemed to be almost a tradition among them (and other arrangements too, when a girl got accidentally pregnant). Sanjay was different; there was something aloof about him, as though he were cautiously keeping himself for his future. He was always more than polite to me – tenderly so: he worried about my health, that I shouldn't eat anything outside or drink unboiled water. 'You don't have the stomach to deal with our stout Indian germs,' he told me (but I never once got sick). When the weather turned in November and we were still sitting out on the lawn, he would hurry inside and get a shawl for me to wear. It irritated Pushpa: 'She's not made of glass,' she said. A little later she herself would start shivering, so that Sanjay had to go in and get another shawl.

Whenever there was a party, Gita and Sanjay argued about inviting Pushpa. 'Why should she come?' Gita said. 'She's not such a great friend of ours that she has to be around our necks every time.'

'She's both a friend *and* a colleague,' Sanjay answered. 'It's important, Giti – we have to stick together, all of us in the services.'

'That's no reason for the rest of us to be bored to death.'

But Sanjay, usually so sweetly yielding with his sisters, was adamant on this point: he could not, would not offend anyone who might in any way be involved in his career.

He was ambitious, yes, but not only on his own account. He sincerely felt that the good of his country depended on people like himself and Pushpa, in charge of its development and progress.

On her twentieth birthday, there was a party for Ratna. It was also an unofficial engagement party, for she and the witty young diplomat who was Sanjay's colleague had come to an understanding. On the day of the celebration, an electrician fixed festive lights in the trees, and Gita ordered a birthday cake so enormous and white that it might as well have been a wedding cake. Good wishes and gifts were heaped on Ratna, along with a lot of teasing. Slight and slender, almost frail – her sister Gita, though also slim, was far more robust – she laughed and blushed; she kept hiding her face in her palms and also leaned forward so that her long hair veiled her completely. There came a moment when it was absolutely necessary for her to be alone with her happiness, and she slipped away as soon as she saw us absorbed in our usual topics of conversation. That never took long: the problems of India were always with us, and no birthday party could make us forget them.

At this time Indian foreign policy tended to lean toward the Communist bloc, and as a representative of the other side, it was up to me to urge the advantage of joining us. Of course they jumped on me – as usual, I had to hear about the decadence of the West and the evils of our capitalist system. But they didn't keep up the attack for long. It was a delicacy in them – I was a guest and outnumbered, and Sanjay was the first to drop the argument and to drift away. The only one who didn't let go was Pushpa; it was not in her nature to let go of anything important to her. And she really did have strong feelings on the subject, as she did on most. Now she became very heated, going beyond the subject of Eastern versus Western political alliance to the perennial matter of the evils of imperialism and how an independent India must free herself totally from the yoke of the West. She had every kind of argument at her fingertips – for instance, the relative figures of the cotton trade before and after Independence – and though I always enjoyed a good debate, I felt at a disadvantage against Pushpa. After all, as she kept reminding me, it was her country that had suffered injustice and mine that had inflicted it. She had raised her voice and others became uneasily aware that the light-hearted spirit of the birthday party was being disrupted. Soon Sanjay came back to us, smiling, a sociable host with a glass of champagne in each hand. But Pushpa said, 'You know I don't drink that stuff.'

Sanjay went right on smiling: 'Then let us drink your health – and the health of the Eastern bloc. Kitty, shall we?' While he and I clinked glasses, he said to Pushpa, 'I'll get you some pineapple juice.'

'I don't want it.' Her face, already puffy from arguing, swelled up even more and her eyes swam as though with tears. Tears at Ratna's party! I felt guilty to have caused them and tried to touch her hand in a friendly gesture. She snatched it away and hid it behind her back, like a fat and angry child. Sanjay and I exchanged helpless glances – she saw us, and now the tears not only filled her eyes but came rolling down her cheeks. She said she wanted to go home.

'But Pushpa, we haven't even cut the cake yet!' cried Sanjay.

'I can't wait. I have to go. I promised Mummy – she's not well.'

'Oh, I'm sorry. Is it her blood pressure again?' When Sanjay solicitously touched her naked arm, she did not move it away. She said, 'I suppose that goddamn driver's disappeared again.'

'Stay a bit,' Sanjay pleaded. 'We'll light the candles, cut the cake – Ratna, where's Ratna? Kitty, please call her—'

'No! I have to go!'

Her voice was so loud, her anger so disproportionate that Sanjay had to save the situation. 'I'll take you,' he said quietly.

She calmed down instantly, and while he left to get his car keys, she adjusted her sari in preparation for departure. Arranging it over one shoulder, she explained to me: 'I get so carried away, I can't help it.'

'I know. I'm sorry.' And I did feel sorry to have worked her up so.

'It's not personal.'

'No, of course not.'

'Only because you're British – and you *have* been here, uninvited I may point out, for two hundred years. He's gone to get his keys,' she explained to Gita who had come looking for Sanjay. 'He's taking me home. I told him not to, but he insisted. Because Mummy's not well.'

Gita brushed away Mummy and Pushpa both; and when Sanjay returned, she flashed at him: 'You can't leave now, not in the middle of our party.'

'I'll be back in twenty minutes.'

Pushpa, now perfectly composed, preceded him to the car. He turned around once to his sister: 'Half an hour at the most. Just keep them all quiet and happy, Giti, all right? I rely on you . . . And you, Kitty.' He singled me out with a smile full of friendliness and charm.

'Can you believe it?' Gita was furious and furiously she said to me, 'Come upstairs. I have to talk to you.' When I gestured toward the guests, she dismissed them impatiently: 'They're too drunk on champagne to even notice we've gone.' She led me through the drawing room and up the stairs to the roof. Here we found Ratna.

She was leaning on the parapet – the way I had once leaned with Sanjay beside me. But of course in her case her dream was fulfilled. She was smiling as she gazed down at the party on the lawn, her eyes fixed on only one person. 'Look at him, flirting his head off,' she said, proud and indulgent. I looked with her: her fiancé had his arm around one of the girls – that was the type he was, always touching girls, teasing them, free and forward. It was what shy Ratna loved him for: his worldliness, his easy sociability, the way he could make everyone laugh – he was doing it now, telling some fantastic story. One hand was on a girl's shoulder, in the other a green-stemmed glass, which he held out for a servant to refill. 'He's going to be so drunk,' Ratna smiled; at that time, being drunk with them just meant being more high-spirited, more irresistible.

But Gita was not smiling: 'That Pushpa, I could kill her.'

'What's she done now?' Ratna said, but indulgent here too, in her happiness.

'Probably she's proposing to him right now in the car and

he's saying yes, you know how he can never bear not to be polite to people.'

That made Ratna laugh, and me too, but Gita saw other undesirable probabilities: 'Or she'll say, Let me drive, and he gives her the keys and she drives like the madwoman she is down to the river and threatens to go right in if he doesn't at once promise to marry her.'

'There's no water in the river,' Ratna said.

'Do you think that would stop her? She'll drive them to the edge of the Jumna Bridge and tell him she'll go over – goodness only knows what she'll do in her craziness.'

'People are crazy when they're in love,' Ratna explained to us. She turned to me, smiling: 'What about you, Kitty?' And when I didn't answer, 'Aren't you in love?' and she touched my cheek with her soft, small hand.

'Well, if you are,' Gita said, 'then please do something about getting him out of her clutches.'

'But what can I do?' I laughed, embarrassed but flattered, hopeful, happy.

'Tell him you'll marry him—'

'Get your car, we'll go after them, catch up with them—'

'And then what?'

'Then you'll say it.'

'Just when she's got to the end of the bridge, we'll shout: "Wait, wait, here's Kitty!"'

'Here he is,' Gita said, looking down.

'Oh, he's back?' Ratna too looked down. 'So she hasn't . . .'

'Driven him off the bridge? No, but who knows what she may not have made him promise . . . Go down now, Kitty. Tell him now.'

They closed in on me eagerly, two beautiful temptresses under the silver sky. Down below, among the colored bulbs in the trees, everyone was laughing at the fiancé's story. He was illustrating it now, with bizarre gestures and dance-steps, and he was trying to pull in Sanjay to partner him. But Sanjay, though enjoying the performance like everyone else, wouldn't be drawn in: he never for a moment forgot himself as the perfect diplomat, a future Foreign Secretary.

'Now,' Gita urged me. 'Go now.'

They were actually pulling me, one from each side, holding my hands; and, though tugged equally from within, I hung back, laughing, blushing: 'I can't, how can I—'

'Oh I would! If I wanted him, I'd tell any man: I'll marry you.' And this was what Gita did, shortly afterward. 'And when I'm sick of him, I'll tell him get out—' And this too she did.

## II

Whatever happened between them in the car that night, Sanjay and Pushpa did not marry. Like myself, Pushpa never married, and Sanjay only did so a few years later when he was well advanced in his career. A beautiful bride was selected for him – a princess from one of the minor royal houses, an educated girl with a degree in art and home science. Two years later Sanjay was appointed to his first ambassadorship, and from there on his appointments grew in importance until he was recalled to New Delhi to become Foreign Secretary. Wherever they were, at home or abroad, he and his wife were famous for their gracious entertainments. Their residences were exquisitely appointed in Indian style – here his wife's artistic training was shown to advantage, as were the fine art objects and miniature paintings she had brought as part of her dowry, along with her hereditary jewels.

In later years, Sanjay sometimes came to visit me when he had meetings in London. I had left the foreign service by then. After India, I was posted to various other countries but never again formed the personal involvements I had enjoyed there. On the contrary, I regarded my contacts with the local population as nothing more than part of my job, and this became so unsatisfactory that finally I resigned and joined the BBC World Service. I bought a little house in a London suburb, and it was here that Sanjay came to see me. I cooked him a hearty meal of chicken in the pot or Irish stew, and we drew our chairs around the fire I had lit for him because he so loved an English open fire. He declared that never anywhere did he feel as cozy and carefree as he did with me. And when he said that, he sighed as if some great happiness that could have been between us had never been fulfilled.

It was many years since I had had any such regrets about him; and anyway, in the meantime I had discovered that I preferred women to men. No doubt he was too worldly not to suspect this, but he was also too tactful to give any sign that he did. Our conversation was all about the past, not about people so much as incidents – charming happenings at parties and picnics. If I asked about a particular person, he would say, 'He's our Secretary of Commerce,' or 'He took a job with the UN.' Most of them had done well and none of them was the same person any more. The one who had changed the most appeared to be Pushpa, of whom he spoke with admiration and respect. She had left the civil service and had stood for Parliament and was now a cabinet minister. But when I mentioned his sisters, his smile of reminiscence vanished; he appeared actually to wipe it away, passing his hand over his face. 'Poor Ratna, what a tragedy, she died so young,' and though he made no mention of how she died, when he uncovered his face, it had settled back into the deep melancholy that, in spite of all his success, had become his characteristic expression. He rarely spoke of Gita, with whom he had quarreled and was involved in a lawsuit.

And he rarely spoke about India – not the way he used to, about the new dams and fertilizer plants. 'Problems, Kitty, problems,' was all he would say. Only sometimes he burst out in misery and disappointment. The country had changed because those in power had changed. They were no longer the young men I had known, who had all gone to the same English-type boarding schools and whom one could talk to and ask to one's parties. Now they were local politicians elected from backward states; some of them could hardly read and write, but they had to be given important posts because they held huge blocks of votes. During the hot summer months, they liked to go on official tours abroad and had to be put up in the Indian embassy, where they harassed the staff. Sanjay himself had had awful experiences with visiting politicians for whom he had had to give official dinners though they didn't know how to use a knife and fork and spat red betel juice on the walls. And then the following year another politician would arrive, with his own retinue of relatives eager to go shopping in foreign countries, with manners the same as the previous visitor, who had meanwhile been charged with bribery and corruption; or the entire cabinet had had to resign on these charges, or the government had fallen and a new one was being elected. But it was always the same types who were elected – no, worse: it seemed to Sanjay that they became worse and sometimes had to be sent back home midway through their tour for causing a scandal, such as getting drunk and harassing air hostesses. It was all too much for Sanjay, not at all what he had expected when he first took up the reins of responsibility; and he was glad, he said, that soon he would be able to relinquish them, for he had only two or three years before retirement. Probably he would be offered the embassy in Washington; he would not accept but retire to the estate his wife had inherited from her father. He would build a golf course there, for he had become an enthusiastic golfer; unlike his in-laws, he did not care for hunting and shooting, although his teenage children were keen on these sports. When he spoke of his family – two boys and a girl – his face cleared again. Each time he brought new photographs to show me, and then he almost became the Sanjay I knew, his sad eyes lighting up the way they used to, with hope and ambition.

Although Gita was married to an Englishman and lived in London for a few years, she mostly avoided me. I think perhaps she didn't want to be with anyone who had known her in other, better times. These were difficult years for Gita. I heard rumors about her, how she was becoming more erratic and reckless. After the tragedy with Ratna, she was completely lost. During this time she visited me more often, to talk about what had happened. She repeated to me over and over how her brother-in-law had called her from Kampala to tell her, 'Ratna has done something silly.' 'Can you believe it!' cried Gita. 'Those were his exact words: "Something silly" . . . Of course he was dead drunk, the pig, wait – wait – wait – he'll hear from me yet.' She had all sorts of mad schemes for revenge, but her weapons of torment were turned inward. Finally she had to enter a clinic for psychiatric treatment, and when she came out, she went back to Delhi, where she remained.

I only twice returned to Delhi – the air fare is very high, and besides, I hardly know anyone there any more. On my second and last visit, a few years ago, I looked up Gita who was living by herself in their old house in the Civil Lines. Traveling in a battered taxi from my hotel in New Delhi, I marveled at the extent of the changes – the wild growth of the city, with high-rise modern office buildings and luxury hotels, a brand-new art museum and a sports stadium; and flowing in and out among these edifices, the squatter settlements for the laborers who were putting up all this new architecture by the old method of carrying bricks on their heads and clambering over bamboo scaffolding. The journey from New to Old Delhi, which used to take less than half an hour, was now twice as long, for the streets were choked with traffic that the posse of policemen wielding bamboo poles were hardly able to control. The buses were still the same old metal wrecks, only now there were many more people jammed inside them, with some hanging on outside. These ancient vehicles emitted volleys of black smoke that mingled with other fumes and shrouded the sky – the once radiant Delhi sky – in a pall of yellow smog with cinders flying around. The vastly increased motor traffic – even the rickshaws had been motorized – must have needed a lot of fixing, for the stalls that had sold embroidered caps and slippers were now given over to spare parts such as hub-caps and brake-linings, fan-belts and clutch-plates.

The Civil Lines area had also changed, with the large family houses replaced by blocks of new flats. Only Gita's house remained, standing in isolation among these flats; all her aunts, uncles and cousins had sold up and moved away. She still had her large garden but the lawn was now patched with brown and the flowerbeds were full of dry earth. Only the trees had grown even more luxuriant and pressed in on the house. It had always been kept dark inside, for coolness, but now, buried in trees, it was as cold and damp as a tomb. Dust had settled in the velvet upholstery and in the cracks of the carved furniture, and there was the smell of Gita's dogs and another smell that may have been bat droppings. Gita simply did not have the staff to look after such a large place, and those she did have she needed for the thriving new business she had started.

She was dying to get rid of the house – to sell it, like everyone else had done, and build flats. 'Do you have any idea how much those flats go for?' she asked me – indignantly, because Sanjay had no idea and refused to sell. That was why she had filed a suit against him and was no longer speaking to him or his family. She went into a long list of her grievances against them – it was the first thing I heard, almost immediately after her greeting: 'Kitty! How thin you are! And my goodness – what's that I see? Grey hair!' Gita's own once auburn hair was dyed a solid black, but it was still shiny and healthy like the rest of her. She was attended by two dogs, huge Alsatians who stood on either side of her. She held herself very erect and with squared shoulders and still tossed her head back the way she used to, in defiance. She tossed it a lot while speaking of her brother. I think it was a relief to her to have someone like me to speak to, who had known him; now their paths had diverged completely and they had no common friends or even acquaintances. 'All he knows are those dull as ditchwater civil servants like himself with their promotions and pensions which is all they ever think about . . . And of course his wife and her family. What dodos, Kitty, you would not believe!' She detested her sister-in-law and her courtly manners – she imitated these for me, the exaggerated courtesies, the exquisite circumlocutions, the obsequious greeting with palms joined under bowed head. 'It's just hypocrisy, that's all it is; like those old Rajputs sticking knives into each other's backs while clasped in brotherly embrace . . . And to think he could have married anyone; he could have married you, Kitty.'

She laughed, and so did I. I asked if we could go up on the roof. She led the way, followed by her two Alsatians. She had transformed the place into a busy workshop, with two tailors cross-legged inside the turret turning their little sewing-machines, while outside on the terrace young boys were sorting and packing bales of textiles for Gita's boutique. She had also begun to export to England and Germany, where she had good contacts. She showed me her goods – all in excellent taste, designed by herself – gave instructions to her tailors, shouted a bit at the boys in what sounded like a racy dialect. She was in her element up here.

I leaned on the parapet the way we used to do. Although the trees were smothering the house, some trailing branches over the terrace, the housewives in the surrounding flats had no difficulty watching us from their higher level. A mild winter sunshine filtered through the smog of pollution sagging from the sky; more gaseous fumes rose from the traffic on the road outside, which had become a main thoroughfare leading to new colonies. The scene was busy and intensely alive, but no longer romantic. Nor were Gita's thoughts when she joined me, though she too leaned her elbows on the parapet in our old way. 'If I could just get rid of this place,' she said. She described everything she would do: build flats and sell them and then move herself and the dogs to New Delhi, near her boutique. She was eager to take me there – it was a whole new development, she told me, with very smart shops dealing in the highest quality designer goods. 'It's all different now, Kitty, you'll see. We're all different.' She told me about the other women who had gone into business; like herself, most of them had escaped from bad marriages, or other unfortunate situations. Instead of waiting for some man to take care of them, they had turned their assets to their own advantage – these assets being their looks, their culture, their brains, and some inherited money. They had started art galleries, the wholesale export of fashion garments designed by themselves, beauty salons selling their own herbal products. Some of them were already millionaires, Gita told me, with pride in her class; and when I asked, what about you, she laughed in a full-throated way: 'I'm getting there.' There was no trace left of the neurotic Gita I had known in London, but she was still in some way the Gita of our youthful days: only even more proud and strong, and with the wary and rather calculating look of someone determined not to be taken advantage of. I admired her, but I was sad too, the way one tends to be when the past has irrevocably changed. I looked away from her over the parapet, but of course everything there had changed too and all I saw was housewives hanging up washing on lines slung across their verandahs.

'Do you remember how we stood up here and told you to marry Sanjay?' She spoke with no nostalgia at all; on the contrary, as of something ridiculous.

'You told me to go down and propose to him. You said I could easily do it if I was in love.'

'Fortunately you had more sense than we did. Love – what rubbish. The only creatures to love are these filthy beasties.' She bent down to rub her face against the heads of her Alsatians, and they responded by licking her face with large and eager tongues.

'What we really wanted was to save him from Pushpa. And now it turns out that it's Pushpa who had the lucky escape – wait till you see her! Success Story Number One.'

'Do you see her?'

'Only in the newspapers. And on TV of course; she loves to go on TV.'

It was not easy to meet Pushpa. I telephoned her several times, and each time was told by a different assistant that she was in a cabinet meeting, or was opening a school fête. But when at last I got through to her – 'Kitty! What a lovely surprise!' Her voice blasted into my ear like a trumpet – she would send a car for me, not to move, her chauffeur would be there instantly. She lived in the old, the imperial New Delhi, in one of the imperial mansions taken over by cabinet ministers and chiefs of staff. She was in her office at the front of the house, and she emerged from behind an enormous desk, which was piled high with papers and flanked by two assistants trying to sort them. She descended on me, arms flailing, hair flying, full of energy though she had grown very fat, and at once began to drench me in a flood of words that never stopped the entire time I was there. She wore a plain white cotton sari, her only ornaments some gold bangles and a diamond stud in her nose. While she talked and gesticulated, her sari kept slipping off her shoulder, till she impatiently pinned it with a huge silver brooch in the shape of an oak tree ('A gift from the President of Poland'). The walls were covered in photographs of her with various such Presidents at official functions, also with national leaders – all of them, including Pushpa, heavily garlanded, smiling, powerful.

She led me across a courtyard dividing her office from her living rooms. These were furnished with Indian handicrafts – she pointed them out to me, the work of the weavers' association and the spinning cooperatives. Under government auspices, giant strides had been made in the development of cottage industries. Her mother, who had suffered a stroke, was wheeled in to join us for lunch and Pushpa kissed her and tried to coax her to take titbits from a spoon ('Mummy is naughty sometimes about not eating'). Pushpa herself ate heartily – Indian-style, with her hands; she had given up using cutlery – and continued to do so even when her assistant entered with a cellular phone, which he held to her ear. She told me everything she felt I ought to know; she was concerned that I should be as fully informed as a press conference on current developments and progress. And this not to show off but out of affection, as though loading me with precious gifts to carry home. By a lucky chance that afternoon she was to address a women's rally – she consulted her watch: 'My goodness! In fifteen minutes!' – and proposed to take me with her. 'Now you will see, Kitty, with your own eyes!' she cried as she whirled out of the house, with me in her wake, doors held open for us all the way.

Ensconced in the back of her official car, she said how she loved to meet old friends and talk about the past – though not one word about the past had we exchanged, or mentioned one single person we had known in it. It was all the future for Pushpa, she drowned us in the future. The rallying ground lay just outside the gate dividing New and Old Delhi. It was the road I had often traveled to and from Sanjay's house –

always, so it seemed in my memory, by moonlight and with romantic thoughts, passing a mosque with a striped dome and a garden surrounding the tomb of an Emperor's sister. But now, when I tried to peer between the satin curtains that shielded Pushpa from the public gaze – as once Moghul queens and princesses had been shielded – she nudged me to take note of a newly constructed colony of low-cost housing for government clerks.

A welcoming committee awaited Pushpa at the entrance of the rallying ground to garland and lead her to the platform. As she passed, women tried to touch her, like a goddess or a film star. I had to sit beside her on the platform – a garland had been hung around my neck too – along with many other people, some of them arguing about their right to that position of eminence. The successful claimants got up one by one to address the crowd. Everyone spoke for a long time and in Hindi. The crowd consisted entirely of poor laboring women, a mass, a living sea of them filling the vast open space. They sat cross-legged on the ground, very old women and very young ones with small children in their laps. Older children ran around, playing games and piping shrilly, which seemed to be their right for no one tried to stop them. Yet all the women were attentive, their faces raised to those who addressed them from the platform at such length, never relaxing their respectful, grateful, listening attitudes. Beyond the rallying ground, I could see the old city gate, now flanked by a statue of a dead national leader in stone waistcoat and spectacles. And beyond him, stretching as far as the river, there was some empty land that Pushpa had pointed out to me as the potential site of a new industrial complex. It was still an open dumping ground, almost a swamp, with kites and vultures circling above it.

At last, when all the speakers had had their turn, Pushpa got up to take the microphone. A current of renewed ardor ran through the mass of women at her feet. I couldn't understand the Hindi she spoke to them, but whatever it was she said seemed to be what they most wanted to hear. They raised their faces higher, in adoration, in worship: those who clutched

slogans scrawled on pieces of cloth held them up and waved
them. Murmurs of assent to everything she said rippled through
the crowd, then swelled into shouts of approval. She swooped
them up to further heights with the chanting of slogans – to
be repeated by them again and again. Huge and fat, perspiring
and inspiring, she flailed about, a many-armed, golden-bangled
goddess with the diamond in her nose flashing in the sun.
The women laughed, they shouted, their hour had come.
I had never seen so many faces radiant with hope – all of
them worn by poverty, overworked and undernourished, some
pockmarked through disease, others bruised with beatings,
a few with their noses cut off (the ultimate act of cruelty
from a vengeful husband), but all of them infused, suffused
with whatever it was that Pushpa promised them. It became
impossible to hear what she said, every word was drowned in
triumphant shouts, and now she was only repeating the same
slogan and making them echo it – again, and louder, louder!
– right up to the polluted sky and into the distance where the
kites and vultures wheeled over the sewage that would soon be
drained and cleared for a new industrial estate of small-scale
industries.

# A NEW DELHI
# ROMANCE

---

Indu had married beneath her, but that was many years ago, and besides, she no longer lived with her husband. Everything else had changed too – her parents, who had so deplored her marriage, were long since gone, her brother and sisters had moved away, and the big house they had all lived in had been torn down and a block of flats built on its site. Indu herself still lived in the neighborhood, almost around the corner from the old house, in a complex of ramshackle hutments that had once been a barrack for policemen. She had lived here for twenty years and the rent was still the same, which was why she stayed on – who could have afforded anything else? – though it was far from her place of work. However, it did have the advantage of being near the University, so that her son Arun, who was a student there, could easily come home if his classes were canceled due to a strike or the death of some important politician.

Arun, taking full advantage of the proximity of his home and his mother's day-long absence from it, didn't wait for classes to be canceled but cut them whenever he felt like it. Lately he had begun to bring his girl friend Dipti there – though only after a struggle, not with Dipti, who was willing enough, but with himself. For one thing, he had to overcome his feelings of guilt toward his mother for doing this in her home; and then there was the shabbiness of that home – he was ashamed of it for himself and his mother, and angry with Dipti for maybe judging it in the same way he did. But Dipti was so happy to be there that she had no wish to criticize it: on the contrary.

Yet Dipti herself lived in a very grand house and was brought to the college every day in a chauffeur-driven car. Her father was a politician, an important cabinet minister, and the family lived in luxury. They gave lavish parties at which everyone ate and drank too much, they brought back all the latest household gadgets from their trips abroad, even a washing machine though they had their own washerman living on the premises along with their other servants. Dipti's mother was always going shopping, for saris and textiles and jewelry, and she bought fresh pastries and chicken patties, so that if Dipti brought her friends home there was plenty to eat, as well as every kind of soft drink in the refrigerator. Long before he decided to bring Dipti to his own house, Arun had been visiting hers. He didn't eat the pastries – he didn't care for them – and made no attempt to ingratiate himself with her parents. But they liked him – approved of him, and of his mother. Dipti's mother was very gracious to her, not at all assuming the role of VIP's wife that she usually played to its full extent, as was her right. She brought Indu home, ostensibly consulting her on a question of interior decoration, and she even pretended to take her advice, though Indu's taste was not at all consonant with her own preference for rich ornamentation.

Indu accepted Dipti's mother's respect as her due and did not return it. But she liked Dipti – how could she not, for Dipti was everything a young girl should be: sweet and pretty and very much in love with Arun. It had not taken Indu long to discover that the two young people spent afternoons in her house. Dipti's floral perfume hung in the air hours after she had left, and once Indu found a white blossom on her pillow, which might have dropped out of the garland wound into a girl's hair. Indu's feelings as she picked it up were mixed: pride in a son's conquest, as well as a movement of jealous anger that made her indulge in a burst of outrage ('and on my bed'). But as she sat on this bed, slowly rubbing the petal between her fingers so that it released its scent, memories of her own obliterated all thoughts of the young couple. She hardly needed the fragrance of the jasmine emanating from between her fingers to recall the secret nights on her parents' roof with Arun's father, when the rest of the household was fast asleep. What more romantic than those nights drenched in moonlight and jasmine – or what more evanescent? The blossom in tatters between her fingers, she flung it away, her resentment now not against Arun and Dipti but against Arun's father; and also against her own stupid young self, who had tossed away all the advantages of her birth for the sake of those stolen nights.

Arun's father, Raju, had for years lived in Bombay, where he was involved in films. He had turned up throughout Arun's childhood, an unwanted guest who stayed too long, and far from contributing to the household or his son's support, borrowed money from Indu. Raju was good fun, especially for a young child – he sang, he played games, jokes, and magic tricks; but later Arun became as exasperated with him as his mother was. Dipti likewise expressed exasperation with *her* father: 'Daddy works far too much! And all those people who come – does he have to see all of them!' But this was a pretence: she was proud of her father and the way crowds thronged to him. At certain hours of the day he sat enthroned on their verandah, an obese idol wrapped in a cloud of white muslin. Petitioners touched his feet in traditional gestures of respect; some brought garlands, some baskets of fruit or boxes of sweetmeats; poor people brought an egg or two, or milk from their cow. There were those who had traveled all night in crowded third-class railway carriages from his native state, in order to present some petition to him; others came only to be in his presence, imbibing his aura of riches and power. He addressed them in a tangy native dialect, and his homilies were illustrated by examples drawn nostalgically from the simple life of thatched huts he had long left behind. He had a reputation for salty humor and liked the sound of appreciative laughter. That was one aspect of him – racy, earthy, a man of the people; at other times, with other guests, he was different. Big cars drew up outside his house; if there were too many of them, special police constables had to be called to supplement the guard on duty at his gate. Then he himself became obsequious – he hurried out to receive the visitors, his big bulk moving lightly and with grace. He led them inside and into his carpeted drawing room where refreshments were served, not by servants but by his wife, her head covered as she offered silver beakers on a silver tray. Sometimes these visitors were led into a further room where a white sheet had been spread on the carpet; here they all sat cross-legged in their loose native clothes leaning against bolsters, some fat like himself, others scrawny from fasting and prayer. These powerful men weighed each other up like poker players, sometimes staying up all night while journalists waited outside; for the game that was being played involved millions not only of rupees but of lives. However, this was never a consideration in the minds of the players who, like all true sportsmen, were wholly dedicated to the game for its own sake.

One day Dipti and Arun's afternoon was disturbed by the arrival of Arun's father. He walked into the living room that opened straight off the main compound around which all the barrack-like structures were grouped. 'I'm here!' he called, like an eagerly expected guest. In the bedroom, Dipti in a state of undress clapped her hand before her mouth and her wide eyes grew wider as she looked to Arun for rescue. As in all relations with his father, he was more exasperated than embarrassed. He got up and, winding a towel around his waist, went into the living room.
     'Ah-ah-ah!' cried the father with delight at the sight of his son; and he hugged him tenderly, held him away for a moment to look at him, then hugged him again. Arun frowned all through this performance – he never liked to be embraced by his father and especially not now, for Raju was full of sweat and soot, as after a long train journey in an overcrowded carriage. But he pretended to have come by plane – 'Indian Airlines is hopeless, hopeless! Two hours late and keeping us waiting without even a cup of tea! . . . How are you? And your mother – I tried to call her in the office to tell her I was coming, but the connection between Delhi and Bombay – hopeless, hopeless! . . . Did

you get my telegram? No? That's funny . . . Why aren't you at college? Is it holidays? Good, we'll have a fine time, you and I, eh, what, ha? Pictures, coffee-house, and so on.'

Arun said, 'I came home to study for my exam.' He frowned more and added, 'With a friend.'

'Ah. A friend. Where is he? . . . Understood!' cried Raju, his eyes dancing with pleasure and amusement as they roved over his son's handsome face and naked chest.

Arun went into the bedroom and, seeing Dipti fully dressed, told her, 'You can come out. It's only my father . . . It's all right,' he said in answer to her stricken look. When she still hung back, he took her hand and pulled her quite harshly through the curtain that separated the two rooms.

But Raju stilled her fears at once. Giving no sign that there was anything out of the way in a young girl appearing with his son out of the bedroom, he greeted her warmly, and with obvious though highly respectful admiration for her beauty. He became the host of the occasion, gesturing grandly to everyone to sit. Apart from the couch on which Arun slept at night, the furniture was scanty and makeshift; but Indu had made everything tasteful with handloomed fabrics draped over oil cans and egg crates, and hanging up reproductions from art books wherever new cracks appeared on the walls. Raju wanted to make a tea party of it, encouraging Arun to go for fritters and potato patties to the stall at the corner, even rummaging in his own pocket for money, but when he came up with nothing, the idea was dropped. He made up for it with his conversation, and while his son rolled his eyes up to the ceiling, Raju enjoyed his own skill as an entertainer and its effect on Dipti. She responded to him the way women, starting with Indu, had done all his life long – they didn't always believe what he said but liked his way of saying it. And he knew how to take the right tone with his audience: for instance, today, with Dipti, in telling her about the Bombay film industry, he did not stress its glamor but only its stupidity and vulgarity, adapting himself to what he guessed to be the opinion of someone like Dipti – a University student and, moreover, his scornful son's girl friend.

'I *like* him,' Dipti later insisted to Arun, and repeated it in spite of his 'You don't know a thing.' She did know some things – he had more or less told her the story of his parents' marriage – but she had not plumbed the depths of his feelings on the subject. And he had not described the scene on that night of Raju's arrival, when Indu got home from work. It was something that happened regularly whenever Raju reappeared in the bosom of his family. When it came time to sleep, he carried his battered little suitcase into his wife's bedroom, on the assumption that this was his rightful place. Arun was already lying on the couch, which had been his bed ever since he had grown too old to share his mother's. He had turned off the light and shut his eyes, pretending to himself that he was too sleepy to listen to the altercation in the next room. He didn't have to: he knew exactly what course it would take. First they would keep their voices down – for his sake – but when Raju kept saying 'Sh – sh,' Indu's rage rose till she was shouting, so that Raju too had to speak up to make his protests heard. That caused her to shout louder till she was shrieking, and finally – Arun waited for it – Raju's little suitcase came flying out through the curtain, and he followed, groping around in the dark to retrieve its scattered contents, while mildly clicking his tongue at his wife's unreasonable temper. Arun continued to pretend to be asleep, and with a sigh of patient resignation, Raju lay down on the floor mat. Arun then got up to offer him his place on the couch, and after some protests, Raju accepted. He was soon blissfully asleep, while Arun lay awake for hours, tossing and seething and aware of his mother doing the same in the next room.

Arun had grown up with such scenes, for his parents had been separated since he was two. Over the years, they had given him much occasion to ponder the relationship between men and women. Now he shared these thoughts with Dipti, though in a purely general way, careful not to give any insight into the particulars on which his theories were based. And that was the way she responded to him – also theoretically, with no reference to what she had observed between her own parents. For that marriage too, though enduring in the face of the world, had its own unmentioned, unmentionable areas on which no light was ever shed. Even in her own mind Dipti had veiled the scenes she had witnessed since her childhood – her father's outbursts when, for instance, a garment was not pressed well enough, or a stud was missing from his shirt: then her mother would cower in a corner with her arms shielding her head against the shoes he threw at her or the blows from his fist. Yet not half an hour later, when the defect in his toilet had been corrected and, starched and resplendent, he reclined among his guests, she was once more the modestly veiled hostess offering sherbet in silver vessels. It was only to Dipti that her mother sometimes whispered, in the dark and in secret, about the shame that it was the fate of wives to suffer: beatings and abuse, and also that other shame – she did not specify it further – that had to be undergone.

But Dipti knew, just as Arun did, that this was not how men and women should be together. They had formed their own idea on the subject, and it was the opposite of what they had observed between their parents. Their plan was to try out their theories on each other, and having already begun at the most basic, or essential, level in their afternoons together, they found that it was indeed a far cry from Raju's suitcase being flung out of Indu's bedroom, or that unspecified humiliation that Dipti's mother whispered to her about. Instead, they learned to grope their way around together in a completely new world that opened up for them, in infinite sweetness, at the touch of delicate fingers and the mingling of their pure breath.

'Yes, and if she gets pregnant?' Having found yet another blossom on her pillow, Indu could no longer refrain from confronting her son. He shrugged – his usual response to any of her questions he did not care to answer. But his father, who was still there and more and more on sufferance, interposed: 'Ah, don't spoil it for him.'

Indu seized the opportunity to turn on her husband: 'Oh yes – having ruined my life, now you send your son out to do the same to another innocent girl . . . Not that I care what happens,' she returned to Arun. 'This time the shoe's on the other foot: it's not *you* who'll get pregnant and have to be married whether you want to or not.'

If Raju had not been in such a precarious position in his wife's household – or if he had had the least bit of malice in him, which he did not – he could have pointed to himself as an unfortunate example of what Indu was talking about: for he, though still a student at the time, and from a very poor family, had been forced to marry Indu when she was found to be pregnant after their months of delight on her parents' roof.

This thought did arise in Indu, filling her with bitterness: 'But of course,' she told her son, 'you can always follow your father's fine example and never spend a single rupee on your child's support – well, what else have you been doing your whole life long!' she said to Raju, as though he had dared utter a word of protest. 'Sitting around in Bombay, running after film stars, while I'm working myself into a nervous breakdown to raise this child and give him a decent education fit for my father's grandson – oh leave me alone, leave me alone!' she cried, though neither her husband nor her son had made a movement toward her. She ran into her bedroom – if there had been a door instead of only a curtain she could have banged it – and flung herself face down on to her bed.

Father and son remained together in silence. Raju would have liked to follow and comfort her but knew that his good intention would meet only with rejection. At last he said to Arun in a low voice, 'Go. Go to her.'

But Arun would not. It was not in his nature to dispense tender consolation to a woman in tears. He loved his mother fiercely and suffered because she did; but at this moment he also felt sorry for his father. Everything that Indu accused him of was true – Raju had got her pregnant and had never been able to provide for her and Arun but had let them struggle along on their own. But this was because he couldn't provide even for himself let alone a family, because he was – so his son thought with contempt and pity – just a poor devil. Raju would have liked to be generous, and if his pocket had not been chronically empty, he would have put his hand in it and

pulled out bundles of bank notes to fling on his wife's table –
'Here, take.'

Dipti's feelings for her father were equally confused. Immensely
proud of him for being what he was in the world, she could
not forget what he was at home, behind closed doors with her
mother. At the same time, she blamed her mother for the way
she submitted to his treatment, crouching under his fury like
an animal unable to defend itself. Yet she was a proud woman.
Haughty and imperious with servants, with petitioners, with her
husband's clerks, she passed among them like a queen, walking
with slow majesty, as though her own massive weight and that
of all her jewels and brocades were difficult to carry.

All this was before the scandal, which broke slowly, with a
minor paragraph in one or two newspapers, and proceeded
to mount with headlines in all of them, and photographs in
the news magazines. At first Dipti's father brushed away the
accusations against him, he joked with the visitors assembled
around him on his verandah and made them laugh at the
expense of journalists and other gossipmongers who had
nothing to do in their offices except kill flies and make up
lies about him. Then, when the stories persisted and questions
began to be asked in Parliament, he grew angry, he challenged
his cowardly accusers – this too on his verandah amid his
friends – to come out with one single fact against him. And
when they did – not with one but with many, how he had taken
money from industrialists, businessmen and foreign investors –
he blustered and demanded proof. This was forthcoming: there
were letters and diary entries as well as the huge unexplained
wealth he had accumulated in movable and immovable properties. Denying everything, he demanded an inquiry where he
could, he said, easily prove himself as innocent as a newborn
child. Cartoons of him in this latter role promptly appeared
in the press. Although his resignation was demanded not only
by the opposition but by his own party, he refused to submit
it and hung on to his position, and to his official residence,
until given the chance to clear himself before a committee to
be appointed from the highest in the land.

During these difficult times, Dipti continued to attend her classes at the University, holding her head high. It was only when she was alone with Arun, during their afternoons in his mother's house, that she sometimes gave way to her feelings – and then only with silent tears, hiding her face against his chest. They never discussed the case and only referred to its essentials – as when she informed him that a committee of inquiry had been set up, or that her father had drafted his letter of resignation. Arun received the information without comment. Like Dipti herself, he had no desire to discuss the affair, and when other students did so within his hearing – and they spoke of it constantly, cynically, with jokes, everyone convinced of Dipti's father's guilt and gloating over it – he harshly reproved them. They nudged each other and grinned behind his back and called him 'the son-in-law.'

He also quarreled with his mother – his father was back in Bombay where he claimed to have been hired as a scriptwriter for a major production – for Indu had strong opinions about the affair.

'What do you know about it?' he challenged her.

'I know what I read in the papers plus what I've seen with my own eyes . . . You're not trying to tell me,' she went on, 'that they were living on his salary? . . . All that vulgar display – tcha, and everything in the lowest taste possible of course, but what can you expect from people like that.'

'People like what?'

She refused to be intimidated by his angry frown: 'Uncultured, uneducated people. Peasants,' she threw the word out with contempt.

'Oh yes, only you're very grand and cultured.'

'Yes I am. And so are you.' She tried to touch his face, glorying in his light complexion, his aristocratic features, but he jerked away and said, 'And what about my father? Is he so very grand too?'

'Forget about your father. Think of your grandfather, who *he* was . . . God forgive me for what I did – dragged his name in the mud by marrying your father – all right, by getting pregnant from him, stupid, stupid girl that I was! . . . Arun, are you sure that you're doing everything – or she's doing everything – you know, so that she doesn't—?'

'Why, what are you afraid of?'

'That you'll ruin your life the way I ruined mine.'

He wouldn't listen any more. He turned his back on her and went out of the house, through the compound, into the street, and walked for a long time through the lanes of the city, all the way to Mori Gate where he sat outside a tea stall smoking cigarettes, immersed in his thoughts.

A few evenings later he had to take the same walk again. It happened after his mother had come home from work and was cooking their dinner in the little attached shed that served as their kitchen. There was a commotion outside, and from the window he saw that the children of the compound as well as one or two repressed little servant boys and the old sweeper woman employed by all the tenants had come running to see the spectacle that was unfolding outside Indu's house. A long shiny car with satin curtains had drawn up; a chauffeur jumped out to open the back door from which emerged Dipti's mother, in all the glory of an orange brocade sari with golden border and her full array of ornaments. Indu too had come to look but went quickly running in again to fix her hair, which was straggling over her forehead damp with perspiration from her cooking. She was in the somewhat stained cotton sari she wore for housework, and with no time to change, she had to maintain her dignity with a display of the breeding and fine manners she had acquired in her father's house and at her convent school. The chauffeur carried in a basket of fruit and several boxes of pastries and other sweets, then returned to his car to chase away the children scratching at its bright blue enamel paint. Arun too had to chase them off when they peered in at the window of the living room to see what was going on. This was not anything that required Arun's presence, so he went out and repeated the walk to the tea stall outside Mori Gate where he sat for a long time, not wanting to return and hear what Indu had to say about her visitor and the mission on which she had come.

But of course he had to hear all about it for days on end. Indu was indignant – 'Yes, now they come running when they're in disgrace and think no one will take the girl off their hands. How old is she now?' Arun didn't answer so she answered herself, 'Old enough to have been married long ago, I'm sure, only now who'll have her?'

'Dipti wants to be a college lecturer.'

'She may want but her mother wants something different . . . Who do they think we are?' She was incensed. 'Who do they think they are?'

Arun did not tell Dipti about her mother's call, or its purpose. Yet she may have suspected it – even seen signs of it on her afternoon visits: for days the pastries that had been brought lay moldering in their golden boxes (Arun didn't like them and his mother, who loved and could never afford them, was too proud to eat them). Dipti pretended not to see them. Secrets grew like a wall between her and Arun, making them often avoid each other's eyes. But as if to make up for the lack of words, their lovemaking became more passionate and they clung to each other as if fearful of being torn apart. They also grew more careless, and when Indu came home from work, she sometimes found an undergarment forgotten on her bedroom floor.

Now she changed her tactics with her son. She sidled up to him with sighs; she took his hand in hers, and when he snatched it away, she smiled and said that yes, he was too big now for her fondling. Smiling more, she recalled their past together, when he had been a little boy and had crept into her bed and kissed her and promised her that, when he grew up, he was going to be a policeman and guard and take care of her forever. He squirmed at these memories – they were like little stab wounds in his soul – but she went right on, talking not of the past now but of the future she had always envisaged. No, he was not going to be a policeman, except perhaps a very high-ranking one who sat at a desk and controlled whole districts. A year from now, after he had graduated, he would take the entrance exam of the Indian Administrative Service and he would pass with flying colors – ah, she knew it! Wasn't he his grandfather's grandson and with the same brains? He would rank among the country's ruling élite, rising from one eminent bureaucratic post to the next. As for marriage – everyone knew that once a boy had passed into that corps, all the best families would come running with their daughters and their dowries. Well, he was free to accept them or not, as he pleased, just as long as he kept himself unencumbered and at liberty to pursue all his advantages.

Arun broke away from her – for while she spoke she had drawn closer to him, winding a lock of his hair around her finger – 'What is it?' he said through clenched teeth. 'What are you trying to tell me?'

He knew all too well, for it was his own thoughts she was expressing, digging up what he was trying to suppress and hide from himself.

Last year on her birthday Dipti had cajoled Arun into coming to her house – 'Yes, everyone knows you hate parties and all you do is sit there like a sick monkey – but you've *got to come*! Please? For me? Arun-ji?' He had sat at the side watching the others dance, their friends from the college and some other friends she had from prominent political families like her own. Dipti herself was a terrific dancer and she had often tried to teach him, but he stubbornly refused to have anything to do with it. He frowned while he watched them, but secretly he enjoyed seeing her spin around on her slim feet, wriggling and waggling inside her tight silk kameez, her hair and long gauze veil flying behind her.

After her father's disgrace, she stopped having parties. In fact, it was Arun who asked her, a few days before her birthday, 'Aren't you going to invite me?' She didn't answer for a while but turned away her face; then she said in a low voice, 'Would you come?' 'What do you mean, would I come?' he answered her, doing his best to sound cross. 'But of course if you don't want me—' Before he could finish, she had pressed her mouth against his, and he returned her kisses, pretending not to feel her tears on his cheek.

That evening he told his mother, 'It's Dipti's birthday on Thursday.'

'So?'

In the past, when he had gone to Dipti's birthday party, it was Indu who had brought the present for him to take. He relied on his mother's fine taste, and she always got a discount at the handicrafts emporium where she worked; besides, he had no money of his own.

'Don't tell me they're having a party,' Indu said. 'Surely they wouldn't, at such a time. And who would go to their house anyway?'

'I'm going.'

'You'll be the only guest then.'

'Good. Get me a nice present to take, that's all I'm asking.'

Later, while they were eating and she was serving him what she had cooked, she said: 'I'll get her something very pretty, but give it to her at college. Don't go to their house,' she pleaded, when he pretended not to understand.

He raised his eyes from his plate and looked at her. He had beautiful eyes, full of manly intelligence. She melted with tenderness for him, and pride, and also fear that he would not fulfill her hopes of him. 'Oh I feel sorry for her, poor girl,' she said. 'And I've always liked her, you know that. But people are very cruel – the world's very cruel, once you've lost your place in it.' She stared into the distance for a moment, as though into her own past, before continuing: 'If you go, her mother will get a wrong idea . . . Why aren't you eating?' for he had pushed his plate away and got up.

'Just get me a present,' he said and walked away from her.

She did bring a very beautiful gift for Dipti – even better than anything she had brought for her before – and Arun took it with him. Although, as Indu had predicted, he was the only guest to celebrate Dipti's birthday, her mother had attempted to reproduce the atmosphere of previous occasions. The servants had been made to shine the silver and wash the chandeliers, and the pink birthday cake she had ordered was as huge as for the previous contingent of thirty guests. But she did not manage to dispel the fog of gloom that had settled over the house – not even when the twenty birthday candles were lit

and flickered on their pastel stems over the lake of pink icing
with its festive inscription in green. Dipti did her best to be
cheerful and smiling, in gratitude to Arun for having come
and also to her mother for her efforts. These never ceased –
the mother bustled about and gave orders to the servants and,
a fixed smile on her face, tried to get her husband and Arun to
join her in singing 'Happy Birthday,' and when they wouldn't,
she sang it herself. But most of her hard work was expended
on Arun, for whom she couldn't smile enough. She had always
been gracious to him, to demonstrate her acceptance of him
as Dipti's friend, but now there was something desperate in
her attitude, as if she were not bestowing but herself craving
acceptance.

Dipti's father too had graciously patronized Arun in the past,
sometimes singling him out among the crowd of admirers to
address him with his pungently humorous remarks. Now Arun
was their sole recipient, for there was no one else to hear them.
And just as the mother had ordered the same size cake as for a
large party, so the father, as voluminous as ever in his starched
white muslin, spread out all his store of comment and conversation for Arun's sake alone. Supplying great gusts of laughter
himself, he did not notice that Arun could only summon the
faintest smile in response to his best jokes. And then, when he
changed his topic and with it his mood, he needed no response
to his words other than his own mighty anger. This was when
he spoke of his case and of his enemies who had brought it
against him: and from there he went on to announce what he
would do to all of them, once he had cleared his good name
and confounded all their schemes and dirty tricks. His voice
rose, his face swelled out in a fearful way. Dipti implored,
'Daddy!' while his wife laid a hand on his arm to restrain
him: 'Leave off,' she said. Then his anger burst like a boil:
'Leave off! I'll show you how I'll leave off when I've crushed
them under my feet and plucked out their eyeballs and torn
out their tongues – rogues! Liars! I'll show them all, I'll teach
them such a lesson—' His hands fumbled in the air as though
to pluck down more threats – and then fumbled in a different
way like those of a drowning man attempting to save himself.

His face swollen to a monstrous color, his words changed to a gasp, he keeled over in the throne-like chair on which he was seated. His wife screamed, servants came running; Dipti and Arun tried to prevent him from falling out of the chair, holding his huge throbbing body in their arms. Bereft of his guidance, everyone was calling out confused orders, several hands plucked at him to undo the studs on his kurta. 'I'm dying,' he gasped. 'They've killed me.'

Dipti's father did not die, but he had suffered a stroke and was taken to hospital. There he lay in a private room, monstrous and immobile, while his wife sat at his feet, moaning 'What will become of us?' The sight and sound of her drove him mad, but he could neither shout nor throw things at her, and she refused to be driven away. His eyes swiveled imploringly toward Dipti, who had taken over the duty of caring for him. Fully occupied with her father, she could no longer attend her classes, and once or twice Arun visited her in her father's hospital room. But he had always been impatient of anyone's sickness – whenever Indu felt unwell, she suppressed it in his presence as long as possible – and the sight of Dipti's father in his present state was intolerable to him. And almost worse, in a different way, was the mother groaning 'What will become of us?' and then looking with begging eyes at Arun, as though he alone held the answer to that question.

The final examination was drawing near, and Arun no longer had time to visit the hospital, or for anything except his studies. His mother was delighted with the way he devoted himself to his work, and she did everything she could to encourage him. She fed him his favorite foods, and in order to buy special delicacies for him, like ham or cheese, she gave up taking a rickshaw to work and went by public transport – though secretly, for she knew how this would upset him, to think of her in the reeking, overcrowded bus, being pushed and even pinched, for she was still attractive enough to attract such unwanted attentions. It was her ambition – and his too, though he never spoke of it – that he should repeat the success of her father who, in the same examination more than half a century earlier, had stood first in the whole University. The gold medal he had won then was one of her most precious possessions. These days she took it out frequently and gazed at it in its velvet-lined case, and also left it open on the table where she served Arun his meals. She was in an unusually good mood, and was completely free of the headaches and depression that so often plagued her.

Unfortunately, Arun's father Raju again turned up unexpectedly at this time, completely broke, for the film script he had set his hopes on had fallen through. But he was as cheerful as ever, and although he tried to be respectful of his son's studies, could not refrain from expressing the thoughts tumbling around in his lively mind, or humming the tunes that came bubbling up there. He inquired after Dipti, and when he heard what had happened and how she had had to drop out of college, he shook his head in pity for her.

His thoughts reverted to her at odd moments – for instance, at night while he was lying on the couch and Arun sat over his studies at the table, he suddenly said, 'But she was a pretty girl. Really special. Intelligent but oomphy too.'

Arun looked up, frowning: 'What sort of word is that?'

'Oh, you know – like in "She's oomphy – toomphy – just my moomphy,"' and he sang it, in case Arun didn't know this popular Hindi film song.

Indu thumped on the wall: 'Are you disturbing Arun?'

'Oh no, I'm helping him with his physics!' Raju called back. After a while, he spoke again: 'How you must miss her – oh oh, terrible! I know with Indu, when I had measles – can you imagine a youth of nineteen going down with measles – for three weeks I couldn't see her and I thought I would surely die with longing for her . . . Yes yes, all right!' he called when Indu thumped again. 'I'm already asleep!'

After a few days of this – 'He's driving me crazy,' Arun complained to Indu. That night, when Raju already lay on the couch that was his allotted space, she called him into the bedroom. Raju raised his eyebrows at his son in pleased surprise; Arun too was surprised, and more so as the minutes passed and Raju was not sent out again. Arun found it difficult to return to his books. His attention was strained toward the other room; he heard their voices rising in argument till they shushed each other and continued their fight in whispers. Finally these too ceased, but by now Arun was completely incapable of concentrating on his work. What were they doing in there? He could not hear a sound. He walked up and down and cleared his throat, to make them remember he was there; they continued silent, as though holding their breath for fear of disturbing him. He was no longer thinking of them but only of the room and its bed on which they were together, as he and Dipti had been together for so many afternoons.

Dipti's father was in the news again when the results of the inquiry against him were made public. He had been found guilty on every count – taking money from interested parties, acquiring properties, accepting imported cars and going on shopping trips to Hong Kong in return for favors received – and the report expressed itself in the strongest terms on his conduct. Although he was named as the prime culprit, several senior bureaucrats were drawn into the same web of accusations, as were other members of the cabinet. The whole government was brought under suspicion, the opposition clamored for its resignation, while frantic meetings were held at the highest level to save the situation. By then he had been discharged from the hospital and lay helpless and speechless on his bed at home, with his wife at his feet and Dipti ministering to his needs. No newspapers were allowed into his room, and when he made signs to ask for them, everyone pretended not to understand. All this time Arun had not seen or spoken to Dipti. He had tried to phone her once, from the college – he had no phone at home – but he knew she was in her father's room, with both parents present, so that it was difficult for him to speak. And while he was groping for words, other students waiting behind him for the phone kept saying, 'Come on, hurry up.' After that he had not tried to contact her again.

When the report about her father came out, it gave rise to a lot of discussion in which he refused to participate either at college or at home. When Indu said she had known it all along, that one look at the way they lived had told her that it was all based on bribery and corruption, he cut her short with 'You don't know what you're talking about.'

'It's all here – in black and white.'

'Oh yes,' he sneered, 'you're just the type to believe everything that's written in some rag of a newspaper.'

'*The Times of India*,' she protested – but he was already out of the house and on one of his furious walks.

He had not yet returned when his parents were getting ready for bed. 'He's thinking of the girl,' Raju said to Indu in the bedroom where he was still allowed to remain. 'He feels for her – poor child, what is her future now? He loves her,' he concluded in a musing, sentimental voice.

'He doesn't see her. Of course he doesn't! He's much too busy studying for his exam to waste his time on a girl.'

Raju smiled: 'Time spent on a girl is never wasted.'

'That's your philosophy, but thank God it's not his.'

'Yes, thank God,' Raju echoed but continued smiling. His arms clasped behind his head, his eyes meditating on the ceiling, he began to recite in a soft poetic voice: '"My thoughts buzz like bees around the blossom of your—"'

'Sh!' she said, putting her hand over his mouth. 'He's come home . . . Arun?'

She had to call twice more before Arun answered: 'What do you want? Why do you have to keep disturbing me?'

'Are you studying?'

'Well, what do you think I'm doing?'

'He's studying,' Indu said to Raju. She took her hand from his mouth: 'Go on, but keep your voice down.'

Raju continued: '"My sting is transformed into desire to suck the essence of your beauty . . ." Do you like it?'

'Is it something you made up? I don't know why you can never think of anything except bees and flowers.'

'Should I turn off the light?'

She assented, yawning to show how tired she was. 'I must get to sleep. I have to be up early to go to work, unlike some people.'

But once the light was off, it turned out she wasn't so tired after all. Although they tried to make no noise, they became so lively together that Arun in the next room had to cover his ears, in an effort to muffle the sounds from the bedroom as well as those pounding in his own head.

Next day Arun had an important pre-exam tutorial, but instead of attending, he went to see Dipti. He prepared himself to find her house as silent and gloomy as on her birthday, but instead it was in turmoil. They were moving out – having lost his official position, the father also lost his official residence, and all its contents were being carried into cars and moving vans parked around the house. In supervising this operation, Dipti's mother had regained her former bustling, domineering personality. She was on the front lawn, fighting with a government clerk who had been sent to ensure that no government property was removed. Whenever he challenged a piece of furniture being carried away, she told him that whatever was not theirs by private purchase had been earned by years of selfless public service, and overruling his protests, she waved the coolies on with a lordly gesture.

Arun found her attitude to himself completely changed. She greeted him haughtily, and when he tried to enter the house in search of Dipti, she barred his way. She told him that her daughter was busy, and working herself up, went on indignantly, 'My goodness, the girl has a sick father to look after, and here we are in the middle of a move to a big house of our own, not to mention other important family matters – you can't expect to walk in here whenever you please to take up our time.'

Arun flushed angrily but was not to be put off. When she turned away to resume her argument with the clerk, he strode past her into the house. He picked his way among sofa-sets, chandeliers and china services, through the courtyard full of packing cases and cooking pots to the family rooms at the back of the house. All the doors here were wide open except one: he did not hesitate to turn its handle and found himself in the father's room. The invalid had been placed in an armchair, with Dipti beside him feeding him something out of a cup.

Her reception of him made Arun even more angry than her

mother's: 'What a lovely surprise,' she said in a bright, social voice. 'And I was thinking of you only yesterday.'

'I was thinking of *you*,' he replied, but in a very different tone, his voice lowered and charged. 'That's why I'm here.'

'I was going to send you a note – to wish you good luck. For your finals. Isn't it next week? You must be so jittery, poor Arun.'

'I have to talk to you.'

'One more spoon, Daddy, for me.' She put it in his mouth, but whatever was on it came dribbling out again.

'I must see you. Alone. Where can we go?' He didn't know if Dipti's father understood anything or not, and he didn't care. He thought only to leap over all the barriers between Dipti and himself – her huge helpless father, the house in upheaval, her mother, and most of all Dipti's own manner toward him.

Her mother came in. She addressed Arun: 'You must leave at once. You can see we're very busy.' To Dipti she said, 'The jeweler has come. I told him it's a bad day, but now he's here, we might as well look at what he's brought. There's not much time left.'

'Not much time left for what?' Arun asked Dipti, ignoring her mother.

Dipti had her back to Arun, and instead of answering him, she scooped up the food from her father's chin back into his mouth.

Her mother told her, 'Don't forget those people are sending a car for you in the afternoon. I said, Where is the need, we have plenty of cars of our own, but they insist. They like to do everything right – naturally, they can afford it. I'll call the jeweler in here, he can spread it out on the bed for us to see.'

'It'll disturb Daddy.'

But her mother went to the door to call for the jeweler. Quick as a flash, Arun drew near to Dipti and bent down to breathe into her ear, 'Tomorrow. Four o'clock.' She still had her back to him, and he laid one finger on the nape of her neck – it was the lightest touch, but he felt it pass through her like an electric current, charged with everything that had always been between them.

✳     ✳     ✳

But it so happened that next day Raju stayed home. Usually he accompanied his wife when she left in the morning and then remained in the center of town for the rest of the day, calling on friends, sitting with them in their favorite coffee-houses, enjoying himself. But that day he had a cold, and as always when he was sick, he looked at Indu with piteous eyes that said 'What has happened to me?' Before leaving for the office, she rubbed his chest with camphor and tied a woolen scarf around his neck. She left tea ready brewed for him on the stove, and two little pots of food she had prepared. He stayed in bed, mostly asleep; but as the day wore on, he became more cheerful, and by afternoon he had almost forgotten about his cold.

Arun arrived just before four, and as soon as he entered, he heard his father singing a lyric to himself, in that swooning way he had when deeply moved by a line of verse. 'What are you doing here?' Arun said, in shock.

Raju stopped singing and pointed to the scarf Indu had tied around his neck. He coughed a little.

'Oh my God,' Arun said in such despair that Raju assured him in a weak voice, 'It's just a cold, maybe a little fever.' He felt his own forehead: 'Ninety-nine. Perhaps a hundred.'

There was a soft knock on the living room door, and Arun ran to admit Dipti. 'Who is it, Arun? Has someone come?' Raju called from the bedroom. Dipti's eyes grew round in distress and with the same distress Arun said, 'My father has a cold.'

Raju came shuffling out of the bedroom, and when he saw Dipti, he held his hands to cover the crumpled lungi in which he had slept all night and day. 'Oh, oh!' he cried in apology. 'I thought you were Indu come home early from the office. She was very anxious about me when she left.'

But he quickly recovered and began to compliment Dipti on her appearance. She was dressed in pale turquoise silk with little spangles sewn on in the shape of flowers; she also wore a pair of long gold earrings set with precious stones – 'Are they rubies?' Raju admired them. 'All set around a lovely pearl. They say that older women should wear pearls, here, around their throat,' he touched the woolen scarf, 'but I love to see them on a young girl.'

'You could go back to bed,' Arun suggested.

'And leave you alone here with this pearl?' A flush like dawn had tinted Dipti's face and neck. 'Anyway, I feel much better. Completely cured by the sight of beauty, which is the best medicine in the world for a poor susceptible person like myself. I don't have a heart,' he informed Dipti, 'I have a frail shivering bird in here, drenched by the rains and storms of passion.'

Arun exclaimed impatiently, but when he saw Dipti, still freshly flushed, smile at Raju's extravagance, irritation with his father turned to anger against Dipti. 'You should ask her some more about those earrings,' he said. 'Ask her if they're her wedding jewelry—' Her flush now a deepest rose, Dipti's hands flew to her ears. 'What was he doing there yesterday with you and your mother,' he challenged her more harshly, 'what had he come to sell?'

'Whatever they are,' Raju said, 'she's come here wearing them for you. I wish I could say it were for me, but even I'm not such a conceited optimist. But I'm really feeling much better and I think I might just lie and rest here a little bit on this couch. I won't disturb you at all – I'll shut my eyes and I shall probably be fast asleep in a minute. But if you're afraid of waking me, you could go in the other room and keep very quiet in there.'

He did exactly what he said – stretched himself on the couch and shut his eyes, so that they could think of him as fast asleep. But they had no time to think of anything – before they had even got into the next room, Arun was already tugging at her beautiful clothes and she was helping him. It was many weeks since they had last been together, and they were desperate. Their youth, their lust, and their love overflowed in them, so that their lovemaking was like that of young gods. It is not in the nature of young gods to curtail their activities, and they forgot about keeping quiet and not disturbing Raju.

He *was* disturbed, but in a way he liked tremendously. He lay on the couch, partly listening to what was going on next door but mostly preoccupied with his own thoughts. These made him happy – for the young people in the bedroom, of course, and for *all* young people, and these included himself. Raju was nearly forty, he did not have an easy life – he told no one about the many shifts he had to resort to in Bombay, to keep himself going in between assignments, which often fell through, or were never paid for. Nevertheless, he had not changed from the time he had been a student in Delhi and used to creep up to the roof of Indu's parents' house. She often had to put her hand over his mouth to keep him from waking everyone up, for in his supreme happiness he could not refrain from singing out loud – he knew all the popular hits as well as more refined Urdu lyrics, and they all exactly expressed what he felt, about her, and the stars above them, and the white moonlight and scent of jasmine drenching the air around them.

But now the sounds from the next room changed: Raju propped himself up on his elbow. 'I'll tear them off!' his son was saying. He was back on the subject of the ear-rings. The girl screamed – Raju sprang up, ready to intervene: he knew there was something in his son that was not in himself – a bitter anger, perhaps transmitted to him by his mother during the years she had struggled to make a living for them both. But somehow the girl pacified him, or it may have been his own feeling for her that made him hold his hand. She pleaded – 'What else could I do? Arun, what could I do? With all that was happening, and Daddy's illness.'

'You wanted it yourself. Because they're rich. Ah, don't touch me.'

'Yes, they're rich. They can help Daddy.'

'Who are they anyway?'

She hesitated for a moment before replying: 'They're Daddy's friends.' He had to insist several times for a more definite answer before she came out with the name. Then Arun said: 'Great. Wonderful.' And Raju too on the other side of the wall was shocked: for the name she had mentioned was that of a tremendously wealthy family notorious for their smuggling and other underworld activities and involved in several political scandals, including that of Dipti's father.

Dipti said with a touch of defiance: 'They helped us when there was no one else.' But her voice trembled in a way that made Raju's heart tremble too; but not Arun's, who continued to speak harshly: 'And you're madly in love with the boy . . . Why don't you answer!'

'I've met him twice. Arun, don't! I'll take them off. Here.' She unhooked the earrings before he could tug at them again. He flung them across the room. One of them rolled under the partitioning curtain into the next room. Raju looked at it lying there but did not pick it up.

Arun said, 'It's like selling yourself. It *is* selling yourself.'

Again she spoke defiantly: 'As long as it helps my parents in their trouble.'

'Yes, and what about being a college lecturer? That was just talk. All you want is to be rich and buy jewelry and eat those horrible cream cakes.'

After a while she said in a very quiet voice, 'That's not what I want.'

'Then what? Don't try and fool me. I know you like no one else knows you. Like no one else ever will know you. You can never forget me. Never. Never.'

'No. I shall never forget you.' Then she broke out: 'But what can I do, Arun! You tell me: what else can I do!'

And on the other side of the curtain, Raju's heart was fit to burst, and it was all he could do not to cry out to Arun: 'Tell her!' He was almost tempted to show him – ah, with what abandon Raju himself would have acted in his son's place, how he would have flung himself at the girl's feet and cried: 'I'm here! Marry me! I'm yours forever!'

But Arun was saying something different: 'I'll haunt you like a ghost. You'll keep reading about me in the newspapers because I'm going to be very famous. If necessary, I'll go into politics to clean up our country from all these corrupt politicians and smugglers who are sucking it dry. You'll see. You'll see what I'll do.'

'I have to go. Let me get dressed.'

'Not yet. Five minutes. Ten.'

Then there was no more talking and almost complete silence in the bedroom, so that when Indu came home, she didn't know anyone was in there and said to Raju, 'Why aren't you in bed?'

He laid a finger on his lips and glanced toward the other room. She followed his eyes and gasped when she saw the earring that had rolled from under the curtain. 'Sh – sh – sh,' said Raju.

'He's got that girl in there,' Indu whispered fiercely.

'You needn't worry.'

'What do you mean not worry? His finals are next week.'

'Oh, he'll do very well. He's your son; and your father's grandson.'

And for the hundredth time in their life she said, 'Thank God anyway that he hasn't taken after you. Let go of me. Let go.' For he had seized her in his arms and pressed his lips against hers – she thought at first it was to silence her but relaxed as his kiss became more pressing and more passionate: as if he wanted to make it up to her for his shortcomings, and then, giving himself over completely, to make it up to all women for the shortcomings of all men.

# HUSBAND AND SON

In his latter days – and even that is now over thirty years ago – her husband was always referred to as 'the old man.' Or 'the old man up there,' for he was by that time living almost entirely on the roof of the family house. The only sound that came from him was the Vedic hymns he sang at dawn; his voice, though cracked, sounded very sweet. Vijay was left to rattle around by herself in their large mansion, with nothing to do except bully the servants. It was her boast that any member of the household could walk in any time – rising from the dead, that is – and find the place just as they had known it. At the beginning of every summer she had the carpets rolled up and stowed away, as though her father-in-law and his guests were still there to be kept cool amid marble floors sprinkled with rose water; and every winter the quilts were stuffed with new cotton, though there was no one now to sleep under them except herself. The old man on the roof just covered himself with a blanket, as threadbare with age as he was.

She spent many hours sitting on her verandah, looking out over the river Jumna. During the monsoon, it regularly flooded, and one year they had had to go up and down the streets in boats. This was before the Ring Road and the fortifying walls and the overpass were built: now you would no longer be able to see the river from their house – but anyway, once Vijay herself had died, less than a year after the old man, the house was torn down and rows of municipal offices built in its stead. Even in her day, changes were taking place. For instance, the mansion at their rear, which had belonged to a prosperous

Muslim family, had been divided up among refugees from Pakistan; straw-roofed huts, selling betel and other necessities, had been built into the niches of its compound wall. And the house next door, where a famous eye-surgeon and his family had lived on a lavish scale, had been taken over by a school of Indian dance, sponsored by the Ministry of Culture.

Vijay welcomed these new activities around her. Despite her age, she was still full of energy and had nowhere to expend it. Her parents-in-law and their entire generation of widowed aunts were dead. Her son Anand – in his thirties now but too busy to get married – was posted in Bengal where he was an important government officer. And the old man was becoming more and more eccentric. He had cut down his meals to one a day, consisting of a few chapattis and a vegetable or a lentil dish, never both, for he wanted to eat no more than the poor could afford. Vijay's appetite had remained healthy and she still needed her regular meals, with meat or fish. The old man did not grudge her this rich food and often came to keep her company while she ate. He read to her from those strange books he had or expounded his even stranger ideas. She didn't understand or even listen much, but it gave her the opportunity to keep a sharp watch on him. Why was he holding his jaw like that? Next day she hauled him off to the dentist, overriding his protests: did horses go to the dentist? he asked. Or when it turned out he had a hernia and a truss was prescribed – did horses wear trusses?

He had always been careless of his health; careless of himself. In the past, when they were both young, it was because he had been so busy, immersed in public affairs. Although he came from a pro-British family – his father had been a High Court judge – he himself had been deeply involved in the Indian independence movement and had spent several years in jail. Later, after Independence, he had been elected to parliament and had been given a cabinet post. Those had been wonderful years for Vijay. They had moved out of the family house on the Jumna to one of the former British residences requisitioned by the new government of India. An armed sentry stood at their gate, supplemented by a whole posse of policemen when the

Prime Minister or other members of the cabinet came to the house. Important decisions on national and international policy had been taken in this house. Foreign dignitaries had been entertained there, or they themselves had been driven in their official limousine to the President's palace to attend banquets in honor of visiting prime ministers, or royal guests from the neighboring kingdoms.

All this was still going on in New Delhi, on an ever larger and more sumptuous scale, but she and the old man were no longer part of it. He had resigned his offices and all his honors after only a few years of holding them, and they had moved out of the official residence back to the family house on the Jumna. She had protested – what was the use of all their sacrifices and his years in jail if they were not now to reap the benefits along with everyone else? But she had acquiesced, because she realized how unhappy he was, disgusted with the politics of power. And she could not bear to see him unhappy: it was his cheerfulness that had from the first drawn her to him, the sprightly way he moved around, humming a tune to himself (Urdu love lyrics it had been then, or Hindi patriotic songs, also the *Marseillaise* and the *Internationale*). Even on their wedding day, when they had sat together before the sacred fire and the rest of the family had been full of the usual marriage fuss and fury, he had muttered irreverent jokes from behind the strings of flowers that hid his face from her as hers was hidden from him; so that, instead of weeping the way brides are supposed to, she had had trouble stifling her giggles. Their marriage had been arranged while he was still abroad, taking his degree in Cambridge (England). The year was 1923. When he returned, the old man – only he was called Prakash then – was twenty-five years old, full of high spirits and high ideas. She liked him immediately. He wasn't handsome but he had a very nice face, with spectacles and a mouth that was always twitching with suppressed laughter. He rarely laughed out loud, as she did all the time. Even during sex – and they had had a lot of it, oh my God what a lot of sex – he had to put his hand over her mouth so that the rest of the family wouldn't hear the racket she made. They had been given a bedroom of their own, but all around them were the rooms of other members of his large family. With the door shut, they felt quite private, and besides making love, they also talked a lot and he told her his ideas, which she adopted as her own. Her eyes blazed when he spoke of the necessity of throwing out the English; and during the years he was in jail, she quarreled with his family and with her own, all of whom, far from throwing out the English, only wanted to be like them and to be allowed to join their clubs. He never argued with his family but only made jokes: for instance, about his mother and aunts – poor things, he said, every day oppressed by three terrible problems: What to wear? Where to go? What to do?

Nowadays, sitting on her verandah and the old man up there on the roof, Vijay found herself beset with the same problems, or at least two of them. What to wear she had settled long ago. For a time, under his influence, she had sacrificed her fine saris for the patriotic homespun cottons he wore; but they felt scratchy and coarse, and she soon went back to her imported silks with embroidered borders. To her regret, he never again wore the suits he had brought from England, but she kept them hanging in her wardrobe – they were still hanging there, and she touched them sometimes, stroking the sleeves of tweed and wool and sniffing at them for the last aroma of the English cigarettes he had chain-smoked.

Every evening she walked by the river and sometimes joined the groups of hymn-singers clustered around a priest or holy person; she was not religious but sang as lustily as all the others. She also sat cross-legged in a circle of friendship with simple housewives whom she advised on birth control and other topics they were eager to learn about from a superior person like herself. Everyone knew and liked her; when she bought from the shops in the compound wall, they told her the correct price, as though she were not rich but one of them. As soon as the dance school moved into the eye-surgeon's house, she couldn't wait to pay them a visit and be shown around and watch the pupils at their practice and lessons. After that, she went every day, she liked it so much. The students were all

young girls – not at all the sort you would expect to be students
of Indian dance (that is, the illegitimate daughters of temple
dancers) but from good families for whom the Indian classical
arts had replaced the piano as part of a girl's accomplishments.
But the teachers were still of the traditional class, hereditary
musicians and dancers transmitting their art from father to son.
They were delighted with this new source of income, especially
the old men who had spent their lives turning over the sparse
coins that came their way from weddings and festivals. Now
they were civil servants under the Ministry of Culture, with
regular salaries and pensions and provident fund. Those who
were too old for the job had sent their sons or nephews, so
that there were a few young teachers too, with whom the girls
fell in love. All day the house was filled with the sound of
ankle-bells and drumbeats, of notes plucked from many lyres
and the laughter of light-minded girls; sticks of incense, rose
and jasmine, burned in honor of the patron goddess of dance
and music.

Vijay, as was her way, made friends with everyone, teachers
and students, but her favorite was Ram, one of the dance
teachers. He came from Jaipur and was the nephew of a
famous exponent of the Kathak form of dance. His mother
tongue was some strange Rajasthani dialect and the Hindi
in which he had to communicate in Delhi was atrocious
and made everyone laugh. Vijay also laughed and she tried
to make him speak more correctly, but he couldn't learn, or
wouldn't. He said he would like to learn English, which she
spoke well and he not at all. He admired her for her higher
education, and for being rich. She invited him to the house,
even sometimes to eat with her; it was good to have someone
share the big meals the cook prepared every day for her alone.
At first Ram was shy because he didn't know how to eat rice at
a table with a spoon and fork. She taught him, and there he
was quick to learn and eager, for it was his ambition to be sent
abroad and perform for foreign audiences in their big halls.

Sometimes the old man came down and joined them. The
first time Ram was astonished to see such a shabby person in
this grand house and even more astonished to learn that he

was Vijay's husband. But when she enlightened him who this husband was, or had been, Ram's attitude changed completely. The next time he saw the old man he stooped to touch his feet in the traditional mark of respect – or at least he tried to, but the old man prevented him by jumping backward and flapping his hands at him, as though shooing away some noisome insect about to sting him. Vijay covered her mouth to stifle her laughter; she had always been amused by the way the old man had dealt with people who tried to pay him respect. When he was a cabinet minister, she had seen him literally turn and flee before a group of citizens advancing toward him with garlands to hang in honor around his neck.

The old man accepted Ram's frequent visits without comment. Perhaps he did not always notice him – sometimes it seemed to Vijay he did not even see or notice her, he appeared so lost in his thoughts or in his reading. He carried his strange books around with him – old books, falling to pieces, out of which he would occasionally read a passage aloud to them. Ram listened with the utmost respect, with reverence, swaying his head in appreciation of what he heard, though Vijay knew he understood even less of it than she did. In the old days, when they were first married, the old man – Prakash – had read to her out of the books he had brought from his studies in England: Tom Paine, John Stuart Mill, Karl Marx – she hadn't always understood them entirely but had grasped the gist of their ideas. Now what he read was way beyond her. But so was the old man himself – she understood him less and less but accepted him wholly in all his eccentricity; and so did Ram, honoring him as supremely noble, a sage who had given up the world. The three of them had begun to form a family group, Vijay and Ram at the dining table enjoying one of the cook's sumptuous meals while the old man read aloud out of his tattered book, about the soul and the Absolute and their identity-in-difference.

These pleasant hours had to cease when their son Anand arrived from Bengal to confer with his superiors at the Ministry of Home Affairs. His official visits occurred two or three times a year and gave him a chance to check up on his parents. He had taken charge of their finances some years ago. This had become necessary when the old man was on the point of giving everything away, including their house to be converted into a beggars' home. Now Anand had settled the house and all monies on his mother, under his personal supervision, relieving his father of the millstone of earthly possessions. When Anand was there, his parents were on their best behavior. The old man remained quietly in his room on the roof; Vijay did not visit the dance school or anywhere else in the neighborhood but stayed at home, supervising the servants. On the first day of Anand's arrival, Ram had come as usual, but after that he stayed away. He knew Anand's type well, for civil servants exactly like him arrived for an inspection every time the grant to the school came up for renewal. Then students and teachers were meek as mice, their lessons went like clockwork, and it was not until the inspection was over that everything reverted to normal. Similarly, it was not until Anand had left (fortunately he was too busy to stay long) that Ram came back to eat his meals, the old man descended from the roof, and the three of them resumed what had become their regular routine.

Vijay had always been proud of her son, who had been a brilliant student and had stood first in the administrative service exam. She boasted that, of course, with such a father, nothing less could be expected of him; but really Anand did not take after his father at all, his brilliance was of quite a different order. The old man had questioned all authority, whereas Anand did everything he was told from above with no questions at all. He blamed his father for retreating into his own eccentricity instead of serving his country. Vijay tried but found it hard to defend the father against the son, for she had never really understood why the old man had had to give up everything – except, as she told Anand, that he had been unhappy with the way power was being misused by those who had seized it. Anand waved this away: personal feelings were of no account at a time when the country needed to be guided by men of talent and integrity. When he said this, his spectacles gleamed the way the old man's used to when he spoke of his ideals; but, strangely, the glass of Anand's lenses gleamed in quite a different way from his father's. Maybe because with the old man you never could be sure whether he was laughing or not, whereas with Anand you could be sure that he was not.

Vijay loved her son dearly, but it had always been difficult for her to express her feelings for him. From childhood on, he hated to be kissed and fondled, hated to have his hair combed by her as she longed to do. Ram was the opposite. His own mother was far away, so were his many sisters, and he missed their endearments. On hot summer afternoons he and Vijay kept each other company, sitting on the marble floor of her drawing room directly under the ceiling fan, which brushed them with a cool breeze like a delicious shiver. He leaned against her knees while she combed his hair, playing with and exclaiming over it. Anand's hair had always been straight and thin (it had begun to fall out when he was still in his twenties), but Ram's clustered over his head in bunches of pitch-black curls that she could wind and rewind over her fingers. Each curl was plump like Ram himself and, also like himself, shiny with scented oil. Inhaling its fragrance, she could not resist kissing first his hair and then his cheek, which was rounded like a peach and rarely needed shaving. He smiled and looked up into her eyes and fondly murmured 'Ma.' From the beginning, he had called her mother, but it was only lately that she had begun to call him not son but 'My sweet son.' Because that was what he was to her, in a way that no one had ever been. When she was tired, he massaged her feet as he used to do to his mother, cracking the toes. The only other person who had done this to her was the old man, when they were both young and forever making love.

Once the old man came in unexpectedly while Ram was doing this to her feet. Usually in the afternoon he stayed on the roof – she never knew how he could stand the heat up there under the tin roof of the little room that he had taken for his own though it was only meant for storage. He refused to have a fan – do horses have fans? – and anyway there was no electrical outlet. Now he had come to read a passage from his book to them, and he did read it; it was about the knowledge that is real and the knowledge that is illusory. She sat up – she had been reclining on a mat spread on the floor – and Ram stopped massaging her feet, while they both listened respectfully. When he had finished reading, the old man shuffled out again, without saying anything more. Ram wanted to continue his massage, but her mood was spoiled, almost as if they had been doing something wrong though she knew they had not.

Later that day she went up to see the old man – she did this at least twice daily to check up on him, once to bring his food and make sure he ate it. But that day she lingered longer than usual, chatting away to him but with pauses to give him the opportunity to say something if he wished to. When he didn't, she herself started on another topic, and finally she talked to him about Ram. She said Ram was the wrong name for him, it was impossible to connect him with that intractable warrior god whose wife had to be so far above suspicion that he banished her, though she was pure and innocent. It was Krishna whom *her* Ram resembled – '*our* Ram,' she said, glaring at the old man when he did not respond: Krishna with his flute and all his milkmaids who loved him though he teased them mercilessly, mischievous boy that he was. Not that Ram, '*our* Ram,' was in the least mischievous: on the contrary, never had she known a boy to show so much respect and devotion to his elders. 'You never ask if my legs are hurting,' she accused the old man. 'Dr Sehgal says it's the beginning of arthritis, but what do you care? I could be lame and blind and you wouldn't even notice, you or your son.' The old man still had said nothing, but he looked up at her and when she looked back at him, she saw that one lens of his spectacles was cracked right across. Exclaiming impatiently, she snatched them off his nose and had them fixed by the optician that same day.

Her friendship with Ram continued to grow. Only it wasn't friendship, it was something else, some other relationship that they often speculated about, deciding that it had been carried over not only from one previous life but several of them. They might have been mother and son in one incarnation, husband and wife in another, brother and sister, even lovers, they teased each other, like Leila and Majnu, or Romeo and Juliet. The emotions of all these relationships had been infused into their veins in this birth, so that they could not help being what they were with each other. In the cool of the evening they walked by the river, his hand in hers like a child's, or their intertwined hands swinging between them like those of friends. The hymn-singers around the holy man made room for them to join their circle, so did the groups of gossiping housewives; everyone smiled on them, on the old woman and the youth, and the way they cared for each other.

The biggest treat for both of them was to go shopping together. She hired a carriage, the prettiest she could find, the driver with a clean shirt and the horse with a little bunch of flowers nodding behind each ear. They drove into the big bazaar opposite the Red Fort, into the cloth-market and the lane where gold-embroidered slippers were sold. The owners sent for iced sherbet, while Vijay and Ram pointed up to the shelves to have more and more bolts of cloth brought down till there was a glittering sea of silks and muslins spread around them. Ram had a fine appreciation of quality – of course he was a dancer, an artiste with a highly developed sense of beauty. She loved to watch him examining the embroidery on a tunic or rubbing a delicate silk between his fingers. What he liked best always turned out to be the most expensive item in the shop, and he would modestly lay it aside: 'No no, it's too much.' She drew it forward again and insisted till he gave way; and then she was doubly rewarded – by his joy in the new acquisition and by the tender gratitude he expressed toward her, the donor.

When, on his next visit, Anand made his usual scrutiny of her accounts, he was surprised by the increase in her expenditure. She easily explained it: there had been visits to the dentist, a loan to the cook who was arranging his daughter's marriage, and then she had ordered clothes to be stitched for the old man – and did Anand have any idea what a chore it was to make him wear them? Anand nodded, he remembered many altercations between his parents, whenever his mother had tried to replace some coat or shirt falling to pieces. For years now she had wanted to throw out the tattered blanket that was his only covering in the winter – she had even tried to steal it, but the old man had made such a fuss that she had had to give it back. Anand was aware of the situation and deplored it, along with all his father's eccentricities. It seemed to him that the old man was getting worse, but what could he, what could anyone do about it? Usually he just shook his head and shrugged; but on this last visit, he detected something in his father that made him ask his mother: 'Is he all right?'

'How do you mean?' She was on her guard immediately; the old man was her responsibility, no one else's.

'He's not sick or anything?'

'Yes, of course he's sick, there are probably a thousand things wrong with him but you try and get him to see a doctor, if you can. All I ever hear is about that horse.'

Anand too had heard often enough about the horse, so he knew it was useless to say anything more, and next day he went back to his district in Bengal where many duties awaited him.

Vijay had not needed her son to point out that there was a change in the old man: didn't she know him better than anyone, every bit of him? All those years ago, when he had become disillusioned with his government post, she had sensed his distress though for two years he had said nothing about it. And now too she detected a sadness in him that expressed itself only in his silence. She listened for this silence – for instance, early in the morning when he had been in the habit of singing hymns to the rising sun. Now the sun rose and he was silent and she fretted. Was he really ill? His cheeks had been hollow for many years now, usually with grey stubble in them; she had recently had the last of his teeth extracted and his mouth had sunk in, which may have accounted for his grieved expression. His spectacles had lost their gleam – probably they were dirty, but when she cleaned them for him, they still looked dull: dull and sad.

When the old man no longer came down to read to them, Ram asked after him, he missed him. Vijay explained that he had these periods of withdrawal when he was very busy with his thoughts, one had to expect it in a philosophical person. Ram looked awed for a moment; then he and Vijay resumed their playful mood, enjoying each other's company in the usual way. In the mornings she often strolled over to the dance school to watch him give his lesson. He had a class of nine girls, all eager to learn his Kathak style of dance. They were not talented and he became very impatient with them, which made them giggle in a mixture of fright and delight. They were all in love with him. Sometimes, exasperated by their ineptitude, he showed them how the steps should be done. They held their breath to watch him – the strength of his stamping feet, the imperious ring of his ankle-bells, the muscles of his round young arms rippling in the godlike movements of his dance. He was always exquisitely dressed now in the Lucknow tunics Vijay bought him; they had also begun to patronize the jewelers' lane in the bazaar, to buy little diamond studs to fasten these tunics. Neither of them could resist the ruby ring he now wore on his middle finger, or the one in his ear, or the gold chain that encircled his neck, smooth as a girl's but sturdy. When he danced, a skinny young musician accompanied him on the drum, beating out the rhythm with frenetic fingers, flinging himself about, long hair flying; no one had a glance to spare for him, all eyes were on Ram dancing and all of them shining, Vijay's along with the girls'.

Alone at night, she imagined what the girls must be feeling, in love with Ram. She recalled the sensations of her own youth, what it had been like to be in love. With her, it had always and only been the old man. She had been very proud to be married – of course, it was every girl's dream, to be a wife with a husband of her own and a bunch of household keys at her waist. She had been especially fortunate. Her father-in-law was rich, the family was tolerant and moderately modern, the house was run on a lavish scale with nothing wanting for comfort or even luxury: it was an atmosphere in which a young wife could bloom and flourish. Best of all was the old man – Prakash – himself. He was terribly in love with her. She was beautiful in those days, with wide hips springing from a small waist, and she had walked around the house lightly on bare feet, her gold jewelry jingling as if in celebration of her loveliness. Before others, he retained his cool manner, his own brand of cynical humor, but when they were alone together – the moment they locked their bedroom door behind them – he became ardent, adoring. He even fell at her feet, though she tried to prevent him, and when she couldn't, she got down on the floor with him and they clung together and rolled around, laughing and kissing. One year, during an epidemic, she had typhoid fever and he would not leave her bedside, changing cold compresses on her head; when she woke at night, tossing and burning, she heard him murmur as if in prayer – but that must have been an illusion caused by her delirium: as a young man he never prayed, it would have been against his principles.

In those years she had slept so soundly – had sunk so effortlessly into deep dreamless sleep – that it was a joke in the family how she could never be made to get up. Prakash woke early and tiptoed around and gave strict instructions that she was not to be disturbed. But nowadays, and especially during the time of her growing friendship with Ram, she spent many hours of the night awake, helpless under the press of her thoughts and memories. She was still in the bedroom she had once shared with her husband; when she felt very lonely, she went up to the roof to see him. He slept on a servant's string cot, which on hot nights he dragged from under the tin roof on to the open terrace; he did not need a mosquito net, probably his blood was too thin for mosquitoes to bother with him. He sat up the moment he saw her, as if he hadn't been sleeping but had been waiting for her. He smiled at her – his toothless smile that was so painful to her that she turned her eyes away. It was not only that it was a very old man's smile but that it held something apologetic in it: yes, as if he were apologizing to her – for what? For being old, for being the way he was now, for everything he had given up and had made her give up? When he had first begun to live as an ascetic, he had also given up sex between them, though they both still desired it. It had been several years before her menopause, and those had been difficult years for her.

'Go to sleep,' she told him, and he lay down obediently,

not wishing to be troublesome. She walked to the front of the terrace with its view of the river; on moonlit nights she could see the water stretching far into the horizon, lambent like the sky itself in its veil of stars. From the other side she overlooked what had once been the eye-surgeon's house and was now the dance school. The terrace was slightly lower than her own, so that she could see the beds placed there side by side in a row. In the summer, the dance teachers and their musicians slept up there; they were all men, some of them young like Ram and not yet married, the older ones with wives left behind in their home-towns. Even when there was no moon, she could make out the row of beds because each one had a white mosquito net that shone in the dark. She could never distinguish who was sleeping under what net, not even when there was a moon; everything was shrouded and still – except when a sudden dust storm blew up, or it rained, and then they would all start up and there was a confusion of white-clad figures scurrying for shelter. She had no time to linger and watch, for she had to help the old man drag his bed into his tin-roofed shed.

A terrible scandal broke out in the dance school: one of the students from good family was found to be pregnant. It was difficult to imagine how this could have happened in their institution. Their schedule was arranged in such a way that no student was ever alone with a teacher; and after hours, the inmates of the school lived a communal life, almost like monks. Nevertheless, what had happened had happened. The girl was already quite big, and under pressure from her parents admitted that she had been with one of the teachers; and under further pressure, she named Ram. He denied it absolutely, vehemently. The girl was a liar, and anyway much too thin and dark-complexioned for him to bother with her. The other teachers agreed with and believed him; but they were in a dilemma. Although the girl's family had sent her away to Simla in an attempt to suppress the scandal, news of it might leak out and reach the Ministry of Culture. Then the school's financial grant would be canceled, forcing them to close and all the teachers to return to their meager, salary-less days. If Ram confessed, he could be made an example of and dismissed. But he refused to confess, protesting his innocence with indignation and with tears.

He tried to hide his trouble from Vijay, but it was not possible. His feelings were too volatile, overflowed too spontaneously – it was part of his artistic temperament – to be concealed from anyone, let alone from Vijay with her mother's heart for him. He sought refuge in her house more often than ever, but his high spirits were extinguished. He stared dully in front of him, and when she first asked – then urged – then begged him to confide in her, he shook his head in dumb despair. Trying to cheer him up, she took him shopping every day now, and on a bigger scale than before. They went straight to the jewelers' lane, where they bought many large and shiny items. Fastening an imported gold watch around his wrist, she felt rewarded to see his eyes light up with some of their old sparkle; but this lasted hardly longer than it took to pay and leave the shop, when again he fell into a deep gloom.

On his next visit, Anand found the house changed – dark and dismal, with the servants neglecting their work and his mother too engrossed in Ram to supervise them in her former energetic way. The old man sat silent and alone on the roof; he no longer came down, not even when Vijay, kept out late shopping with Ram, forgot to bring up his meal. As for Ram, instead of tactfully disappearing during Anand's visit, he stayed close by Vijay's side, looking at her son with eyes that begged to be allowed to stay. But the worst was when Anand examined his mother's accounts. Unable or unwilling to explain the enormous increase in her expenditure, she became defiant and shouted at her son. He tried to shush her – 'The servants will hear' – so did Ram – 'Maji, your health' – but both pleas only incensed her more. 'Let them hear, let everyone hear, what sort of a son I have brought into the world!' And on the matter of her health, 'So who cares when my own son is making me die from grief and heartache.' The noise she made brought the old man down to see what was happening; but when she told him, 'Nothing to do with you,' he turned, silent as always nowadays, and went back to his place on the roof.

When Anand scolded the servants for their neglect, they looked sullen. At first they only muttered, throwing out hints that he should look further than a bit of dust on the furniture. Soon they became more voluble, they spoke of the shopping expeditions, drew his attention to the gold watch and the diamond studs in the new tunics. And the meals that had to be cooked for the visitor, not just one meal now but three a day with cold drinks and snacks in between. But they were not the kind of servants who should be expected to serve this kind of person (a low-caste dancer). Moreover, if they were to reveal what they knew about the goings-on next door, the accusation against him – and then they did reveal it, every detail of the scandal that they had learned from reliable sources like the school's sweeper woman and the shopkeeper who sold betel and cigarettes and knew everything.

When Anand told his mother, she rejected the information outright. She ran first to the girl's family – who, anxious only to save their good name, denied everything. Ram too denied everything. She made him swear on what was most precious to him and he swore on her life. Anand took action on his own. He used his influence with colleagues in the Ministry of Culture to institute an inquiry into the affairs of the school. This done, he left for his district and let matters take their course. Thus the scandal was uncovered, and the official report advised the withdrawal of the grant and the closure of the school on the grounds of moral turpitude. However, this verdict was subject to appeal provided the miscreant was exposed and immediate disciplinary action taken against him. Then Ram's dismissal could no longer be delayed. That very day he had to pack up his belongings in three bundles and leave the school forever.

Carrying his bundles, he went to say goodbye to Vijay. She was deeply shocked, she would not accept the situation. But he was innocent! He hung his head, he said nothing. He was innocent, she cried again – had he not sworn on her own life! For answer, he fell to the floor at her feet and lay there, absolutely still. He resisted all her attempts to make him rise, to speak, to answer let alone assent to her protestations of his innocence. At last realization dawned on her. She said in a cold dead voice, 'Get up.' He obeyed; when he glanced at her face, he saw it closed against him as against a stranger. He begged her: 'Maji,' but her expression did not change. When he tried to take her hand to hold against his cheek as he had done a thousand times before, she snatched it away. He burst into tears but she continued to sit rigid, with her big knees planted wide apart as if made of stone, and her eyes, fixed on the wall above him, also made of stone.

Although she said nothing, asked nothing, he poured out his confession. He did not try to justify himself: yes, it was the girl who had taken the initiative, had tempted him, but he had followed her lead, and with abandon. Every night he had crept from under his mosquito net and let himself out of the house, so silently and secretly that neither watchman nor sweeper ever caught a glimpse of him. And silently, secretly, he ran to her house three lanes away, where she was waiting to let him in. While the household slept two storeys above them, they had done what they did together right there in her father's house, on the gold brocade sofa of his drawing room where he entertained his guests; the smell still lingered of the kebabs that had been eaten and the whisky that had been drunk. She knew where the bottles were kept, and not only did they fornicate but they drank alcohol together, till the household began to stir at dawn. And this not once but night after night, for weeks together – those same weeks when he and Vijay walked hand in hand by the river and went shopping in the bazaar. And more, more – for he was now in a confessing mood and all his wickedness came rushing out of him – sometimes they were so overwhelmed by their desire that even in the school, after her class with him, they crept into a cubby-hole where winter clothing was stored in a steel trunk and they lay together on this trunk, in the dark and holding their breath if they heard voices or footsteps passing outside.

After he had told her everything, he remained standing before her with his head bowed. He did not dare ask for her forgiveness, nor did she offer it. She remained sitting there as before, stonelike – until suddenly she rose and her arms flailed as she beat him about the head and shoulders. He put up his hands to shield himself but did not utter a sound. When she had finished beating him, she abused him: she called him thief and scoundrel, who had insinuated himself into her house and her heart for what he could get out of her, for the money she spent on him, the jewelry with which she adorned him. When she said that, he said, 'No, Maji,' in a still, broken voice. 'And you laughed about me with her – with your prostitute – you said wait till you see what the old woman will buy for me.' 'No, Maji,' he said again, in the same voice. She slapped his face: 'Don't lie to me! All this time you've lied to me and I believed you.' 'I never lied to you—' But she slapped him again: 'You said you were my son, that you loved me like a son.' 'It's the truth. I love you like a son.' 'Liar! Liar!'

Silently, he bent down to his three bundles and untied them. He took out everything she had given him – the clothes, the gold-thread slippers, the ornaments. When he had finished, there was only one little bundle left and he tied it up again. The rest of the things he placed in a pile at her feet; lastly, he took off his new watch and laid it on top of everything. He picked up his remaining bundle and went to the door; there he turned around to her – not as if he hoped to be called back but perhaps for just one word, not even of forgiveness but only one word from her. She said nothing and he left, the mark of her hand still red on his cheek.

During the following days, there were times when she wanted to call him back. She had no idea where he had gone, and when she went to the school to find out, it was as if he had never been. A new teacher was taking his class, an ugly squat pockmarked man whom the girls teased till he lost his temper with them. Ankle-bells still tinkled, drums and lyres played, but now all this was unbearable to her. That day she went to the railway station and picked her way among the crowd to peer at the figures lying asleep on the platform with their cloth bundles of food and their water jugs, waiting for trains that had not arrived or not departed. But Ram's train, if he ever took one, must have started long ago and he had already reached his home-town and the musicians' alley with the broken-down house where his mother and sisters lived. Or he was still on the train, crammed into his third-class seat, with his bundle on his knees and the red mark on his cheek, remembering what he had left behind or looking forward to what lay before him.

As for her, she had nothing to look forward to. It was like that time when the old man had first resigned his office and they had had to give up the perks and pleasures of power that she had begun so much to enjoy; and the silent years that followed and her lonely solitude as he withdrew more and more. Now that he had even stopped singing his Vedic hymns, the silence was total; whenever she went up there, she found him perched on his bed, his head sunk low and to one side, like a sorrowing bird. Some days he did not eat his food, but she was too depressed to rally or scold him. There were times when she neglected to take her bath and sat on her crumpled bed with her grey hair hanging loose. At night she wandered around the house, and when she thought the old man was asleep, she went up on the roof. She found him lying on his side with his knees drawn up. She had no thought to spare for him; she came to look over the parapet, not at the river or the sky, both shining and beautiful, but over the other side at the terrace of the dance school. She saw the white mosquito nets standing in a rank that was serried and unbroken. There was no movement, no sign of life, but she knew that under each net a figure lay stretched out, chastely asleep.

But one night there *was* movement. A net in the middle of the row of beds stirred; a leg was cautiously thrust out, then a man emerged – although everything was flood-lit by an almost full moon, she was too far away to make out whether it was one of the old teachers or a young one. It may even have been the stocky, pockmarked Kathak master who had replaced Ram. She watched him glide past the other beds – perhaps he was only going to the toilet? But the way he moved like a thief he seemed intent on a less innocent excursion; once he stopped stock-still – maybe one of the sleepers had stirred, and he stood there with one foot still raised in the air. Then he continued, crouching low now. She wanted to shout out a warning – was it to the others, or to him, to let him know that someone was watching him? He reached the stairs leading down into the house and disappeared. She waited; if he had only gone to the toilet, he would return. She waited and he did not return.

She continued to stand by the parapet. Her eyes were still fixed on the row of white nets, but in her mind's eye she was following the other's stealthy progress – out of the house, down the lane, into the next lane; tonight he would have to be very careful because of the moon. When he reached his destination, there would be someone to let him in. And then what? She let her imagination roam, beginning with what Ram had told her – the brocade sofa and the bottle of whisky: until suddenly she was plunged into her own ocean of memories, and it was not the girl and Ram she saw, but herself and the old man – Prakash! In their marital bedroom, with the door locked and the electric fan whirring furiously but unable to cool their hot bodies; his hand was over her mouth to muffle her irrepressible laughter.

She left the parapet and went to him where he lay curled up on his side. When she touched his shoulder, he sat up immediately, as if he had not been asleep at all. She said, 'Why didn't you eat your food today?' There was something in her voice that made him raise his drooping head. 'If you don't look after yourself,' she said, 'what will happen to you? . . . And to me?' She touched his face: 'And when did you last shave?' She spoke severely but bent down to his cheek, brushing the grey stubble with her lips. He smiled, toothless, blissful. She sat on the ground by his rickety bed, leaning against it; they talked together and were silent together. Although it was very late when they parted, he was up at dawn and he was singing again. This is what he sang:

> As bees pile honey upon honey
> O Kama! Thus in my own person
> O Kama! Let honey flow
> Let lustre, brilliance flow and strength!

# UPPER EAST

*Beaver Street, off Wall Street, New York City*

# THE TEMPTRESS

All the young people Tammy knew in New York had odd family backgrounds, so it was not necessary for her to give much thought to her own. And unlike many of her friends, she did have a home, or a base, even if there was no one in it except herself and Ross, whom she had inherited from her mother. Again unlike many of the people she knew, Tammy never really felt lonely or adrift: maybe because she was always either looking forward to or looking for something, so what was actually happening in the present wasn't of overriding concern to her.

In earlier years, when they had been college room-mates, her friend Minnie used to say that Tammy's serenity came from never having had to worry about money. But now that Minnie too had money – a poor girl with a lot of personality, she had married a rich man – she herself had not attained serenity; on the contrary. When her marriage broke up – her husband had turned out to be a rotten bastard – Minnie was tremendously restless and traveled all over the world, first for pleasure to places like Venice and San Raphael, then further east for enlightenment. Tammy had sometimes joined her on both kinds of expedition and had enjoyed them much more than Minnie. But it was Minnie, all by herself, who found and brought home Ma – though it was Tammy who inherited her, as she had inherited Ross.

Ma was in her sixties: an ordinary Indian housewife with extraordinary powers. By feeling a person's pulse, she was able to locate a sickness anywhere in the body; she had a clear view over past births, reaching back many centuries, as well as (though this was a power she used sparingly) future prospects in this birth; she could cure snakebite by transmitting a verbal talisman over the telephone; and a number of other such specialities, which however were all secondary to her main work. This was to give peace to people who came to her in need of it; or spiritual enlightenment to those who felt themselves ready for it, as Minnie did. On one of her excursions into India, Minnie had been taken to Ma's New Delhi home in a row of whitewashed structures, their balconies overhung with a lot of washing. It was a government housing colony, Ma's husband having been a clerk in the Ministry of Disposal and Supplies; and after his death, no civil servant dared turn Ma out of these quarters, for by that time she had reached something of the status of a holy woman, though without ever laying claim to it. She said she was there for her friends, that was all; that they should feel free to visit and sit with her and talk with her and occasionally to sing and rejoice with her. And that was what happened in her house: people came and, leaving their shoes on the threshold, sat on a sheet spread in her living room, while she spoke sometimes of quite mundane matters, like the quality of the year's mango crop, and sometimes of higher things. It was not for what she said but for the effect of her personality that people came to her: at first only a few friends from the neighborhood, then more from other neighborhoods, and as news of her spread, they came from farther away, until she was so well-known that even foreign tourists were brought to see her, Minnie among them.

On her return to New York, Minnie told everyone about Ma; and the way she spoke of her, her friends too longed to come within Ma's aura. Minnie tried to describe this aura, but words failed her except for common ones like fantastic, and out of this world. That was exactly what being with Ma was, Minnie insisted: like not being in this world at all but in a completely other, different one. At that, Tammy could not repress a cry: for it was exactly what she herself was always wishing for, to get out of this world into a completely other one. Minnie described how, when Ma had laid her hands on

Minnie's head, the effect had lingered for days, for weeks, and it was still there, she said. So then all the friends agreed that Ma must be brought to New York, and it did not take them long to collect her fare and other expenses; she would of course be staying with Minnie, who had first claim on her. Ma herself was surprisingly compliant with all their plans for her, which she said came from above.

Minnie had described her as a homely, comfortable, house-wifely figure, but when she arrived, they were all surprised by the way she glittered. It was as if she had done herself up the way a star would, when on tour for a series of gala appearances. She had repossessed herself of all the gold jewelry – the bangles, the bracelets, the ear-rings, the hair ornaments – that she had had to lay aside as a widow; her cotton saris were replaced by effulgent silks with huge borders of gold thread; no traces of grandmotherly grey remained in her hair, which shone black as night except for the parting adorned with henna. Her manner was effusive, brimming over with gratitude for all their kindness to her. She called them her children, her little ones; she read wonders in their palms; she told them all the old stories, about Krishna teasing the milkmaids and Vishnu churning the ocean. She also laid her hands on their heads, the way Minnie had described – but though they waited expectantly, nothing happened. The fact was, Ma fell flat; she was a failure; by common consent, Ma was a bore.

Meanwhile, Minnie was stuck with her. She had installed her in the master bedroom, which had once been her own marital chamber ('Don't remind me,' said Minnie). Minnie herself slept in the second bedroom, but this turned out to be too close to Ma, who got up at dawn and sang very loudly, giving Minnie a headache that lasted the entire day. Ma was moved into another, smaller bedroom, and from there farther away to the maid's room at the back of the kitchen, but still Minnie's headaches continued. For it wasn't only Ma's song that pervaded the place, it was her smell too – 'All that scent she uses,' Minnie complained to Tammy, 'and twice a week she has an oil bath, smearing herself from head to foot in some ghastly stuff that makes me want to puke—' 'Sh,' warned Tammy, for at that moment Ma entered, radiantly bearing a plate of very greasy fritters she had just fried for them. She thrust her offering at them, smiling with pleasure at the pleasure she was giving them. But Minnie drew back – 'No thank *you*,' she said. Ma's smile gave way to an expression of such disappointment that Tammy felt she had to take one of the oil-drenched balls and, with Ma's eyes fixed on her expectantly, to chew right through to the slice of raw onion inside and then to swallow that as best she could.

The situation became impossible for Minnie: she said Ma would have to be sent home. But Ma wasn't ready to go home. She felt she was still needed here, also that she hadn't yet had her fill of shopping and nice restaurants and all the lights coming on in the theater district and the advertisements flashing and the many different cable channels and flavors of ice cream. Inside the tiny room that was now her lot, she kept as quiet as she could, even muting her morning hymn so as not to irritate Minnie. She never complained that no one gave any more dinner parties for her, nor that Minnie's friends had ceased to call on her. When they came to visit Minnie, she was as sweet with them as before, pressing the heads of those that would let her and maybe failing to notice that most of them now shrank away. Tammy was the only one who managed not to yawn when she told the beautiful old stories; and Tammy became her favorite – she recognized very special qualities in her, so that day by day it became clearer to her that her mission in New York lay with Tammy. Ma was grateful to Minnie for bringing her here, and for her hospitality and all her goodness. But Minnie was on a different path where she was unable to benefit from the help that Ma had come to give; and finally one day Ma had to break the news to Minnie that she could no longer stay with her but was needed at Tammy's.

Tammy's apartment on the West side was as large as Minnie's on the East side, but nowhere near as pristine. Minnie had hired an interior decorator for hers, also contributing some wonderful ideas of her own; but the rolls of wallpaper specially made for her in Paris had only just arrived when her marriage ended and she began to spend more time traveling around than living in the apartment. Tammy had inherited hers from her mother, and she left it the way she had always known it: sofas and ottomans upholstered in unraveling tapestry, a tattered wall-hanging of silk thread, the marble busts of early Presidents, the Venetian mirror with black spots on it, the collection of dead clocks handed down by a great-grandfather who had been an envoy to Russia. From time to time Tammy bought a plant to cheer things up, but it always died, and even the hardy desert ones drooped and collected dust in their fleshy wrinkles. There was only one other person living there, and that was Ross – 'Is he your uncle?' Ma asked Tammy, who said no but didn't know how to explain him.

Ma asked a hundred questions about Ross: who is he? Why is he living here? Doesn't he have a wife? Children? What is his income? Why is he called Ross – is it his own or his father's name? The only one Tammy could answer was the last; she knew Ross was a corruption of something else: Rosenthal? Rosenbaum? He was a refugee of a vintage so outdated – so old hat – that no one wanted to hear another word about their stories of escape or survival. 'Ross' was what Grace, Tammy's mother, had called him; sometimes she said 'Rosie,' not affectionately but to tease him. As far as Tammy was concerned, he had arrived from nowhere: one year, when she had come home from school for the summer vacation, he was there. 'I found him in the park,' was all Grace said by way of explanation. It may have been true; Ross spent a lot of his time, even now, sitting in the park. 'How do you like my new beau?' was something else Grace said about him, but this was hard to believe. Grace had been tall, aristocratic, haughty; a ruin of great beauty. Ross was tiny and bald and spoke with an accent that was a compound of languages spoken in European countries with ever-fluctuating borders.

Grace's brother in Philadelphia – this was when they were still on speaking terms – used to warn her that Ross was a dangerous character out to bilk her of her fortune. It was true that Grace had a fortune, but it was safely buried in trust funds from where she was not inclined to dig it out for anyone. Ross had difficulty getting even his cigarette money out of her, and it amused her to make him beg for it – sometimes literally, holding it high above his head so that, looking up pleadingly, he resembled a pet dog standing on its hind legs for some promised morsel. But she must have been fond of him, for she let him stay with her for over six years – the last six years of her life, when she had quarreled with everyone else. They were each other's only companions, except when Tammy came for vacations; and in the last years, when Tammy started traveling, Ross and Grace were mostly alone, entombed together in the vast apartment in the vast old Gothic building. Tammy knew that he took care of her mother as far as anyone could; Grace had almost stopped eating, all the cigarettes she smoked and the vodka she drank must have killed her appetite. Of course he couldn't make her happy or contented – all he could do was hide her hoard of pills, though not successfully, for in the end she managed to get hold of enough to kill herself with an overdose.

When Tammy told her some of these facts, Ma put her hand to her cheek and cried, 'Oh! Oh! Oh!' She almost blamed herself for not coming earlier to save Tammy's mother. But she now understood that the purpose of her mission (we move in one direction, she explained, and then we are moved in another) was to do whatever she could for Tammy. While engaged on this work, Ma settled in very nicely. That was one beauty of her character, that whatever her circumstances, she accepted them gladly. Never for a moment had she murmured when demoted to Minnie's maid's room; and she installed herself as equably into the dark, dusty, cavernous bedroom allotted to her in Tammy's apartment. She made it her own, spreading her ambience over the furniture – as roomy and gloomy as coffins – that had come down from Tammy's maternal ancestresses. Soon there were all the smells of incense and oil that Minnie had objected to; also little statues of gods that she tended and sang to with jubilant hymns; and the jingle of her bangles, and the silks of vibrant orange and purple in which she swished around the house.

Ma also loved roaming the streets. She was completely

uninhibited by the city, which she treated as her neighborhood bazaar. If she saw something of interest on the opposite side of the street – it might only be a colorful display of fruits – she would not hesitate to cross against the lights, holding up her hand to stem the torrent of traffic. She was always intrigued by what people were selling out of cardboard boxes on the sidewalks, and after some decent haggling, she came away with their, often stolen, goods. She brought home trinkets for Tammy – not that Tammy didn't have everything in the world, but as a gift from Ma's own hands, and what did it matter that this was paid for out of Tammy's money (they had made a tactful arrangement about Ma's expenses). She also came home with some purchase she had made for Ross – her first present to him was a T-shirt with 'You're My Best Grandpa' printed on it.

It was of course a joke. He never wore T-shirts, he was always in jacket and necktie, which would have looked natty if they had not been frayed. 'Put it on,' urged Ma, snapping her fingers at him as if to give him rhythm, 'you must be a little bit with-it.' But she grew serious when he pointed out that he was nobody's grandpa. She said that, on the contrary, he was everyone's – that he and she had both reached a stage where they were only there to help others along their paths. She said she knew of what great service he had been to Tammy and waved aside his disclaimer that, in view of the fact that he had no money at all, it was the other way around. As if that mattered a hoot, exclaimed Ma. He admired her attitude of complete nonchalance about who paid the bills, having never really got used to being unable to pay any himself.

It was not difficult for the three of them – Tammy, Ma, and Ross – to live together because they never got in one another's way. Tammy was taking a variety of courses in psychology and religious philosophy; Ross followed his own routine of reading the papers in the park, or in the coffee-shop where he ate all his meals; Ma went out on her excursions, cooked spicy little messes for herself, had long afternoon naps, and watched TV. She felt fulfilled in the knowledge that she was of use to Tammy. She encouraged Tammy in her attendance of classes and was disappointed if she dropped one, as she often did. When Tammy expressed disappointment with what she was being taught, Ma said that it was always good to learn – she had great respect for book learning, possessing very little of it herself. But Tammy longed for something quite different. She couldn't say in words what that was, but her face took on an expression of yearning. Tammy had a very pure face, with clear eyes and clear skin; her head was small and reared up from a long neck, so that she seemed always to be straining upward, in the direction of something beyond her reach.

One day Ross was sitting in the park reading the afternoon paper; he had already read the morning one. It wasn't really a park but a triangle of grass set at the intersection of four busy crossroads; here he was in the middle of the city's traffic without being a part of it. Looking up for a moment from his paper, he saw a strange sight: this was Ma escaping from a car that was about to run her down. She was going as fast as she could, making for the safety of the little park. But she was laughing as if it were a game, one hand hitching up her orange sari, so that her brand-new golden shoes were visible; she clutched a handbag under one arm, a red umbrella under the other. Still laughing, she made it to the park where she stood and shook her fist playfully at the driver of the erring car. She sank onto the nearest bench, which happened to be the one occupied by Ross. 'Did you see that? The rascal,' she said, as though about a favorite grandson. She was tugging at her sari, which had come partly undone in her flight, and she adjusted something at the front and tied a string at the side, pulling her garment together. 'He saw me perfectly well but he said let me have a game with this old madam. But I won – you saw me win? Oh, it's you,' for she had thought she was addressing a stranger.

'He had the light.'

'What light? He could wait for a minute, my goodness, what is there? And for a person my age.'

'You run pretty fast for a person your age.'

Having fixed her sari, she began on her hair, sticking a lot

of hairpins into her mouth, which however did not inhibit
her from talking. He had noticed her habit of commenting
on whatever happened to float into her mind – in this case,
the little park in which they sat: 'How refreshing,' she said, 'a
small paradise of peace in all this hubbub.' It did not seem
to bother her that the grass was worn away in big patches,
and was anyway not very green, or that several benches were
broken and all of them unpainted; besides herself and Ross,
the only occupants at the moment were two bundled figures,
one stretched out, one hunched up, both asleep.

She showed him her red umbrella: 'I bought it just now
from a man who let me have it very cheap. When it rains,
at once the price shoots up, so I said better buy now, why
waste? Oh shame!' she cried, for having opened the umbrella
to admire it, she found it torn at the center spoke. 'Cheating
an old lady! And such a nice boy from Ghana with a big big
smile – wait till tomorrow, he'll hear from me so he'll forget
to smile.'

'Tomorrow he'll be back in Ghana. And there are plenty
of umbrellas in the house, since you don't believe in waste.'

'I love this pretty color.' Probably she was thinking, as he
was, of the huge old umbrellas in the brass stand at the entrance
door, some with animal heads, none of them colorful or ever
used, the property of people who had died. This silent thought
led her on to others that were spoken: 'Did you see the pretty
moonstone ring I bought for Tammy? Of course it was not
costly, but I wanted only to give her something in return, as
you do. You've given her so much.'

'That's not the general opinion,' said Ross.

'Oh, she's told me how you loved her mother and cared
for that poor soul! And I've seen with my own eyes how you
love Tammy, sitting up for her every night, waiting for her to
come in. No need to be shy,' she interpreted the expression
on his face.

'How would you know I wait up for her? You're always fast
asleep and snoring.'

She laughed: 'Yes, I can sleep in peace because I know
you're awake to welcome the child when she comes home.

That's what makes it home for her – that you're there. Again you're shy. You should be proud and glad.'

Now it was his turn to laugh: proud and glad! Never had such scintillating words descended on him.

But it was true that, however late it was, he was always awake when Tammy came home. This was due both to insomnia and habit: or perhaps the insomnia had become a habit from the time he was always starting up, listening into the night for what Grace might be doing. He had not trusted her for a second. And what a relief it had been when Tammy was there in her vacations to ask, 'Is she asleep? Is she all right?' That was all he wanted, someone to care with him, for a moment. Not that he meant to burden Tammy or have her carry a share of his burden of her mother – on the contrary, it was his ambition to keep her as she was, young and free.

Even now, four years after her mother's death, it was what he wanted for Tammy. That was why he asked: 'How long is she staying?'

'Who?' Tammy asked. 'Ma?'

He grimaced at that name: he didn't call her that – he didn't call her anything, and the first time he had heard Tammy say 'Ma,' he had asked 'Whose Ma?' with the same face as now. 'Has she settled down for good, or what?'

'She likes it here. Well, it's all right, she's not disturbing us – unless you mind all the smells, her oil and so forth?'

'They're potent, although one could get used to them, if one had to. But does one have to?'

'She's got nowhere else to go, that's the thing. And we brought her here. It's not her fault it didn't work out. And she still thinks we need her. Ma is very simple, really. But of course if you want her to leave, Ross, then she'll have to.'

Ross had been living in the apartment for ten years. When he first came, Tammy was thirteen and at boarding school, since no one knew what else to do with her. After Grace died, she left everything to Tammy and nothing at all to Ross – it had been one of her taunts to Ross when she was alive: 'He's hanging around because of my will, but just wait and see,' which had made Tammy feel ashamed. She had felt generally ashamed about the way Grace had treated Ross; and when she didn't leave him anything, Tammy was relieved to be able to make some amends.

The day after she bought the red umbrella, Ma showed up again in the little park, with a green one. She waved it at Ross from the middle of the street – this time the traffic stopped for her – and when she joined him, she said, 'See, I made him change it. He was a good boy, after all.' She sat down and chattered away, though he didn't look up from his paper and rattled it ostentatiously whenever he turned a page. That didn't make any difference to her, she continued to share her thoughts with him. Suddenly she poked him with her green umbrella: 'How is it you're not married and no children?' she repeated the question she had been asking since the first day she met him.

He brought his paper closer to his nose, but she was undaunted: 'Look at me: five children and twenty-one, no, twenty-two grandchildren.'

'Why aren't you with them?'

'Tammy needs me.' When he lowered his paper to look at her, she nodded to confirm he had heard right: 'Tammy needs a mother.'

'Tammy has had enough of mothers.' He folded his paper, not that he had finished it but to show he was departing. She put out her hand to hold him back – it made him jump, maybe because her hand was preternaturally hot, or because he was not used to anyone touching him.

It had been in this same park that he first met Grace. Even then the grass had been patchy, and though the benches had been intact, the people sitting on them had looked derelict. He himself must have looked the same; he had just lost his job – the wholesale clothing firm where he had been employed as accountant had gone bankrupt – and at the same time, by the sort of mischance he was used to, he had been turned out of his place to live. Grace had sat down at the other end of his bench, as far away from him as possible – she never wanted to be near anyone, and like himself hated to be touched. But she had started a conversation with him; it

was her habit to talk to strangers in a way she never would
to anyone closer to her. He had felt flattered that she should
address him – this tall, beautiful, aristocratic, *poetic* woman:
for this was the impression she conveyed right till the end.
She wasn't particularly well-dressed, she had bought no new
clothes for years, but whatever she wore took on a stateliness
as of sculptured drapery. And she spoke in the lazy drawl of
someone who was used to being listened to with admiration,
adoration; also without looking at her interlocutor, dropping
her words into space for him to catch as best he could. And
then, as abruptly as she had sat down by him, she got up to
leave, and he gazed at her in panic, thinking that he was
never going to see her again, that she would remain to him
as only this moment of vision. But she invited him to come
along home with her, and she might as well have rubbed
two fingers together and made sugared sounds to induce him
to follow: he trotted along beside her, with no reflection but
ready to give himself up to her body and soul.

During the years of living within the Gothic ruin of her
apartment, he had felt the need for occasional excursions
out of it, as for daily doses of fresh air. Yet he never strayed
far – only to this little park and a nearby coffee-shop and
a few utility stores – so as always to be, as it were, within
earshot of the grotesquely ornate, turn-of-the-century, scrolled
and sculptured corner block where she lived. And he remained
tethered to this routine after she died: it was still the same places
he went to, and also at the same hour every day, so that he could
be easily tracked down, if anyone had had any such intention.
In addition to the little park, Ma began to show up in the
coffee-shop where he ate his meals. The customers here were
like himself, regular and solitary, and they were all served by
the same elderly waitress, Stella, who knew everyone's order
without being told. She was amazed when, for the first time
in all the years he had been her customer, Ross was joined by
another person – and what a person! At first Stella was haughty
with her, as she was with any new customer, and especially
one who could not be socially placed. But Ma melted her

with motherly fondness, calling her her child, though Stella was as old as she was. Ma desired a hot chocolate; it came out of a machine and had a froth of synthetic cream on top, which adhered to Ma's upper lip. And from under this white fringe she smiled at Ross and congratulated him on the coziness of his little dining place, though it was a dark hole with two serried rows of glass-topped tables, which could be easily wiped off by Stella whenever she happened not to have her hands full.

As usual, Ma was not in the least put out by his lack of response – she carried right on talking and asking her perennial personal questions. Only today he countered with, 'But aren't you supposed to be a wise woman who knows everything about everybody?'

That made her laugh: 'I know everything about *you*,' she said, and suddenly she seized his hand. As before, a shudder ran through him at her touch, and especially when she began to slither her forefinger along his palm to read the lines written there. He snatched his hand away and wiped it on a paper napkin. Just then Stella arrived with his meal, and she asked eagerly: 'Do you tell fortunes?'

'Yes, my child,' said Ma. 'Was there something you wanted to know?'

Fearfully, Stella put her hand before her mouth and nodded. Ma moved over on her rexined bench, inviting Stella to sit next to her; and after a swift look around – but there was no boss, the coffee-shop was part of a chain and a supervisor only came around twice a week – she slid onto the seat and, opening up her hand, she whispered: 'Should I have the operation on my kidneys? My daughter says I should but what if afterward I can't serve the tables, what'll happen then?'

'Wait wait wait,' soothed Ma, studying the palm stretched out like an offering to her wisdom. And she did look worthy of the awe and trust with which Stella regarded her – not an ordinary fortune teller, not a gypsy, though there was something of both in her bright apparel (today she was in deep plum-purple) and her frizzy hair dyed black as ink: but truly a being from some other, probably superior place, where superior knowledge was available.

Ma's study was prolonged, and some customers were already impatiently banging their flatware on the glass-topped tables for service. But at last Ma looked up – with satisfaction, for she had good news to give: Stella's operation would not only be successful with regard to her kidneys but would also regenerate her whole system, so that she would be fulfilling her function here more splendidly than ever and for many years to come.

'You have a nerve,' said Ross, when Stella, already rejuvenated by these tidings, had returned to her duties.

'What's wrong? I've given her hope and optimism, which everyone needs, including you.'

'Kindly leave me out of your hocus-pocus. And now she'll go in for a dangerous operation on the strength of your lies.'

'You don't know that I don't know,' said Ma, and she looked at him mischievously, roguishly, while licking off her creamy mustache – a disappointment to him, for he had enjoyed not telling her that it was there.

It seemed to Ross that Ma was everywhere – in the apartment too, which was big enough for her to keep out of his sight instead of constantly appearing in it. Whereas for her outings she still dressed up gorgeously, at home she was now usually in dishabille, in some old Indian cotton housecoat torn under the armpits, or in the short blouse and waist petticoat she wore under her sari. Although the gloom of the apartment blurred details – often, when he had encountered Grace in the passage, she had been like a young woman walking toward him – Ma never appeared as anything but old and fat. Yet, unlike Grace who had thrown her shoe at a mirror because of what it showed her, Ma could be seen admiring her reflection – posing with one hand on her hip – in that same mirror that still hung over the mantel with a crack right across it.

To hide from her, he began to creep around stealthily, but as she too moved around silently – she never wore shoes in the house – she was always surprising him: catching him was how he thought of it. If she failed to trap him in the passage or one of the other rooms, she did not hesitate to track him down to his bedroom. This was a triangular corner room at the rear end of the apartment, allotted to him by Grace to be as far away as possible from her own bedroom. Ma never came in on him by surprise – she announced herself by calling out to him from her room at the other end, and then she padded down the corridor, calling all the way ('Ross! O Ross!'), so that by the time she reached his room, there was no need for her to knock but only to open the door and say, 'There you are.'

What did she want of him? The only person with whom he could share that question was Tammy, but Tammy was at this time greatly preoccupied. Minnie had returned from Copenhagen, bringing the Doktor, who was just too marvelous to leave behind. They all became very excited about him: he had evolved a completely new set of techniques which, for the first time in the history of mankind, harnessed scientific method to the cause of spiritual attainment. This called for arduous training and was altogether a far cry from Ma's homely little get-togethers in her house in New Delhi, where she had talked a bit, sung a bit, burned incense, and performed some harmless miracles. Minnie laughed at herself now for ever having been taken in by Ma; but she explained to Tammy that it was because they all had such personal difficulties – were such lost souls – that they had grasped at the easy security offered to them by this matriarchal figure.

Tammy was as enthusiastic about the new teacher as Minnie and the other friends, and she spent long hours with him in the place that had been taken for him in a monolithic ultra-modern new apartment tower. She came in later than ever at night, but Ross was always awake and waiting for her to come in to talk to him. Ross loved seeing her the way she was at that midnight hour – alternately very serious or laughing at herself for not being able to express what she felt in anywhere near adequate words. Well, he loved seeing her anyway, always had done. It seemed to him that she hadn't changed much over the years: although now in her twenties, she was still the same budding young girl, impossibly light, swaying with every breeze of emotion rippling through her, her head rearing heavenward from the stem of her neck like a flower thirsting for rain or dew. Year after year he had expected her to fall in love – any day now, he thought, that would be the subject of her breathless confession: but though the emotion was ineffably there, it never was for a person but always for an idea, for a promise of something beyond what one human being could receive from another. He was disappointed but realized that he would have been more so if she had rested, or arrested, her yearning in some ordinary young man.

When Minnie had first brought Ma to be their guide, Tammy had spoken of her in the same terms that she now spoke of the Doktor: but by this time they found it incredible that they had once believed in that fat old gypsy woman smelling out the apartment with her hair-oil and fried messes. Now when Ross asked, 'How long is she staying?' – and he asked several times more – Tammy said, 'Oh, the poor old thing, where would she go?' But the last time he asked – for Ma was really getting on his nerves – Tammy said, 'Well, if you want, we can tell her to go,' quite carelessly, and then she continued at once talking to him about the Doktor.

After a while, Ross interrupted: 'Should we tell her?'

Tammy said, 'I said if you want. It's up to you . . . You see, Ross, his method is to reach that point in us where we merge with the universal—'

'Do you want me to tell her?'

'Yes, but do it in a nice way, please, Ross.'

Although the idea of Ma being endowed with special powers had always struck him as ludicrous, he had been ready to grant her some form of heightened feminine intuition. But now it seemed to him that she was exceptionally obtuse. He only had to think back on his own years of living on sufferance in other people's houses to remember how acute and immediate had been his perception of the moment when he was no longer wanted. But Ma didn't notice a thing: every day she settled in a bit more happily – she gave herself oil baths, she walked around in her slatternly housecoat, she hardly ever bothered to wear her teeth, and she sang her hymns of praise now not only in the morning but all day long.

And she seemed to be following him everywhere; even when he stood in line for the cinema, she was suddenly there. He often went to see films with subtitles, which he didn't need to read – he spoke many European languages – and she couldn't read fast enough, so that she nudged him to explain till he got up in disgust and left halfway. She followed him willingly, for she found these sort of films very dull; whereas she hugely enjoyed the other kind that played in the big picture palaces where popcorn was to be had. Here she only nudged him to help himself out of the giant tub she had bought, and if she liked what she saw on the screen, she cheered and clapped, or she cried out warnings to the hero to guard against the menace behind him. All the time, while she was engrossed in innocent amusement, he thought of how to tell her to leave; once or twice he began to approach the subject but in ways too devious to succeed. Then he would continue plotting – he knew of so many openings, of excuses he had often heard himself, of how other guests were expected. And in rehearsing these openings, he found his thoughts constantly occupied with her; and suddenly she would appear beside him, a scented, solid, brilliant embodiment of these thoughts.

'Have you told her yet?' Tammy would ask. And one day Tammy said, 'You'll *have* to tell her.' She made it sound so urgent that he began to protest the difficulty of turning someone out of doors.

'But you said you couldn't stand her another minute.'

'Maybe I could.'

'Poor old Ma,' Tammy said. 'We should never have brought her.'

'Yes, but now that she's here—'

He and Tammy looked at each other: they both felt bad about the situation. Yet he saw something else in Tammy's face besides guilt. Her eyes danced, the corners of her mouth twitched – he felt that she wanted him to know something and was deliberately suppressing it, like a beautiful secret she was keeping not from but for him.

Meanwhile, he and Ma spent more and more time together. He ceased to avoid her and even began to seek her out, to find opportunities to broach the subject of her departure. She had so much to say that it was difficult for him to say anything at all. Occasionally he got as far as opening his mouth to speak, but never much further. He was by no means the only person she addressed. Often, in the park, she called out to strangers, though they might be too sunk in drink or misery to hear her. In the coffee-house she spoke to everyone within earshot; but here she was listened to eagerly, for she had built up a little reputation. Stella had undergone her operation and was on her feet again, which was ascribed to Ma's good offices, so that now others also sought her advice. She was very ready to give it, whether it was to the cook – a young man suffering from boils who was breaking up with his live-in friend – or salesgirls from the neighboring discount store who came hurrying between customers with their urgent problems. Ma dealt with everyone in the manner of one used to hearing strange and even terrible things without letting herself be overwhelmed by them. This attitude had a soothing effect; and so did her words of reassurance, even though they had no basis in fact, or any bearing on the situations to which she applied them. She was also ready to give more advanced treatment, consisting of whispered spells or little talismans secretly passed under the café table; for the most drastic cases she performed some circling motions with her arms and then cracked the knuckles of both hands against her temples.

Patients began to arrive at Tammy's apartment. Ma seemed to take this for granted – she was used to people in need seeking her out – and she had given orders to the doormen (they too sometimes consulted her) to let everyone in who asked for her. Her visitors sat rather shyly in the darkened drawing room; it was a grander place than they were used to, though dusty and derelict. The brocade upholstery, already frayed and worn, now began to split open with people sitting on it, and a couple of antique chairs collapsed from the same cause. Ma clicked her tongue at the damage done to Tammy's property, and once Ross found her up on a ladder repairing a curtain that had been torn from its rings (long ago, when he had chased Grace around the room to get some pills away from her).

Tammy asked more often, 'Have you told her yet?' and each

time he had to admit he had not. Tammy bit her lip, as one who had something difficult to say and could not. She was distracted, her thoughts elsewhere – of course they usually were, Tammy characteristically had something rapt, distant, inattentive about her. So it was not surprising that she failed to notice signs of change in the apartment; sometimes people were still sitting in what had become a waiting room late at night when she came home. Ross, who now constantly looked and felt guilty, muttered in explanation that they were waiting to consult Ma. 'Oh yes,' Tammy said, as though this were the most natural thing in the world, and then she said again, reverting to what was important, 'Have you told her yet?'

But one day Minnie came and was appalled by what she saw: 'Who *are* all these people?' she accused Tammy, for it was in the afternoon and the place was crowded.

'They're waiting for Ma,' Tammy said, with the same guilty air as Ross.

Minnie was speechless – but only for a moment, she was never speechless for long. Although Minnie and Tammy were such close friends and shared the same interest – that is, spiritual improvement – they were opposite types. Minnie was far more forthright than Tammy – one would have said more worldly, if her business had not been so specifically in the cause of unworldliness. It turned out that it was for this cause that Ma, and now all her retinue, had to be cleared out of the apartment: 'Next month,' said Minnie. 'He'll need to move in next month.'

'Who'll need to move in?' Ross asked, looking at Tammy; and at the same time Minnie also looked at Tammy, who blushed like a rose between them.

'Don't say you haven't told him,' Minnie said.

'I will. I'll tell him today. Truly,' Tammy implored.

'Just see you do. Good God, there's so little time left and this place will need some straightening out, I tell you. Pooh,' said Minnie, wrinkling her nose against the smell she had so disliked in her own place – Ma's hair and cooking oils – now mixed with that of the visitors, who included a few homeless people.

Later that night Tammy spoke to Ross. She told him that the work they were doing with the Doktor was advancing by leaps and bounds; that so many people were coming to his lectures and workshops, and to live under his tutelage in the place taken for him in the apartment tower, that they were in urgent need of more accommodation. 'Like Minnie says,' Tammy urged, 'this place is perfect. I mean, it's just too big for only the two of us to rattle around in, and Ma wants to go back to India, she needs to.'

'She thinks she's needed here.'

Tammy made a gesture that was affectionately dismissive: 'She doesn't understand that everyone has changed.'

'You've changed,' said Ross – but it wasn't true, Tammy was the same only more so: more yearning, more straining upward.

'Of course I've changed!' she cried, her voice too straining upward to a higher register. 'That's what it's all about – his technique,' she explained. 'It's incredibly hard work – he says it's like drilling through rock, the rock being the calcified self. He's really helping me, Ross.'

'Why should you need help?'

'Because I'm a terrible person,' said Tammy, a cloud of despair darkening the pure heaven of her face.

'Is that what he's told you?'

'It's what he's shown me. He makes you turn inward, and the horrors you see there! Not only what your own past has deposited but everyone else's too, all the generations before you – you have to break them down because you're responsible for them, for what they were and did. We'll have to get rid of all the furniture, Ross. Because it's charged with everyone's bad living; and dying.' She laid her own cool hand on his and whispered, 'We'll both feel better when it's all gone. You'll see – it'll be like everything's been purged away, exorcised.'

'I don't know that I'd want to exorcise Grace out of her own apartment.'

'But it's so different already.' Tammy sniffed the air as Minnie had done. 'It's even got in here – is it oil or incense? You'll really have to tell her, Ross. We have to clear the

place out. His work is so fearfully hard inside that outside
he absolutely needs a neutral space.'

However, as news of Ma spread in the neighborhood and
beyond, the apartment became more and more crowded. It
wasn't only through the people in the coffee-shop that Ma
was getting to be known; those clients brought new clients
and those in turn brought others; the doormen too had friends
and relatives; and finally a new sort of clientele came from
the other inhabitants of the building. This mighty pile, with
its Gothic façade, its marble entrance halls, its Boston palms
and areca ferns, was chock-full of troubled people. Some of
these had inherited their apartments from their grandmothers,
others had bought them from other people's grandmothers, or
from heirs who had had to sell to pay the inheritance tax.
Their furniture was of the same vintage as Grace's, their lives
too not unlike hers, each with a quota of madness, suicide,
even in one instance a hushed-up murder. The most recent
owners were the wives of businessmen who had made a lot
of money very quickly and were now in jail for financial fraud
on so enormous a scale that their sentences ran into decades.
At first all these neighbors had complained about the rag-tag
jamming up the mahogany-paneled elevators on their way up
to Ma; but one by one they became curious, and some of them,
and then more, came to see what she would do for them.

All this could not be managed without some organization,
and Ross found himself handling that end. He arranged Ma's
timetable and allotted the appointments for special sessions.
It was years since he had had a job – he had usually been
employed by more successful fellow refugees, whom he had
helped over some delicate matter in their accounts; for, though
not highly qualified, he was trustworthy. Now again he was in
a position of trust as Ma's right-hand man; he was kept very
busy, and of course so was Ma, and there was no time for any
private exchange between them.

Tammy too was under pressure, for it was past the date
when the Doktor was due to have moved in. Meanwhile the
apartment had become transformed into what was almost a
public meeting place; people felt free to walk in and out and

to stay as long as they liked, and they liked to stay very long. When Tammy came home at night, she had to thread her way through the passage, saying 'Excuse me,' very politely to the people blocking her way; she made straight for Ross's corner room. Instead of asking him, 'Have you told her yet?', she would ask, more of herself than of Ross, 'What can I tell him?' for it seemed the Doktor was expecting to move in at any moment.

One day Tammy said, 'He'll say it's my fault. And he's right – I've let him down and let you down and let Ma down and everyone. It just shows I'm a failed human being – I am, Ross, unfortunately. I can't do anything right because I'm not right inside myself. I'm very poor material for him to work on.' She gave a wan smile. 'I've been with him long enough to acquire some self-knowledge. Failing yourself is one thing – but failing him and Sally and the children – his family,' she explained to Ross's look of inquiry. 'Well, of course he has a wife and children – he's a fully developed man, that's what makes him what he is. He's about fifty,' she answered Ross, 'but you would never in a million years think it. Sally's his second wife – I mean, the second one he's had a ceremony with or whatever – but of course everyone who submits to his guidance is his wife. You know, like the soul and the spouse.' There was a silence. 'Anyway,' she continued, 'all that's just technical.'

Ross looked down at the floor, and there was another silence.

'It's not fair,' she accused him. 'When Mother said that about your being her last lover, I never asked is it true or not, so why are you asking me?'

'I'm not asking anything. What am I asking?' He waved his arms around as he did on the rare occasions when he got excited.

'You *cared* for her like a lover, took care of her, that's what was important. Is important.'

'Is that what he does for you?'

'Of course he does,' said Tammy, wiping her eyes. 'Guiding someone psychologically means taking care of them – caring for them–' In spite of her efforts to brush them away, tears flowed – so many that Ross had to help wipe them away. She leaned against him while she went on: 'He has this wonderful gift of being with you even when he's not – like you think he's busy with someone else? Like he might be with Minnie or someone for hours and you think you've been completely forgotten and then next thing you realize he's never for a moment stopped thinking about you and knows exactly what's going on inside you. I can't stop crying, I feel stupid. I never used to cry, did I, Ross? Not at the worst times so why should I now when the best thing in the world is happening to me?'

Later that night – very late at night – Ross made his way to Ma's room. He had to step over several bodies asleep in the passage, for some visitors had developed the habit of staying overnight. They slept very peacefully, and the only sound to be heard was the snoring from Ma's room; and when he reached there and had slipped inside, the sound was so loud that it was like being in the engine room of an ocean liner with everything churning to keep the ship afloat. Ma was on the high mahogany bed between four bedposts; her window and curtains were wide open, spilling in a mixture of moonlight and streetlight, both white. She had fallen straight on the sheet without changing her clothes and lay spread-eagled on that snowy surface, forming a mound that, with each snore, appeared to heave higher to the ceiling. Ross called out, 'Hey!' (he still refused to call her Ma, so had no name for her at all) and shook her shoulder till she started up.

He said, 'We have to help Tammy.' He explained the situation, but – perhaps she had been too abruptly awakened out of her deep sleep – she only yawned and stretched, so that her sari slipped from her upper body and spilled in a pool of violent, violet silk around her. She seemed terribly to want to go back to sleep.

Ross became more explicit: 'She wants you to leave.'

'And you?'

He grimaced: 'There's always a corner for the poor old dog.'

That sounded like a good joke to her and she laughed at it.

Her mouth was like an empty cavern but her teeth smiled all by themselves in a glass by her bedside. He began to be very irritated with her.

She said, 'Well, I'll have to find somewhere else.'

'Where would you go? And with all these people?'

'If I go out of this door and into the park and sit on that broken bench you like so much or under a tree or anywhere I choose, they'll follow me. Don't ask me why. I don't know why.'

'Neither do I. You're setting up as this wise woman and you don't understand the most basic situation. You can't even help one single person.'

'You mean yourself?'

'No, not me,' he said, now more irritated at her obtuseness. 'What help could you give me?'

'No, none,' she agreed. 'But if Tammy wants me to go, then I'll have to.'

'I would have thought you'd have some better solution after all your promises. Yes,' he overrode her, 'when Minnie sent you packing, that's what you promised: that you were here to help Tammy.'

'But now Tammy is sending me packing, so what can I do?' She laughed again and then she chucked him under the chin in the most familiar manner. Offended, he turned to leave, with her calling after him: 'But why are *you* angry? It's I who should be angry that you've come into my bedroom in the middle of the night, making people think all sorts of things that should not be.'

But only a few nights later, it was she who came to his room. She entered silently on her bare feet, only her bangles jingling. She climbed nimbly on to the end of his bed, and tucking her feet under her, she said, 'So what are you arranging for me? . . . What, nothing? First you tell me to go, then you have nowhere for me to go to – you're a fine first-class business manager.'

'Business manager,' he repeated: he had never had such a grand title and didn't think he could live up to it.

'Well, who else has been arranging my business here, and doing it quite well too? I think you have a future.'

'With you?'

'If you care to come with me, certainly.'

He took off his reading glasses; he said, 'But where are you going?'

'I'm asking you! I thought you'd have arranged a place by now. That's why I've brought all this: look.' She lifted her sari; a cloth bundle was hidden there, tied to her petticoat string. She unfastened the bundle and shook it out on his blanket: hundreds and hundreds of bank notes of all denominations fluttered down, together with crumpled checks and money orders. 'This is for a deposit: you get us a nice place and the rest of the money will come. That's easy.'

'So you've had a fund-raiser.'

'I only said, "Children, I need another home where you can all come visit me." Everyone gave. Some stood opening doors at the supermarket collecting in a paper cup so as to have something to give. They needed to give – some more than others.' She smoothed out one of the crumpled checks, which was for an astonishing amount: 'From the lady upstairs, the one who has all the lawsuits with her son. She needed to give very badly . . . And meanwhile you've done nothing.' She clicked her tongue at him but playfully, and playfully she shook his toes under the sheet. When he indignantly withdrew them – 'How proud you are,' she pretended to pout. 'Here I've come to you past all these people looking on and suspecting, now what are those two up to again? And you won't even let me touch your feet . . . I think you only think of her: Grace. You live with a ghost.'

'You've laid her ghost long ago.'

'Then what's wrong? Don't you like to be with a living person – even if she is a bit fat and old?' To prevent herself laughing, she sucked in her lips, which disappeared right into the pit of her mouth. She swept her hand over her black, black hair and coquettishly turned her profile. When he laughed, she laughed too, releasing her lips and opening that gaping pit: she looked like a hundred-year-old witch but like a temptress too, gleaming and glittering with oil and silk and gold.

'Oh my God, that *smell*!' said Minnie as usual, on entering the apartment. She was right: besides everything else, a lot of cooking went on in there now, and volunteers had been taught by Ma herself to deep-fry fritters and breads and onions and spices. Along with hot meals, she was also glad to offer bathing facilities, expounding the benefit of oil massage for body and scalp, so that all the bathrooms were in constant use, including Tammy's, Ross's, and what had been Grace's.

'Listen,' said Minnie, 'you'd better get her out of here, but quick.'

'Yes,' Ross agreed. 'As soon as we've found a suitable place to buy.'

Tammy gazed at him, startled, and so did Minnie, who asked, 'You're looking for a place to buy?' He nodded casually, and narrowing her eyes a bit, Minnie regarded him with more interest than she had ever shown him: 'How much are you thinking to spend?'

It turned out that she was looking to sell her apartment, which her lawyer had managed to get for her as part of her divorce settlement. She hardly stayed there nowadays, spending most of her time with the Doktor, and anyway the place held horrible memories for her from her horrible marriage. But when she took Ross there to view it, it didn't seem as though it could have any memories at all. Even the paintings had been chosen by the designer, who came in regularly to check up that everything was kept as he had arranged it, including the dining table set out according to his specifications, though no one ate there any more. Minnie gave Ross a guided tour, pointing out the French wallpaper, the rugs handmade by inmates of a jail in Kabul, the Tibetan wheel of life over the king-size bed. With regard to this bed – 'I cannot tell you what went on there,' she said and went on to tell in detail. 'And I thought I was marrying this decent guy who liked girls.' But thank God it was all in the past – a bad dream – and if only she could get this place off her hands, off her mind, out of her life – if only someone would come up with the money . . . It was a lot of money, but Minnie could hardly let it go for less, it was owed to her, after what she had paid for it in suffering.

Ross said he would take it. After another fund-raiser, he was able to pay for it in cash. The lady from upstairs actually sold her ancestral apartment and all its contents to pay for Minnie's, so that she could move in there with Ma. Ross agreed to buy Minnie's furniture too – he knew it wouldn't be in their way, they would all just dispose themselves around it, the way they had done at Tammy's. Tammy's furniture meanwhile – the detritus of a hundred years – was appraised, and as soon as Ma moved out, it was carried off to the auction houses. Here it was sold for a very handsome amount (the proceeds went to the Doktor's movement), for it was from a period much in fashion, and even the cracked mirror fetched a good price. Ross agreed to stay on as caretaker, though his bed and wardrobe had been sold – they were too valuable to leave behind – and he slept in a sleeping-bag Tammy lent him and kept his belongings in his two old suitcases. He was now the only occupant, for Tammy was too busy preparing for the Doktor's move to have time to come home; anyway, her bed had been sold too.

Workmen moved in – painters, carpenters, plasterers, electricians – to get the place ready for the Doktor. They stripped and purged the apartment into its furthest corners, including Ross's corner room, sweeping him out along with all the roaches, which had come scuttling out from under cracks and water pipes and broken tiles. Minnie was there to supervise the work. She had changed completely: far from the restless seeker she had been, she was now very busy, efficient, a businesswoman; only her manner had remained the same – alternately effusive and rude, depending on whom she was addressing. Tammy followed behind her; she was supposed to be taking notes but did not do it very well, so that Minnie kept snapping at her. When they reached Ross's room, Minnie found some fault in the ceiling, and stretching up to point this out to the delinquent plasterer, she stubbed her toe against Ross's suitcases. She glared at them angrily and asked, 'What's this?' and when Ross acknowledged them, she glared at him: 'I guess you're taking them away today? Tomorrow? When are you moving out?' Ross had bent down to take his possessions out of her way, and by the time he straightened up, she had swept on with her troupe of chastened workers. Tammy stayed behind – she helped Ross with his bags, but when she tried to put them in the closet, he said not to.

She peered into his face: 'You're not really leaving?'

He was embarrassed, he shuffled his feet and said, 'She needs me in the other place.'

Minnie was irritably calling for Tammy; Tammy called back that she was coming. Stepping closer to Ross, she whispered, 'You can't leave me alone here.'

'Then come with me.'

Tammy sighed; she shook her head: 'The work is here now, not with Ma . . . Don't look like that, Ross. You've never met him; you've never met anyone like him. I don't blame you that you don't believe me – I'd have felt the same had anyone told me what would happen; how he would change me.'

And by now she *had* changed. Her head, once hopefully raised toward a higher region, now hung from her neck like a flower wilting on its stalk. When Minnie again shouted for her, even more impatiently, she called back in apology, and letting go of the suitcases she had been trying to wrest from Ross, she began to hurry away in answer to the summons.

But now he held her back; he said, 'Won't you come with me?' It was only a shy suggestion, giving her the chance to turn him down. And sadly she did so, shaking her head, turning toward where Minnie was yelling for her.

He had no words to dissuade her. Just as he could never tell her mother outright 'Please don't kill yourself' but only by indirection – for instance, by making her laugh, mostly at himself – deflect her from her purpose: so now he could only catch hold of Tammy's hand to halt her in her flight from him. Her hand lay very lightly in his, so that, if she had wanted, she could have drawn it away; but she left it there, a pale, live, frail thing that could easily be crushed by a stronger hand than his. *His* hand was as small as her own, and she could nestle there till there was another call from Minnie – 'Let me go,' she whispered, as though she hadn't the strength to draw away herself; so he released her and picked up his two suitcases and left.

\*          \*          \*

When he arrived at Ma's new place, she had one of her song sessions going. He found all the people who used to come to Tammy's assembled here. But Minnie's interior decorator could have walked in and been perfectly satisfied that nothing had been disturbed: even the tables were still laid, and the little porcelain fruit-tarts unchipped. Ma's people had simply flowed over the design like water over a grotto, leaving it perfectly preserved while drowning it forever. Only the hi-fi system had been disassembled – there was no need for it, since Ma's voice was more powerful than any high-tech machine; and the table on which it had stood now served as her seat or throne on which she sat as she had on Tammy's dining table, with her legs tucked under her. From here she conducted her sing-song; sometimes hers was the only voice to be heard, for the others had forgotten the words and trailed off till she started them up again. She was not totally absorbed in the performance but dropped from time to time into conversation, encouraging everyone to lift up their spirits along with their voices, or only inquiring if the lentils had been stirred. When she saw Ross entering with his suitcases, she called to him gladly and invited him to sit up front; but when he preferred to remain at the back, she explained to the others, 'He's shy. And he won't sing.'

'I can't,' Ross said.

'You won't,' she said and smiled in that flirtatious way she had with him.

But now her song was ascending to its climax, and she opened her arms wide as though to sweep them up to its height. What was it that she was making them sing? No one understood the words, she had never translated or explained them. Nevertheless, they all did their utmost, gathering strength and voice to follow her lead. Only Ross sat silent. He could still feel the touch of Tammy's hand in his, and when Ma's eyes sought him out in the crowd to exhort him to sing, he shut his palm as though it held something precious that he did not want to let go. Ma was singing with all her might, so that he wanted to stop his ears against her; nor did he dare raise his eyes to her but kept them lowered to his hand balled into a fist.

'Sing, Ross, sing!' she exhorted him and sang and swayed and shone and shimmered, till he knew he could not withstand her. He scrambled up from the floor, and without a glance in her direction, he picked up his suitcases and escaped into the elevator. Her voice followed him down twenty-seven storeys and even into the street – or was that just his fancy, and fear? Anyway, he did not feel safe till he was in the opposite part of the city, the part he knew so well, and outside Tammy's apartment building and then inside that marble vault, where the doormen were all new, for the old ones had followed Ma and had lost interest in holding down their jobs.

# A SUMMER BY THE SEA

Lying on the beach, I could hear their voices all day long. Sometimes they sounded like bird song, but when I opened my eyes they were all men. He – Boy, my husband – was very happy in their company. How everything sparkled on those long days on the beach: the ocean, the sky, the sand, and that group of handsome men in swim trunks, their bronzed limbs glistening with drops of water and grains of sand, scattered all over them like pearls.

Then there were the days when my mother was there with us. Those were not so good. She bothered them and she bothered me. By myself, I was happy just to lie near them, mostly with my eyes shut, and to hear their voices. I didn't expect to take part in their fun, and didn't really want to or need to. But Mother hated to be left out. She liked talking and laughing, but what she said bored them, and what they said bored her.

'What *are* they talking about?' she would ask me. 'What's all that rubbish? Giggling like a bunch of kids.' She would get disgusted with them and go off by herself, splashing in the ocean and making friends with other people. She usually joined some group, and we could hear her voice shouting above theirs and, looking over at her, we saw her – very bright in her bright bathing suit, with her gold-red hair and her jewels glistening in the sun, and her too-white skin that never tanned, and the operation scar showing over the top of her bikini.

She suffered from insomnia, and she would walk the house at night, looking for someone to talk to. Boy and I would lie very still, not daring to turn on the light or talk or read, in case she found us awake. The nights were very long and boring whenever she was there. The days weren't so bad, because I would pretend to be busy looking after the friends, or to be asleep on the beach, so that Mother couldn't ever really get hold of me for one of her tête-à-têtes. But sooner or later she managed it, and then it would always be the same – about Boy, and our marriage, and his friends, on and on, as it always had been from the beginning and even before.

Yes, even before we were married she liked to question me about Boy. He was quite different from any son-in-law she had expected. She had disliked his family almost from the beginning – his mother and two sisters ('those crazies,' she called them) – but she could not dismiss Boy, not just because he was part of me and so part of her but because he fascinated her. His good looks and his refinement were like heirlooms that had come into the family, and she wanted to have them appraised. She could not ask me enough about him, and the longer we were married the more pressing and intimate her questions became.

Boy used to teach a course in art history, but since our marriage he's been concentrating on his own research. That leaves him with a lot of time on his hands and makes him very dependent on having friends. Hamid has been his special friend for some months – they had got very close in New York, where they both liked to go to afternoon movies – but Mother hadn't met him until she came to stay with us in this cottage on Nantucket that Boy and I usually rent in the summer. She and Hamid got on very well together. They kidded around and seemed to have the same sense of humor, and Mother really became like a girl, with all that teasing and joking they did together. He called her by her first name, Bea, and treated her as if they were the same age. Naturally, she liked that and opened up to him completely. What she didn't know is that behind her back he called her Golden Oldie, and laughed at her with Boy and the others. I tried to warn her, but of course she wouldn't listen; she knew better.

'You don't understand, Susie,' she said. 'You don't know

anything about these things. You never did.' I am her only
daughter, and it's one of the regrets of her life that I haven't
turned out to be fun-loving and sexy, like her. 'He's my type,'
she told me about Hamid. 'We have the same chemistry.'

Hamid had a lot of chemistry. I am not usually sensitive
about this (as she has told me often enough), but I could
feel that. There was a change in our circle after he entered
it. Before that, it was always Boy we were all centered around
– not that Boy is bossy or selfish or anything but just because
we all wanted to do what he wanted and we didn't really get
any fun out of anything unless he was behind it heart and soul.
Perhaps this was because we all loved him so much. But I guess
Hamid had a stronger personality than the rest of us, including
Boy. Or maybe it was because he is a foreigner, an Oriental –
someone different in an exotic way – and we kept looking at
him with fascination to see what he would do next.

At first we thought he must be some kind of prince, on
account of his looks, but he was too poor for that. He never had
any money at all. Not that it bothered him, because there were
plenty of people eager to pay for anything he needed. Boy said
that maybe he came from one of those very ancient royal lines
that were extinct now, except for a few last descendants working
as coolies in Calcutta. Or maybe, Boy said – he has plenty of
imagination and also quite a bit of oriental background, thanks
to his study of art history – Hamid was a descendant of a line
of famous saints, dating back to the thirteenth century and
handing down their sainthood from generation to generation.
When I said that I didn't think there was anything saintly about
Hamid, Boy said, 'Oh, no? Just have a look at his eyes.' So the
next time he was near me I did, and while I had to admit they
were very beautiful, I couldn't see anything in them except an
eroticism so deep that he had to keep it partially curtained by
lowering his black satin lashes.

Mother always got up later than the rest of us, and then it
took her a long time to get herself ready to appear on the beach.
'Here comes Golden Oldie,' Hamid would say to us, but when
she got closer he would call out to her, 'Good morning, Madame!'
in a cheerful voice. 'Or should I say "Good afternoon"?'

'You can say "Good evening," for all I care,' Mother replied pertly, and they carried on from there, topping each other with childish jokes, and always looking over each other with impudent, knowing looks. The other friends would pretend to be engrossed in their own doings. One was reading Baudelaire's *Intimate Journals*, and another building something in the sand, and Boy lay face down, with his head buried in his arms. I kept my eyes shut; I didn't want to have to see Mother, with her face – so carefully made up, with green eyelids – exposed by the blazing light from sea, sun, and sand.

'Can't you stop her?' Boy sometimes asked me. I wanted to say, 'Can't you stop *him*?' For Hamid was leading her on, no doubt about that. He needed a lot of reaction from people, and although he got plenty in our house from Boy and Boy's other friends, perhaps he needed women as well. In that department, there was only Mother and me, and he had given up on me quite quickly.

Very late one night, when Hamid and Mother were sitting together out on the porch talking in low voices, Boy suddenly went rushing out there in his pajamas. I heard him say, 'What are you *doing*, for Pete's sake, out here in the dark?'

'Ah-ha-ha!' replied Mother playfully, but with a hysterical note in her voice.

By the time I came out, Boy had turned on the light. There was Mother in full regalia, in a silver-spangled halter dress and actually wearing her dangling diamond earrings, and Hamid was stretched out on the painted wooden porch floor at her feet, in his very short shorts, with grains of sand still clinging to the hairs on his thighs.

'Can I speak to you?' Boy said to Hamid. 'For a moment?' He seemed rather frail in his pale blue pajamas. His fair and (unfortunately) thinning hair was tousled, from drawing his hands through it in his nervousness.

Hamid sat up on the floor. He looked powerful and almost angry. We all waited for him. At last, he reacted favorably. He said, 'Okeydokey,' and heaved himself up from the floor, using Boy as a support. They went in together.

'How can you *stand* it?' Mother said to me.

We could hear them arguing inside – or, rather, Boy arguing. He tried to keep his voice low, so that we couldn't hear what he said, but that just made it more intense and passionate. Hamid made only an occasional remark, in a soft voice, as if he wanted to cool him down. But Boy was not cooled down.

'Well, *I* can't stand it,' Mother said at last. She went down the porch steps, onto the beach, into the dark. I could see her pacing up and down there, like a firefly in her spangly dress and jewels.

I didn't want to join her but I knew she expected me to. As soon as I did, she fell on my neck and wept. She said it was for me. But that was an old story, and these tears came from somewhere new. Unexpectedly, she began to talk about Daddy. 'I keep thinking about him these days,' she said. 'Not like he was later, with all those tarts he had' – she pulled her familiar sour face – 'but in the first years.'

Of course, I had heard all about those early years, when Daddy had been making his first million and Mother had given up a promising (she said) singing-and-dancing career to be married to him. The fun, the jokes! I never quite made out what these had been, because usually she laughed so much remembering them that she couldn't get out the words.

'How he'd have hated it here!' she said now. 'He'd have been bored to death. And so am I. I don't know how you can like it.'

'You know I like it,' I said. Boy and I had chosen this house on a remote section of the beach.

'Daddy liked being by the sea, too, but only if he could look at it from the terrace of some Grand Hotel,' she said. 'Sitting there with his binoculars – he looked at some other things besides the ocean, I can tell you that. Well, I guess that was his nature. He had these strong, manly appetites, God rest his soul.'

I went right to the edge of the water. I looked and listened to the waves and really enjoyed that. But she came and stood next to me.

'Can I tell you something?' She said it like a secret. 'He reminds me of Daddy. Hamid. Not that they look alike or anything, but there is *something*. Maybe it's because they're both strong – strong, sexy men. He was telling me about his first experience today. He was only twelve, can you believe it? He was seduced by a servant girl, but she stank so much it put him off women for years. Everyone knows they're ambidextrous over there. It's all right over there. It's expected.'

'Can we go back in now?'

'You know something, Susie?' she said. 'You're a moral coward. I wouldn't have believed it that a daughter of mine and Daddy's – Because we always did *everything* we wanted to.'

I said, 'How do you know I don't?'

The next morning, Boy sat gloomily on the beach while Hamid laughed and joked with the other friends. When Mother came to join us, in a new lavender bikini and a matching headscarf, Hamid turned all his attention on her. Of course, she was delighted and reacted twice as much. Neither of them seemed to care when Boy got up and went away. After a while, I followed him into the house. He was in the kitchen making crêpes – he tends to start cooking when he's upset.

Boy is so sensitive that when he is emotionally worked up he quivers all over. It is as if his body is just the thinnest, finest sheath around his soul, totally inadequate to protect him against the roughness of this world. That's why I feel I have to do everything to protect him, even though I know that I'm just as inadequate and unprotected. Boy hates me to see him when he is upset. He doesn't want me to know these things about him, so I have to pretend I don't.

I sat down at the kitchen table, talking to him about his damn crêpes and pretending I was interested in whether he was going to make them Suzette or Gil Blas. And he pretended that that was all he was thinking about, too, frenziedly beating the batter. But he couldn't keep it up, and finally he sat down next to me at the table and said in a low, mean voice, 'Get her out of here! I can't stand her another minute.'

I knew how he felt, but I also knew how Mother felt. I murmured, 'It gets awfully lonesome for her in New York.'

'I don't *care*!' Boy said.

This was ludicrous. Boy cares more than any other human being in the world. He is so imaginative that another person's unhappiness is as real and painful to him as his own. He is always asking me, 'How's your mother? Did you speak to her today?' A lot of the time, he phones her himself, to make sure she isn't dying of loneliness in that big apartment of hers, with the gilt furniture.

Luckily, I remembered something just then. I said, 'Your sister Evie phoned last night. I forgot to tell you. She was—'

'What?' he asked in apprehension.

'Well,' I said, 'she seemed okay, really. She spoke about going to visit Bobby at his summer camp, but then she – she—' I was upset, but I couldn't help laughing. Evie had told me that she had to call the doctor in, because there were birds roosting in the valance of her dining-room curtains. She was in one of her disturbed states, and spoke very seriously.

'Is she bad?' he asked. 'Did Linda phone?'

Linda is his mother. Every now and again, when Evie gets very bad and has to go away for a while, Linda and her other daughter, Paula, are constantly on the phone to Boy. He is the only male left in the family. His father is dead (drowned while drunk, at East Hampton), and Evie's and Paula's husbands left years ago.

'I guess Linda would have phoned if she was really bad,' he said, putting that problem aside for the moment. 'That leaves *your* mother.'

When I started to defend her again, he said, 'Doesn't she realize how it looks? That everyone's laughing at her?'

'Who's laughing?'

At this point, Terry came to join us in the kitchen. He is an English boy, studying architecture in New York, and he had come to stay with us for the summer, along with some of the other friends. It's a big cottage, and they all like to be together. Terry was forever following Boy around, and that was why he came to join us in the kitchen. But Boy, wanting to be alone to talk with me, got rid of him quite fast. Poor Terry! How different it had been last year, when Hamid had not yet appeared on the scene and Terry had been the apple of Boy's eye.

'Everyone is,' Boy said, as if no interruption had taken place. 'To see an old woman like her making a fool of herself over – The whole beach is laughing. By the way,' he said to me in a different tone, 'can't you tell her not to wear a bikini? That scar – I mean, we all know, poor thing, but it makes you feel *sick*. Hamid asked me about it. He said, "Who slit her up?"'

'Does it make him feel sick?'

'No, it makes him laugh. Everything about her makes him laugh. He thinks she's a ridiculous, ludicrous, silly old hag. He hates her,' Boy said. He held his head in his hands.

I wanted to stroke his hair – which would have made him mad – so to resist the temptation I took the bowl of batter and began to beat it as hard as Boy had. After a while, he took over again – a good thing, because nobody makes crêpes the way he can, and also it was therapy for him, so by the time everyone came in to eat he was feeling better and was awfully nice to Mother, as if he wanted to make it up to her for having spoken unkindly behind her back.

Later, Linda, Boy's mother, did phone to say that Evie was bad again. She wanted Boy to come to the city to persuade her to go back in the hospital till she was better. His sister Paula also phoned, with the same message. He usually goes when they call him, but this time he was more reluctant than usual. He just couldn't bear to leave Hamid, especially when Mother was there. It was a dilemma – he and I were very much aware of it, and so was Mother. (She wanted him to go, of course – very much.) I don't think Hamid knew what was going on, though he knew something was up. That was typical of him. He was remote from us and our problems, but at the same time he was extremely sensitive to what everyone was feeling.

When Linda phoned again to give the latest report about Evie, Mother tapped the side of her head and said to Hamid in an undertone, 'His sister.'

'She is . . . ?' And Hamid also tapped his head.

'Completely,' Mother said.

I began to protest. I said Evie only had these spells, but Mother shouted me down. 'Of course she's nuts, completely and absolutely gone,' she said. 'The whole family. You're not trying to tell me,' she said, turning to me again, 'that other sister of his, that what's-her-name, that *she's* normal? Or if it comes to that, what about Linda herself?'

'Linda? Why, she's the sanest woman I've ever met. She's so – so—' I didn't have the word for my tall, bony, thin-lipped, determinedly energetic mother-in-law, who is always frenziedly engaged in some practical job, like cleaning out the linen closet.

'She's the most screwed-up of the lot,' Mother said emphatically.

'Who is?' Boy asked, coming in after speaking to his mother on the telephone. We all looked at him, but he told us nothing.

'Well,' Mother said, 'are you going?'

Boy looked at Hamid, who said, 'Of course you'll have to go if your sister is . . . not well. If your family is expecting you.'

Boy looked at him, and so did I. There was nothing in Hamid's eyes except solicitude for Boy. Mother was smoking frantically, dropping ash into her coffee, but Hamid was calm and gentle, at that moment caring only for Boy and his family problem and wanting everything settled. So when Boy left later that morning – Hamid and I dropped him at the airport – he went with a relatively light heart.

Whenever Boy is away, I keep myself occupied with all the household jobs I can think up. As soon as the plane left, I went off to buy pounds of peaches, and later I was very busy making jam that no one would ever want to eat. I was so busy I didn't wonder where Hamid was or Mother was. 'Don't you *care*?' Terry asked me. He himself cared terribly. I guess that was why he had stayed behind; the other friends had scattered when Boy left. He wanted to see what would happen – to spy, if you want to look at it that way, or to look out for Boy, if you prefer. He kept following me around to report on his findings, and it irritated him that I didn't want to know.

'Don't you care?' he kept saying.

Actually, Terry himself was one of the people who taught me that it's not good to care too much. I was like him once –

for instance, when he and Boy were very much involved with each other – and I used to torment myself by spying, speculating, finding out. But now I don't do that any more.

It turned out to be the wrong day for making jam. It was terribly hot, with no breeze coming in from the ocean. Mother stayed in her room all afternoon, sometimes calling to me to come in and talk to her. She was sprawled across the bed, and she seemed both exhausted and excited. She was still in her morning wrap, which had fallen open, exposing her thighs. She said she wished she were back in New York – at least there was air-conditioning there, so a person could breathe – but I could see she didn't mean it. She didn't want to be in New York, she wanted to be here.

'When is he coming back?' she asked me, and then she answered herself: 'I guess he has to put his sister away first. My God, Susie, what sort of a family have you gone and married us into?' She has said this so often that it's almost become a refrain. And almost in the same breath she said, 'Did you see Hamid? He was out on the beach in all that heat. I called to him from the house. I said, "You'll get sunstroke!" but he just laughed and waved. he's used to the heat – it must be even hotter where he comes from. I don't know how people stand it. He seems made different from us, don't you think, Susie? Don't you have that feeling about him?'

'I don't know,' I murmured, pulling at her wrap to cover her thighs.

'You don't know anything,' she said, pushing the wrap off again. 'Sometimes I envy you. I mean, it must be a lot easier to be made the way you are. Wouldn't you think I'd have got over all that by now? Wouldn't you think so? That a person would be allowed to cool off? But no such luck, no such luck.' Suddenly she cursed herself and struck the side of her head, like a peasant woman.

I had often seen her do that, when I was a child, only then she had been cursing Daddy, who was usually away somewhere with someone else – someone younger. At that time, Mother had still been very pretty, so quite often she would get up and go over to the mirror to look at herself, and then she'd ask me,

'I look okay, don't I? What's wrong with me?' And I would tell her that she looked fabulous. But now she didn't go to the mirror or ask any questions.

Terry came in, with his rather sharp nose pointing out of his thin face, so that he seemed to be sniffing the air for information. When he saw that Hamid was not there, his expression changed from inquisition to distaste. Boy also looks like this whenever he comes into Mother's bedroom. I don't notice it myself, but I guess the feminine smell around her *is* rather strong, with all those perfumes and creams she uses and the little underthings she has discarded lying scattered around the room.

Just then the phone rang, and I went running out. It was Boy. I asked, 'How is she?'

'Oh hell, Susie, don't ask,' he said. 'What are you all doing?'

'Mother's lying down and Terry's—'

'Hamid's not there? Listen, ask him – Oh, I'll call again later. Tell him – I've got to *go*, Susie,' he said as I began to ask him about Evie again.

Terry had followed me, and he stretched out his hand for the receiver. When I told him that Boy had hung up, he said, 'Did he ask to speak to me?'

'His sister's very bad,' I said apologetically.

Terry said, 'What are you going to do about tonight?'

Unfortunately, I knew at once what he meant. I had already made up my mind that if Hamid and Mother got together there was nothing I could do about it. Actually, I had planned on taking a sleeping pill. I usually do that anyway when Boy is away; it helps me over having to sleep alone.

It never cooled down that night, and we kept everything wide open and wore the minimum of clothes. I forgot about the jam, and it burned and stuck to the bottom of the pan, and the house was filled with the smell of this blackened, sugary mess of peaches. I went into my bedroom and took a sleeping pill. But before it could take effect, Hamid came in and lay down on Boy's bed to talk to me. It seemed he had gone to see a movie in the afternoon, and now he was telling me the story, which was about a mother and daughter, both in love with the same guy. He slept with both but was really in love with another guy, who was an actor who played cowboy roles. All this seemed very strange to Hamid, and I must say it sounded strange to me, too, and I wondered whether he had got it quite right or whether I was beginning to feel very drowsy with my pill. He went on telling me about the movie, and then I think he told me some incidents from his own life, but by that time I was in a state where I couldn't quite keep the two apart.

When Mother came in, he said to her, 'Listen to this.' So she sat on the side of the bed where he was lying while he went on telling his story. I think it really was his story now, because Mother said, 'Well, what do you expect, with looks like that?' and she fondled him with real respect – reverence, even – for his beauty. And he let her do it, as if it was quite ordinary and what he was used to. He was telling her how, some years ago, his visa had run out and he was going to be deported, but there was this very wonderful lady he met. He went to live in her house, and she arranged everything about his papers, so that he could stay. She looked after him very well, and he was grateful to her and enjoyed being with her in her various houses, which she went to from season to season.

'Where is she now?' Mother asked, tangling her fingers in the hair of his chest.

The end of the story was not as good as the beginning. For reasons he didn't specify, he had had to leave her, and this gave rise to some very bad scenes. At one point, the police had been called in, and for a while his immigration papers had been endangered again. But it had all been straightened out, thanks to some other friends he had made in the meantime, and after a while she was all right, too, and had been able to leave the hospital, where her daughter had placed her. It made him sad to remember all this, and he freely admitted that he had not acted well. But it had all been out of ignorance, he told us – youth and ignorance (he had been just eighteen). He had been unaware that it was this bad time for her, when certain physical changes occur in women of her age. If he had known then, he said, what he knew now, of course he would have acted with far greater delicacy and care for her. Then it seemed Mother needed comforting, and I saw him sit up to rub her back. My pill had really begun to work by then, and I was more than half asleep, and after a while fully asleep.

The weather changed, and a wind sprang up from the sea and came blowing through my open windows, so that I woke up for a moment to cover myself. It was still night, and Mother and Hamid had gone from the other bed and I was alone. Terry must have been alone, too, and I could hear him in the living room playing some of last year's records.

The next day I spent a long time scrubbing out the pan in which the jam had burned. But the smell must have lingered around the house, because the first thing that Boy said when he came home was 'What's that smell?' Unfortunately, Terry was there to overhear, and he said at once, 'Well may you ask,' in his very English accent, so I knew he was only waiting to get Boy alone to tell him all sorts of things. But it wasn't as easy as all that for him to get Boy alone. Hamid was not in when I brought Boy back from the airport, but shortly afterward I saw him making his way from the beach up to the house. Boy saw him first, and he didn't waste a second. He ran down the porch steps and straight as an arrow down to the beach toward Hamid. They met halfway. Terry wanted to join them, but I held him back. He was furious with me. He said, 'Aren't you going to tell him?' and then, 'If you don't, I certainly will.' But, as I said, he didn't get the chance so easily, because Boy would not let Hamid out of his sight.

Mother had seen the meeting on the beach from her window. 'It's disgusting,' she told me. 'He ran like a – like a—'

'Like a lover,' I said.

'Disgusting,' she said again.

And she really was disgusted. Mother has always liked to think of herself as a woman of the world, knowing all there is to know. I used to see her and her friends huddled close together with flushed cheeks and the tips of their tongues showing, as if tasting something nice, while the maid, pretending to be busy with the tea trolley she had rolled in, would cock her head in their direction and her cheeks would flush, too, at what she heard. When I was small, Mother would say, 'Go away, Susie, go and watch your program,' and when I was grown up, she said, 'Oh, Susie wouldn't know anything about it. She's just stayed a great big baby.'

Mother doesn't drink an awful lot, usually – only when she is upset, to make herself feel better, and then, because she isn't used to it, she gets high very quickly. That was what happened on the day of Boy's return. In the evening, when we were lying on the floor listening to records, she came and stood in the doorway and said to Boy, 'You haven't told us about your crazy sister.'

Although she said this in a very loud voice, the record almost drowned her, so she stalked over and turned it down, and then she repeated what she had said.

Boy went white and bit his thin lips even thinner. He said, 'I'm not going to discuss my family affairs.'

'I thought we were all family here,' said Mother, looking around at us all, but especially at Hamid and Terry.

I was afraid of what else she might say in her state, so I went toward her, hoping to take her away to her bedroom. But she pushed me aside.

'Susie is healthy,' she informed Boy. 'A healthy, normal human being like her mother and her father and everyone in our family.'

'Why don't you ask her about last night?' Terry said to Boy in a cool, smiling way. 'That should be interesting.'

Hamid, who had continued to lie on the floor with his eyes shut, sat up and blinked like one awakened from deep sleep. 'Who turned the music off?' he said.

'Or you can ask him,' Terry said.

Hamid got up from the floor and went over to the record-player and turned it up again. Now he and Mother were the only ones standing; the rest of us were on the floor looking up at them. Hamid made sensuous movements to the music. 'I wish I could dance,' he said.

Mother, completely forgetting about Boy and her anger with

him, said, 'You can't? I'll teach you.' She even had to show him how to hold her.

'What happened last night?' Boy asked Terry.

'I was making jam and it got burned,' I said.

'Oh really, Susie,' Boy said impatiently. 'Are you a fool or something?'

Mother was laughing loudly at Hamid, who was playing dumb and doing everything wrong – on purpose, I think, to amuse her and, if possible, the rest of us, too. 'It's like teaching a bear to dance,' she said. Then he pretended to be a bear and lurched around the room. Mother went after him, laughing her head off, trying to make him come back and hold her again, but he got away from her. However, the room wasn't big enough for him to escape her for long, and she soon had him cornered by the bookcase. Then he made quite a clever move. Still pretending to be a bear, he shook her off and lurched across to me and said, 'You teach me.'

Well, I'm not much of a dancer – not like Mother, who is fantastic – but I saw that this was the best solution, so I got up and let him lead me. He danced quite well, it turned out. I can't say I enjoyed it and I guess he didn't much, either, but the other three were staying quiet, watching us, so we just went on dancing.

Later, Mother let me take her away and help her undress and get into bed. While I was doing this, she kept moaning, as if she were in pain or as if someone had just died, but otherwise she was quiet and seemed only to want to be put to bed like a child. And like a child, lying there in her nightie, she let tears flow down her nose in a natural, unashamed way, and childishly she said, 'He married you for your money. For Daddy's money.'

This was a familiar accusation, which I no longer bothered to answer. And it is true that Boy is poor – so is Linda and so are the two sisters. Their father lost everything with terrible speculations, before drinking and drowning. It is also true that Boy has very refined tastes and needs money. But he likes me, too – and yes, he needs me, just as much as he needs the money.

He came into the room now, and saw Mother in bed. 'Is she all right?' he asked.

'What do you care?' said Mother, letting the tears flow.

'Of course I care,' Boy said.

He sat near Mother's bed and told us about Evie. He spoke quite freely, in a quiet, restrained voice, about her terrible and unhuman behavior. He made it clear that he wanted to hide nothing from Mother and me and that he considered it our right to know.

Mother was horrified. I think that once she had heard him out, she would sooner not have been told. Boy explained that at first they had tried to get Evie to go to the hospital voluntarily, but she had resisted so violently that it wasn't possible. So then they had to call the people from the hospital to take Evie away. I saw Boy tense up inside himself as he said this – she had had to be taken away like that once before, and he had been there that time, too, and he had told me that he never wanted to see it again.

Now Mother really had something to cry about. So many things! Boy and I sat on either side of her bed and she pressed both our hands and said, 'Children, children.' All that crying completely washed away her make-up, and she suddenly looked her age.

'Poor Linda,' she said. 'Oh, poor soul. What shall I do for her? Does she need money? Can I send her a check?'

'I'll let you know,' Boy said. He would, too. His mother always needs money. She is really hard up, and he couldn't afford to let such an opportunity go by.

'I wish I lived closer to her, so I could help. Or if she lived near me. Do you think she'd want to? I have this goddamn stupid apartment. My God, who *needs* all those rooms?' Now Mother was really getting carried away. The idea of those two, Mother and Linda, living together . . . Boy and I caught each other's eye and had to look away quickly. But Mother seemed to like her line of thought. 'We wouldn't have to see each other every day. We wouldn't even have to cook or eat together, except maybe like Sunday brunch or something. And you two could come, too – it'd be fun. Just Sundays. And if you had –

if there were some kids . . . Lots of people adopt kids. It doesn't make any difference, they say; you love them just the same. How would you like me as a grandma – what do you think? Grandma Bea?' She giggled.

Hamid could be heard calling outside the door. Mother let go of our hands. 'Don't let him come in!' she said frantically. But he was in already. Mother quickly turned out the light by her bedside. Boy had stood up.

Hamid said, 'What, all finished? Everyone gone bye-byes? Then I will go bye-byes, too. Good night.'

Boy said, 'We could go for a walk. On the beach? There's almost a full moon.'

He was excited and entirely different from the way he had been only a moment before. Mother, too, was entirely different. She called out from the semi-darkness of her bed, 'Yes, let's go for a walk in the moonlight!' She tried to make her voice youthful, but it cracked on too high a note.

'Why are you in bed?' Hamid asked her. 'Are you ill? And in the dark . . .' He leaned over to switch on her lamp, but she caught his hand and said, 'It hurts my eyes.'

'Come on!' Boy said urgently to Hamid.

'Wait for me!' Mother cried. 'I'm getting my clothes on!'

As soon as they had gone, Mother jumped out of bed. She began to dress feverishly. Nothing I said could stop her, and her only answer to me, as usual, was 'You don't understand.' She quickly pulled on some white jeans and a candy-striped sailor blouse.

I went out and sat on the porch. I could see Boy and Hamid walking by the edge of the ocean, and then I watched Mother running in her high-heeled pumps to join them. Terry was still inside, playing records, but after a while he came to sit with me. 'Why don't you go with them?' I asked him.

'Why don't you?' he said, and then he answered for both of us: 'We're not wanted.'

He spoke bitterly, and no wonder. Last summer, it had been different. Then it had been he and Boy walking on the seashore in the moonlight. But it hadn't been any different for me, because I had still sat here on the porch, watching them.

Only then it had been Mother who was sitting with me, and Mother had been angry, indignant. She said, 'What the hell are you doing, staying with him?' She wanted me to go away with her. She offered to help me pack, and we would both leave and I would stay with her in my own old room in the apartment.

And now Terry was saying, 'I don't know how you stand it, Susie.'

And I said, as I always say to Mother, 'Oh, it's okay. I don't mind.'

But I'm getting tired of people deciding for me what I can stand and what I can't. How do they know? Maybe I like things the way they are. No one ever tells me that it's wrong for me to love Mother for the way she is and not for how she is supposed to be. Then why not Boy – why can't I care for him the way he is?

# GREAT
# EXPECTATIONS

Pauline was a New York real estate agent – middle-aged and comfortably settled. It had taken her many years to reach her present plateau of contentment, also to build up her own business, after having worked for other people. Now she had a tiny office which was almost a store-front – it had been an unsuccessful dry cleaner's before she had rented it and was in a row of other commercial establishments, including a deli, a nail spa, a newsagent, and a jewelry boutique about to go out of business. But Pauline had converted her interior into what was almost a cozy little parlor, with flowers, prints, and little armchairs done up in striped silk. The windows had curtains from inside, but from outside they were plastered with notices offering apartments in terms so attractive that passers-by often stopped to read them, even those who didn't need new accommodation.

However, there were enough people who did to give Pauline a comfortable income and a devoted clientele of her own. She took a very personal interest in her cases – as she humorously called them – and several of them remained her friends after she had accommodated them. These were mostly single women – though, unlike herself, not by choice but as a result of divorce or abortive affairs, so that they were often in need not only of apartments but of solace and friendship.

And of all the needy cases who came to her, Sylvie was the most desperate. It wasn't that she was poor – some of the others were in really tight straits because of unfavourable divorce settlements forced on them by their husbands' lawyers. But Sylvie's husband had remained supportive. Of course, there wasn't only Sylvie to consider but also their daughter Amy. Sylvie and Amy came as a pair, a team: this was how they had first presented themselves in Pauline's office, two waifs in tatty but chic little frocks, so desperately in need of help that they sat in dumb despair, winding locks of their long blond hair around their fingers.

It was Pauline's specialty to know just how to cater to the needs and means of a client. But although Sylvie always said, 'It's lovely, Pauline,' to whatever she showed her, and Amy echoed, 'It's lovely, Pauline,' they never took the place. Something was always somehow wrong; neither of them could say what this was. So they said, 'Lovely,' or 'Fabulous,' or 'Fantastic,' and then looked vague or blank, or miserable at not being able to oblige Pauline by signing a contract.

Yet their situation was hazardous – they really had to have a place, for they were under duress to vacate their present quarters, belonging to a friend who was no longer a friend. 'Mona is so hostile,' Sylvie said and then clamped her lips tight, indicating that she did not want to say anything derogatory about anyone. And even when they were forced out – legal threats were involved – Sylvie still did not utter a word of complaint, but she and Amy came to Pauline's office with their bundles and suitcases, and they sat there, silent and forlorn.

Pauline had no alternative but to take them home to her own apartment. She did not want to at all. Pauline liked – she loved – her privacy, a preference it had taken her many years to achieve. In her youth she had been like everyone else and had craved romance, or at least companionship. When these were not forthcoming, or their promise was blighted, she had slowly come to accept her solitude and self-reliance. These became an absolute necessity after her mother died. Although they had not lived in the same city for years – the mother had remained in Kansas City – Pauline had visited her home-town at least three or four times a year, and they had spoken almost daily on the phone. Pauline had a married brother in Washington, and in the first years after their mother died, she was expected to spend Christmas and Thanksgiving with him and his family. But soon it was only Christmas, and then one year Pauline decided that it was easier to stay home; and after that she spent all her Christmases at home, and usually alone – which she grew actually to like: that was how independent she was.

Sylvie and Amy stayed in her second bedroom. They were very considerate and tried to make themselves useful, which was not easy with someone of Pauline's settled temperament. Pauline didn't like the way they made beds, or washed and put away her dishes, so when she came home in the evenings, she undid everything they had done – rather grimly, for she was tired after her day's work. And she didn't like the way they cooked either – well, it wasn't really cooking, they usually prepared some sort of salad and beans (both of them were vegetarians), so that Pauline had to run down and buy herself a steak. By the time she had cooked and eaten it, she was completely exhausted and in no way inclined to be sociable or even agreeable. She went to bed long before they did – Amy was only ten, but she kept the same hours as her mother; and Pauline could hear them showering together, or laughing at the TV, and though they shushed each other and tried to walk on tiptoe, they kept her awake long after she needed to be asleep.

Still, she endured the situation. As all her friends and acquaintances could testify, she was a good sort who was always glad to help people out in their troubles. Besides, she knew the arrangement was only temporary, and that as soon as she found them a good apartment, she could have hers back again to enjoy in undisturbed comfort. This business of finding them an apartment had become a professional challenge: for whatever she came up with – and she came up with many, many – they continued to find unsuitable for their particular needs. She began to wonder somewhat bitterly how those complicated needs could possibly be satisfied in her spare bedroom: but of course they did have the place to themselves the whole day and could make full use of its many advantages, such as her washer and dryer, which were always full of their panties and T-shirts.

Unfortunately, besides laughing and showering together, they also had fights. Out of deference to her, they tried to keep their voices down, but getting excited, they began to shout and bang doors. They fought like children – well, Amy *was* a child, and Sylvie reacted as if she was, too. They called each other names like stinkbag and went over old grievances, such as when Amy ruined two pairs of Sylvie's jeans with bleach. These fights often ended with Amy stuffing some tu-tus and her fluffy giraffe into a back-pack, saying she was leaving, she was going to her Daddy. However, this did not appear to be feasible, for she soon allowed Sylvie to unpack again and then they both went to sleep, earlier than usual because of being exhausted from their fight.

Pauline had met Amy's Daddy once or twice, when she had come home earlier than expected, and she suspected that he spent more time in her apartment than they wanted her to know. It must have been a convenient place for them, better than strolling around the streets and shops and cafés, which were their other alternatives. This was because Sylvie was not welcome in the place where her ex-husband lived – in his mother's very grand Park Avenue duplex, where Amy went to visit, by herself, every third Sunday.

Sylvie's ex-husband, whose name was Theo, was so much like Sylvie herself, and like their daughter, that Pauline wondered they had not stayed together. They certainly seemed to enjoy one another's company, and when Theo was there, the three of them did the same sort of things Sylvie and Amy did on their own. Theo even looked like them – he was slender and pale and fair-haired; and when he accompanied them to view the apartments that Pauline was hopefully showing them, he reacted with the same 'It's lovely,' and the same unspoken opinion that it was not for them. He was also a vegetarian – in fact, he and Sylvie had met in India, in a guru's ashram where, let alone eggs, not even root vegetables, such as onions and potatoes, were allowed.

*     *     *

On the Sundays when Amy visited her Park Avenue grand-mother, Sylvie was so depressed that Pauline felt obliged to cancel her usual Sunday arrangements and devote herself to Sylvie. But she never succeeded in making her feel better. There was the time when she had taken her for a walk in the Park, hoping to console her among the holiday crowds in spring clothes come out to enjoy the blossoms flying through the air like pink raindrops. Sylvie was in one of her long flowing pastel dresses – a bit faded because of being washed so often – and people looked at her with pleasure: only to look away again at once, shocked to see this embodiment of youthful enchantment in tears. Pauline was embarrassed, as if people were blaming her for her companion's misery. And in a way she felt guilty that it was she who walked beside this girl and not a youth as fine and fair as Sylvie herself: not, that is, someone like Theo – or indeed, Theo himself.

This was the essence of their tragedy: that they could not be together. Every third Sunday Sylvie said it, or hinted at it, in a different way; but she always ascribed the fault to fate, or destiny, or plain bad luck, never blaming their separation on any person. Yet she could, it seemed to Pauline after several of these Sundays, very easily have named Theo's mother as the agent of their malevolent fate – Pauline herself was inclined to do so, after piecing together Sylvie's various hints on the subject. But as soon as Pauline said anything subversive about his mother, Mrs Baum, Sylvie begged her to be silent; she put her hand on Pauline's and said in a gentle voice, 'No, she's Theo's mother; she's a good person.'

'She hasn't been good to you,' Pauline said in her out-spoken way.

Sylvie shook her head and smiled: 'She's good to Theo and to Amy.'

She did not mention the fact – very clear to Pauline by now – that she herself was never invited to accompany Amy, or ever visit the Park Avenue place at all. Gradually Pauline came to realize that Sylvie had not even met Mrs Baum. Yet she always spoke of her with admiration: what a grand lady she was, who gave the most fabulous parties, never for pleasure but always for a good cause or for some cultural purpose, for she sat on many boards – for the opera, and the ballet, and for the educational advancement of disadvantaged youths in the inner city. She was also the chairman of her late husband's company, which was a huge undertaking for a woman alone, so that she needed all the support she could get. And the way things were in the business world, Sylvie said, looking grave as though repeating a thought that was too big for her to handle, you were surrounded by sharks wanting to swallow you and all your assets, and the only people you could trust were your own immediate family.

'That's Theo?' Pauline said.

'She has no one else. No one in the world.'

'What about you?'

But again Sylvie shook her head, smiling: 'Oh, you know how I'm just this airhead.'

Pauline said, 'I don't know anything of the sort.' This was on another Sunday, when they had gone to a museum and were looking at pictures. Pauline's favorites were sunny landscapes with graceful young people walking in them in eighteenth-century clothes. Sylvie didn't seem to have any particular favorites – but she would suddenly be transfixed by a picture and would stand in front of it as in a trance; and when she finally managed to break away, it was evident that she had had a deep experience.

Obviously, under such circumstances, it was not possible for her to look at many pictures, and they often sat out, either in one of the galleries or under the glass roof of the loggia where fountains played and sometimes splashed them with cool drops.

'No, I'm not very bright,' Sylvie said. 'Of course I never had the chance to go to college, though I'd have loved to study something. Painting, or psychology.'

Pauline put out her hand to tuck a loose strand of hair behind Sylvie's ear. 'Oh, you're wet,' she said, feeling her cheek. 'Should we sit somewhere else? I'm getting splashed too.'

'No, I like it, don't you? . . . Maybe Sanskrit. Or religion. I've always been very interested in religion. But I never even finished school. It wasn't my fault,' she said, looking sad, as she usually did when talking of the past, or that part of it.

Pauline had picked up some details of this past on a succession of previous Sundays: Sylvie's difficult childhood with a divorced mother, who had nervous breakdowns and finally died in a psychiatric institution – a private one that had absorbed most of her funds, leaving Sylvie only just enough to take a trip to India in pursuit of an interest in Hindu religion.

'I bet if you had finished school you'd have done something,' Pauline assured her. 'I think you have a lot of talent.'

'Oh really?' Sylvie's interest was stirred enough for her to turn her face and focus her eyes, vague but luminous, on Pauline. 'For what? Or are you just saying it?'

'I mean it. I think you could do anything you put your mind to.'

'You think I could paint?'

'I'm sure . . . And you'd be very good at business too.'

For a moment Sylvie looked at Pauline as if she were crazy. Then she lost interest in her and the subject completely; she turned away her face again and let her eyes wander, filling them with the light filtered through the glass roof and through the springing silver cascades of the fountains.

Pauline, in her anxiety to recapture her attention, became light-headed: 'If you were to come with me in the office, you'd learn the business in no time.'

'Real estate?' Sylvie laughed but was quick to explain: 'I'm laughing at me, not you. I mean, it's so fantastic, me learning real estate.'

'What's fantastic about it? Only you'd have to come in the office with me every day. To see how things are done,' Pauline explained.

There was a moment's silence between them; then Sylvie did turn her face toward Pauline again: 'Are you offering me a job?'

'Yes.' Pauline spoke resolutely, although the thought had never till that moment occurred to her. And she went further – she heard herself offer Sylvie a full-time job in her office, and when Sylvie asked, 'With a salary and all?' she said,

'Oh yes, and commissions. That can work out to a lot of money.'

'How much?' Sylvie said, not so much out of interest as out of courtesy, to keep the conversation going.

'It depends on the sale. For instance, if you were to sell a two-bedroom, two-bathroom in a good location at 450K – but I don't want to confuse you with figures—'

'No, don't. I was never any good at sums. Arithmetic and stuff. Hopeless.'

'You wouldn't have to be. Nowadays, with computers and calculators, you hardly need a brain – I'm not saying you don't have one, Sylvie, on the contrary, I think you're a very intelligent person and that's why I'd like you to come work for me. With me,' Pauline said, like a suitor ready to promise the earth.

'Let's not talk any more now. It's so wonderful just sitting here.' Sylvie raised her face to the glass roof, letting the light stream down on herself. 'It's like being under water. Like we were two mermaids,' although it was only she who looked like one.

They did not mention the subject of Sylvie working in Pauline's office for several days. But Pauline found herself thinking about it more and more – especially in the afternoons, when she suspected, or rather knew, that Theo was with Sylvie in her apartment. What did they do there? She supposed they made love – and yet, it was difficult to think of them doing so, at least not in the way other people did it. There was something otherworldly about them; they seemed to talk to each other on an ethereal level – when they talked at all. Mostly there was a charged silence between them, which neither of them seemed to want to break with anything more substantial than 'Divine, isn't it,' while the other breathed back, 'Out of this world.'

Yet their problems were substantial. They were divorced, for one thing, or separated – Theo's mother had insisted on this, and she had also arranged the settlement, which gave Sylvie nothing more than child support. Sylvie and Theo had had to agree to everything because Theo himself had no money and was completely dependent on his mother. In any case, his mother had suggested that they weren't really married at all – which was ridiculous, as far as Theo and Sylvie were concerned, for no one could have had a more beautiful marriage ceremony. This had been in India, where they had met, in a holy place in the Himalayan foothills, with a holy river running through it. This river was turgid and had all sorts of suspicious things floating in it – the funeral pyres were built on its banks – but nevertheless everyone bathed in it, including Sylvie and Theo. They had first seen each other in this river, at dawn, pouring water over themselves out of brass vessels and praying to the rising sun. As this rose, it suffused part of the river in a pool of light; Theo saw Sylvie standing in such a pool, as if she had just risen out of it and was pouring not water but light over herself.

Sylvie was alone – she had taken a room in the town, in a hotel given over mostly to pilgrims. She ate food in the bazaar, even raw fruits, and never got sick. Theo lived with a guru in an ashram; he had quite a high position there, as one of the guru's right-hand men. But after he met Sylvie, he was no longer so interested in the teaching, although it was what he had come to India for. He put his case to the guru: how it was through their love that he and Sylvie could achieve the ascent to the Good and the Beautiful, which the guru himself taught was the purpose of all human life. The guru was not quite convinced by this interpretation of his own message, but he was sympathetic, and in fact performed the marriage ceremony. This was very beautiful, with all the members of the ashram singing while the guru chanted the benediction and Sylvie and Theo walked around the sacred fire. They were completely covered in flowers, strings of marigold and jasmine hung down over their faces, but nevertheless at the end everyone threw more flowers at them, showering them with fragrant blossoms. After all that, it was ridiculous to say they were not really married.

Pauline became restless, and it got worse every afternoon when she thought of Sylvie alone with Theo in the apartment. One day she decided she had a headache and needed to go home. Unfortunately she had an appointment with a client, which she had to cancel, but that couldn't be helped. She did have her health to consider; and it was just one more proof that her business was simply getting too big for her to handle alone, and she really needed an assistant. She decided to reopen the subject with Sylvie as soon as she got home – but when she did, there was only Amy there, back from school and lying on Pauline's bed, eating corn chips and watching an adult program on TV. Pauline's entrance did not disturb her – she gave her a friendly little wave, then settled herself more comfortably on the white chenille bedcover.

'Where's Sylvie?'

Amy pointed at the screen, indicating that what was going on there precluded conversation. It was only when Pauline insisted that she answered, 'She's out . . . Do you mind?' she said, pointing at the screen again.

'Yes, I do mind.' Pauline was grim: she minded Amy lying on her bed, she minded the greasy corn chips she was scattering over it, and most of all she minded Sylvie not being home. 'Is Theo with her? . . . Where've they gone?' When Amy didn't answer, Pauline turned off the TV.

Amy was silent for a while. Then she said, 'Well. That wasn't very polite.' She spoke with quiet reproach so that Pauline felt a bit ashamed and began to make excuses: 'I don't think it's the sort of program you should be watching. And I have a headache,' she remembered.

'Oh, I'm sorry.'

'Yes. That's why I came home. Why aren't you at school?'

'They sent us home early. Someone died . . . I could give you a head massage. I do it for Sylvie all the time.'

'No thanks. I don't think you should be eating on my bed. Making crumbs.'

'Oh, sorry.' Amy got up at once and made token gestures of brushing off crumbs. 'We have some herbal stuff if you like that, but don't take aspirin whatever you do.'

'Why shouldn't I? . . . Is she with Theo? Where did they go?'

Amy answered only the first question: 'It does horrible things inside your stomach. Toxic things.'

'Oh rubbish, Amy.' Pauline went out impatiently, and Amy followed her, saying, 'I swear to God. It's been proved.'

Pauline sat down heavily on her living-room sofa. She felt disconsolate: to have left her office, canceled and maybe lost her client, and now to be trapped here with Amy. It wasn't that she had anything specifically against Amy: it was really, though she never admitted this, that she didn't like children in general. That had been the trouble with spending Christmas in her brother's home. She had done all she could to make herself liked by his children, bought them expensive presents and so on, but she had heard them making fun of her – she had rather heavy ankles and they told each other that she had elephantiasis and amused themselves with imitating the walk of such a person. It seemed to her that children were cruel, and if you did not measure up to their standard, they despised you. She had several times caught Amy looking at her in a way that told Pauline she was contrasting her with Sylvie.

Pauline looked up now and saw Amy's eyes fixed on her; but it turned out to be with compassion: 'You look awfully sick,' Amy said.

'Yes, that's why I'm home.' And Pauline did feel sick, with disappointment. She said, 'Do you think they're coming back soon?'

'I wouldn't know. There was no one here when I got back. It's not very pleasant for me, to come from school and there's no one here.'

'No. You're right. It's not.' Pauline spoke as a fellow sufferer – though in the past she had enjoyed nothing more than to come home to an empty apartment and be alone there and still.

'Do you want to know how I was born?' Amy said.

Pauline wanted to say no, but instead said, 'If you want,' without encouragement.

'I was born in India,' Amy said.

'What – in that ashram place?'

'Oh no. Theo and Sylvie didn't live there any more – they'd gone up in the mountains to be by themselves in a hut. They didn't have any water or electricity or anything. They washed in a mountain spring.'

Amy was sitting next to Pauline by this time, quite close, as if craving company. 'I'll just do it for a minute, shall I? I'm really good at it but you can tell me to stop if you don't like it. Okay?'

She began to massage Pauline's head. It *was* soothing, although Amy's fingers were a bit greasy, probably from the corn chips. She was so close to Pauline that she was almost sitting in her lap, enveloping her in her smell. Some of this was like Sylvie's – they used the same shampoo and soap – but some of it was peculiar to Amy: natural, in the sense of non-artificial, also somewhat dewy and damp like the wool of a lamb that had been out in the rain.

'So were you born in this hut?'

'Sylvie wanted to stay, but with there being no doctor or anyone near, Theo took her down to the town – it was a holy town called Hardwar so that was all right. And they say I was so good I just waited till they had gotten her in this hospital and then guess what? I came out so fast they said it was like kittens coming out of a mother cat so we needn't have been in the hospital at all and I could have been born in the hut.'

Amy had now climbed right into Pauline's lap – this was in order to press her fingertips against Pauline's brow. It was simultaneously soothing and disturbing: Pauline was really not used to having anyone sit in her lap and touch her face so intimately.

'But then we did go back to the hut, Sylvie and Theo and I, and they were so crazy about me they couldn't stop looking at me and they'd get up at night and *wake* me up, just so they could play with me some more and count my fingers and toes.'

'Do you remember all this?'

'They told me but I think I remember it too. I *think*. I was only seven months old when we left. It was snowing all the time and they couldn't find any more firewood. Anyway, by that time Granny had found out and we had to leave. Leave

India, that is, and go to New York. Because of Granny. Are you feeling better now?'

'Yes, I think so. Thank you very much, Amy.'

'I do it well, don't I? Sylvie likes me doing it even when she doesn't have a headache. She's very sensuous, Theo says.'

Late that night Amy and Sylvie had one of their fights. Pauline, who was already in bed, propped herself on her elbow to listen, but they were showering together so most of what they said was drowned by the sound of the water. Next morning was as usual a big rush, with Sylvie having to take Amy to school. When she returned from this mission – for which she had merely thrown a raincoat over her nightdress, which anyway wasn't much different from her usual kind of frock – she went straight back to bed. This too was her custom, so that she was always asleep by the time Pauline left for her office. But today Pauline wouldn't let her; she followed her into the bedroom and said, 'We have to talk.'

Although warm and nestled between her sheets, Sylvie roused herself to face a serious and perhaps not unfamiliar situation: 'I know, I know – and I swear wc'll go the moment we find a place, I promise.'

'It's not that,' Pauline said. 'It's not that at all.' She was silent – not that there were no questions to ask but that there were too many. For instance: where had Sylvie gone yesterday with Theo? What had they fought about, she and Amy? Instead, when Pauline spoke, it was to say: 'What I asked you the other day? In the museum?' When Sylvie looked puzzled – 'Because I really do need someone, and if you can't do it or would rather not . . .' And still receiving no answer, Pauline worked herself up a bit: 'When someone offers you a job, the least you can do is say yes or no. I mean, it would just be common courtesy.'

'Oh Pauline. I never thought for a minute you were serious.'

'Why wouldn't I be?'

'It's such a terrific compliment – to think anyone would think *me* capable of a *job*. When I told Theo, he laughed and laughed.'

'Who's he to laugh? What's he ever done for you except come around here to my place in the afternoons or whatever – where did you go yesterday? Where were you when poor Amy was sent home from school and no one here to meet her? I think that's shocking. Absolutely shocking.'

Sylvie hung her head and plucked at the satin hem of the bedsheet. It was not possible to tell whether she was ashamed or offended.

For fear it might be the latter, Pauline went on: 'I know it's none of my business but I'm so fond of you both, you and Amy.'

'You've been an angel to us, dearest Pauline. You *are* an angel.'

'Well, you see, I love you.'

'Of course you do,' Sylvie said. 'And we love you. Very, very much,' she added, but this, for Pauline, only made her reply less satisfactory.

Although Pauline felt herself so overwhelmed with work that she was ready to hire an assistant, a few days later she again shut her office early and went home. This time she found what she expected – Sylvie was there, and Theo was with her. Pauline could hear them splashing in the bathroom, but when she opened the door, she quickly shut it again. Theo was washing Sylvie's hair; she had her head bent over the basin while he massaged soap-suds into it; both were naked. But when they came out, Theo had wrapped a towel around his waist and Sylvie was in a white bathrobe. They looked like twins.

'What a surprise,' Theo said, referring to Pauline's unexpected arrival; he made it sound like a joyous surprise.

'Yes, well, you see, I have to talk to Sylvie on a very important matter.'

Theo was rueful: 'I'm afraid I can guess what it is, and I promise you that the minute we've found a halfway nice place we're going to move out and meanwhile I cannot tell you how terrifically grateful we all are to you, aren't we, Sylvie? Do stop that and listen to Pauline,' for Sylvie was vigorously rubbing her hair with a towel.

'But it's all *wet*,' Sylvie protested. 'I'll drip on her rug and ruin it.'

Theo said, 'Oh you mustn't. It's such a pretty rug.' He looked down at it and Pauline could tell from the politely sweet expression on his face that he didn't think so at all. She had had the same impression before when she had encountered Theo in her apartment. Although she had taken a lot of trouble with her furniture and fittings – matching colors and so on – in his presence everything appeared drab, lower-class.

Ignoring him, she addressed herself only to Sylvie: 'You still haven't given me an answer – I don't think you realize how important it is, important for the business, that is, for me to have a proper assistant.'

'You're talking about the job you offered her, and that again I must say shows your incredible kindness.'

Pauline said, 'I hear it made you laugh no end.'

'Made *me* laugh—?' Unable to believe that he might be the person referred to, he put both his hands on his chest. His chest was naked, giving him an almost mythological appearance. He looked as if he might be living in a forest and carrying a bow and arrow, not to shoot down birds or other living creatures but apples from a tree for Sylvie to eat.

Theo had turned to Sylvie: 'Did you tell Pauline that I laughed?' Sylvie began to defend herself, they argued with each other, softly, sweetly, while Pauline stood by. She realized that it was hopeless to try to intervene – they would only have listened to her politely and then turned back to each other. She could not come between them, no one could; perhaps not even Amy.

Amy turned out to be receptive to the idea of Sylvie taking a job. She at once asked Pauline, 'What'll you pay her?'

Sylvie said, 'Amy, that's vulgar.'

'No it's not,' Pauline said. 'It's realistic.'

She was relieved to have been able to return to the topic in Amy's presence and away from what she could not help feeling was Theo's negative influence. But Sylvie still seemed to be under the latter: 'We don't need money,' she told Amy.

'Yes we do. We need heaps.'

'What for?'

'You know very well what for,' Amy said.

She and Sylvie exchanged a conspiratorial look that excluded Pauline. Yet Pauline too wanted to ask, what could they possibly need money for? It was not in her present interest to point out that they lived rent-free, or that she paid their grocery bills – though it was true that these had hardly increased since they had moved in with her. Their vegetarian diet of cereals and pulses was as frugal as if they had been living on bird seed.

Sylvie said, 'Theo gives us whatever we need.'

'Theo doesn't have anything to give,' Amy said.

'He will though,' Sylvie said with quiet confidence.

'Not till Grandma dies. Which she won't.' Amy raised her voice to defend her facts: 'She's terribly healthy and she has all these doctors giving her vitamin injections and all these people coming in doing massage and things on her and you know she goes swimming every afternoon because that's the only time Theo ever gets to come visit you.'

'That's not true,' Sylvie said.

'It is so! *And* she plays tennis but Theo can't get away then in case she needs him for a partner.'

'You'll have to forgive Amy,' Sylvie turned to Pauline. 'Sometimes she just doesn't know what she's talking about. No you don't! You're a silly brat, that's all.'

'*I'*m a silly brat, look who's talking. *I'*m the only one who earns any money. And I give you all my pocket money from Grandma to put in our savings and you haven't put in one single dime.'

'I haven't got one single dime.'

'Then why don't you take Pauline's job! She'll pay you—'

Pauline gladly said, 'Of course I will.' But when Amy at once came back with 'How much?' she became more cautious. She said to Sylvie, 'You'd be on a starting salary at first, but later of course when you really know the business—'

'How long would that take?' Amy asked. 'Because we haven't got very long. *You* think we have,' she turned again on Sylvie, 'but I'm not going to that shitty school forever or stick around here when you *promised* – you *promised*—'

'Amy, shush, darling, it's our secret.'

'Don't *pinch* me.' But Amy bit in her lips so that no further words should escape her, not even in answer to Sylvie's 'I did *not*.'

Next day Pauline lost another client. Unfortunately it was one whom she had been nurturing for several months, for a bigger sale than usually came her way – a converted brownstone in the East Fifties, and Pauline had made an appointment to meet her client there for what she hoped was a final and decisive viewing. But just as she was about to leave on this mission, Theo came into the office. 'Can we talk?' he said to Pauline after a pleasant greeting. When she hesitated, 'You're busy. A pity, but never mind. That's just our bad luck. Sylvie's and mine.'

Pauline hesitated again, but not for long. She dialed her client's number and left a message on the machine to postpone the meeting by an hour. Then she allowed Theo to lead her away. Although this was her neighborhood and not his, he knew exactly where to take her. It was not a place she would have chosen herself – a stone garden created between mammoth buildings with an artificial waterfall trained to run down a brick wall.

'Isn't this fun,' said Theo, bringing two styrofoam cups of coffee from the refreshment window, and also, in case one of them felt hungry, a Danish in plastic wrap. There were only a few elderly people sitting around, some reading the newspaper, some dozing, one or two staring straight into the waterfall but probably seeing other things. The chairs were white metal, small and uncomfortable with criss-cross seats like egg-slicers.

Theo said, 'I shall have to take them away.' For a moment Pauline didn't know what he was talking about, and when she realized, she cried out much too loudly, 'You're crazy!'

He smiled sadly: 'It is a shame.' Then he assured her: 'You're not to blame. You meant well, but things don't always turn out the way we intend.'

'And may I ask,' she said, 'what is it that hasn't worked out?'

He gestured into the air, indicating that the matter was too delicate to be put into words. But she wanted words and didn't care if she appeared crude and indelicate. She felt that way anyhow, in his presence. She was dressed in a very good business suit, with a blouse that had cost her a good deal of money, but beside him – though all he wore was jeans and a shirt – she felt badly dressed. It couldn't be helped; she was what she was; so she repeated her question.

He was courteous and tried to give her a fair answer. He said, 'You see, we have to be careful. Amy's very high-strung.'

'Amy? What have I done to Amy?'

'Please. I said it wasn't your fault. But once Amy gets something in her head, it's one hell of a thing to get it out again. It was a mistake, you know,' he said. 'Asking Sylvie to work for you. You know Sylvie better than that. She can't. She wouldn't be able to.'

Pauline swallowed – controlling her rising anger for the sake of a higher good. 'I thought she might like to; to give her something to do; pass the time while Amy's at school and you're with your mother.' When he made no response, she went on – quickly, before the subject could be considered closed: 'But of course it was only an idea. She doesn't have to at all, and we'll just go on as before.'

'Yes, but now there's Amy.'

'What does Amy *want*?'

'Amy wants money. Ridiculous child.' He smiled.

Drops of water fell on them from the artificial waterfall. It reminded her of sitting with Sylvie by the museum fountain. Why should they have this association with water, with cool crystal drops, as though their place were by the side of a mountain spring? In spite of his clear eyes, his graceful figure as of a young hunter, he did not at this moment give her the impression of purity; on the contrary.

'That's why I have to take them away,' he said. 'But don't you have to meet someone? Your client?'

She gave a start. She had truly forgotten. But now she said, 'It doesn't matter.'

'Oh but it does. You mustn't neglect your business – certainly not on our account. You want all the money you can get. Everyone does.'

'Including Amy?'

'Amy wants it so badly that she's willing to send poor Sylvie to do a job she's absolutely not fit for. Not physically, not temperamentally, not in any way. I know you acted from the noblest motives – out of love and affection for us – but I wish you hadn't started this whole thing. Now Amy can think of nothing but money, a salary, all that.'

Pauline pleaded: 'It wouldn't be very hard work.'

'I'm sure not, but unfortunately Sylvie's not capable of any work.'

'She could stay home. It wouldn't be any different from what it is now.'

'You mean you'd pay her a salary for staying home? Only for staying with you? . . . You really are a saint. An angel.' In gratitude, he undid the Danish for her from its plastic wrap, but then advised her not to eat it as it was stale.

For the past few years Pauline had considered herself comfortably off. She had built up her business and was able to pay herself a good salary out of it. But now, after losing several clients – she told herself the market was bad – her income was declining. This was especially unfortunate now that she had begun to pay Sylvie a salary, which, after negotiation with Theo, turned out to be almost as high as her own. Often there was nothing at all going on in her office, so that on several afternoons she had just locked up and gone home. She always went hopefully, but when she arrived, Sylvie was either not there, or she and Theo were together in the second bedroom where Pauline could not disturb them. She didn't even let them know she was there but tiptoed out again and went to a movie she had no particular desire to see. At such times, she remembered other home-comings, evenings in the past before they had moved in with her, when, after a long busy day in the office, she had lain on the sofa in her old wrap with a gin martini she had mixed for herself, savoring her silence, her solitude, her peace. Now she had no peace – whether they were home or not home. She didn't even have it when she was away from them, in the office or alone at the cinema, because of thinking about them all the time, wondering where they were, what they were doing; wanting to be with them.

But even when she was with them, she still found herself alone. Sylvie and Amy always seemed to have so much to do – their laundry, Amy's homework, cooking their gruel which needed hours of stirring – and also so much to discuss, arguing and, more and more nowadays, fighting with each other. They continued to be careful to keep their voices down, so that she could never make out what they were saying, however hard she strained to do so. And that was all she was capable of doing now – straining to hear what they were saying, to discover what they might be up to. It had become impossible for her to concentrate on anything else, like her accounts or a book. If some old friend telephoned, she hardly had time to talk, she was so afraid of missing something going on between Sylvie and Amy.

More than anything, Pauline looked forward to the Sundays when Amy was away at her grandmother's and she could have Sylvie to herself. But on each of these Sundays Sylvie became progressively more miserable. She sat hunched in a corner of the sofa, twisting a strand of hair between her fingers, and staring ahead with large scared eyes. If Pauline suggested one of their usual outings, she declined – terribly politely, the more remote she was the more polite. She said Theo or Amy might telephone and she didn't want to miss their call. They never did; and when, perhaps desperate with waiting, she herself dialed their number, she put the receiver down before anyone could answer. 'They don't want to be disturbed,' she explained; once she said, 'His mother doesn't like me to phone.'

The resigned way she said this angered Pauline: 'How long are you going to stand for this?'

'What can I do?' Sylvie said. 'We have no money. Only she has.'

'And what I give you? Your salary?'

'You're so kind, Pauline,' Sylvie said, courteously acknowledging what could only be considered a mere trifle.

Pauline bit her lip – to her it was not a trifle at all; in fact, the way things were, she had difficulty paying it. But she longed to be able to say that she would increase the amount, that she would give Sylvie as much as she wanted – suddenly she said, 'You know everything that's mine is yours;' but she blushed scarlet and was breathless, as if this statement had been literally wrung out of her.

'I do know it,' Sylvie said with sincere gratitude. 'We're such a burden on you, Pauline – yes we are – but I promise you it's only for now. Like Theo says, we only have to wait.'

'Wait for what? For his mother to die – that's what you're waiting for, don't tell me.' Sylvie hung her head in shame, so that Pauline's heart was filled with pity and she said, 'We don't *need* Theo's mother.'

Sylvie raised her head and stared at Pauline: 'Who's we?'

'You and I – and Amy of course.'

Pauline waited for her, expected her to say, 'And Theo?' But she did not. His name may have hung in the air, but it was not spoken. Pauline welcomed this silence, which she interpreted to her own advantage.

By the first of the next month, Pauline found herself in trouble. Her rent was due for the office, her maintenance for the apartment, she had to have her own salary and the amount she had agreed to pay Sylvie. She did not know where anything was to come from; she had made no deals for the past four months and the business account had run very low. She considered all the payments essential except her own; and for this latter, to cover her domestic expenses, she was forced for the first time to break into her savings. She did so with a heavy heart. Her savings were sacrosanct to her, they were her future, her freedom from friends, family, from all the world except herself; they were the ground on which she stood. However, for one month it wouldn't matter; she would try not to spend more than was necessary to keep their household going. It was easy to do without a new summer outfit, and also she wouldn't be taking her usual vacation in the Berkshires this year. She always stayed in a good hotel, which she could afford on her own but would be excessive for three of them – that is, if Sylvie and Amy would consent to accompany her, which they probably wouldn't. And she knew that, without them, she would not be able to derive her usual joy and consolation from her holiday, her solitary walks in the cool woods, her morning coffee under a maple tree on the summery green grounds of the hotel.

Two months later, there were still no deals, and the office account had reached an all-time low. By taking an overdraft, she might just be able to squeeze out the rent and the maintenance, but the salaries, hers and Sylvie's, would again have to come out of savings. She had already taken a substantial cut in her own salary; and she was now trying to broach the subject of a possible reduction in Sylvie's too. 'Only for this month,' she was planning to plead. 'Only till the next deal comes through.'

To say this, she had waited for the Sunday of Amy's visit to her grandmother. But Sylvie was so edgy – waiting for the phone to ring, dialing and then putting down the receiver – that Pauline could not find an opportunity all day. In the evening Amy returned in a very bad mood. Although she handed over her pocket money as usual, she did not spread out her presents for Sylvie to see but locked herself into the second bedroom, so that Sylvie had to stand outside, calling softly for admittance.

Pauline said, 'What's the matter?' And when Sylvie parted her lips so that her teeth showed in a smile indicating everything was fine, she went on, 'Then why has she locked herself in?'

'Oh you know,' Sylvie said with the same smile.

'I wish I did,' Pauline said.

Sylvie moved away from the door. She arranged a flower in a vase, then patted a cushion or two, to show how happy and comfortable she was here with Pauline in the apartment. But soon she was back by the bedroom door, calling through it, 'Let me *in*,' in a way that made Amy open the door, though only just enough for Sylvie to slip in.

Pauline stooped to put her ear against the keyhole; she felt she had to do it, low and mean though she considered it to be, for the sake of their future. But soon she didn't have to listen at the keyhole, their voices rose enough for her to hear. And then they screeched in such a way that Pauline felt compelled to thump on the door, and when they failed to answer, she tried the handle – it was unlocked, the door flew open, and the two stood revealed, each tugging at a hank of the other's long blond hair.

Pauline rushed between them, and though herself receiving some pinches and slaps, managed to separate them. They stood on either side of her, looking away from one another, both of them flushed and pouting with angry self-righteousness. And to Pauline's repeated inquiry of what had happened, each tilted her chin in the other's direction: 'Ask *her*.'

'Yes, ask her,' Sylvie said at last. 'Ask her why she's so mean and horrible.'

'I'm not giving it,' Amy said. She glared at Sylvie and Sylvie looked back at her with the same face. Amy said, 'All you ever do is give it to him! And he just keeps it for himself.'

'Oh wicked, wicked,' Sylvie said, bating her breath at so much wickedness.

'Then what's he do with it? Why doesn't he do what he promised for ages and ages? With my money and with what Pauline gives you?' And in response to Sylvie's shushing sound, she stamped her foot and cried, 'I don't want to have a secret any more!' Tears of rage were in her eyes.

'I'm sorry, darling,' Sylvie said. 'I've upset you. It's my fault.' To Pauline she said, 'I keep forgetting she's only a child.'

'You always say that when I want something you don't want!' Amy brushed at her cheeks, ashamed of the tears that had begun to roll and were of sorrow now more than rage.

Sylvie started forward to embrace and comfort her. But Pauline remained between them; she even stuck her elbow out to prevent Sylvie from approaching Amy. And it was Pauline herself who embraced Amy and encouraged her to bury her face in Pauline's bosom. She pressed Amy's head against herself so that she could not raise it to meet Sylvie's imploring gaze.

                    *        *        *

Most afternoons, since Sylvie was busy with Theo at that time, Amy was brought home in a car pool; but on that following day Pauline again shut her office early and waited for Amy outside the school. Amy's mood was still sullen; she hardly greeted Pauline and walked beside her, kicking at the sidewalk. But Pauline had a treat in mind for her. She took her to a palatial new hotel with a lobby that was all gold and glass and flowers in purple vases as tall as Amy. The tea-room was upstairs, reached by a curving carpeted staircase, and it made Amy gasp at its beauty. Golden angels floated in a sea of glass and crystal; they played lyres and wore garlands of plaster of Paris fruits and flowers wound around their ankles. Although the lyres were inaudible, celestial sounds came from a lady harpsichordist in a chiffon gown. The waiters were handsome and dressed as for a wedding; one of them held Amy's chair for her, but before daring to sit on it, she whispered to Pauline: 'Do you think I'm okay?' She was in her uniform and was rather grimy from a day of working and playing at school.

'You're fine,' Pauline assured her. She had never seen Amy's eyes shining so brightly.

'Wouldn't Sylvie love it here,' Amy said, looking around with those eyes.

'Yes, I wish she were with us. But I guess she's with Theo.' Pauline watched the brightness fall from Amy's face. But Pauline pressed on: 'They're together every afternoon, aren't they, when you're at school and I'm in the office. Do you think they have a lot of secrets they don't want us to know about?'

'They've got one secret and I know about it.'

'I don't,' Pauline said.

A waiter smilingly held out a silver tray of little sandwiches to Amy who took one in a very refined way and said, 'Thank you,' in the same way. Pauline encouraged her, 'Take more than that, they're so tiny.' Amy did so – it was a ham sandwich, but Pauline did not tell her.

'I don't think it's nice when people have secrets from their friends,' Pauline said. 'I think friends should tell each other everything.'

'Yes, but if they've promised their other friends that they

wouldn't—' Amy frowned as one trying to grasp and state a metaphysical problem.

Pauline said, 'Oh of course, no one must ever break a promise.'

Amy frowned more: 'But what if they break *their* promise . . .'

'I'm sure they wouldn't. What are you doing?' For Amy was taking the tops off her remaining sandwiches to examine the contents.

'I want one like the pink one I ate. What was it?'

'I think it was tomato. Take mine.' Pauline put her own ham sandwich on Amy's plate. She said, 'They love you too much ever to break a promise they've made you.'

'That's what you think.' Amy chewed; she brooded; she appeared tempted to say more. Pauline sipped her tea, seemingly indifferent, enjoying the harpsichord music, and Amy gave in to temptation: 'They've promised and promised and they still haven't done it.'

'Haven't done what? But if you tell me, you'll be giving away the secret and you mustn't. You know what? I'll tell *you* a secret, but will you promise not to tell *them*? All right: the sandwich you ate? The two sandwiches? They were ham.'

'What's ham?'

'It's meat. It's meat from a pig.'

The harpsichord, sweet and mellifluous, played into the silence between them. At last Amy said, 'So what. I don't care. I liked it. I can eat meat if I want.'

'Yes, but they don't want you to.'

'Only because of going there. They say when we're there we can only eat fruit and nuts and everything pure like that . . . In India, in the hut where we lived when I was born. They said we're going there as soon as we've gotten enough money, and I've given them my pocket money for years and years and you're giving them money and we're still here. Ask him if he has another sandwich like that. I'll eat all the ham I want and I'll tell them and they can do what they like.'

'You said you wouldn't tell. You promised,' Pauline reminded her.

But it seemed Amy no longer believed in promises. She told

Sylvie that same evening, and went on, 'And I'm going to eat steak too like Pauline and hot dogs and hamburgers and stuff like everyone else eats every day.'

'You know what that means,' Sylvie said in a warning voice.

'Oh sure, yeah. It means I can't go to India with you.' And when Sylvie shot a look in Pauline's direction – 'She knows. I told her. And I told her how you're not going anyway like you said and all you do is take my money and her money and give it to Theo.'

Sylvie, a hunted doe, glanced around wildly, wondering where help was to be found. Amy's arms were crossed defiantly; she remained adamant. But Pauline, touched by Sylvie's pale distress, said: 'He's probably keeping it in a savings account for you to earn interest so you'll have more money.'

'Yes, more money for him,' Amy replied.

Sylvie pleaded, 'And for you and for me. So we can go.'

'He doesn't want to go,' Amy said. 'He likes being here with Granny. You don't know, you haven't ever seen them! He's always messing around with her silver and stuff and those pictures she has like that stupid Picasso that's supposed to be such a big deal.'

'It is a big deal, Amy,' Sylvie said. 'And one day it'll all belong to Theo and to you and to me.'

'But I keep telling you! You can wait till you're a hundred thousand years old and she still won't be dead, she'll be swimming in her swimsuit from Bendel's and it's you who'll be old and die. You'll die and leave me,' Amy ended very differently from how she had begun.

And in response Sylvie too changed: 'I'll never leave you,' she said, utterly confident, scornful of any such idea.

Next day, while Pauline was sitting idle in her idle office, she was surprised by a visit from Sylvie. Sylvie was in a long buttercup yellow dress and a straw hat with a buttercup yellow ribbon. Involuntarily, Pauline rose in her chair, and then found herself blushing: she didn't know if it was in embarrassment or from the tide of warmth that surged out of her heart and suffused her.

But Sylvie at once said, 'Why did you give her ham to eat? And telling her it was tomato.'

Although this was an accusation, Sylvie spoke as usual in a mild voice; and Pauline lowered her own rather harsh one to ask, also mildly, 'Does it matter so very much?'

'It's a principle, Pauline.' Sylvie looked around her: 'It's different in here.'

It was different. The pretty striped armchairs appeared to be dusty; a bulb had gone out on one of the Chinese vase table-lamps, leaving it to the other one to light up the rather dim interior.

'Is it?' Pauline looked around abstractedly. 'No, it's just the same . . . Whose principle is this? Is it Amy's?'

'In a way . . . When she was born, she was – I can't tell you – so shiny white, it was like you could look through her, like she was an angel. We said, we must give her nothing but angel food – it was a joke really, but we were eating very simple food ourselves, so my milk I was giving her came out as pure and white as she was . . . I don't know what she eats at school; what the other girls give her. Children always want to do the same as everyone else. If only we could get her away.'

'She wants to go, more than anything.' Pauline leaned across her desk: 'But do you want to?'

'Of course. That's what we're saving for, putting everything away . . . That reminds me.' She was embarrassed; so was Pauline: it was past the beginning of the month and she had not yet paid Sylvie. 'I'm sorry to ask you,' Sylvie said, acutely apologetic, 'but it's important for us.'

'No, I'm glad you did because I was going to mention it myself . . . I was going to ask you if you would mind very much waiting maybe till the middle of the month, or when I get paid for something I'm putting through now.'

Sylvie tried the switch of the table lamp; but the bulb really was dead, and moreover when she withdrew her hand, it was dusty. 'Don't you think, Pauline, you should – maybe – you know – a little bit, so it would look nice for clients who come in.'

'What clients?' This escaped Pauline, with bitterness, before she could stop herself.

'Why, Pauline, you've got hundreds of clients! And you just said there's a big deal coming through in the middle of the month – not that I care about getting paid, if you can't you can't, I mean *I* would be happy to wait—'

'But Theo wouldn't?'

Sylvie leaned back in her chair with a sigh. It was so difficult to explain, but she tried. 'There's two things. One is that Theo is really quite businesslike, he doesn't look it but it's the sort of family he comes from and that's how they've made a lot of money. It's sort of in his genes.'

'And the other thing?'

'The other thing is Amy and I. He's doing it for us, saving and so on. So he can take us away. Well! Aren't you sick and tired of us, even though you are a saint, you must be counting the days till we move out.'

'And will he take you where Amy wants to go?'

Sylvie smiled, her sad smile, as at something too desirable to be possible.

'Because if he doesn't, I will.'

Pauline hadn't thought she was going to say this – she hadn't thought of it at all – but now suddenly it was there: a possibility, something she could do, something not fantastic but within her reach. Too excited to stay still, she got up: 'Let's go home,' she said. It was Sylvie who protested it was only the middle of the afternoon, that a client might come: Pauline turned off the one remaining lamp and then shut the office door behind them and padlocked it.

And next day she did not reopen it. She had too much to do. She had spent the previous evening elaborating her idea, explaining it to Amy, talking it over with her and Sylvie. Amy was wild with enthusiasm, and between them they swept Sylvie along. Pauline conclusively proved to them that it was something that could be achieved within a short time. All Pauline had to do was dissolve her savings and her pension fund; and she could sell her apartment, or rent it out furnished, and maybe she could sell her business too, to some big company, and if she couldn't, she would just lock up and go away; at least she would be saving the overdue rent on it, and the landlords could do what they liked. She became light-headed, she was so busy proving to them that Theo was not the only one who was practical.

First thing in the morning, she started phoning around the airlines, to get a price on fares; from there on they could work out the rest of their budget. Amy wanted to stay home from school to help her – anyway, she argued, what was the use of continuing with school now? Pauline helped Sylvie persuade her to leave; though afterward she wished she were back again because, without Amy there to prop her up, Sylvie began to falter. She kept biting her underlip and saying, 'Are you sure it's all right, Pauline, that you want to do this?' until Pauline, in between her telephone calls, replied, 'I've never been so sure of anything in my life.' And truly it seemed to her that she had shaken off the burden of her past and her personality – and was ready to step out unencumbered into a new world of freedom and light.

However, this mood vanished when Theo appeared in the afternoon. It was left to Pauline to tell him of their plan while Sylvie sat by, biting her lip. When Pauline had finished, Theo laughed; and then Sylvie laughed too, though glancing nervously at Pauline.

'Yes, isn't it a hoot,' Pauline said to him. 'You've kept them hanging with your promises for years together, and when I come in, it's all done within hours. Here are the figures: an economy couple ticket for Sylvie and me, and half-fare for Amy because she's under twelve.' She held out the yellow pad on which she had been scribbling all morning.

Theo peered at it, as if he were near-sighted, which he was not. He said, 'Yes, you've got it all worked out.' He looked up and at Sylvie: 'Pauline's got it all worked out, for you and Amy and herself . . . I'd like to come, I really would,' he said to Pauline. 'But I do have obligations here – unfortunately one can't just pack up and leave and turn his back on everything. Sylvie understands that.' He put his arm around Sylvie's shoulders and looked apologetically at Pauline.

Again it struck Pauline how alike they looked, like twins, a boy and a girl – though from another planet, a different one from Pauline's. But she spoke up courageously, as if there were hope of communication: 'Does Amy understand? You've been promising her since the day she was born, almost.'

Theo said, 'If you promise a child Santa Claus, you're not exactly obliged to deliver him on Christmas Day.'

'So that's all it is: Santa Claus.' Pauline looked toward Sylvie, not hopefully, not really expecting help.

Sylvie spoke gently to her, as if she felt sorry for her and wanted to explain things: 'Without Theo, it's only a hut on a hillside, and anyway it's probably fallen down by now.'

'We can always find another hut,' Pauline said.

'But why should you? When you've got this nice apartment—' Theo looked around, the way he always did, with that set smile that told Pauline what he really thought of her modest little interior. 'Two bedrooms, and everything so cozy and tasteful, not to speak of your office—'

'Pauline doesn't want to keep her office,' Sylvie told him. 'She says she owes the rent and is not making any money.'

'Oh?' Theo said.

'She says she can't pay me anything this month,' Sylvie said.

'Of course I can!' pauline had jumped up. 'And next month I'll be able to give you more, there's some big deals coming up.' She waved Sylvie away impatiently before she could even speak. 'You don't think I would ever give up my office, turn my back on it, just pack up and leave? That's not the way I was brought up.' She was going to say more, but Theo put up his hand in warning. They all three listened to the key turn in the lock of the front door – it was Amy, delivered by her car pool, letting herself in.

'Don't tell her,' Sylvie whispered. She held out her hand for the yellow pad Pauline was holding and looked around for somewhere to hide it. Theo took it from her and slid it inside the back of Pauline's sofa. Then all three turned to face the door with that false smile of adults who have promised children something that they have no intention of delivering. Only Pauline had difficulty keeping up her smile: for Amy entered with a radiance of expectation that Pauline, settling for a lesser good, had only just managed to extinguish within herself.

# PARASITES

Paul opened the door of the brownstone, and Dora asked, 'How is she?'

'Stella's fine! Great!' Stella called in a stentorian voice from the stairs.

Actually – she knew it, everyone knew it – she was dying. The doctors had said six months. So when she claimed to be fine and great, Dora, her niece, looked wry. She went into the drawing room, and in the few moments before Stella could get down the stairs, Paul said to Dora, 'She really has been all right – not bad at all!'

'Guess who's here, upstairs,' Stella said to Dora, smiling to herself with pleasure.

Dora couldn't guess who it was, and Paul didn't give her any help. He was very busy dusting some of Stella's treasures – her Mogul box, her Wedgwood bowl – doing it carefully and with pursed mouth, like a dutiful servant. He tended to turn himself into a servant whenever he wanted no part in something, and no one could object to that, because, as a matter of fact, he *was* paid for his services.

'It's Annette,' Stella said finally. She stretched out one stout leg to the small fire in the fireplace and smiled down at it, still with that same mysterious pleasure.

Paul continued dusting, giving no help to Dora, nor did he look up when Annette herself came in.

'Dora, darling!' cried Annette, in a rather high, shrieky voice. 'All grown up! A real big grown-up lovely girl!' She seized both of Dora's hands and looked up into her face with dancing black eyes.

Annette was small, smart, and animated; Dora rather stringy, somewhat dowdy. When Annette called her a lovely grown-up girl and looked at her with those amused eyes, Dora knew that she was really thinking something quite different. She disengaged her hands from Annette's tiny, plump, warm ones as soon as she could.

But Stella was so obviously pleased at this meeting, at having her favorite niece and her favorite friend (not to mention dear Paul) under her roof at the same time, that they all knew they would have to make the best of it.

Annette, in any case, did not have to pretend to be pleased to be there; she really was. She loved Stella's house. It was a heavy, five-story brownstone in Murray Hill, with a broad, old-fashioned front stoop, and brass railings that ran up the stone banisters. Although in recent years the neighborhood had grown shabby and decayed, Stella's house had retained its well-kept appearance. Inside as well as outside, it was as polished, as prosperous, as comfortable as it had ever been. Stella did not stint on her living arrangements, and Annette knew how to enjoy them to the brim. Nor did Annette hesitate to make full use of Paul's services, since these happened to be available. After all, she might have argued, that was what he was being paid for – to cook and clean and look after Stella and her guests.

Dora had an apartment of her own, and also a job to go to, in the conservation department of a small museum, but she came every day to see her aunt. And every day she saw that Annette had dug herself in a little deeper. Paul and Dora realized that Annette had come to stay till the end – till Stella's end.

Dora's mother had phoned often from the Vineyard, where she now lived year-round, to ask about her sister Stella. 'Should I come?' she asked. 'Does she want me?'

'Not yet,' Dora kept saying.

Dora's mother was much disturbed by Annette's presence in the house. It had been enough, she felt, with just Paul there, but now this other one as well . . . The whole family, all Stella's relatives, were upset. The only counterbalance was the presence of Dora, and for the first time the family really appreciated her and no longer thought of her (in contrast to her successful, married cousins) as poor Dora.

Apart from Dora, Stella had never cared for her family. She had gone her own way and made her own friends. These had always included one special friend – usually someone like Annette, many years younger than herself. Before Annette, there had been a German woman called Lisa, and before Lisa various other women, almost all of them Europeans of assorted nationalities (though once there was an Indian girl, a great beauty). But after Annette left her, eight years ago – walked out on her, actually – Stella did not make any more special friends. Perhaps she felt too old by then, perhaps she had been disappointed too many times. Also, her illness (though at that time undiagnosed – indeed, unsuspected) may have begun secretly to undermine her. In those years, the person she drew closest to was Paul, who had been a waiter in an expensive and fashionable hotel restaurant that she frequented. He left that job when she invited him to come and live with her. Although he was quite a young man – about Dora's age – Paul was extremely responsible and took good care of her, and of her house and possessions, which he loved passionately. Between him and Dora, she had all the company she needed in these last years, and she had seemed more contented than she had ever been before.

Nevertheless, she had sent word for Annette to come back again. 'As soon as I got the letter,' Annette told Dora, 'I gave up everything and came at once. At once,' she added, satisfied at her own behavior. She did not specify what it was she had given up. She had been living in London, and she also didn't specify what she had been doing there. But that was typical of Annette – the details of her life were always left vague, a subject for the speculations of anyone who cared to speculate. But she herself was a very definite little person.

She told Paul, 'I came because she needed me.' Paul didn't ask why Stella should have needed Annette, when he himself was there. Paul was a disciplined young man, and he did not allow himself to ask questions that people might not wish to answer. Instead, he tightened his face and busied himself with household tasks; there was always something to do around the house, and he did it. His discipline was partly that of a conscientious servant and partly of a military officer – not that he had been in the army, but he was German, and it must have been something in his blood. Though of humble origin, he looked like a German officer. He held himself very erect and had brushed-back fair hair and clear eyes and thin lips.

Never would he allow any word of complaint to escape through those lips. He did not like Annette – he could not stand her – but since she was there, a guest in the house, he was prepared to serve her. He cooked her meals and cleaned up after her and cleaned out her bathtub, silently, uncomplainingly, and very thoroughly. Annette took all this for granted – or, rather, she didn't even notice it; she was the sort of person who ate and drank and dressed herself, and walked away and let someone else clean up after her. If there was no one, then she lived in such disorder, such squalor, that sooner or later she had to abandon that place and start again somewhere else.

Dora didn't like to see Paul do so much for Annette. But when she told him this, one afternoon, he said it was all right, he didn't mind doing his duty. Dora bridled at that last word, but before she could say anything more he said, 'Sh-h-h, *she's* coming.' Although they were in Paul's own room at the top of the house, where they might have thought themselves private, Annette had not hesitated to follow them up there, and she walked straight in.

She began at once to question them about Stella. She was always doing that, wanting to know exactly what the doctors had said, what was wrong with her, and was it really true that she had only a few months to live. This last Annette would not believe at all; she pooh-poohed it as one of those doctors' things – doctors trying to make themselves important and then sending in fat bills. And anyway, she suggested, everything was changed now that she had come. There wouldn't be any more nonsense – she would see to that. And she looked at Paul and Dora as if they were part of the nonsense. It was no use their giving her medical details about Stella; she wouldn't listen to them. 'Well, we'll see' was all she said. She seemed to be mentally rolling up her sleeves, ready to clear up this mess that they had managed to create during her absence. Then she looked around Paul's room, which was very comfortable, with some of Stella's excellent pieces of furniture in it, and she said, 'So this is your room,' as if it were one more thing that might have to be looked into and changed.

It really was true that with Annette there Stella's condition seemed to improve. Annette certainly kept her very cheerful, from early morning on. In the few weeks since she had arrived, Stella had spent a large part of each day in bed, and in the morning Paul would come in with her breakfast tray and open the curtains and tidy the room. Annette was a late riser by nature, but from the day she came she made a point of being up at Stella's breakfast hour and going down to her room and slipping in next to her in the big double bed. So now Paul had to bring in two breakfast trays every morning, and while he worked he had to hear the cheering chatter that Annette made to amuse her sick friend. And there was no doubt about it, Stella *was* amused. She just loved every moment of it, having Annette next to her, being so wonderfully loving and entertaining. Most of Annette's chatter pertained to their past together – 'Yes, and what about Saratoga?' 'Annette! No, please!' – and the fun they had had together; and Stella bloomed and thrived in living it over again. Paul listened, too, grimly dusting, except when Annette said, 'Darling Paul, I think we need some more toast, thank you, darling' – holding out the empty toast rack to him by dangling it from her finger like bait. He would take it from her without a word and go down to the kitchen, his special domain, and make the toast, and more coffee, too, and when he came back Stella would often be blushing and smiling like some big, heavy girl, and she would say, 'Annette, Ann*ette*' – half reproving, half approving – and Annette would toss her head, bold and unrepentant, and say, 'That's the way it was, and I'd do the same tomorrow.'

Dora's mother telephoned. 'Is she still there?' she said to Dora.

'Of course she is,' Dora said, challenging the distressed silence at the other end. 'You don't think she'd come all this way and then go off again tomorrow? She's here to stay. Anyway, what's wrong with her?'

'What's *wrong* with her!' Dora's mother repeated incredulously.

So then Dora had nothing to say, until her mother went on, 'And he? I suppose *he's* still there?'

'Paul? Things would be in a fine mess if he weren't.' Dora hung up indignantly.

Annette had the idea, which she shared with Stella, that Dora was in love with Paul. Stella liked this idea and made Annette give her more details. And then Stella asked, 'And he?'

Annette gave a little laugh at that. 'Naturally, he's pleased. He likes it.'

'Yes, but does he feel the same way?' Stella asked.

'Goodness, Stella, if you're in Paul's position, you don't ask yourself such questions. You take what falls down from heaven and keep quiet. Thank you, darling. Just what we needed,' she said as Paul returned with more toast, and she began to butter it at once.

Stella watched Paul and Dora together, but it was difficult for her to see what Annette saw. Paul was always reserved, and as for Dora – Stella knew that she was, like herself, a person of deep feeling; but everything in Dora's training, her nature, even in her physical presence, was calculated to hide this. 'Poor thing, what do you expect, she's so dreadfully repressed,' Annette said when Stella complained she couldn't see anything of what Annette had described. 'Probably she doesn't even know it herself. What she needs is opening up – the way I opened you up,' she said to Stella, who then blushed and smiled again in that big-schoolgirl way.

Whatever their feelings for each other, Paul and Dora certainly spent a lot of time together in the house. That may have been partly because Annette now monopolized Stella. She had taken Stella's regime in hand, and it was she who decided that now it was time for Stella to have her nap, and now it was time to play chess with Annette, and now, perhaps (all bundled up in furs and boots), what about a drive with Annette through Central Park? So it didn't matter whether Paul and Dora liked being together – they had no alternative. They always had plenty to talk about – mostly about Annette, or Stella and Annette. It wasn't long, then, before Paul told Dora about the big scene that had taken place between Stella and Annette eight years earlier. He had never talked about this to anyone, even though it was by no means a secret, for it had been enacted in front of the whole teatime crowd assembled in the hotel restaurant where Paul had at that time been a waiter.

He knew Stella well; she was a regular patron. She was very generous with her tips and always had a friendly word for the staff. She had quite a large circle of friends – most of them rich, clever, middle-aged women like herself – but after Annette appeared this circle gradually shrank, and after a while she came only with Annette. Stella didn't seem to mind the loss of her other friends. She appeared very happy, feasting herself on the presence of Annette and basking in her high spirits.

But on the day of the big scene Annette had not been in high spirits. She was an avid consumer of teatime pastries, but on this afternoon she was eating compulsively, angrily. She was still licking up the remains of one rich, squashy cake when she imperiously waved her hand for the trolley to be wheeled over to her again. Stella also had a fondness for these pastries, but she had to be careful of her weight. When the trolley was summoned for the third time, Stella made a selection of her own, but Annette (her mouth sticky with whipped cream and chocolate flakes) turned on her. 'Are you completely out of your mind!' she cried. 'Stuffing yourself when – look at you – you're already the size of a buffalo. It's disgusting.'

All this was said in front of Paul, who was refilling their cups with tea, and the trolley waiter, who stood there gaping. Paul took charge then, waving his colleague away and also removing himself and his teapot discreetly to other tables. But he kept an eye on Stella. He had always liked her, and he felt protective about her. He thought of her as a wonderful American lady, and admired the expensive suits and shoes she wore, from the best shops. He also watched Annette; he knew *her* type only too well, unfortunately. After those first words, he kept his eye on the two of them as best he could, although it was a very busy time and the place was packed. Every time he looked again, he saw that the scene between them had advanced a stage further, and he was appalled. Annette appeared almost to have lost control of herself. But Paul knew that she hadn't, really; she couldn't afford to. A person like her had always to be in control of herself, and of others, and of situations. She could only survive by manipulation. So she must have deliberately let herself fly into a terrible rage, and although Paul couldn't hear what she was saying (she was almost shouting, but luckily much of what she was saying was drowned out in the teatime roar), he knew it was mercilessly cruel. He could tell this from the expression on Annette's face, which was frightening. Even as she was shouting at Stella, she continued to attack the huge piece of Black Forest cake she had selected from the trolley; her mouth dripped with it, so that she looked like a beast of prey – cruel and greedy.

When Paul looked next, Annette had gone, and Stella sat alone. And now he didn't care how many tables were clamoring for him; he went straight over to her and stood between her and the rest of the restaurant, shielding her with his back while pretending to pour tea for her. 'Now,' he said, 'now, now.' She had completely disintegrated. Her shoulders were hunched within her tailored suit, her face was ugly and red, and huge tears rolled down it. 'Now, now,' he said over and over, not so much to say something as to prevent the sounds that came from her, the helpless sobs, from being heard at adjoining tables.

'I guess I know when that was,' Dora said when Paul had told her this story. And Paul confirmed that it was eight years ago when Annette had walked out on Stella and gone off to London with one of her businessman friends. Paul guessed that she had staged the scene in order to rid herself of Stella. In any case, within a day or two she had packed her bags and moved out and flown to London. It was then that Paul began to be really close to Stella, and gradually it became his life's task to take care of her.

Annette said it was a wonderful arrangement. She said this often – to Stella when they were in bed together and Paul was serving their breakfast, and to Dora, too, looking at her out of the corners of her merry black eyes. 'Such a nice person,' she said about Paul. 'So helpful and good.' And once she added, 'Of course, he's very lucky, too. He's fallen on his feet here. What a chance for him – a person from his class.' She turned her mouth down in utter contempt.

'What class is that?' Dora said coldly.

'Oh, darling,' said Annette. Again she looked at Dora with dancing, teasing eyes. 'I wonder what your family thinks of him,' she went on. 'Not quite what they're used to, is it? A waiter.' Again she pulled her mouth down. 'A proletarian.'

'A what?' said Dora.

Annette repeated the word for her, relishing her own contempt.

Dora, of course, did not report this conversation to Paul, but she did ask him what he thought Annette's own background had been. Now it was Paul's turn to pull his mouth down, and he grimaced just as Annette had done when she spoke about him. 'Yes, yes,' he said, 'we all know what she is, where she comes from.'

'She says she's Russian,' Dora said.

Actually, Annette was vague about her lineage. Sometimes her parents were White Russians who had fled their homeland and settled in Paris, leaving vast estates behind; sometimes only her father was of Russian ancestry, and her mother was a French ballet dancer.

'Yes, yes,' Paul said again. He added, 'And about her age.'

'She says she's thirty-five.'

'All right,' Paul said. 'Sometimes a lady likes to take off a year here and there. That is quite natural; we all understand it. But to take off fifteen years!'

'Fifteen years?'

'That's really shameless,' Paul said. 'She is quite shameless.'

After that, Dora looked more closely at Annette. She could

not believe she was fifty. Of course, Annette used a lot of make-up, and her hair was not its own color, but all the same there was a youthful vitality in her face and in her plump, active little body. Dora herself, who was not quite thirty, felt almost middle-aged beside her, and of course dowdy. Annette often commented on Dora's appearance, usually in front of Stella. She would study her, with her head to one side and the tip of her rosy tongue thoughtfully protruding. 'Yes,' she said once, speaking about one of Dora's discreet dresses, 'it's nice, smart – but wait!' She jumped up and dashed away, to return with one of her own bird-of-paradise scarves, which she quickly wound around Dora's neck. 'There!' she cried in triumph. Stella nodded and smiled, and Annette said, 'Paul likes it, too, don't you, Paul?' And when Dora pulled the scarf off, Annette cried, 'Oh, why? It looks so *chic!*' and Stella echoed her.

Stella and Dora, as aunt and favorite niece, had always had a lot in common. They liked the same books and in the past they had often gone to concerts and exhibitions together, and had usually come away with the same reactions. Stella had appreciated the girl's mind, her good taste, and her quiet, withdrawn, modest behavior. But now she no longer seemed to value these qualities, and, like Annette with the bright scarf, Stella began to suggest changes. She wanted Dora to go out and enjoy herself. 'Why don't you go to a play tonight – Off Broadway! And supper afterward?' Or, 'The stores are open late tomorrow. Why don't you let Annette take you shopping?'

'Oh, yes, yes!' cried Annette.

'I don't need anything,' Dora said.

Another time, it might be Annette who suggested an outing – to a film festival, to a musical, to a newly opened restaurant. When Dora refused, Annette would say, 'Paul can take you, if you like. He can have the evening off, can't he, Stella?'

'Oh, my dear,' said Stella, in horror at the idea that Paul should have to ask for such a thing.

But neither Paul nor Dora had any inclination to go. They preferred to stay with Stella.

Dora's mother telephoned more frequently from the Vineyard. 'How is she? Is she still there? Should I come?'

Dora always told her not to. She said it was all right – Stella was the same, no change. But in fact there was a change; Stella was not the same. She had kept active as long as she could, and got dressed at least once a day in her skirt and cardigan, and came downstairs to sit by the cozy log fire Paul had lit. But now, as her illness progressed, she was forced to stay more and more in her bedroom, and Paul lit a fire in there. In the evenings, when Dora first came home from her job in the museum, it was the place where they all congregated, with Stella in bed as their centerpiece. Annette spent most of her days in there. She had an armchair and little table by the fire, and there she sat, playing solitaire while Stella dozed. Excellent meals were brought in on trays by Paul, and snacks in between, and Annette seemed to be perfectly content to sit there throughout the day and let Stella watch her, when she was awake. It was mid-winter; the snow fell outside, and the one tree visible from the window was stripped and dead, so it seemed nice to be sitting inside, even in a sickroom.

Sometimes, when Stella was asleep, Paul and Dora became restless. They had a lot of things on their minds and no one else to share them with, so they tended to sneak away together, usually up to Paul's room. Sometimes when Stella woke up, she asked, 'Has Dora gone home?' And Annette would kick a log into the fire and say, 'No, she is with Paul, upstairs.' Stella saw Annette's face lit by the flickering flames, and a smile flickering there as well. Stella, too, was pleased to think of Paul and Dora together; it gave her satisfaction to imagine what happiness might be going on between them in her house.

There was no fire in Paul's room. There was a little fireplace, but he liked to keep the room cold, with the radiator turned off and, whenever possible, the window left open. And though Dora usually felt the cold very much, she was glad of this outer coolness, because she felt there were fires within her. The moment they were alone together, they began to speak of Annette. Dora did her very best to be fair and to assume that Annette was living in the house and keeping vigil in the sickroom for love of Stella, for noble motives. But whenever she said that, Paul took on the knowing sneer he always had for Annette. 'Listen,' he said, 'Dora' – there was always the slightest hesitation when he said her name, for she had only recently managed to persuade him not to call her Miss Dora – 'listen, she is not the type to do anything for love, that I can tell you. She can't afford to.' His thin lips went thinner, and his cold, pale eyes looked at Dora now with dislike. 'I'm afraid you wouldn't know about that . . . Dora. About a person like her, the way she has to live all her life.'

'How?' asked Dora, curiously excited.

'On her wits, on what she has up here,' he said, slapping his forehead. 'Yes, and of course, what she has down there, too,' he said, pointing downward with a coarseness very unusual for him. 'Excuse me,' he said immediately but in an unrepentant tone. 'That's the way it is. If you don't have' – and he rubbed two fingers together in a moneylender's gesture – 'then that's the way you have to make do. I've seen hundreds like her – thousands – all over the world. They used to sit around in the restaurants I worked in. They were the first to come and the last to leave. They could never go home, because there was the landlord downstairs waiting to be paid, or maybe the people they were living with had told them to leave. You don't know what that's like, Dora – when you're asked to leave by your host. When they want to be polite to you, they say they've got other guests coming. But they don't always want to be polite; they don't need to be, do they? For instance, now, if this house were yours and you wanted someone to leave, you wouldn't have to pretend anything. You could just say, "Go." You could say it to Annette, you could say it to me. "Go" – just like that.' He had grown very pale, and Dora, too, grew pale.

Stella's doctor paid regular visits, and he talked gravely to Dora afterward in the drawing room. Annette was always there, and her right to be there was by now indisputable. Each time, Dora had to recover from what the doctor had told her, waiting downstairs to collect herself before going back to

Stella. Annette waited with her, to comfort and strengthen her, but if Dora stayed too long, sitting there in silence, with her head bowed, Annette got restless and began to pace the room. There was a cashmere shawl thrown over a grand piano in one corner, and sometimes Annette took it off and wrapped it around herself and modeled it before the pier glass. Once she sighed and said, 'How beautiful,' and, picking up a silver box, she sighed again and opened it and shut it, looking at her reflection there, too, for Paul had polished the box to perfection. 'He keeps things well,' she murmured to Dora. 'Quite the little housekeeper. He's going to miss all this, you know. When it's no longer here.' She gave a third deep sigh, and, unwinding herself from the shawl, replaced it on the piano – though very slowly, letting her hand linger over the soft wool, as if reluctant to let go.

'What are you going to do with all of it?' she asked, indicating the drawing room and all of its contents – all Stella's beloved screens, fans, clocks, and mirrors. 'Sell it, I suppose,' she went on, now almost talking to herself. 'No use keeping it, and, my goodness, it should all fetch a pretty penny. A pretty penny,' she repeated, wistfully.

Dora still hadn't spoken, sunk in thoughts of Stella and the doctor's prognosis.

'And what about us?' Annette asked. 'What are you going to do about us, Paul and me? We won't fetch much, I'm afraid.' She laughed at that – a deep, cynical, unfeminine laugh – and, looking at her, Dora believed for the first time that Annette was fifty, for this laugh seemed to come out of years of disappointment.

Annette caught Dora's look of surprise, and she went on, 'She's not going to leave much to us, you know that – to Paul and me. It's all going to you, naturally. Naturally,' she repeated. 'Money like that doesn't go out of the family. It never does.' And again she seemed to speak out of long, long experience.

Dora's mother said, 'How is she? I could come over for the weekend.'

'Mother, it's all right,' Dora said into the telephone.

'Dora, are you telling me everything I ought to know? My own sister, after all.'

'It's all *right*,' Dora repeated.

Dora had always had a room kept ready for her in Stella's house, and now she moved into it, locking up her own apartment. She wanted to be there with Stella all the time. Stella had shrunk so much that her own bed seemed to overwhelm her. Her booming voice, too, was down to its own echo. One day, Annette fell asleep by the fireside, and Dora sat by Stella's bed, holding her hand. For the first time in a long while, aunt and niece had the opportunity to talk privately together. Stella talked about Annette; she kept looking at her fondly as she slept. It was the afternoon of a winter day and the light was failing, so that Annette was mostly in shadow. Her head was supported on her hand, her face was flushed by the fire, and she breathed peacefully.

'She's so kind to me – you have no idea,' Stella said. 'But that's nothing new. She's always been like that, all goodness and kindness.' She smiled at her memories. 'Of course, we had our little difficulties sometimes, but everyone has those, don't they? If they're really close to each other. That's part of it – hurting each other because you love each other so much. It's different when people don't care for you, or only pretend to.'

'Mother calls every day to ask after you,' Dora said.

Stella nodded, as if she knew that and also knew what it was worth.

'I wish – I wish – I wish—' said Stella, after a long silence, swinging Dora's hand about. This by-play was one of the things they had between them, as if they had spent their childhood together.

'What?' said Dora, smiling.

'I wish that *you* had someone you cared for more than anyone else in the world,' said Stella. 'I wasn't ever really happy till I had someone like that – a very special person of my own.' Again they both looked at Annette, cozily asleep. 'I'd like you to have such a person,' Stella said to Dora in her weakened whisper, which made everything she said into a significant message.

Paul came in with Stella's supper tray. He wanted to turn on the light, but Stella said it would disturb Annette. Now it was almost dark in the room, except for the warm and glowing space where Annette sat by the fire. The window framed the last gleam of winter daylight, through which snowflakes could be seen falling.

'We were just talking about you, Paul,' said Stella.

'Nothing but good, I hope,' said Paul with his stiff humor.

'Tell him, Dora,' said Stella. 'Tell him what I wish for more than anything in the world.' She squeezed Dora's hand. 'Isn't it lovely to be here all together? Isn't it the coziest thing? God bless this house,' she said, 'and all of you in it.' Annette stirred in her corner, and Paul and Dora remained quite still in the still room, with only their thoughts rustling inside their heads.

At night, in his bed, Paul slept like a lead soldier laid to rest in his box. He slept very soundly, so that Annette had to call him several times that night before he woke up. Then he sat bolt upright and called out like a sentry.

'Sh-h-h,' said Annette. 'Sh-h-h, sh-h-h. Don't be a fool.'

'Something's happened to her,' said Paul, and jumped out of bed in a great fright.

'Nothing's happened,' said Annette. 'Not yet.'

Paul realized that Annette had come to him on a personal visit, which might be of some duration. He put on his dressing gown and sat down on a chair, facing her.

'And when it does happen?' she asked him. 'What will you do? You'll have to do something.' When he shrugged, she said, 'Oh, I see. You'll get another job in a restaurant and share an apartment with one of the other waiters. Off Amsterdam Avenue? Or downtown? One of those houses cut up into rooms, with very dark stairs and a lot of security locks? Charming. After this.' She indicated his room, which had two armchairs, three oriental rugs, a Persian wall hanging, and a walnut desk with an enamel inkstand on it. She leaned toward him and looked into his face. 'The girl's not bad,' she said, with a shrug. 'Some would say you were very lucky. I think you are. My goodness, yes.' She gave her harsh laugh.

Paul cleared his throat. 'It's a very difficult position for me,' he said.

'I would like to be in such a difficult position,' Annette went on. 'What's the matter with you? Don't you like girls? I've wondered sometimes.' She continued to look into his pale, stubborn, handsome face. 'That's nothing,' she assured him. 'It doesn't matter a damn.'

He stared ahead of him. His Adam's apple worked up and down very slightly; otherwise he was motionless.

She said, 'You learn to ignore little things like your own personal tastes when you get to my age. Which is thirty-five,' she added in parenthesis, smiling at him broadly and tapping her foot. 'When you get to that, you don't care the teeniest little bit. Remember when I went off to London? I learned my lesson there, all right.'

'I've got nothing to learn,' Paul said, still staring over her head.

'You soon will have. You heard what the doctor said.'

'I thought you said that was all nonsense.'

'We have to be ready for all weathers – that's another thing we learn.' She tapped his knee and leaned even closer. 'I'm on your side, don't you know that? I'm with you. I want to see you stay here, where you like it so much. Just look at you,' she said, amused, watching his knee twitching where she had kept her hand on it. 'What are you afraid of? It doesn't hurt with a woman – here, I'll show you.' Dexterously, she slipped from her chair onto his lap, and, taking his face between her hands, she pressed her mouth against his. She kept it there a long while and did all sorts of expert things, and when she had finished she laughed and gave his cheek a little slap and said, 'There. You see, you've got nothing at all to worry about. You're doing it very well. Absolutely right,' she assured him.

Annette's visits to Paul were repeated several times, and then one night she was pleased to find his room empty. She put her ear to the door of Dora's room and heard Dora talking. Annette rolled her eyes in amusement. Dora was just the sort of girl to lead a discussion group in the midst of life's business. Stella had had the same tendency, before Annette had taught her better.

If Annette had bothered to look through the keyhole, she would have been even more amused to see the two of them – Paul on a Victorian love seat and Dora on the carpet, with her arms clasped around her knees. Dora was talking as she hadn't since she was a girl at boarding school. She was telling Paul everything about her life – which wasn't much, except that she felt it all with such intensity. She told him about her family, too, and this was the part he liked best. She seemed to dwell mostly on their shortcomings – their conventionality, their narrow outlook – but what he wanted to hear about was her money and family genealogy. It made him shudder with pleasure to contemplate how the proper investments of one ancestor – a tea importer – had of their own accord and with great dignity (so he liked to think) grown and grown, so that there was now a river of money that flowed without cease for the benefit of the descendants. It gave him an emotion more profound than sexual pleasure to contemplate Dora in the light reflected from this river. But for her the thrill was to think that none of it mattered – the family, the family's position, the family's money. Only she and Paul mattered – Paul who possessed nothing except himself, and she, Dora, sitting there so simply on the floor, hugging her knees and revealing herself to him in her entirety, with whatever inward splendors she might have.

Dora's mother was almost beside herself: 'Why aren't you in your apartment? Is she worse? Is that why you've moved in? *Tell* me, Dora.'

'She's not worse,' Dora said, spacing her words. 'You don't have to come.'

'I can be there on the next plane.'

'You – don't – have – to – come. Mother, *please*?'

Dora told Paul how her mother and Stella, although they were sisters, had never got on. They were different from each other in just the same way that Dora was from all the other girls in the family. It made her indignant that her mother should now wish to come into this house, as if she had a greater right to be there than those who truly loved Stella.

'Your mother doesn't like me to be here,' Paul said, casting his eyes downward, as if admitting with shame that Dora's mother had reason not to do so. 'She doesn't like either of us – me or Annette.'

'As if you had anything in common with Annette.'

Paul kept his eyes cast down.

Stella's nights were restless now, and Annette made Paul install a bed in Stella's room, so that she could be with her. Although by nature a very sound sleeper, Annette woke at the least sound from Stella. She seemed to be waiting and watching, not just for Stella but for the others in the house as well.

'What is it? What are they doing?' Stella asked one evening, noticing Annette alert for sounds from elsewhere.

'He is in her room,' Annette said.

'Ah,' breathed Stella, full of satisfaction.

She dozed off for a while, and when she woke again Annette was still sitting on the side of her bed, although it was very late in the night.

'How good you are, how kind,' said Stella, devouring Annette with eyes of love. There was a night light in the room; the snow had again begun to fall.

'The family won't like it,' Stella said dreamily. 'They'll hate it. But I've told her, to hell with the family. When you've found a treasure for yourself, you don't give it up for them. Wouldn't I have been a fool to give *you* up? And not have you sitting here *now*?' She squeezed Annette's hand in gratitude and shut her eyes.

Annette kept her hand in Stella's, but she didn't pay much attention to her. She was still listening for sounds from the rest of the house. It disturbed her to hear the door of Dora's room open downstairs and then Paul going softly up the stairs, past Stella's door (Annette was so alert that she could hear him breathe), and up to his own room at the top of the house. She waited for Stella to doze off again, and then she disengaged her hand and went up to join Paul.

She was quite rough with him. 'What's the matter with you?' she said. 'Why aren't you with her?'

'We've said good night,' he answered defiantly.

She gazed down at him as he lay in bed in his striped pajamas. 'Move over,' she said.

He was getting quite good with her – so good, in fact, that he had learned to put his hand over her mouth so that her cry could not penetrate the rest of the house.

After a while, she said, 'Now go to her.' But he didn't move from her side.

'What shall I do with you?' she said, in loving despair.

He had his eyes shut, stretched out beside her like a knight on a tomb. 'Just stay with me,' he murmured.

'Yes, that would be nice, wouldn't it?' she said sarcastically. She knew only too well that it would be glorious, but she could not afford to indulge herself.

'Get up!' she ordered. 'Go down! Why not? You like her.'

'I respect her.'

She laughed. 'And not me?'

He turned his face to her and sank his teeth into the soft, middle-aged, yet still full and luscious flesh of her naked upper arms.

She didn't urge him any further but gave in to the luxury of staying beside him. She knew that Stella might wake at any moment, but she didn't care. It was he who had to remind her.

'Let her wait,' she said. She was silent, and her thoughts made her bitter. 'We can have these five minutes. We're not going to get much else. Not if you don't go down.'

'She doesn't want to,' he said.

'Doesn't she!' Annette gave her bark of a laugh. 'They don't know what they want, those parasites. We have to teach them everything – what to do with themselves, their time, their money. Even that they don't know! When I first met Stella, I took her shopping. I made her buy all sorts of things: little purses and scarves and some nice pins and a lot of underclothes – mine were in tatters – and at lunch we got a little bit drunk on Martinis, and then I felt like going on one of those buggy rides around the Park, so we did that, and, my God, she loved it! Her big fat face went all red, and she said, "Isn't this fun, Annette?" Such a stupid, silly thing, which she could have done every day if she wanted! But they don't know how to enjoy anything. And me, who was born to enjoy a lot more than a buggy ride around the Park, I had to sit there jog-jogging along with her. Tchk-tchk, tchk-tchk,' said Annette in disgust, making coachman noises, while her naked arms above the bedclothes pretended to hold reins.

'I think she's calling,' Paul said, sitting up in bed.

'Who cares?' She pulled him down again. 'All right, so you'll go back to being a waiter. You'll meet someone in a restaurant – a man, a woman – someone who'll like you and want to take care of you, and you'll start all over. But what'll I do?'

'What you've always done.'

'I need to rest, Paul.'

The way she said that made him look at her, and he saw that her face was old. But he took no pity on her. He said, 'She *is* calling. You'll have to go.'

'I don't want to. I've done enough for her.'

He pulled the bedclothes back from her, but still she wouldn't get up. Stella was calling louder. Paul leaped over Annette's naked body, and, struggling into his dressing gown, went to the door. At the same time, Dora's door opened below. 'Is Stella calling?' she asked.

Paul came down from his room and Dora met him on the stairs. 'Something's happened,' Dora said. 'Where's Annette?'

Then she looked up and saw her. Annette stood in the doorway of Paul's room, plump and nude, filling it completely; she had one arm raised against the doorpost. 'You'll have to give her her pills,' she called down.

Dora went in and searched around for the right pills, but it was Paul who knew where they were. It was also Paul who got the water and supported Stella in bed to help her take her medicine. He spoke soothingly to her and said that Annette would be coming soon. Dora saw that Stella was in good hands for the moment, so she went to the telephone and dialed the Vineyard, and when her mother answered, she said, 'You'd better come now.'

# FIDELITY

When the doctor told Sophie that her disease was incurable, she would have liked to share the information with her husband. But she knew that Dave had many troubles – like his business and his creditors and his young girl friend – to which she did not wish to add yet another.

She also failed to confide in the other person closest to her – Dave's sister, Betsy. But she kept thinking what Betsy would have done in her situation – how she would have thrown herself into everything that gave her pleasure: eating all the cream cakes she wanted, going back to her two packs a day, buying masses of wonderful clothes, even trying alcohol which she didn't care for. On the other hand – and this too was part of Betsy's nature – she might have done nothing like that but only exactly what the doctors ordered, so as to keep alive a little while longer and have the chance to enjoy everything again.

Sophie and Dave lived around the corner to Betsy, on Park, and after Dave moved out to be with his girl friend, he took another place nearby, on 79th. The three of them spoke every day and often saw each other, so that each always knew exactly what the others were doing and also, with Betsy and Dave, what they were thinking. Sophie didn't have as many thoughts as the other two, nor their gift of volubly expressing them. Sometimes she imagined Dave's reaction if she told him her present piece of news – how everything in his mind and heart would come rushing out, washed ashore on a flood of tears. Dave had this ability of bursting into tears – it was a facility almost, anyway it helped him to feel better, so that when the outburst was finished and the last tear wiped away, he seemed to be almost happy with himself.

The first time Sophie had discovered Dave to be unfaithful was when they had been married less than a year. They were living in her grandparents' apartment, which was waiting to be sold – a vast old mausoleum stuffed with their heavy German furniture and thick with the smell of the heavy German meals they had eaten till they had sunk into their graves with repletion. It was an anomalous setting for someone as alive as Dave, but he soon filled it with himself, the way he did every place he inhabited. He was already running his family's carpet business and expanding it beyond all previous limits. This kept him busy till late into the night when, to relax, he joined his friends in a poker game. He and Sophie often ate at midnight, and he told her about his whole day and mimicked the people he had met and himself talking to them. He was up early in the morning, and when he saw she was awake, at once began talking to her again. He also sang something like 'I can't give you anything but love, baby,' and performed a little dance shuffle in his underwear. His legs were hot hairy columns and his sexual organ bulged as though wanting to burst out of his tight shorts. He shaved with an electric razor, as closely as possible, though by late afternoon his beard had begun sprouting again. He doused himself in cologne and put brilliantine on his hair but dressed very quickly. He was always in a great hurry because of everything he had to do.

She didn't mind being left alone all day, especially as he phoned her every few hours – yes, with all his business, she was always in his thoughts. He kept her informed of his whereabouts, usually rather vaguely; but if he was going to be very late, he would cite some particular place where he could be contacted. Once it happened that someone from such a contact place phoned to ask where he was – people were always trying to find him – and laughed when she said, but he is with you. Then she became anxious and phoned several other places where he said he had been that day; none of them had seen him. When he finally came home – still shiny and scented and just a little bit more disheveled after his busy day – he found her sitting very still in a corner of her grandparents' sofa. When he lied, she said nothing, and then he told her the truth, more or less – he wanted to tell it, to spill it into her lap together with his tears, until he felt the touch of her forgiving hand on his head.

In the beginning she had never analyzed why she loved him so much, and his sister Betsy too, though later she realized it may have been because they were so different from herself. They were full of a vitality that had been drained out of her before she was born. Dave and Betsy were exotic, semi-oriental – they were Sephardic Jews – whereas Sophie's family were German Jews and had been comfortably settled in small Westphalian towns before migrating to America, at the beginning of the century, for even greater opportunities. Although they had married only among themselves, they had brought with them the prominent pale blue eyes and thick ankles of the German community whose hospitality they had enjoyed for so long. Sophie had inherited these; she was not pretty at all and was prepared for people to say that Dave had married her for her family's money – which they couldn't say for long, because he very quickly made (and lost) a fortune of his own.

During those early years Betsy was living in Los Angeles. She was married twice, and both her husbands were in films, one in production and the other on the distribution side. For a while she had enjoyed the premieres and the film festivals and the stars, but they had palled, especially as she was not at the glamorous center but on the commercial periphery. It might have been different if the husbands had been better, but they ate too many business lunches and had too many huge business worries that gave them huge ulcers. Finally, disgusted at them and at whiling her time away in her lovely Beverly Hills home vying with other wives in theirs, she had returned to New York with her son Michael and taken an apartment on Madison Avenue around the corner to Dave and Sophie. Michael was just starting college, so Betsy lived alone with not much to do once she had furnished the new apartment. Lavishly spending her alimony on it, she created a bower of fruits and flowers for herself – some real, in silver bowls and vases, others a cascade of glass grapes or silk hydrangeas; even the antiques she bought were of shiny gold and looked freshly made.

Betsy's son Michael – Michael Goldstein – did not take after his mother or uncle, nor after his father, the first of what Betsy characterized as her animal husbands. It would be difficult to describe Michael in positive terms. He had grown up in Hollywood, and while going to school with other children whose parents were involved in films, had remained completely free of their needs – he didn't even want a car and had never learned to drive. He had no difficulty getting into Harvard, but here too he kept himself aloof from its expectations, and in fact dropped out in his junior year. Then he began to travel. He almost became a Zen Buddhist in Thailand and almost a Tibetan one in Dharamsala. He spent time with Sufis in upstate New York and with Hasidim in Brooklyn; he read Meister Eckhart and St John of the Cross. Betsy said he was nuts – 'I'm sorry, he's my own son, but Michael is nuts.'

He had been twenty – it was the year he dropped out of college – when Dave left Sophie for the first time. By then Sophie had been married to Dave for twenty-five years and had been through many forgiveness scenes with him. She had also suffered several miscarriages and a few unsuccessful operations to correct the obstruction in her womb. Over the years, her heart had taken on a stone-like quality, not so much in hardness as in heaviness. And just as it is impossible to draw blood from a stone, so it is to draw tears, and it was always left to Dave himself to supply these, which he did in abundance.

And it was Betsy not Sophie who supplied the indignation when Dave went to live with his young girl friend. 'Men are animals,' she told Michael.

Michael replied, 'A man has to be an animal before he can become a human being.'

'What? What are you talking about?'

'A quote: Aquinas,' Michael said – at twenty, he still prided himself on his erudite reading.

But his mother, who was as impatient of these interests as she might have been of comic strips or video games, cried,

'Why can't you be serious!' Convinced it was a waste of time to talk to him any more, she rushed to the telephone to talk to her brother – the culprit himself. They had one of their famous fights that they both enjoyed, throwing all their energy into it. Once curvaceous, voluptuous, Betsy had with age grown very thin, as though consumed by her own intensity, which also seemed to issue out of her in sparks – literally, for she smoked far too much, and when agitated, she flicked wildly at her cigarette, scattering ash and fire in all directions.

Her indignation – her intensity – were often directed at Michael himself. Once, when he shaved his head preparatory to becoming a monk, she developed such high blood pressure that he had to give up on the idea, and instead of entering a monastery, had stayed with her in the Madison Avenue apartment. Here his hair had grown back in stubbles, which made her laugh every time she looked at him. But she was very affectionate with him at this time, trying to steer him back toward a respectable life that would make her proud of him. For instance: 'Why don't you become an artist, Michael?'

'But I can't draw.'

'Of course you can. You used to make such sweet pictures for me. You made an acrobat and a clown and a fish in a fishbowl, don't you remember?' She was perched on his chair, stroking his stubbled head.

He did remember – himself solemnly drawing with crayons while she watched over him, finally unable to refrain from hugging and kissing him, so that he frowned at being disturbed, which made her kiss him more. 'Where are those pictures?' he said.

'Oh, I don't know – they might still be in that house on Woodrow Wilson Drive unless your disgusting father has thrown them out. Really,' she said, her mood spoiled, 'what is this, hair you're growing or pins and needles?'

The weeks after Dave moved out, Betsy kept encouraging Michael to visit his aunt. When he asked, 'But what should I say?' Betsy answered, 'What do you mean, what should you say? Haven't you got any feeling?' Michael said nothing; he couldn't very well admit that he really had no feeling for this particular situation. It seemed to him that by now his aunt Sophie should be glad to be rid of his uncle Dave.

Although he liked his aunt, he found her company dull. Perhaps she was too much like himself, without natural high spirits and needing to be sparked up, ignited by someone else. In his case, this had so far been only his mother. At twenty, he had had a few girl friends, all older than himself, but with no particular enthusiasm, causing Betsy anxiously to ask Dave, 'He's not gay, is he?' Of course, if he had been, she would have been the first to march in parades along with other, similarly situated mothers. Or, if his interests had led him to chant with a tambourine and a huge shaved head at street-corners, she would have clapped and sung along and dropped money in his collection box, encouraging other spectators to do the same.

Michael was prone to depression, for which he used to take pills, and sitting with his aunt in her dark apartment tended to aggravate his condition. Sophie was no longer in her grandparents' apartment where she had spent her first married years, but in another, similar one, inherited from her parents together with some of the Biedermeyer furniture that the parents themselves had inherited from the grandparents. Sunshine did not fall on this side of the building, but would anyway not have been encouraged: Sophie had grown up with the idea, passed on by parents and grandparents, that it had to be kept out lest it fade the upholstery. Her pictures were also dark, and even when they featured fruits and flowers, their glow was extinguished by a center-piece of dead game or glassy-eyed fish. Once, when Michael was there, his uncle Dave unexpectedly arrived. First thing he did he tugged at the curtains to pull them apart: 'Okay, so let the wallpaper fade, better than sitting in a tomb!' When the light fell on Sophie, it showed her eyes shining as though with the tears she hadn't shed in years. 'Now what's the matter?' said Dave, pretending exasperation. She tried to smile: 'No, nothing – only I'm glad you're here.' 'But I'll always be here, you know that; always be here for you,' he said and held her face against his chest. He looked over at Michael, who was surprised to see that the tears that had failed to rise to Sophie's eyes were spilling in large drops out of Dave's.

A few years after moving out of Sophie's apartment, Dave moved back in again. A lot had happened in the meantime – principally, that Dave had been in jail. He had been convicted of fraud. Betsy and Sophie never got the details clear, and Dave swore (on his mother's grave, his usual oath) that he had been framed. This may have been true – his business affairs were conducted in shadowy areas where, as far as his wife and sister were concerned, anything could happen. He was sentenced to three years in a minimum security facility, and they were able to visit him every fortnight. They sat with him in a large, bleak reception room, among other prisoners surrounded by their families. Dave introduced them to some of his fellow inmates – he said most of them were very decent people caught up, like himself, in situations beyond their control. They all chatted with their visitors in low voices, under the surveillance of two guards; the atmosphere was not unlike that of a boys' boarding school on Parents Day, an impression enhanced by the blue uniforms worn by the prisoners. But there was also – and this was not like Parents Day – a pervading sense of shame, of an imposed humiliation that made inmates and their visitors avoid each other's eyes. One old man sat in a corner with his visitor, an old woman who kept stroking his hands, looking away from him and not speaking a word.

Dave, as subdued as the rest, was quite unlike himself. He had lost weight but nevertheless bulged rather ridiculously out of his shirt and knee-pants. When it was time to leave, all the prisoners gathered in an enclosed space off the parking lot for a last glimpse of their dear ones driving away. They crowded each other, and those closest to the wiremesh fence pushed their fingers through and waggled them in farewell. Sophie and Betsy drove mile after mile in silence. Betsy at the wheel stared tensely at the road ahead of her; sometimes her lips moved, but she was speaking to herself and all she said was, 'Thank God Mamma's gone,' and she sighed from some place inside herself where her heart was breaking. But when after a couple of hours they came to a roadhouse, she always stopped, and with another deep sigh conceded that they had better eat something; and inside she was picky about the menu, saying the cheeseburger she had had last week had been stale and she would try their spaghetti Bolognese this time.

During his two-year absence – one year off for good behavior – the apartment Dave had bought to keep his girl friend in had to be sold to pay his fine and legal fees. The girl friend herself disappeared, so when he came out, it was natural that he should return to live with his wife. Sophie's one desire was to restore him to himself, so neither by word nor look would she make the least reference to his former behavior, or the mess it had landed them in. His sister was not so reticent; on the contrary. He welcomed her reproaches, which he said he fully deserved, and assured her that his sentence had done him good, by giving him the chance to review and renew his character. And there was a sort of renewal about him – he wasn't just resilient but seemed to jump even higher than before, as if his enforced period of inaction had charged him up with fresh energy. He threw himself into what he had missed in his absence – for instance, dinner-dance in his favorite hotel. It was like he and Sophie were on honeymoon again, and he booked a fine table and ordered a bottle of champagne, which they had difficulty getting through for they were not serious drinkers, and neither was Betsy. Betsy always had to make a third with them because, though he had tried and tried to teach her, Sophie couldn't dance. She stayed behind at their table, among their crumpled napkins and half-drunk glasses of champagne and the gravy stains on the white cloth where Dave had too eagerly helped himself to the veal sauce. Entirely unmusical, she could not help tapping her foot, not so much to the sound of the band as to the rhythm of Dave and Betsy dancing together. It didn't matter that both were middle-aged – everyone else was too, or even elderly, no younger person could afford to come here. Dave was too fat and Betsy too scraggy, but they were both terrific dancers, better than they had ever been, charged up and indefatigable, Betsy flashing lights from her diamonds, Dave from his cuff-links and rings; his pomaded hair was dyed blacker than it had been in his youth and shone like his patent leather pumps that twinkled on the dance floor.

With the same exuberance, he started up his various businesses, taking on a new side-line in parquet flooring that yielded him a lot of money. Soon Dave was rich again and was himself again – which meant that he was out from early morning and came back late every night after his poker game. But he did not neglect to call Sophie at intervals throughout his day to tell her where he was and what he was doing, and though she did not always believe him, she was always glad to hear his voice. However, within two years he was obsessed with another young girl and had to buy another place to keep her in. Again he moved out of Sophie's apartment, while resuming his regular visits to her to keep reassuring himself of her forgiveness.

Around this time Michael showed up on one of his periodic visits to New York. It was a time of crisis for him too – now in his thirties, he was discovering that the freedom to pick and choose among religious traditions could be as unsettling as switching between graduate programs. Of course his mother understood nothing of this and anyway would not have had time to listen. She was entirely preoccupied by what was happening with Sophie and Dave, although she claimed that she had given up on her brother, whose pitiful sex life she said was no business of hers. And neither, she continued – for when Michael came home after his prolonged absences, Betsy talked non-stop – was it her business what Michael's father Harvey Goldstein was doing, which was more or less the same as her brother Dave. That was the way it was now, Betsy told Michael: in the old days, fathers would sneak out to eat a ham sandwich in an automat, that was about the extent of it, but today nothing less would do than a twenty-year-old blonde fresh from Kansas City.

'At least you lead a clean life,' Betsy said to Michael – but she looked at him suspiciously (Is he gay? Frigid?). 'You should talk to them a bit, give them the benefit of whatever it is you're studying – not that they'd understand a word of it . . . What do you talk to them about anyway, when they take you to one of

those grand lunches, your father or your uncle? Not that they'd
have time to talk, they'd be too busy stuffing themselves with
all that risotto and rubbish they shouldn't be eating.'

This wasn't a bad guess. Michael's father, who made frequent
business trips from Los Angeles, felt obliged to see
his son whenever their visits to New York coincided. He had
other sons – a new family altogether – but Michael was his
oldest, maybe his smartest, certainly his oddest. He appeared
ambivalent about Michael's oddness – both embarrassed and
intrigued by it. The embarrassment usually won out, and his
father spent most of their time together with his head bent
low over his plate, grunting with the effort and pleasure of
eating, so that Michael was reminded of Betsy saying, 'Men
are animals.' As if guessing his thought, his father would lift
his head – licking away a trickle of sauce from the corner of his
mouth – and meet his son's eyes, washed clear by meditation:
he tried to explain himself, making a philosophy out of his
cravings – for food, sex, a terrific deal – because what else was
there, he asked, what better thing than for a man to enjoy the
fruits of his hard work and success.

His uncle Dave took Michael to similar packed and noisy
luxury restaurants – it may even have been the same one, it
certainly had the same sort of clientele pressed together on rows
of velvet banquettes too small for them. Dave also shoveled a lot
of food into his mouth very quickly, but when he took time out
to look up from his plate, it was to explain that he had been
tempted sometimes to leave all this – he waved a fatty hand
with rings on it at their surroundings – and to devote himself
to higher values the way Michael did: and as he spoke, there
was a yearning in his eyes as for something ineffable – but this
may have been because his eyes were dark, oriental, seemingly
fathomless, so that anything could be read into them.

Sophie continued to keep her secret, although every day
tempted to disclose it. One day she even left some of her
medicines in view – strong drugs and painkillers – as if hoping
to be questioned about them. However, as usual, Dave had too
much on his mind: principally, his new girl friend who wasn't

worthy he said, to kiss Sophie's shoe. Never in his life had he met anyone so selfish and lazy – well, of course, it was to be expected from young girls, that they would want to stay in bed cocooned in that deep warm sleep out of which nothing could rouse them except the phone ringing and someone inviting them for lunch or to go shopping at Bendel's, and then how they would jump out of bed and wriggle into their tights and try one ridiculous little short outfit after the other while spraying clouds of scent under their armpits and into the hollows of their knees. While he said all this, Dave was too excited to sit still but wandered around, in and out of various rooms, including Sophie's bedroom.

'What's all this?' he asked, stopping short for a moment by the array of medicine bottles she had left out on her bedside table. 'Why are you taking all this stuff?'

She came up behind him, quickly swept them into the drawer where she usually hid them.

He rebuked her: 'You know how I feel about people taking pills.'

'Yes I know, but these—'

'Some bicarbonate to settle your stomach, maybe an aspirin sometimes, but the rest – all they do is poison your system.'

'These are just vitamins.'

'Well okay, vitamins – that's good, you have to keep up your strength, I need you, dear. Nobody will believe this, but I need you more than ever.' He kissed her brow, and when she shut her eyes, he kissed the lids.

One day Michael saw an ugly sight in the cross-street where Dave lived with his new girl friend. It was Dave himself in an argument with a girl. This was presumably his girl friend whom none of them had ever met, for Dave was always careful not to mix family and other matters. She was certainly a type he would have gone for – platinum blond, and with terrific legs stretching out of a very short skirt. Dave himself wore a smart double-breasted suit that set off his stout figure wonderfully but was a bit too young for him. He was trying to explain something to the girl, talking fast and gesticulating with his hands like the Middle Eastern businessman he was. The girl didn't respond at all but kept on walking – till suddenly she stood still and, without a word, began to hit him around the head with her crocodile handbag, so that he had to put up his arms to protect himself. Then she walked on, very briskly on her high heels, her blond hair swinging furiously; and he followed, pleading, protesting, running behind her as though attached to her and pulled on a leash.

Although Michael did not mention this incident to Betsy, it was easy enough for her to guess that, besides business troubles, Dave was also having personal ones. He complained to her, 'Young people don't understand.'

'You mean they don't understand that you need money,' Betsy answered him. He had borrowed from her and she had given him all she could, but she realized it was nowhere near enough to cover his present difficulties.

'He'll have to sell the apartment and put her somewhere else she won't like so much,' Betsy said to Michael, who guessed that this may have been the cause of the scene he had witnessed. Anyway, selling the apartment no longer appeared to be an option Dave felt he could exercise; and in considering others, or another, he became increasingly agitated, gnawing at the skin around his thumb and driving Betsy crazy with anxiety. He jumped every time the phone rang, even at Betsy's, and said, 'I'm not here.'

'Who says it's for you?' she said as she went to answer it – and it always was for her. But she wondered what could be happening to him that he wouldn't tell her – 'You're not involved in another case, are you?'

'What case? What are you talking about?'

'Anything is better than if he has to go inside again,' Betsy said to Michael. 'I couldn't stand it – and Sophie couldn't stand it, so I'm sure she'd a thousand times rather lend him the money. He only has to ask,' she concluded, as if this were the easiest thing in the world though perfectly aware that it wasn't. Dave's relation to his wife was an affair of the utmost delicacy to him. He considered his love for her as the only pure and selfless part of him, which he was reluctant to

tarnish with a request for money to keep him out of jail. Yet
Betsy knew that, like herself, he could not help thinking of
Sophie's wealth, quietly accumulating in portfolios that had
been growing in value over two generations, but at present as
inaccessible, and useless, to him as any precious metal hidden
in the bowels of the earth.

'You ask her,' Dave finally begged his sister. She resisted the
idea, although it had already occurred to her. She dropped in
on her sister-in-law every few days, giving her the latest news,
mostly of a personal nature. Like Dave, Betsy was completely
unconscious of the effect she had on people, simply taking
it for granted that she cheered them up. She was equally
unaware of any influence outside herself – of anyone else's
mood or ambience – so that whenever Michael said that he
found Sophie's apartment oppressive, she didn't know what
he was talking about. 'Do you have any idea what all that
furniture and stuff is worth?' she asked him. But now she too
found herself oppressed; and twice she visited Sophie without
being able to utter a word of what she had come to ask.

'Not yet,' she answered Dave's anxious inquiry after each
of these visits. 'Give me time,' she pleaded, and he pleaded
back, 'I haven't got much time.'

There was something so uncharacteristically piteous about
the way he spoke that she resolved to do it at once. Perhaps
it would be easier over the telephone – rapidly dialing the
number with her skinny, nervous fingers, she listened to the
ringing at the other end. No one answered for a long time,
and she imagined it echoing through an empty apartment as
through hollow space. And when Sophie at last answered, her
voice seemed to come echoing from just such a hollow space,
as deep and dark as the grave. 'Don't tell me you've been asleep
– at this time of day!' cried Betsy in her cheeriest voice.

'Kill me but I can't do it,' she confessed to Dave. He
understood; after all, he felt the same himself, more strongly.
He sat on Betsy's sofa with his shoulders slumped in despair.
She came close to him, took his hands and stroked them in
silence. Then she remembered having seen this same gesture
in the prison visiting room – a woman stroking a man's hands,

both of them silent as she and Dave were now silent. And as if he too remembered that scene, he said suddenly, 'It won't be minimum security this time. Not for a second offense.' He spoke what was, for him, dryly – that is, tonelessly; also without the tears that came to him so easily.

Betsy cried: 'My God, it's only money!' Just then Michael came in and she told him, '*You* ask her,' and before he could say a word – 'Don't you want to keep your uncle out of jail? You could do something for once in your life – something practical instead of just praying for people. Or whatever it is you do!' she shouted when he laughed. 'All those hours sitting on the floor with your eyes turned up, what good is that supposed to do anyone?'

'No no,' he protested, 'it's only supposed to do good to me.'

'Well, I wish we could see some results then,' she pretended to grumble.

But it was because he was the way he was – uninvolved, innocent where everyone else carried a weight of past mistakes – that she felt she could send him to Sophie with their request: as a neutral messenger. Fair, spare, and clear-eyed, he *looked* neutral – she suppressed the word neuter, though it lurked in her mind.

Dave began to stir out of his mass of despair. He looked at his nephew with a flicker of hope; and with Dave it never took long for a flicker to become a leaping flame. 'Tell her anything you want, Michael,' he said. 'Every bad thing about me. I made a mistake and I'm paying for it. Tell her I'm paying for it, Michael. I don't sleep nights and I can't enjoy my food. I'm losing weight.' He went up to his nephew and put his arms around him: 'Tell her I love her.'

When Sophie had disposed of all her business – with her lawyer, stockbroker, and accountant – and was satisfied that she was leaving everything in the best possible order, she felt she could give in more to her illness. She knew that, on the days when Dave or Betsy telephoned, they did not feel it necessary to visit her; so on those days she went back to bed and lay

FIDELITY                    261

there, sinking into the sickness and the drugs prescribed for
it. Strange bruises had appeared on her body; they looked
like blows inflicted on her, though not from outside by any
physical violence. She was careful to dress in such a way that
they should be invisible, unknown to everyone except herself
and the doctor who had explained their cause. Although it
took her longer and longer every day, she continued to struggle
into her full regimen of clothing and underclothing; and then,
after Dave and Betsy had telephoned and she knew neither of
them was coming, she struggled out of them again.

Michael arrived unexpectedly. Her maid opened the door,
and with her finger on her lips, motioned him toward Sophie's
bedroom. This lay at the end of a whole series of rooms, each
one shrouded and unused. Her bedroom alone appeared –
not alive but at least serving a purpose, if only as a shelter or
retreat. The curtains were drawn here too, but they were of
some gold-textured material that allowed a faint light to filter
through. Sophie lay white, old, and alone in the marital double
bed. She was asleep, her head to one side, her mouth open
and emitting heavy, labored breathing sounds. But something
inside her was alerted to his presence: she opened her eyes
and at once jerked herself up and into activity – twitching
at her bed-jacket, fumbling at her hair, all the tiny motions
with which she had, since her girlhood, kept herself scrupulously tidy.

'I thought you were Dave,' she admitted at once. 'He called –
I said are you coming, but he said not today. He didn't come
yesterday either, or the day before. He must be busy.' She
smiled: 'He'll never stop.'

'No, he'll never stop,' echoed Michael but not smiling, so
that she asked at once, 'There's no trouble, is there?'

'There is trouble,' Michael said. 'And it might get very bad
for him—'

'Like before?'

'Worse than before.' She drew in her breath, and he plunged
on: 'He needs money; a lot of money.'

'But it's all there,' she said – in plaintive impatience, as
though arguing with someone unreasonable. 'I spoke to Mr G.

only the other day – Mr G. is the accountant. It's what Dave calls him: G. For Good. Because what he dispenses is good. It's our joke. Has he sent you to ask me?' she said. 'Well, you can tell him it's all right. I've done everything with Mr R.B. The lawyer: Mr Rotten Bad. Another joke.'

Michael said, 'He needs it now.'

'Now?'

'In the next few weeks. As soon as possible.'

After a short silence, she became querulous: 'I don't know why he doesn't come to see me. He hasn't been since Tuesday. Tell him to come tomorrow. Tell him I'm not well.' And before Michael could ask anything, she went on rapidly: 'Why go into all that – just tell him I need to see him. Surely it's not so hard to understand,' she said, turning herself into a cross old woman, 'that I want to see my own husband sometimes.'

'How do you know?' Betsy challenged Michael's report. 'You wouldn't know. You're not a doctor or anything.' However, after only a few moments, she said: 'If she knows something, wouldn't she tell us? Dave would move heaven and earth, take her to every specialist in the world – my God, nowadays there are treatments for *every*thing . . . At least we could try.'

Michael said, 'But if she doesn't want to try?'

'Everybody wants to live.' She blew out a volley of smoke from her cigarette. 'Dave's my own brother and I'm not defending him, but there's one thing you can't take away from him: whatever he's done, he's always had feeling for her. Michael, I wish your goddamn father had ever in his life had one-tenth that much feeling for me. Maybe I know better than anyone what it's like to be married to a bastard – two bastards! – but I've still plenty, I've everything to live for, and if *I* thought anything was wrong with me—'

'There isn't, is there?'

'I said if if *if*!' She laughed at the expression on his face. 'Come here,' but it was she who went to him and took his face between her hands.

He cleared his throat but still his voice came out husky: 'Try that smoke-enders program again. You *have* to quit.'

'I will. Don't worry. I intend to live forever.' She stubbed out her cigarette, but then she said, 'If there's really something wrong with her, we'll have to tell Dave,' and with this worry at once lit a new one.

Dave reacted with complete disbelief. He even began to quarrel with Betsy: 'How would Michael know? He has no experience of that kind of thing. He's just a boy.'

'He's thirty-four years old,' said Betsy, narrowing her eyes at her brother in a dangerous way.

'But he's never done anything except study and so on.'

'So by you that's nothing? Tell me what's something then – how many blondes do you have to fuck before you've done something?'

'Betsy, Betsy, is this a time to get in a fight?'

She realized it was not but continued sullen: 'If you don't believe Michael, you'd better go talk to her yourself. Anyway, she wants to see you today. Because Michael told her. About the hole you've gotten yourself in again.'

He sat holding his big head between his hands. He was bowed with shame. Although she was angry, disgusted with him, Betsy also felt sorry for him. 'Well, you'd better go. Michael's done some of the dirty work for you, but the rest you'll have to do yourself.'

'I love Michael,' he murmured out of his deep self-abasement. 'Michael is wonderful.'

'Yes, and I thank God every day that he hasn't taken after you.'

'Me too,' Dave said. 'I thank God too.' He got up and, as though leaving on some great enterprise, lumbered toward Betsy to embrace her. But she pushed him away – 'Go on, she's waiting for you' – and stood by the window with her arms folded and her back to him before he had even left the room.

But when he had gone, she became melancholy. This was uncharacteristic of her and also at variance with the bright rooms in which she lived. Even now the sun was streaming

in through her windows, spilling its light over all her shiny
objects and her richly blooming carpet. But it failed to light
up Betsy's heart, which was at that moment full of the dusky
gloom pervading the place where her sister-in-law lived. And
her thoughts strayed toward that other apartment where, any
moment now, Dave would be entering: Sophie would give
a start as he drew apart the curtains and the light came
in and lit up both the room and her face. Betsy covered
her own face, as if the light from that other place were
blinding her.

Next moment she shattered her mood by calling out to
Michael in a loud voice: 'Are you home or not!' She knew
he was but guessed he might be in his meditation, where
she was not allowed to disturb him any more than if he
were a lawyer working on a big case. She lit another cigarette
and sat down by her telephone. The first two numbers she
dialed were answered one by a maid and the other by a
machine, but at a third try she reached a friend who shrieked
with joy at hearing Betsy's voice. They talked of matters of
common interest for a while till the friend strayed to the
subject of her latest relationship, with a man in his sixties,
three times divorced, children and grandchildren all over
the place. Betsy listened in fascination – the conversation
became completely one-sided and lasted half an hour – but
when she put down the receiver, other feelings overcame her.
At first she voiced them as disgust – 'At her age and with a
hysterectomy' – but then again that unfamiliar melancholy
seeped into her, and she sat quiet for a long time, just thinking
and smoking.

Today Dave did not open Sophie's curtains, nor did he rush in.
It was her maid's day off, and letting himself in with his key, he
tiptoed through the silent apartment as far as the living room,
which was empty. 'In here!' came Sophie's voice: for however
drugged she was, and however quiet he tried to be, any sound
from him at once detonated a response in her.

'Why are you in bed?' He spoke to her from the doorway – too timid to approach. There was something remote

about her lying motionless amid the white sheets of their double bed.

'Oh, I'm being lazy – just for today,' she smiled. She patted the side of her bed but had to do it again before he ventured to perch there, and then gingerly, on one big buttock. They were silent, taking each other in, shy like a couple just getting to know each other.

'Michael was here,' she said at last.

'I know. He told me.'

'What did he tell you?'

He answered with a question of his own: 'You're sure you're doing okay, Sophie? You're not hiding anything from me?'

'What would I hide from you?' She smiled again – he knew her teeth were not her own but had never seen her without them. His eyes shifted to her bedside table. There was only one bottle of pills on it today. 'Yes, I know you told me not to take anything,' she intercepted him, 'but I haven't gotten around to throwing them out.'

'Why don't you tell what's-her-name to do it? Your girl – that's what she's here for.' He took the bottle and held it up, trying to read the label. 'I haven't got my specs,' he said, replacing it. They were in his top pocket – she could see them – but what was the use of putting them on, for even if he could read the label, he didn't know one medicine from another.

She said, 'Michael told me about you.'

'Forget it. It's not important. What's important is your health.'

She lifted her hand where it lay on the sheet and touched the lapel of his suit. He looked down at her hand: it was the broad, heavy hand of her German ancestry but now reduced to its bony frame, big bumpy knuckles pushing through the paper-like skin.

She whispered, 'Why don't you open the curtains so we can see each other?'

'No. It's nice this way.'

The light filtering through the golden bedroom curtains

veiled the two of them in a pale haze that made them look
spectral. She kept on whispering, and this seemed right because
what they had to say to each other was outside of ordinary
speech.

'I'm afraid,' she whispered.

'As long as I'm here, nothing will happen to you.'

'But what if something happens to you – like before?'

He seized her hand, still on his lapel. Although he meant his
grasp to be firm, strong, and reassuring, his hand was trembling
more than hers. They held on to each other.

'I won't let it happen,' she whispered.

He repeated: 'Forget it. It's not important. Only your health.'

'I told you a lie – those pills? The doctor prescribed them.
He says I have to take them.'

'And then you'll be okay?'

'Oh yes. But you know how bad I am with taking pills.
Throwing up and so on.'

'How many do you have to take?'

'All of them in the bottle.'

'All at once? The doctor said? Dr Blum?'

She nodded. 'But he said Dave has to help you.'

'That's what I'm here for.'

'I want to sit up.'

She tried to do so by herself, but he wouldn't let her. He
put his arms around her and lifted her and then kept holding
her. Frail in his arms, she seemed to be made of some other,
ethereal substance; her fine white nightdress enhanced this
impression. Her mouth was very near his ear and her words
came wafting into him on her breath: 'Mr G. knows what to
do, and Mr R.B.'

'I don't need to hear this,' he whispered back. 'You're not
to think of any business till you're absolutely one hundred per
cent again – understand?'

She nodded, shutting her eyes. Joy and suffering lay so close
together, they were really one and the same.

'Should I get some water? Or what do you want to take
them with?'

'I'll try with fruit juice. That – what's it called? Apricot nectar. Or is it Ambrosia? It's in the ice-box. But just one more minute. Hold me for one more minute.'

'As long as you want. Forever, if you want.' Tears had already gathered in his eyes, ready to flow and ease him.

# BOBBY

After her last man friend, when the situation with Bobby became very difficult, Claire preferred to have only women friends. And as the years passed, and Bobby grew into his full and frightening manhood, his mother only felt comfortable with her oldest friend, Madeleine, and spent most of her time with her. That suited Madeleine better than anything. When they were at school together, Madeleine had had a crush on Claire that never entirely wore off, though their lives had diverged completely and there were years when they had lost touch. But now that the main activity of those years had ended and they were back, at least geographically, where they had started, the old relationship could be resumed.

It wasn't as though either of them had changed all that much. They found that underneath everything – that is, underneath their transformed physical appearance – they retained the character of the schoolgirls they had been. They had a lot of fun together even now. Madeleine, who had lived abroad for many years, bought an apartment in New York in the same building and on the same floor as Claire's. At weekends they drove to the place in the country that Madeleine had inherited from her parents. It was a two-story house, built in the twenties, and they could have comfortably lived there all the time. Madeleine wanted to, but Claire said she would miss the plays and concerts in the city. But it wasn't that at all – they could have easily driven in for the day; it was Bobby. It was always Bobby.

Sometimes he joined them, but mostly he stayed in the city,

and then Madeleine had Claire all to herself in the house in the country. It made her more happy than she had dreamed, during her bad years, she ever could be again. She got up in the morning and prepared breakfast for when Claire woke up. It wasn't until she had given the last touch to the table laid cozily in the breakfast nook that she tramped upstairs to Claire's bedroom. She stood over Claire and said, 'Up with you, lazybones.' From within the delicious warmth of her bed, Claire looked up at her; and if Katze was curled on the comforter, then Madeleine would grab and squeeze him hard till he miaowed in indignation.

'You'll kill him,' Claire warned.

'Yes, kill him with love,' said Madeleine, making big threatening eyes at Claire in bed.

'You will,' Claire said. 'You don't know your own strength.'

'I'm not like you – look at your ridiculous little wrist.' Madeleine took it and spanned it between two fingers. 'I could snap it in two if I wanted,' she said, sounding as though she might.

'Help,' said Claire lazily; making her wrist go limp, she left it where it was in Madeleine's big hand.

At first Bobby had hated Madeleine. He jeered at her appearance – her big shapeless body and the way she dressed it in long peasant gowns. He asked, what was she, an Old Believer, or a prophetess? With this he was also hitting out at the way Madeleine had spent her life. She had been companion-secretary to a philosopher and had traveled around with him all over the world. People thronged to his lectures and workshops, for his philosophy was as attractive as his personality. Both were totally absorbing to Madeleine, and she had dedicated herself to him; but then he took on a younger secretary and the situation changed. Madeleine had returned home to the States, and all that was left of her years of devotion was a trunk full of the peasant gowns that he had encouraged his women followers to wear.

When Bobby taunted Madeleine, Claire was ashamed and would have stopped him, if she hadn't known that this would only make him worse. She was grateful for the patient way

Madeleine, who was not patient by nature, pretended to take it all as friendly kidding. It turned out to be the best way to deal with him. Losing interest in her, he ignored her, which could be interpreted as tolerating her – anyway, that was how Madeleine and Claire interpreted it, enabling them to continue building up a life together. Madeleine made it scrupulously clear that the house in the country was as much Bobby's home as it was hers and his mother's, and that he was free to come there whenever he wanted. But of course it was best when he didn't come.

At first Madeleine and Claire used to drive back on Mondays, but one week Madeleine said, 'Why not stay till tomorrow?' Claire said nothing, but after a while she went up to her bedroom, shutting the door. Madeleine knew she had gone to phone Bobby, to ask his permission, and she waited nervously. But when Claire returned, she said: 'There's no answer.'

'He's out having a good time,' Madeleine urged in false cheer.

Claire continued to frown anxiously. It may well have been that Bobby had gone out, but equally well he might be at home not answering the phone – for any number of reasons: because he didn't feel like it; or because he knew it was his mother and it gave him pleasure to think of her worrying where he was, what he was doing. Or he may have been asleep, he often slept through the day after taking God knows what, a legitimate drug prescribed by his doctor or something else. Or perhaps he wasn't asleep – didn't Madeleine know every tormenting thought that formed behind Claire's delicate forehead? Perhaps he *couldn't* answer the phone because – well, anything could *happen*: 'We'd better go,' Claire said, and Madeleine knew there was nothing she could say to keep her.

But the following Monday Madeleine decided to stay back and let Claire return alone. It was both a wrench and a relief: to let her go, and yet not to have to be with her in the city under the cloud of Bobby's presence. They spoke briefly on the phone several times a day and had long conversations in the evening. In the background Madeleine could hear the rock music that Bobby always played at an earsplitting level. On Friday afternoon Madeleine drove to the station to collect Claire. Her heart leaped when she saw her step off the train – stylish and slim, laughing with some silly thing that had happened to her on the way. They both laughed, like a couple of madcap schoolgirls, Madeleine driving the car rather recklessly. Then Claire said, 'Bobby said he might join us this weekend,' and Madeleine said, 'Oh good,' getting a firmer grip on the wheel because the front tires had skidded with her careless driving.

He arrived the next day in a cab from the station. It was early evening, and Madeleine and Claire were sitting idyllically under an apple tree, shelling peas for their supper. Behind them the sun was setting in a mild glow of gold. The moment she saw Bobby arrive, Claire put down her bowl of shelled peas and went to pay the cab driver. She kissed Bobby, who turned away from her to face Madeleine – not with his usual scowl but with a sort of triumphant smile that may have meant no more than 'Here I am.'

He was carrying his big metal stereo. He never went anywhere without it – loud, reverberating sound was his inescapable accompaniment. Madeleine had almost gotten used to it. It was difficult to tell where the music ended and his own personality began, for both hammered mercilessly through whatever space he occupied. That weekend happened to be calm for him. He sat for many hours, frowning over a book of which he rarely turned a page; when he looked up, his eyes were clouded with thoughts that seemed to have welled up not from any reading but from some abyss inside himself. That impression may have been subjective, Madeleine had to admit, formed by her vision of him as a darkly brooding presence. Whenever he went on one of his long solitary walks, she imagined him throwing a sombre, terrible cloud over this golden landscape of streams and hills and immaculate white clapboard houses. But she knew it wasn't right to think of him that way, for what was he but a youth enjoying a day out in the country? The impression of shadow, of darkness may have been due only to his complexion, which was a throwback to his father's Italian ancestry.

They gave him one of the bedrooms on the second floor, a charming, simple room with white furniture and flowered wallpaper matching the curtains. He lay, sweet and pure, with his head on the white pillow. Claire sat on the side of his bed and Madeleine stood in the door, watching them. 'How handsome you are, my darling,' said Claire, brushing the hair from his high arched brow, which would have been noble if it hadn't been for the scowl lowering there. But now he was calm; he let her stroke his face; he loved her. 'Shall I read to you, my darling?' she asked. She often read to him – fairy tales of princes bewitched into monsters until redeemed by love; or plays she would have liked to act in – before her marriage she wanted to be an actress – or would have liked him to act in, for wasn't he handsome like an actor, a star? Again she stroked his face, kissing her own fingertips where they had touched him. She loved his looks, and to draw Madeleine's attention to them. Sometimes she compared him to his father, whom she had described to Madeleine as pale, emasculated, deracinated, not only in appearance but in character too: a weak, weak man. But Bobby was strong, with a broad chest and back matted in luxurious black hair. His father's hair had begun to thin before he was thirty; and his father had long thin hands like the artist he had pretended to be, though settling for a safe job with an international organization. Bobby's hands were huge and strong, they were those of the Italian farmworkers his family had been, several generations ago. Claire stroked them where they lay on the sheet; she said, 'Do you like being here? Madeleine loves having you here, she's so grateful you've come – aren't you?' she said, smiling to her standing in the door, and Madeleine smiled back and said yes.

By next day Bobby was bored with being in the country, so his mother returned with him to the city. Madeleine stayed through the week – this had become a regular pattern for her, along with her daily calls to Claire. But on one of those calls there was something odd in Claire's voice, off-key. Madeleine phoned again an hour later, and still that inflection was there, but of course when she said, 'Is everything all right?' Claire gave a light laugh and said: 'Why shouldn't it be?' Madeleine knew many reasons why. By evening she was so restless that she got in her car and drove to the city. The moment she let herself into her apartment, she felt a difference. During her absence, Claire always came in to water the plants; but as soon as she opened the door, Madeleine knew that someone else had been there. And not only been there – had lived there – had turned it into his lair! In her bedroom the mattress had been dragged from the bed to the floor; dirty underwear was stuffed into the sides of an armchair. Her photographs, of her parents and a brother who had died as an adolescent, were thrown face down on the dresser. She thrust open the window to get rid of the feral smell that lay thick in the air.

When she felt calm enough, she went to Claire's apartment down the hall. She rang the bell and called through the door, 'It's me.' Claire opened and said in a shocked voice, 'What happened – why have you come?' She let her in, quickly turning aside her face but not before Madeleine had seen the injury on it.

Madeleine said in a calm, normal voice: 'I have to see my tax man tomorrow, so I thought we might have dinner tonight, you and I.'

'Oh great,' said Claire; and then: 'You haven't been to your apartment yet, have you?'

'No, I came to see you first.'

They moved around each other like pugilists, Claire trying to hide her face and Madeleine to get a better look at it. At last Claire said, 'Why don't you sit down, you're making me nervous.'

Madeleine sat down in the center of a graceful little sofa; she occupied almost all of it, for she was big and sat with her thighs apart. Claire stood by the window as though there were something interesting happening in the building opposite. She said, 'What do you feel like – spaghetti? Chinese? Or we could just go to Rami's. It's up to you.'

Madeleine said, 'Why don't you turn around and let me see your face?'

Claire kept on looking out the window. After a while,

she said: 'I fell.' And after another while: 'Leave it; forget it.'

Madeleine went over to her. She made her turn so that she could study her face. There was a cut over the cheekbone, a large dark bruise around one eye. The way Claire looked at her through this bruise brought a sob welling up in Madeleine's chest. To stifle it, she pressed Claire against herself, and they stood close together, trembling as with one body.

When she let Claire go, Madeleine spoke sensibly: 'We can't go on this way. It's not as if it's just you and he now – I'm here too. And I'm not going to sit by and watch all this. I can't bear it.'

Claire's disfigured face jeered at her: 'You can't? Then what will you do? What do people do when they can't *bear* something?' She gave a dry laugh: 'They bear it.' But next moment she changed to a much lighter tone; she said, 'I really did fall – all right, don't believe me, but that's what happened. All he did was throw a statue at me and it got me – here – and then he was coming after me and I ran and slipped and hit my face against the table.'

'What statue did he throw at you?'

'Oh, just that soapstone Buddha you have—' After a pause she said, 'Yes, it was in your apartment because he's staying there. Only for a while, Mad, as long as you don't need it. Because it's nicer for a boy, isn't it, to be on his own sometimes and not have his mother fussing at him all the time . . . Of course I'll have it cleaned up, you know how messy boys can be – and in fact, that's what the fight was about yesterday.' She laughed, as at a not unamusing incident: 'I was trying to get him to let Teresa in to clean, and he wouldn't. He's getting to be really possessive about your place, Mad. He really likes it,' she assured her in a bright voice, as at something to be pleased about.

Madeleine persuaded Claire to return to the country with her the same night, which was a Thursday, a day earlier than usual. They had several flawless days together. They stayed mostly outdoors where everything was in full summer bloom. Madeleine watered, weeded, and tried to take the scum off the pond, while Claire sat near her in a garden chair, reading and ruminating. Katze chased birds and squirrels. For hours Madeleine and Claire hardly spoke, but then there were moments when they had so much to say that Claire flung aside her book and Madeleine sat on the grass, leaning against Claire's chair. They remembered their schooldays and beautiful summers like this one, and how they had gone to some romantic spot for a picnic and had looked up at the sky and felt the earth pressing against them through their light frocks. They had spoken of their ambitions and plans, which had been wide open, infinite. Claire was going to be an actress, she was the most talented of their group and also one of the prettiest, so that many girls had wanted to be her friend. Often Madeleine had had to sit dumbly on the outskirts of their circle, with no one taking notice of her; so that when Claire spoke of those years with joy, Madeleine thought secretly how much better it was now that there were only the two of them in her fragrant garden with birds chirping around them, sparrows and swallows, and not excited, jealous girls.

When Claire talked about the past and the people in it they had known, she made it all so amusing and alive that Madeleine exclaimed: 'You *should* have been an actress!'

Claire shrugged, smiled – a little melancholy but proud, too, of the talent she had had. Then she said, 'Maybe, if I hadn't been a fool and got married to a fool.' Her face hardened as always at the mention of her ex-husband: 'He couldn't stand it that I did anything better than he. *He* had to be the one always, no one else. I tell you, Mad, he had a huge personality problem – still has. This is his latest.' Clouds had floated over the sun, she frowned at the sudden shadow and chill and said, 'Let's go in.'

But Madeleine pressed her back closer against Claire's legs. Absently, still frowning at her own thoughts, Claire let her fingers play over Madeleine's crop of hair. 'Bobby must have written to him,' she said. 'I don't know what he wrote – he didn't even tell me about it, but good Lord, a boy has the right to write a letter to his own father, I sincerely hope.' She stopped, and took her hand from Madeleine's hair. Madeleine waited breathlessly for her to put it back, but Claire was by now engrossed in her own indignation: 'So I have this letter from him saying on no account can Bobby come to stay with them in Geneva, going into this long thing about his boys' school exams – his boys! As if Bobby isn't! But he's never understood Bobby; never. He's just not fit to understand any personality more complex than those vapid kids he has with his little Swiss housewife – oh, they're okay, I suppose, quite nice if you happen to care for white mice, but nothing, I tell you, nothing compared to my Bobby.'

Madeleine looked up at the sky clouding over. 'Maybe we should go in.'

'It'll be an eternal mystery to me where Bobby gets his looks from. Don't you think he has *star* looks? Really stunning? Those eyes – and his physique, Madeleine, his shoulders – you can't deny that he's incredibly handsome, you can't deny it, can you? . . . You don't like him, that's why you're not saying anything.'

'I said *yes!*'

'No you did not; you said nothing. Because you're against him, like everyone. Is it any wonder that he is the way he is, with the whole world against him, including his own father?' She pushed Madeleine aside so that she could get up. She went into the house and didn't look back when Madeleine called after her. Madeleine stayed sitting on the ground, tearing up clumps of grass with dandelions in them and crushing them inside her fist.

By the time she followed, Claire was busy pottering around the kitchen. Claire said at once: 'I'm fixing dinner tonight – I'm making my pesto sauce, and you just go inside and put your big feet up. Go on now.'

Claire's cooking was much better, more subtle, than Madeleine's, so that night they had a delicious meal for which Madeleine opened one of the special bottles of wine still left from her father's cellar. Afterward they stayed in the living room, dark and crowded with old family furniture and family photographs and an oil painting of a very early ancestress in a mob-cap; there was a rosewood piano that Madeleine's mother

had played, with her music still lying on top. Madeleine sat
on a hard leather settee where her father used to take cat-naps
behind his newspaper. Now it was Claire who squatted on the
floor, with her back resting against Madeleine's legs; and the
moon shone in through the open windows between the lined
velour curtains they had left undrawn.

'You're not like me,' Claire was saying. 'You've always been
self-sufficient. You haven't needed people.'

'Ha-ha-ha,' said Madeleine.

'Not in that way,' Claire insisted.

'What other way is there?' Madeleine said. She knew Claire
was hinting at her relationship with the philosopher, so she
said: 'For all his talk, in the end it came to the same thing. It
was all personal. He manipulated us, just like a lover with a
lot of mistresses.' Claire reached up her hand and Madeleine
grasped and held on to it. She swallowed as though there were
a painful obstruction to what she went on to say: 'He made
us believe it was all for a higher cause, for his philosophy, for
a better world . . . Yes, a better world for *him*,' she sneered,
making herself more bitter than she really felt. 'He's the only
one who got anything out of it.'

'But you cared for him; you did care for him.' Claire gave
Madeleine's hand a little shake, to admonish her that it had
not been all for nothing.

'Of course I did; we all did; that's what he relied on. Making
us his slaves – I don't only mean working for nothing *and* giving
our own money: he never had any poor disciples, he couldn't
afford them – but chaining us to him by our feelings, that's
what's so horrible, that he made us his slaves by what was
best in us.'

Madeleine was shaken through and through – physically
through her strong body, and through all the fortifications she
had built up around her memories of the past. But consolation
was immediate, for there was Claire and their hands were
intertwined.

'Come sit beside me,' Madeleine said. 'Don't sit on the floor
– he was always doing that, making us get down on the floor

at his feet. And of course we liked to do it, we *loved* it. I know what you want to ask me.'

Claire had come to be with Madeleine on the leather settee; they were side by side, chastely holding hands while the moonlight streamed in on them.

'No, I never slept with him,' Madeleine said. 'It was all on a much higher plane – laugh if you want; I feel like laughing myself, now . . . But then of course I took it dead seriously. It made me proud; exalted, if you know what I mean, that I was *overcoming* myself. That was part of the philosophy, overcoming yourself. It wasn't always easy, I tell you. I spent a lot of time with him, in intimate proximity, and he was a very attractive man, sexually attractive . . . Sometimes it was physical torture. But the worse the torture the better I felt – that I was doing this for him. I thought everyone else was doing it too, and it was only afterward that I found out he was sleeping with people right and left. Of course only the better looking ones.' She was silent; her face sagged.

After a longish pause, 'I think you're nice looking,' Claire said. 'I'm not just saying it, it's true . . . Not in a conventional way, not just silly-pretty, but you have real character in your face. That's because you *are* a real character; a really kind good person.' And moved by her own words, Claire leaned toward her friend and kissed her cheek.

Madeleine burst out, 'Thank God I have you now; oh thank God.' And then she threw everything to the wind – all calm, restraint, the good-girl way they were sitting side by side – she put her arms around Claire and began to kiss her hair, and her face all over, impetuously raining down kisses that sometimes missed their mark. And Claire laughed and cried out: 'Stop it, Mad, have you gone crazy!' but it wasn't till she cried, 'You're choking me!' that Madeleine let go.

Claire smoothed her hair and clothes, which Madeleine had mussed. She gave an embarrassed little laugh: 'I told you, you don't know your own strength.'

'You're absolutely right,' Madeleine admitted. She waited a moment: 'Take off your clothes.'

'You *are* crazy.'

'Please. I want it. I want it so much. Only to see you, that's all.'

'Oh for heaven's sakes, Madeleine: do you know how old I am?'

'Yes; four months younger than I am, and I'm fifty-two. Go on, take off your clothes. I'll help you, shall I?' She undid a button here, a zip there, Claire protesting all the way – but amused too, for it wasn't much more than a game that two girls might play together.

Then Claire was stripped naked. She was slender, small-breasted, and illumined only by moonlight she might have been young. Madeleine ran her hands down Claire's hips, touching her reverently.

'Now you,' said Claire.

'Me!' Madeleine guffawed. 'You don't want to see me, I'm like a buffalo.'

'Go on.'

'Promise not to turn on the light.'

'Of course I won't. Go on. You have to. Otherwise it's not fair.'

It didn't take Madeleine a moment – all she had to do was throw off her peasant gown; she wore nothing underneath. 'Oh God,' she said, stark naked, covering her eyes so as not to have to see herself. 'I *told* you.' But she too was transfigured by moonlight. The two of them stood looking at each other; they had clasped hands as though about to circle in a game of ring-a-roses. Katze humped his back and rubbed himself against their legs, so that they laughed out loud and gave little skips into the air to escape his tickling fur.

On Monday Madeleine didn't drop Claire at the station but drove her into the city. She found it impossible to part from her. But Claire was not pleased by this decision and sat tight-lipped and silent beside her. Madeleine tried to keep up her own high spirits by talking cheerfully and playing a lively tape as she drove her car over the winding wooded parkway. It was only when the beautiful landscape began to degenerate into New York City that Madeleine's mood began to match

Claire's; and by the time they reached the Bronx, waiting by the crosslights where a brand-new McDonald's had sprung up on what had been a basket-ball court for unemployed adolescents, Madeleine said gloomily: 'I wish I hadn't come.'

'Yes, why did you?' Claire snapped back at once, as though this was what she had wanted to say the entire way.

Youths with wet cloths had sprung forward to wipe the windscreen. Madeleine furiously waved them away, but Claire lowered her window and held out money to them. Just then the lights changed and Madeleine drove forward with a jolt. 'You shouldn't encourage them,' she said in an angry voice.

'What's a dollar,' Claire retorted in the same voice. Both of them stared straight out the windscreen, though there was nothing beautiful to see now – condemned buildings with their windows boarded up, a warehouse selling off furniture from a closed-out factory. Claire said: 'You don't care for young people, that's your trouble, you have no feeling for them.'

'Not for young criminals I don't.'

'You don't know they're criminals. And what's wrong with trying to make a little money cleaning people's cars? It's better than stealing.'

'My window was perfectly clean.'

It took a long time to get across to the Upper East side where they lived. Again and again they were stuck in dense traffic; heat, noise, and fumes filled their car; they sighed and shifted their thighs where their dresses stuck to them with perspiration. At last Claire broke out: 'You didn't have to come – I *had* to, but you didn't.' She was not speaking in anger now but exasperation.

'I know,' said Madeleine. She cursed briefly as again they missed the green light, stuck behind a removal van. She thought longingly of the house in the country, the shadows of her trees lengthening on the lawn, the splash of water as a startled frog jumped into the pond.

'And there's something else,' Claire said in a gentler, con-ciliatory voice.

Madeleine said at once: 'That's all right – he can stay on in my apartment, I didn't expect him to move. It's hardly worth

it—' she slid her eyes toward Claire – 'since we'll be going
back on Thursday.'

'Yes, or Friday,' Claire said.

Bobby seemed glad his mother had come back and was
indifferent to Madeleine's presence. He took it for granted
that he would stay on in Madeleine's apartment; the idea of
moving didn't occur to him. Claire showed Madeleine into
the spare bedroom in her own apartment, which was really a
maid's room, but Madeleine preferred it to sleeping in what
was usually Bobby's. Anyway, she soon joined Claire in her
bed; it was what they had gotten used to since the night they
had skipped around in the moonlight. But that first night in the
city Claire was constantly alert, listening – 'What's the matter?'
Madeleine asked.

'The door's locked, isn't it?'

'You locked it yourself.'

Nevertheless, Claire got up to make sure. When she returned
to bed, she was shivering with cold or fear. She slept fitfully,
and before dawn she insisted that Madeleine return to the
maid's room.

After such a disturbed night, they both slept late and it was
almost noon when they had breakfast. Bobby was still asleep
in Madeleine's apartment; he rarely got up before afternoon.
'He's awake all night,' Claire explained, 'that's why I never
put the chain on my front door. So he can let himself in if
he wants.'

Madeleine finished her toast, chewing slowly, and then she
said: 'But he never comes in your room? He doesn't disturb
you? I hope not.'

'Oh no – usually he just bangs around the kitchen for something to eat. He only wakes me if he really needs me. If there's
something he really wants to share with me. He gets some of his
best ideas at night.' She gave a shy glance at Madeleine. 'You'd
be surprised – he has some very original theories – scientific
theories about sound waves? – well, it may all be a lot of
nonsense, I don't know, you remember what an absolute idiot
I always was with math and physics. But Dr Stein says—'

'Yes? What?'

Claire shot her another look and went on bravely: 'He says that Bobby could have been a genius. He has that sort of brain, only there's some chemical imbalance, that's why he has these personality disorders or whatever it's called. I don't really understand it, but anyway that's what Dr Stein says.'

'How often does Bobby see Dr Stein?'

'Not very often . . . Actually, he hasn't been for some time. It was Bobby's own decision, I think he feels that he no longer needs Dr Stein, and he's right because I think he's much much better, don't you, I mean calmer, I mean last night at dinner, don't you think he was—' she answered herself, 'absolutely normal and nice;' and she jumped up and busily cleared away the breakfast dishes.

Claire had a very fine platinum chain, which always got knotted up. 'Bobby's the only one who can undo it,' she told Madeleine that evening. She took it off and gave it to him, smiling, and continued to smile as she watched him apply himself to this task. Madeleine too watched, and it was wonderful to see the way his large peasant hands so delicately picked at the dainty chain. It took a long time, but he was patient and painstaking, a perfectionist. When at last he finished, he looked up with a happy smile. How his face cleared with that smile – how handsome it was and open; his brooding eyes were candid under his nobly arched brow. He said to Claire, 'Come here.' She stood with her back to him while he put the chain around her neck. They were almost the same height, for he was not very tall though broad-shouldered and muscular. He fastened the clasp and she asked, 'All right?'; she didn't move but waited, her head bent as for execution. He too stood a while longer, and then he ran his finger along the nape of her neck: Madeleine, who had done the same herself, knew that under his finger he could feel the frail down of hair where it started on Claire's neck and then continued all the way to the small of her back.

He didn't leave till after midnight, so it was late before they got to bed. Even then, Madeleine couldn't fall asleep, and when she went in to Claire, she found her awake too.

She locked the door and got in with her, but Claire shifted uncomfortably. 'This bed's too small for two of us.'

Madeleine said, 'I'm going back tomorrow.'

'All right,' Claire said. 'I'll see you Friday.'

'I don't want you staying here alone.'

Claire said, 'I'm not alone . . . Sh,' she said, her ears far more finely tuned to sounds in her apartment than Madeleine's. 'Turn off the light,' she whispered – so urgently that Madeleine obeyed before she heard the sound herself: of the front door closing, of steps in the hall.

The two women listened while the steps approached their door. They heard the handle being turned, gently at first, then not so gently when the door was found to be locked. There was a pause. Again the handle was turned, and again – and then the door was being rattled, insistently, furiously. 'I'll open it,' Madeleine said in what she tried to make a normal voice. Claire whispered, 'No, no!' and the fear in her angered Madeleine so that she jumped out of bed, shouting, 'Wait!' She unlocked the door and flung it open. 'What's wrong with you?' she scolded Bobby. 'We're trying to get some sleep, don't you have any consideration?' He looked past her toward Claire, sitting shivering on the bed. He seemed reassured when he saw her, as though the only reason he came was to make sure she was there.

Claire said, 'Go to bed, darling. I wasn't feeling well, so I called Madeleine.'

He said, 'Do you want an aspirin or something?'

'No, no, darling, please don't worry. Go to sleep. Madeleine's here.'

'Okay,' he said, seemingly satisfied, and turned and went back out again.

But next morning Claire said she would return with Madeleine. They left before Bobby woke, and the way Madeleine drove it was as if they were fleeing the city. When they pulled up before the house, they looked at each other and laughed, the way people do when they have outwitted everyone and got away. Katze was sitting on a green cushion on a wicker chair right in the middle of the front porch, and his only greeting was a narrowing of his glinting eyes. 'Can't even say hi decently,' said Madeleine, and in her exuberance she tipped him off his chair so that he indignantly stalked away. That made them laugh, but so did everything that day; they were so glad to be there. The hushed, orderly house seemed to welcome them home, even to be grateful for their return – including Katze, for all the superior airs he gave himself. He followed them around as they went from room to room and up and down the stairs; they straightened photo frames and emptied vases, all the time calling to each other – always for some ostensible purpose but really just to hear each other's voices filling this loved and loving house.

It wasn't till next morning at breakfast that Claire said, 'He'll probably come this weekend.'

'Of course,' said Madeleine, in a calm, matter-of-fact way. 'You know he's always welcome. It's his home as much as it's yours and mine.'

Claire took Madeleine's hand, where it lay between them on the table, and kissed it. Madeleine snatched it away: 'Don't do that, silly.' Her big face had flushed scarlet. Their eyes met. 'Silly,' Madeleine repeated, in a husky, scolding voice.

He arrived that same evening. Madeleine found herself scanning his face, gauging his mood, in the same way as Claire. When they went to bed that night, Claire said how she was looking forward to a nice long lazy sleep; Madeleine understood and stayed in her own room – anyway, she wanted to, she felt safer there. He kept playing his music till late into the night. Madeleine put the covers over her head, but there was no escaping the sounds that struck through the house like blows from a hammer. Once she thought she would get up and storm down and turn it off, but she felt afraid; and that made her furious, to think she was afraid in her own home. She leaped out of bed and was already on the landing when she thought better of it. She returned to her room, lay down again. She thought of Claire in her bed, penetrated by the same sounds – and not only now, but forever, inescapably. Then Madeleine thought, if you can stand it, so can I, and this idea filled her with a feeling of peace, even contentment: to be enduring together with Claire, both of them nailed down and battered by the brutal music, as though they were not two persons but one.

Next day Bobby's mood was ugly. Even Katze felt the danger. When Bobby got up in the afternoon and came into the kitchen for his food, Katze slipped off the window sill where he had been contemplating birds and squirrels on the grass outside; but before he could slink out the door, Bobby caught him – 'Ah-ha! No you don't!' He was gentle with him – Madeleine watched his huge hands stroking Katze's fur, to and fro, from head to tail, back and forth. Katze was not happy, Madeleine could see, but he kept still, maybe not daring to move. Bobby went on and on; his caressing hands appeared to take on a life of their own. Claire laughed: 'That's enough now, Bobby. Eat your breakfast or lunch or brunch or whatever you want to call it.' To Madeleine she said, 'Bobby loves animals.'

Madeleine remembered how Claire had once told her that Bobby was usually kind to animals. When he was a child, she could buy goldfish for him and keep them in a tank and he would remember to feed them; once he had been given a canary, but it had died in its cage, a natural death. It was when he had been around other children, Claire had gone on to admit, that she had been nervous. It was usually all right when she took him to the park where the swings were, but there had been incidents, so that she preferred not to go to places where there were other children. 'It wasn't his fault,' Claire had explained, referring to one such incident when he had struck a little girl on the head with his fist repeatedly so that people had had to come running. 'She must have said something to him – you know how kids can be, awfully mean sometimes. He was just defending himself.'

That weekend he turned on Madeleine. She tried to suffer it patiently. He insulted her in the same way he had before he got used to her being around. He sneered at her physical appearance, at the peasant gowns she wore, at what she was, who she was, everything about her, including her past. 'Tell me about your philosopher,' he taunted her. 'What sort of philosopher could that have been – what sort of philosophy would *you* understand?'

'Oh no, of course not,' Claire replied, with a wink at Madeleine to show it was all good fun. 'We're not high-powered brains like you are, darling, we don't understand these abstruse things.'

'You can say that again,' he agreed. 'Straw up here, that's all you have, like all women: straw. Okay!' he shouted at Madeleine. 'If you've got more than straw, tell me what was this great philosophy you learned from your philosopher, just tell me.'

'Well, I'll try,' said Madeleine good-humoredly.

He folded his arms in challenge, and now *he* winked – at Claire, to draw her in on this joke against Madeleine. And Claire smiled with him.

Madeleine said, 'It was like this: he had a Latin tag he had learned – probably at school, like the rest of us. Remember Latin with Miss Coffin?' she asked Claire.

'Oh my Lord!' Claire exclaimed. 'Miss Coffin! Will I ever forget her, in her baggy Jaeger skirt—' but with Bobby's frown on her, she broke off and said to Madeleine, 'Go on then.'

'It was *nihil humani* – you know what that means,' she said to Claire.

'Nothing human,' Claire said.

'You keep quiet,' Bobby said. 'Let *her* talk. Let *her* explain this wonderful philosophy.'

'It was a load of rubbish,' Madeleine said. 'Nothing human *ab me alienum puto* – do I think alien to me – that's what he used to preach at us: to accept everything that anyone did because we had the same thing in us potentially, every evil there could be. It took me years to find out that it was his private license to take whatever he could from people – their own thoughts and personalities, not to mention their money and whatever else they had, including of course sex.'

'Did he have sex with you?' Bobby demanded, and added

at once, 'I hope he had better taste.' Claire tried to admonish him, but he was suddenly in a good mood, laughing loudly at his own joke, which amused him so much that he repeated it— 'I hope he did: have better taste than sleep with you.'

'I guess he did,' answered Madeleine, laughing with him, pleased to have put him for the moment in a better humor.

Claire and Madeleine began to snap at each other. Early next morning when Madeleine entered the kitchen, she found Claire feeding Katze. 'What are you doing?' she yelled. 'I've fed him already – do you want to kill him or what!'

'Well, to hell with you!' answered Claire, slamming down Katze's saucer. 'I thought I was doing you a favor, feeding your fat old cat.'

Madeleine controlled herself. She began to get breakfast for the two of them, cutting bread with a martyr's air that made Claire say, 'Don't cut any for me. I only want some orange juice.'

'At least some *toast*.'

'I don't want it! And such thick slices – I don't know why you can't – here let me—'

'No thank you,' Madeleine said. 'I *like* thick slices, and since you don't want any, I hope you'll let me eat what I like, even if it is thick and coarse.' Claire groaned in exasperation, which made Madeleine continue: 'But that's me – I am thick and coarse, by your standards, I'm sure.'

Claire sat down in their breakfast nook. Madeleine slammed around the kitchen a while longer, but soon she was stealing glances at Claire sitting at the table with its checkered cloth and little vase of flowers that Madeleine had picked an hour earlier. Claire's slight, small profile was outlined against the window and the blossoming tree and patch of pure pale sky that could be seen through it. Somewhere a woodchuck chucked through the calm, utterly peaceful morning air. Bobby slept upstairs; there was no sound in all the house. Madeleine sat in the chair opposite Claire; she buttered a toast for her and Claire ate it. They silently savored their moment together.

By the time Bobby got up, Madeleine was at work in the garden. She dug into a neglected patch of ground, treading down on the spade to force it into the stubborn earth. It was hard work, man's work, and she kept having to stop to wipe the perspiration running into her eyes. Her blood pounded with the exertion, so that she hardly heard the sounds coming from the house – of hard rock music, and also she thought of voices raised in anger. Not wanting to hear them, she kept on digging, perspiring and panting with the physical labor. At last she was so exhausted that she flung aside her spade and lay face down as though burying herself in the earth. She heard and saw nothing but fell into a sleep as black and profound as a pit. When she woke, it was dark, and Claire was standing over her, calling her. Madeleine sat up with a start. 'What's the time?' she said.

'It's nine o'clock. I called and called you to eat, you wouldn't wake up.'

'Where's Bobby?'

'Inside. Can't you hear?'

His music blasted through the garden, drowning out all natural sounds. But not, for Madeleine, drowning out something in Claire's voice – 'He's hit her again,' flashed through her mind. But she wanted to know nothing of it, and if there was any injury on Claire's face, she didn't want to see it. So she continued to sit on the ground, slumped over, not looking up at Claire standing there; she yawned widely to show how tired she still was.

'What's the matter with you?' Claire said. 'Did you take something? You were lying here like a corpse.'

'I was out to the world. You said you called me? I didn't hear a thing.'

'Nothing? You didn't hear anything?'

'Not a sound, I promise.'

Claire said nothing; she didn't believe her. Madeleine still refused to look at her, but even if she had, she would have found it difficult to see Claire's face, which she kept averted and in shadow.

Claire said, 'He has these bad spells. Usually he's fine –

you've seen him yourself, how sweet he can be. But then there are these *days*, and then I don't know what to do.'

'Never mind,' said Madeleine to the despair in Claire's voice. 'It'll pass.'

'Oh yes, of course it'll pass! But meanwhile I'm sorry that your weekend is spoiled . . . I'll make it up to you, you'll see – we'll have our own nice times again, you and I. It's only today – tonight – you won't mind if I just go to bed? I might even take a pill to help me relax and get a really sound sleep.'

Madeleine agreed that this would be a good idea. They said goodnight in tender friendship. Claire went in, but Madeleine didn't follow her. She wanted to stay outside, away from the house, and as far as possible away from the music. But after a while, surprisingly, the music ceased. The house was silent. Then all the lights went out except for one on the porch, and one up in Claire's room. Then the latter too was extinguished. Except for that one dim little porch light, the house was in darkness. It was the grounds that were brightly lit, for there was a full moon pouring down light that was harsh and metallic, as though artificial. Still unwilling to go into the house, Madeleine wandered around. She flitted among trees that, floodlit, looked flat and unreal; she herself looked unreal, ghostlike in her long gown. It struck her that Bobby's bad spells might be connected with the full phase of the moon, and she thought no wonder, for the bright white beams seemed to penetrate deep into her brain, breeding sick, unnatural thoughts. She was also ravenously hungry, having missed supper; with her big healthy body, she needed her three meals a day.

Claire had kept a casserole in the oven for her, and she had laid a place at the table with salad and bread and wine, and all Madeleine had to do was sit and eat. She did so, filling her plate and glass several times. But still something – hunger or restlessness – gnawed her. The unusual silence was eerie, and so was the moonlight flooding harshly through the windows. She went around the house to draw all the curtains. Downstairs, the only sound came from the grandfather clock keeping its steady time, but when she went to draw the curtains upstairs, this ticking could no longer be heard. Nothing could be heard. Where was Bobby? She stood outside his door; she even dared rap on it, and when there was no answer, she went in, to draw the curtains and keep the moonlight out. The room was empty and in the usual mess in which he lived. She went out again quickly, and now she stood outside Claire's room. She put her ear against the door: not a sound. She was frightened. She thought of Claire lying on the bed, exposed to the influence of the moon pouring in on her; perhaps she had taken too many pills. But when Madeleine tried to go in, she found the door locked. She tried again, she rattled it; she rattled it more, she pounded on it; she called to Claire.

Claire opened the door. She said, 'What are you doing? You'll wake him.'

'Why is he with you?'

Claire shut the door, preventing Madeleine from seeing inside. They both stood against this closed door. Claire was wearing Bobby's robe, which she appeared to have thrown over herself in a hurry, for she was still tying it. She led Madeleine away from the door, down the stairs. Madeleine, following, said again, 'Why is he with you?' and again received no answer.

They sat in the living room, side by side on the hard-backed leather settee. With the curtains drawn, it was almost totally dark, and neither made a move to turn on the light. Madeleine said gently, 'He hit you again today, that's why you're not letting me see your face.'

'You can see it if you want, what's it matter.' Claire got up to draw aside the curtain, but she had only just parted the heavy lined material when the moonlight struck inside – and it was Madeleine who covered *her* face, shouting, 'No, don't!' She couldn't bear that harsh light coming in on her, stabbing into her brain.

Claire drew the curtain shut. She sat down again next to Madeleine, as before, with her hands folded in her lap, the same way as Madeleine; they might have been two middle-aged matrons on a social visit. Claire said, 'I told you he has these bad days, but they don't last. Tomorrow he'll be all right.'

'How do you know?'

Claire shrugged. 'Of course I know. I know everything there is to know about him, every little bit of him, better than anyone.'

'Better than a doctor?'

'A doctor is for sick people . . . Why won't you let me open the curtain? Don't you remember how nice it was, in the moonlight, with Katze?' She made her voice soft, flirtatious, recalling that happy time to Madeleine. When Madeleine didn't respond, she said, 'Where *is* Katze?'

'He must be hiding somewhere; he does that when he's scared.'

'Stupid Katze, what's he scared about?' Just then the grand-father clock struck the hour – one beat, one o'clock – and Madeleine gave a jump that made Claire laugh and tease: 'Now *you're* scared.' Madeleine didn't deny it.

After a long pause, Claire gave a sigh in preparation for what she had to say. It took another pause before she started. 'He's *not* sick, that's where everyone is wrong. Including you, Mad, though you're so understanding in every other way. He's *different*, not sick. He's more charged than other people, that's what it is – his brain is more charged, like with high voltage energy, and his body too – well, what do you expect!' she broke out. 'He's not neutered like your poor old Katze – he's a healthy young man in the prime of his life! What should he do? You tell me – what should he do!'

'What did you let him do? . . . No, don't touch me!' Madeleine cried out and snatched away her hand when Claire laid her own on top of it.

Claire withdrew her hand and repeated wryly, '"Don't touch me" . . . *Noli me tangere*,' she translated. 'There's another bit of Latin for you from Miss Coffin days. And what was that tag your philosopher taught you—'

'I told you it was a load of shit,' Madeleine interrupted harshly. '*He* was a load of shit, so don't remind me of him because all I want is to forget him.' She got up. 'I'm going to bed. I want to at least try and get some sleep before that music from hell starts up again.'

'I'll take him home tomorrow,' Claire promised. She kept sitting by herself on the settee, listening to Madeleine's footsteps dragging up the stairs. Madeleine's bedroom door closed, heavily.

But when Claire herself went upstairs, the door opened again and Madeleine came out. She barred Claire's way – 'What do you mean – you'll *take* him home? He can go by himself and you can leave on Monday.' When Claire tried to pass, she added: 'I'll drive you, if you want.'

Claire didn't answer but insisted on going past Madeleine to her own bedroom. Now it was Madeleine who listened to the door close. After a while she followed her. She knocked; when she tried the handle, it opened, but she did not go in. She called to Claire to come to the door and urged her: 'You will stay, won't you? Even if he goes.'

'Well, it's up to him,' Claire said, shrugging. 'Let's see what he wants to do in the morning.'

Madeleine stood in the half-open door. Claire was still in Bobby's robe that she had thrown on and tied securely around herself. Madeleine wanted to tear this robe off her and expose the body inside – was it naked? She wanted to beat and batter it.

But when she spoke, it was quietly: 'Ask him to stay.' She paused, gathered her strength, went on: 'Tell him we want him to stay. We both want him to stay.'

'All right, I'll try . . . Why don't you come in?' She opened the door wider, and when Madeleine hesitated, she said, 'He's asleep. He's all right now. He's fine.'

She encouraged Madeleine to enter and to approach the bed. Bobby was lying asleep in the middle of it. In the dimly shadowed darkness – for Claire too had drawn the curtains to keep the moonlight out – his naked torso appeared luminous, and so did the white sheet with which the rest of him was covered. His dark head lay sideways on the pillow; he had one hand lightly curled on his chest, which breathed up and down most peacefully.

'He's certainly nice-looking,' admitted Madeleine. 'Isn't he?' proudly smiled Claire. The two of them were holding hands as they stood looking down at him, their attitudes almost reverent.

# BROKEN PROMISES

'Reba's more the intellectual type,' Donna would say, whenever her friends talked about their own daughters. It wasn't
strictly true, but how else to account for the fact that Reba
had no visible boy friend and wore blue jeans and lumberjack
shirts? If she was visiting when Donna had her friends in,
Reba would sometimes open the door where they all were;
and though they looked around at her and smiled and nodded
so that their earrings swung and their coiffures swayed (some
of them wore wigs), Reba didn't join them but quickly shut the
door again. Then Donna would have to apologize – 'Reading
some book, I guess, she's always into them;' and her friends
set their perfect pearly rows of teeth into a smile and com-
plimented her, 'Lovely girl,' and 'You're lucky.' Nevertheless,
Donna realized that her friends really pitied her: although
their own daughters may also have had problems, these were
normal ones, like ex-spouses who didn't pay child support or
boy friends who wouldn't marry them.

But unlike her daughter, Donna's husband conformed to
type, for Si had moved out of the apartment and in with his
latest girl friend. Many of her friends were similarly situated,
so they knew what it felt like and could be a comfort to
each other. They always had plenty of good things to eat at
their lunches, and each went to endless trouble when it was
her turn: for what was there now except eating, and maybe
keeping yourself nice with a new hair shade, or shopping for
new clothes that only your friends of the same age and sex
would even notice, let alone appreciate. All the same, there

were frequent fallings-out among these friends, and then they
wouldn't be speaking for months or even years.

Reba could never keep up with these relationships. Once,
when she had come to see her mother, Donna tried to get her
to come to a show with her. Reba didn't want to and suggested,
'Why don't you go with Celia or someone?'

'Celia!' Donna's face grew turkey-red under her golden hair.
'I don't go to shows with snakes.'

Reba kept quiet. Her mother had high blood pressure and
couldn't be allowed to work herself up. Besides, Reba knew
about best friends turning overnight into snakes – for some
remark they had made behind Donna's back, or preempting
a favorite masseuse or upholsterer.

'Next you'll be sending me with that Foxy,' Donna went on,
referring to another friend fallen from grace. 'Anyway, I want
to go with *you*. Nothing wrong in that, I hope: wanting to be
with your own daughter . . . All right, dear,' she sighed next,
'I know when I'm not wanted. Same as with your father.'

Reba said, 'I have to go.' She slung on the cloth pouch in
which she carried her possessions. 'See you next week, I guess.'
She pecked near her mother's cheek in her usual farewell, but
this time Donna clung to her and said, 'I can't take it any more,
Reba; really I can't.'

'You have to,' Reba said. She spoke brusquely but stood
perfectly still so her mother could hold on to her; and also if
possible to give her some of her own strength and sturdiness.
Donna was taller than Reba, but she was fat, soft, whereas
Reba was muscular like a workman.

But after they parted, Reba took longer to recover than
Donna. Driving her battered pick-up to the country where
she lived, Reba couldn't stop thinking of her mother left
to grow old alone in her luxurious apartment. But Donna,
walking around that apartment, still crying a bit and wiping
her tears, called a friend in the hospital and heard all about
her operation, then called another friend to report on that and
make a lunch date, had a little snack from the ice-box, called
the storage people about her furs, finally sat down with Lina
her housekeeper for a cup of coffee and a forbidden cigarette.

Later Si called – he did this practically every day and often she wished he wouldn't, but if he didn't, she got tense and had to take pills.

'Reba's been here,' she told him. 'I'm worried about her.'

'Well, what do you think I am?'

This was their standard exchange about their daughter and led to Donna's next retort, which was bitter: 'She should have had a better example from her father.'

Si said, 'You want to talk to me or not?'

'I didn't call you, you called me.'

At the end of their conversation, Donna had to lie on the sofa for a while. Then she dialed Reba's number in the country. There was no reply, though Reba must have reached home by now. Maybe she was in one of her moods where she didn't pick up the phone, or she was wandering around in those goddamn woods she lived in. Donna let the phone ring and ring and was finally rewarded by Reba snatching it up and shouting 'Hello!' in an angry voice.

Donna said straight off, 'Your father's driving me nuts again.' She pretended not to hear Reba's groan.

'He doesn't look right, Reba. A man his age with a suntan like that on him – it's all done with lamps of course, but ever heard of skin cancer? And all that exercising at the spa, that's not going to do his heart any good.'

'I hadn't heard there's anything wrong with his heart.'

'There isn't, except it's rotten to the core.'

By the time she had finished talking to her daughter, it was dusk outside and quite dark inside, which Donna hated. She went around turning on all the lamps and overhead lights so that everything was brilliantly lit, her white and gold furniture, her tulips and tiger lilies from René the florist, Si's art collection on the walls. From her windows she could see the lights shining from unbroken rows of prime real estate, full of lawyers, developers, and psychiatrists. She imagined them all eating dinner inside their expensively decorated apartments, and that reminded her to call Reba again – 'Do you have anything to eat up there? Well,' she defended herself against Reba's angry shout, 'you don't usually, not anything I'd call *food*.'

Reba, who was vegetarian, wasn't about to get into that argument again; and besides, she didn't want to talk at all, she wanted to go on sitting in the dark. Unlike her mother, Reba loved being in the dark and delayed turning on the light in her little cabin till the last possible moment. In warm weather, she sat on her doorstep; all around her there was nothing but trees, with birds asleep inside them and the last little pool of daylight draining away in a gap between the branches.

Although her father was forever asking her to let him make her an allowance, Reba was entirely self-supporting. Several times a week she stripped people's furniture or the walls of their houses to get them ready for painting. Her cabin was rent free, for though she may have lived there, as her mother always said, like a wild man in the woods, these woods were part of an estate owned by an investment banker and his friend. Reba was employed as the caretaker; she didn't have to do much but had a list of phone numbers for plumbers and electricians, in case anything went wrong in the big house. She rarely saw the owners – they mostly left notes for her on their hall table – and their house was invisible from her cabin, so that she really appeared to be living in solitude.

On Saturday night she drove as usual to the station to meet her friend Lisette arriving on the last train. Lisette couldn't come earlier because Saturday was a very busy day in the gourmet cheese store where she worked; and she was so exhausted from being on her feet all day that she was asleep before they got home to the cabin. Reba just picked her up and carried her to bed, tenderly lifting Lisette's long pale limbs to get her clothes off without waking her. Reba always associated Lisette with something out of a fairy tale – especially when she was asleep, with her long ginger hair spread on the pillow around her pointed little face. She was Reba's idea of the little Match Girl, or Cinderella before the Prince found her – someone pale and deprived who had to be taken care of.

Next day was a perfectly beautiful Sunday in early summer, and they had the whole place to themselves – the woods, meadows, ponds, and apple orchard – for the owners were away in the Bahamas where they had another estate. The leaves had that fresh look of translucent green that would grow heavy and dusty as the season matured; the lilac was out, so were pure white, sweetly fragrant clusters of bridal wreath. It had rained a lot in spring, so the grass was as moist and washed as the sky with its tufts of clouds. The swimming hole was full and the water uncluttered by the weeds that would infest it later; surrounded by trees and bushes, it was a completely private place, so they just stepped out of their clothes and dived in naked. It was cold inside, and Lisette – a pale shape flitting around in the dark green water – soon began to shiver; and Reba, though she herself didn't feel cold at all, made her get out and wrapped her in the big white towel she had brought for her. They sat at the water's edge, on stones embedded in moss, while Reba carefully dried each strand of Lisette's hair and kissed her damp shoulder where it emerged from the towel. Then the mosquitoes came humming – Lisette was always their first victim, with her sweet blood, so Reba snatched up all their clothes and they ran as they were, two shimmering naked girls, to their cabin where they threw themselves on the bed and Reba went perfectly wild. They dropped into a deep sleep, in the middle of that warm afternoon, and when the phone rang, Reba – guessing it could only be Donna – didn't answer, and when it kept on ringing, put her hands over Lisette's ears so she wouldn't be disturbed.

On that same Sunday afternoon Si had come by to see Donna; he usually made time to do this, not liking her to be alone the whole weekend. She at once spoke about Reba: 'Why can't she have a boy friend like everyone else.' Of course Si was the only person in the world she would say this to. She knew he felt the same, though he denied it. 'It's okay,' he said. 'Leave her alone. It's better than if she was with some jerk who wouldn't know how to treat her decently.' Next moment he could have bitten his tongue off, for – 'Plenty of those around,' she took the opportunity to say.

He engrossed himself in looking at his paintings on the

walls. Along with everything else in the apartment, he had left them behind when he moved out. But he loved them very much – for themselves, and also for what they proved about him, that he had learned to appreciate and spend his money on them. Donna never had learned, and in front of him, she derided them: 'Looks like some kid of five's been messing around with a pot of paint.' What he didn't know was that, before her friends, she boasted how he had bought them when no one else had known their worth. She became very indignant if any friend made the remark about the kid of five, and then she explained the paintings; it would have made him smile to hear her, as he used to smile about her in the past, in appreciation of her charming, childish ways.

Donna fussed around noisily emptying ashtrays, and at last she said, 'Who've you come to see, me or those pictures? Well, sit down then, you're making me nervous.'

He sat in one corner of a vast custom-made sofa; she sat opposite him on its twin. She stared at him and thought how unfair, my God. He looked so good with his suntan, artificial or not, his body kept in check at the spa, his stylish clothes: a man only just past his prime. She was two years younger than he was, but sometimes, catching herself unawares in a mirror, she thought with a shock: 'It's Gran.' Her grandmother had died of a stroke in her sixties; by that time all they would let her do was feed the chickens, and she walked around scattering grain for them and making clucking noises, her stockings fallen around her ankles.

'Oh don't, please,' said Si, for big tears were rolling down his wife's cheeks.

'It's my health,' Donna said. 'I feel bad all the time.'

Si said, 'I'm going to speak to Dr Abramson first thing in the morning.' At the same time he was thinking of *his* grandmother. Not that she had looked in the least like Donna – Si's grandmother had been thin, with ghetto eyes and a scarf on her head: but that was the way she had cried, just letting the tears roll down her face. He had assumed that she had wept like that, without words, because she couldn't express herself much in English (for instance, on the subject of Donna, dance hostess from Michigan, daughter of Italian truck-farmers). But now he thought that maybe it was the way old women cried – silently, having no language left for all they had to say.

Slapping his thighs in a determined way, he got up. 'You should get out more, Don, see your friends—'

'I have no friends.'

'See Reba – go to her place, get a car and go there, see what she's up to.'

'She doesn't want me . . . No she doesn't. She has that girl there.'

Donna sighed – differently from how she had sighed for herself; and in spite of his determined good cheer, Si's mood also clouded over, and when their eyes met for a moment, it was with the same expression. Si mumbled, 'As long as she's happy,' but it didn't seem to convince him any more than it did her.

The day after Lisette returned from visiting Reba, Donna went to see, or look at her in the cheese store where she worked. It was easy to see Lisette, all one had to do was buy a piece of cheese. That was how Reba had first met her – Donna cursed the day but it had been her own fault, she herself had sent Reba there to pick up a quiche for lunch. It was Donna's best cheese place in the whole world, and just around the corner from her, on Madison. Although in the past Lisette had not been Donna's favorite assistant, now she always hoped that she would get to be served by her. On this particular day, Donna's lot fell to the manageress, an older woman. Most of the customers, including Donna, had been coming there so regularly that they acted like family friends; and they were all expected to know the manageress's personal history – 'How's Trudy?' Donna inquired obsequiously, as soon as she had given her order. She didn't listen too carefully to the answer, for her eyes were on Lisette – on Lisette's hands cutting cheese for another customer; these hands were too large for the rest of her and also reddened as though they had washed a lot of dishes. A kitchen maid, that's all she is, thought Donna, unaware how imperious she looked at that moment, a real grande dame, which of course she was no more than was Lisette; but she had had money for a long time now and by constantly buying quality goods had taken on some of their aura.

'I told her from the start,' the manageress was saying, while her hands worked independently packing Donna's purchases, '"Trudy, mark my words, that guy's bad news." But who listens to me, I'm only the mother, right? So who am I to give good advice to my own daughter.'

'It's true what they say,' Donna said. '"When they're small, they break your arms, when they're grown, they break your heart." The brie looks nice and moist, maybe I'll take a piece. Sometimes it's like they do it on purpose, taking up with people that they know it'll hurt the parents. Really low company,' she said, the last three words dead slow; and she watched Lisette's hand tremble as the knife she was holding sank into a wheel of cheese. She'll cut her finger off, Donna thought, watching expectantly, but Lisette was too professional to let emotion undermine her skill. The knife made it to the end, the piece was weighed and packed, and Donna said, 'Oh Lisette, I didn't see you, how are you, dear? You look well – have you been in the country? That's right, make the most of it, the good weather won't last forever.' She swept out, and on the same momentum went down the Avenue, proud of herself and the way she looked. There weren't many people on this ordinary weekday morning dressed up like she was – in her silk suit cut amply to accommodate her figure, shoes and purse matching, and a little summer hat swaying on the topmost mast of her bouffant of burnished gold.

But later that day she was defending herself to Reba: 'What did I say? I was talking to what's her name about Trudy. Well, why shouldn't I go there? My heaven, I've been going there long before she ever – and how do you know I was there? Does she call you every five minutes to report on all that's going on in the store?'

Reba hung up on her – because she was mad at her and also because she wanted to get back on the phone to Lisette and calm her down. Donna was unrepentant – 'What did I do?' she muttered defiantly at her own reflection in the mirror, but quickly altered her expression to a nicer, softer one.

When Si next came to see her, she complained to him – 'Now she won't even let me go in my own cheese place.'

Si said, 'It's because she knows you don't like her friend.'

'Her friend! You should see her – she's just this starved little rat. But I guess *you* would like her. You'd like anyone as long as they're under twenty-five. Making yourself ridiculous,' she ended on a change of subject.

Instead of answering, Si went off to look at his pictures again. In a way her accusation that he came not to see her but his pictures was true, though not entirely. These paintings and his feelings for her – what used to be his feelings for her – were mixed up together. He stood in front of one of his earliest acquisitions – *River By Day: II.* He couldn't have explained the subject – it didn't *look* like a river – but he knew he had to have it the moment he had seen it in a gallery many years ago. He had already at that time made a lot of money – in the window-shade business – and he was going to make a lot more. He was in big business and reveled in it, but at the same time there was something in him that kept aloof, untouched by everything he did – strange feelings that possessed him when he saw, for instance, the sun blazing on the ocean; and most of all, and the essence of it all, his feelings for the vital young wife he had married, in spite of all his family and his ancestry, because he had desired her more fiercely than anything else in the world.

And there she stood behind him now and said, 'What's she like?'

For a moment his eyes, still full of *River By Day*, rested on her: but then he lowered them and walked away from her and on to his next picture, hanging there pristine and unchanged. She followed him and said again: 'What's she like?'

It was a question she had asked him before and he had answered it, as he did now, with a vague and vaguely helpless gesture. Then he flung himself on one of the sofas, and she came and sat not opposite now but right next to him, and asked it for the third time. But he said, 'Did you go to Dr Abramson like I told you?'

'Yeah. I went. Same old story: "Donna, I'm warning you, the one thing you're not to do is get upset. Take it easy. Be happy. Sing. Laugh."' She threw back her head to laugh, and next moment she said, 'How old is she anyway?'

'Twenty-three,' he answered, as if he hoped not to be heard.

But she heard, and 'Twenty-three,' she repeated, in a soft, nostalgic way. Then she said, 'Reba's getting on for twenty-five.'

'I know,' he said. 'I know that.' They spoke in low and gentle voices to each other – maybe because they were sitting in such close proximity on the sofa. She moved her knee a little closer to his, just touching it, and he made himself not move away. Clearing his throat a couple of times, he said in a different tone now, more conversational: 'I wanted to talk to you about Reba's birthday.'

'It's not till September.'

'I know it's not till September: you don't have to tell me. But I want to start moving on setting up a trust fund for her. So she'll have some money, for God's sake. Let her go on working as a cleaning woman, okay, it's her choice, but that money's got to be there for her, if she wants it or not.'

'Oh. Yeah. Wonderful.' Donna moved her knee away from him. 'That's all we need: so she can pack up any day she feels like it and go off to Mexico or wherever with whoever. No thank you.'

'That's her business.'

'No it's not; it's mine.' Donna left him and went to sit on the opposite sofa. 'I have my one daughter, after all the miscarriages that's all I have, and I'm keeping her. As close by me as I can.' She hit her fist against her breast, to show how close. But the heart under her resolute fist was jumping violently and there was the familiar pounding in her veins.

Si had always recognized every tremor passing through her and he still did, though they were different tremors now. Dr Abramson had told him, 'Don't get her excited, Si, see she takes it easy, or I can't be responsible.' The way things were, Si knew that to spare her meant to leave her, relieve her of his presence. He no longer asked her as he used to – not only out of courtesy but from real concern for her – how she would spend her day, what she would eat. He had learned that this upset her more than anything, so now he went away without asking, feeling bad she was alone and wishing she had plans for the evening, as he had.

Si didn't call Reba as often as her mother did, and for such an energetic, successful man of the world, he was very shy with his daughter: 'I'm not interrupting anything? You've eaten dinner?' Unlike Donna, he didn't ask what she had had for dinner and then quarrel with her for not eating meat. Instead there was a hesitant silence, and then he asked her to lunch with him on any day she chose; he knew she knew it had to be lunch and had to be a weekday because evenings and weekends belonged to his girl friend. Reba said she would meet him on Friday, at one o'clock – no, wait, one-fifteen.

She drove in early that day to take Lisette out for her lunch break at twelve. She left her car in a parking lot and went to the store, but she had to wait, for Lisette was still busy with customers. Reba liked watching her at work. It was how she had first seen her, and though Lisette had appeared quite homely in the white coveralls she had to wear and her ginger hair tied into a thin pony-tail, even then, before she even knew her, Reba had recognized the real Lisette beneath this disguise.

Now, as soon as Lisette was free from her last customer, the two girls walked down the street to a little walled garden, which had been scooped out of the surrounding buildings. Lisette took possession of a couple of wire-mesh chairs, while Reba lined up at the refreshment booth to buy jello and cream cheese sandwiches for herself and Lisette, who had also become a vegetarian. Reba was going to have lunch with her father, but she liked to eat together with her friend; besides, she had a big appetite and was always ready for something.

'But why does she hate me?' Lisette was saying, for she

was still rankling from Donna's visit, though it was an almost weekly event.

'She doesn't,' Reba answered, as usual. She began to explain Donna's psychology and then Lisette sighed and talked about *her* mother, who had started drinking again. They couldn't hear each other too well because of the loud rushing sound from the waterfall, which had been made to cascade over ridges built into a stone wall. Also, the little stone garden had filled up with office workers enjoying the fine day during their lunch hour and old ladies come out of their apartments to stretch their veined legs to the sun. All the same, Reba felt very private with Lisette. She kept taking glimpses down her friend's back, exposed by the dress she was wearing. It was a sundress, held up by two thin straps and as ill-fitting as most of Lisette's clothes (she usually bought them on sale); but inside it her back was lightly freckled down to the top of her tiny flowered panties, which was as far as Reba could see.

'If she doesn't watch out,' Lisette was saying, 'she'll have to go back to that place where they dry them out. She hates it but she's sliding right back in there and he's helping her: Uncle Jack. I blame him really. You're not listening.'

'Yes I am, and I know I have to get you out of there. And I'm going to. I'm going to do it.' Reba sounded ready to do it right there and then, swoop up Lisette and carry her off. And it wasn't as if Lisette didn't want to be carried off. It was a very difficult situation for her with her mother and her mother's boy friend, who fought together and then made up over drinking together, till they got drunk and started again. And working in the cheese store wasn't all that wonderful either – Lisette was nervously looking at her watch to make sure she wasn't overstaying her hour, and it made Reba say: 'Don't go back at all – just get in the car and come home with me. Why *not*? What is it? Don't you like the country or what? Or is it me? You don't like me.'

While saying this, Reba continued to look down Lisette's back; and getting carried away, she put out her hand to take off the rubber band tying Lisette's pony tail. But at once Lisette shook her off and sat up straight so that her back was covered

by her dress. Reba blamed herself; she knew perfectly well
that any fond gesture in public made Lisette thin-lipped and
prim – a poor girl, genteel and guarding her honor: and in this
guise, Reba loved her more than ever, she became crazy with
love for her. But she restrained herself and spoke as sensibly
as possible: 'We don't have to live in the cabin; we don't have
to live in the country at all; we can go anywhere. I can borrow
some money, if that's what's worrying you, my father's dying
to give me some and then I can take you. We can go away.
Anywhere you like,' she ended up on a tempting note.

'Where?'

'Mexico. Brazil. Anywhere.' She saw that Lisette's eyes were
shining and her face and bare shoulders had flushed a faint
pink. Keeping outwardly cool, Reba continued: 'We'll be on
the beach and go up in the mountains. We could go to Nepal
– China, if you like – we'd be gone for as long as we wanted.
One year; two years . . .'

She allowed her voice to trail off and drown in the sound
of the waterfall. She didn't want to get carried away and say
too much. She knew how easily Lisette's good mood might
disappear, and then the light would fade from her eyes, leaving
them remarkably dull. Now she was just enough roused to
keep her in pleasant anticipation till Reba was ready with the
next move. So Reba frowned at her watch: 'Don't you have to
get back?' Lisette sighed and wished she didn't have to. 'You
don't want to be late,' Reba said and got up, so that Lisette
had to too, still sighing. Reba even made her farewell rather
cool as she sent Lisette back to the store and hurried off in the
opposite direction. Reba's nature was open and entirely frank
– almost blunt with sincerity – but when it came to Lisette,
she had learned to be manipulative, and cunning.

Si's favorite restaurant was very fancy, and Reba's appearance
struck a discordant note there. He wasn't willing to change his
eating place any more than she her clothes, but they put up
with each other. As soon as Reba came in – five minutes early,
but Si had made a point of being earlier – he leaped up to meet
her and hugged and kissed her hard right there in the middle

of the restaurant. Both Reba's parents were demonstrative. The maitre d' stood ready to draw out her chair, politely ignoring her workman's clothes. Si had already discussed the menu with him, so that Reba could have the vegetables she was used to without having to read her way through the gourmet dishes on the menu.

'This is such a treat for me.' Si glowed at her across the table. He came here almost every day with business associates, but with Reba it was like being on vacation in a place where he wouldn't normally be, a hut up some green hills; and though they brought him his usual Bloody Mary, he imagined he could taste the pure spring water she had ordered. Overcome with enthusiasm for her, he said straight off, 'I want to do something special for you, and you can't refuse me, Mousie. I won't hear of it.'

Both he and Donna were used to their daughter tensing up whenever they offered her anything, for mostly it was what she absolutely didn't want. What she did want was either something you couldn't buy, or would prefer not to – like the heat-gun she had asked them for, so she could hire herself out to strip walls and furniture.

He went on resolutely. 'You have a birthday coming up, and this time I'll make sure that you get something behind you. Some cash,' he said and paused, glancing at her nervously for her usual negative reaction. But to his surprise she was listening with attention, looking at him with her steady brown eyes. Was she really going to be twenty-five? To him she looked like a child, like the picture of her in his wallet next to his heart at this very moment, when she was eight years old, stocky and solemn; even her haircut was the same, a square fringe, with the tips of her ears showing. 'Okay, do what you want, live where you want, in some hole downtown or in the woods, but – no, listen to me – you *have* to *have* money.'

She floored him by saying, 'Yes, I need some money.'

'Good,' he said. He hid his amazement, helping himself to the dish held out to him by the waiter. He ordered wine for himself and more mountain water for her. At last he asked, 'Any idea how much?'

'Quite a lot,' she replied calmly, and continued: 'I want to go on a trip; sort of take time off and find out about other places and I guess about myself too. I'll pay you back, of course.'

'Mousie, Mousie, you're talking to your father.'

'Well okay, but I feel I ought to. In theory anyhow, though I don't suppose I'll ever earn enough in actual fact, not with the sort of jobs I do.'

He was silent. In college, Reba had taken subjects like sociology and economics. Her aim had been to devote herself to the under-privileged by joining some international relief agency, and though Donna hadn't thought too much of any of that, Si had backed their daughter entirely. But then Reba had gone through a crisis and dropped out of school, deciding that, before engaging in good works, she had to become better inside.

It occurred to Si that maybe she considered herself ready now, so he said hopefully, 'If you should ever want to go back, to Yale or some place else, I'd be happy to—'

'Why should I? I don't believe in any of that – degrees and stuff – it's a waste of time. You didn't need it. No, of course not; you did fine without.'

'I guess.' Si smiled, but regretfully: he truly missed an education, and for all his success and wealth, when he was in the company of an educated person, he felt inferior. 'Well, okay then,' he sighed, giving up on Reba's education as well as his own, 'but where were you thinking of going? And for how long?'

'A year; maybe two.' She saw the shock on his face and defended herself: 'I told you I need time out to think, sort of rethink myself if you see what I mean, and also,' she said out of her deeply truthful nature, 'I want to be with my friend.'

'Have you told your mother?'

'No; that's next. I can't make plans, can I, before I know if you're going to give me the money.'

'What makes you think I wouldn't?' he said – with good reason, for he had never refused her anything; though of course she hadn't asked for anything, except the heat-gun.

'Mother doesn't like Lisette. She's just awful to her. She goes

out of her way—' Reba had blazed up and now checked herself:
she hadn't come here to complain about her mother.

'She's not well,' Si made excuses for Donna, 'she's not
herself: you know that.' His eyes were lowered guiltily.

Reba nodded, recognizing the situation and not wanting
to embarrass him further. But she did want to go on talking
about Lisette: 'You have to be careful around her because she's
very sensitive. Shy and sensitive. She's extremely intelligent,
extremely, but she hasn't been to school all that much, there's
her mother and all kinds of problems you don't want to hear
about. But you'd like her; you really would.'

'I'd like to meet her,' said Si with his eyes still lowered.

'Of course she's just this kid – only nineteen years old, but
sometimes I feel she's older than I am. Older and wiser. She's
had to be, you see, because of the situation with her mother,
but in other ways she's quite naive and impressionable and
I feel I want to – not exactly educate, who am I to educate
anyone, but – well anyway, do something for her . . .' Reba
stopped in frustration, unable to find words for this longing.

But Si said, 'You work it out how much you'll need and let
me know.'

'Yes okay, I will. As it is now,' she started again, swept away
by gratitude to him as well as by her own strong feelings, 'I
never get to see her enough, she has this stupid job five days
a week, of course we talk on the phone all the time but it's
not the same. You want to actually *be* with the person you
feel close to, the whole time really . . . Are you sure all that's
good for you, Daddy?' she asked, for he had allowed both his
plate and his glass to be refilled and was eating and drinking
voraciously. His mouth was full, his cheeks bulging, but as
soon as he could he said, 'Yes yes, I can handle it, I can eat
all I want and more, nothing wrong with my digestion.' And
he laughed, gloating over his unimpaired vitality.

'You don't *need* all that meat, you know. No you do not.
Lisette used to eat horrible things at home, liver and stomach
and all that stuff, but since she's been with me she's become
completely vegetarian. She's still thin, of course, delicate,' said
Reba and paused and delicately smiled, 'but her health is one

hundred per cent improved – like she used to get these colds? She was sniffling all the time, and it went up in her sinuses and was really miserable, but now she hasn't had a cold in six months, and all because of not eating meat.'

'I believe you,' he said, 'but I still need something more than squash and nuts.'

'I bet I'm stronger than you are – I bet you: want to try?'

They challenged each other across the table, then they pushed their dishes aside – waiters hurried over to help them, Si winked at them: 'Ignore us, we're crazy' – she rolled up her sleeve and planted her elbow on the table and was ready. He first had to be helped out of his jacket and to undo one jeweled cuff-link; the arm that emerged was sturdy and tanned, matted in manly hair which was still mostly black. They interlocked their hands and strained against each other. Smiling waiters watched, people turned around from other tables, acquaintances of Si's called out to him in mocking encouragement: but father and daughter were intent only on each other. Their similar brown eyes – hers pristine and clear, his slightly bloodshot – met in a stare, their lips twitched in amusement though at the same time their faces grew red with effort. Beads of sweat appeared on Si's brow, but he didn't let up, wouldn't, not for anything; their hands swayed a little but the elbows supporting them stood firm. But then it seemed to Reba – she wasn't sure if this was a physical sensation or came to her in some other way – that if she were now to exert one more ounce of her unexhausted strength, he would have to yield. She felt as if he were ever so slightly tottering, no more than a tremor but one that she could, if she wished, follow up on, seizing the advantage and forcing his hand down on to the table, victorious. She didn't; instead she laughed, let go, said, 'Pretty good.' Then he laughed too, slightly shaky with relief, and said, 'Not bad for an old Dad,' and was applauded from neighboring tables. The waiters beamed and pushed up the dessert trolley, and Si, wiping his handkerchief all over his face, rewarded himself with the biggest piece of chocolate cheesecake there was, and even – why not – let them pour cream all over it.

\*        \*        \*

Informed of Reba's travel plans, Donna had a hysterical fit. She screamed, tore at her clothes – a sumptuous dove-grey two-piece she had just come home in from the theater – snatched off her string of pearls and flung it across the room. Reba retrieved it. She was familiar with these fits and considered them part of her mother's nature. Reba had been five years old when she had first witnessed such an outburst. She had been playing on the rug where she had set out her menagerie of farm animals, and she didn't even bother to glance up at her parents who were arguing above her head. She was used to their screaming at each other, they did it every day. But that time, just as Reba was trying to fix a cow's broken leg, there was suddenly a different sound, and when Reba looked up, she saw that her mother had laid back her head to emit this fearsome animal cry. And it was like an animal that she leaped forward and fastened her nails into Si's throat while he tried to wrestle her off: and Reba jumped up and yelled and danced around them. It had been like a parody of what they often did in that very room on that very parquet floor – danced to the record-player, Donna swaying and humming in Si's encircling arm, following his skilled lead, for he was a terrific dancer, incredibly light on his feet for a man that heavy; and Reba, with her bear in her arms, danced alongside and around them, though they were too engrossed in each other to notice her except for a perfunctory 'Bless her.'

And during their fight too they failed to notice her while they wrestled with each other and yelled so loud that they didn't hear Reba's screams below them; and it wasn't till she began to drum her fists against her father's leg that Si looked down at her and bellowed at Donna, 'Are you crazy – in front of the kid!' She didn't even hear him, so he struck her and she fell down; it was then she began to tear at her clothes and flail her fists about her face. Si picked up Reba and carried her to the big double bed in the master bedroom where she came when she got scared at night. He shut and locked the door. 'It's okay, Mousie,' he said, 'we were dancing. It's a new step.' Still sobbing, she said, 'There wasn't any music.' 'This one you do without music,' Si said. He kissed her and rubbed his rough cheek against hers, which usually made her laugh and squirm. It soothed her – did she fall asleep in his arms? – and when she woke up, both her parents were on the big bed with her. They were laughing, so he must have been telling the truth and they really had been dancing. Si was lying on top of Donna: 'You know what you are,' he was, saying in a rich low husky voice Reba had never heard him use before. 'You're the one they warned all the little Jewish boys against.' He brought down his mouth to bite into Donna's shoulder where her nightgown had slipped off. Donna carried right on laughing, so he couldn't have hurt her, and Reba went back to sleep, reassured that her parents were friends.

But after she told her mother about going away with Lisette, Reba had to deal with her on her own. She was frightened and ran off to get Donna's blood pressure pills. She knelt on the carpet where Donna was flailing about and tried to make her take them. 'No, let me die,' said Donna, wrenching away from Reba. Next moment she snatched the bottle from her, and shaking the pills into her palm, made to thrust them into her mouth. Reba struck her hand aside so that they scattered. She put both her arms around her mother and held her fast while Donna struggled and cried to get at her pills. She couldn't keep it up for long though, she was physically too weak. Reba felt her slacken and soon found that she didn't have to hold her so hard. Donna's loud cries had softened into sobs; she said, 'You couldn't do it to me,' and then, 'You wouldn't, would you? You wouldn't leave me.'

Reba wanted to carry her into her bedroom; but Donna was too heavy for that, so she coaxed her up and gently led her there. Donna allowed herself to be undressed – to be eased out of her gorgeous silk, then out of her slip, the vast support bra to be unhooked, her panties and girdle slipped off; and Reba did it all tenderly, as much as possible averting her gaze from her mother's body, remembering how once it had been tight and strutting in the latest style swimsuit. Reba dressed her in her nightgown and tucked her between her sheets, and now Donna obediently swallowed two pills.

'You can't do this,' Reba at last admonished her. 'You can't carry on that way; you'll kill yourself.'

'I'd be doing everyone a favor then. Including myself.' Donna went on, 'And he's actually giving you the money to go away? He's doing that? There – see, I'm right: he wants to kill me. He'll have no rest till he's done it and I'm out of his way.'

'Si loves you,' Reba declared. She leaned forward to kiss Donna propped against her pillows.

'No,' Donna said, and she spoke in a calm, accepting voice. 'It's not true and why should it be; I can't expect it. I'm not twenty-three years old no more – any more,' she corrected herself but was unsure and repeated again, 'No more.'

'As if that's got anything to do with anything,' Reba said, but she knew she was not speaking the truth. She only had to think of Lisette and how different everything was when she was with her – and here Reba remembered one Sunday night a few weeks before. Lisette had already fallen asleep but Reba was still restless, excited. She went to the window and drew aside the curtain – at once the moon struck into the room, and when Reba turned around, she saw that the bed with Lisette sleeping on it was afloat and swimming in the white light. The effect was heightened by the white bedsheet with which Lisette had covered herself. It had taken Reba some time and skill, at the beginning of their friendship, to coax Lisette out of her fussy nylon nighties and persuade her to sleep naked the way Reba herself did. But even on very hot nights Lisette took care to cover herself entirely with the sheet and always woke up and struggled a bit when Reba tried surreptitiously to take it off her. This had become a game between them, and Reba wanted to play it now. She tiptoed to the bed and began ever so gently to tug at the sheet; when she had got it about halfway off, Lisette stirred and clutched at it. 'Let me,' Reba softly pleaded, and 'No,' Lisette murmured, half in her sleep, and went on struggling a while longer; but she was really much too tired, and Reba too persistent, and soon Lisette's hands fell away from the sheet, allowing Reba to strip it right off her. Lisette lay exposed and flooded in moonlight,

her hands up and curled on either side of her head the way
infants sleep, her face sideways so that one cheek was buried
in her spread-out hair; her long slender body seemed to be
shining not only with the moonlight but from within its own
perfect whiteness, making it translucent. Reba's breath failed
her, she sank to the side of the bed and buried her face in it,
and thought it's like dying and being born again, or dying and
going to heaven: unearthly, divine.

'I think I'll have to have another pill,' Donna said in a small,
scared voice.

Reba too was scared – she hurried to get the medication
and water to take it with. She watched Donna swallow it,
not taking her eyes off her face; she said, 'I'm going to call
Dr Abramson.'

'No no, what can he do? Just stay with me.' She caught hold
of Reba's hand: 'You're not driving back tonight, are you?'

'Of course not. Who wants to drive back at midnight? I
was planning to stay with you anyway; that's why I came.'
When Donna guided Reba's hand to let her feel her heart,
Reba pleaded again, 'Let me call the doctor.'

Donna shook her head and pleaded in her turn, 'Don't
go.'

'I'm not. I told you: I'm not going anywhere.'

'You're all I've got.'

'Well, I'm here. I'm not leaving you.'

What was she promising? Reba didn't let herself think about
it. She gave her mother her usual sleeping pill and sat on the
bed watching her grow drowsy. Donna was still holding her
hand, and whenever Reba shifted even slightly, her mother
tightened her grip. But it wasn't enough, and after a while
Donna whispered, 'Get in with me.'

Reba hesitated – it was many years since she had slept with
Donna, though as a child it had been a great treat to get into
this same big bed and lie between both parents.

'Get in with me,' Donna said again. 'It's been so long.'

Reba stepped out of her jeans; she would wait till Donna was
asleep and then go to her own bed. But when she slipped under
the covers with her, Donna made her put her arms around

her and hold her close. Even so, hour after hour, Donna kept murmuring, 'Hold me.' Each time Reba answered, 'I *am* holding you.' She became impatient, as well as hot and uncomfortable, but whenever she stirred Donna said at once, 'Don't leave me,' so all night, over and over, Reba had to promise not to leave her.

On Sunday Reba helped Lisette draft a notice to quit her job. Lisette formed her letters very carefully, like a child who has only recently learned them; also like a child she stuck out the tip of her tongue while concentrating on her task. Sometimes she asked Reba how to spell a word – and whereas she used to be defensive about her own ignorance, now she easily conceded that Reba knew better than she. Nor did she mind it when Reba leaned over her to correct some error; she even looked up to smile at her own stupidity, so that Reba couldn't help kissing her uptilted face. Today Lisette was entirely open to Reba, physically and in every other way. Later they got out a map and sat close together with their heads bent over it. Lisette hadn't even heard of some of the countries they were traveling to, or had thought they were somewhere completely different.

That same morning Donna had got up telling herself she needed a day in the country. She always fulfilled her own wishes, so it wasn't long before she had hired a limousine and chauffeur from her usual car service, stopping off at Colette's to buy a whole lot of cakes and pastries. On arrival, the limousine had to be parked some distance from Reba's cabin and the rest of the way taken on foot through the wood. Donna walked to the cabin in the floating floral dress and the big white hat she had put on for the country; the chauffeur came behind her, carrying the many boxes she had bought. She called out, 'Yoo-hoo!' to announce herself, but already there was a stir in the wood, with a squirrel crackling over twigs to escape up a tree, and the birds changing their tune, so that they seemed to be not singing but shouting in warning.

The girls leaped up from where they sat poring over their map – suddenly the tiny cabin was very full, with Donna in her pearls and shimmering silk directing the uniformed chauffeur where to place the piles of pastry boxes; there didn't seem to be enough surfaces in that bare little space to accommodate them. The girls watched in silence, and only Donna's voice rang out as she first ordered the chauffeur around, then argued with him about what time to pick her up again. His departure left an awkward silence – Donna had not yet explained why she had come nor had Reba said she was glad to see her. Donna made herself bustle around a while longer, opening all the boxes to let the girls see what she had brought.

'Why so much?' Reba said at last, in a hard ungrateful voice. 'Who's going to eat so much?'

'It'll be gone in no time,' Donna urged. 'From Colette's, I went specially. You'll love it.'

'Lisette doesn't eat anything with sugar.'

'She doesn't?' Now Donna's voice had become hard. 'Is she diabetic?' She stared at Lisette, making her shrink against the wall. 'I'd have said anemic,' Donna concluded; she licked her finger where a bit of mocha cream had come off the top of a cake.

'Sugar doesn't do anything for you except clog up your veins,' Reba said hotly. 'I've stopped eating it too.'

'Then why don't you just throw it all in the garbage,' Donna said. 'I'll do it right now: where's your trash can?' She seized a box and stood ready to throw it. Reba took it from her. 'I wish I hadn't sent the car away,' Donna said, 'but I can take the next train back if you'll drop me at the station.'

She spoke with dignity; she was still standing – no one had asked her to sit down – considerably taller in her high-heeled alligator sandals than the two barefooted girls. Then her eyes fell on the map spread open on the table; before she could ask anything, Reba said, 'Lisette and I were planning the route we're going to take.'

'Take where?' Donna's dignity left her. 'You're not going anywhere. You said you weren't. You promised!' Her voice had risen; it rang shrilly around the cabin; Lisette shrank further against the wall.

Reba stepped up close to Lisette. 'Go outside,' she told her.

'Go swimming: I'll come in a minute.' The light that had been in Lisette's face while studying the map had faded completely. She looked dull and pale. 'Don't worry,' Reba said. She put her hand on the nape of Lisette's neck; the skin felt damp with fear. 'We're going no matter what,' Reba promised. She drew Lisette forward so that she could seal that promise with a kiss, right on the lips and right in front of Donna.

When Lisette had gone, Donna sat down at last. She had to, because her legs were shaking. She said, 'Let me go home.'

Reba was brisk with her: 'You're here now so you might as well stay. You can watch us swim, if you like.'

Donna said, in a whisper, 'You promised.'

'What did I promise?'

'You said, "I won't leave you." You said it all night. You did! You promised!' Far from a whisper, her voice had become a shriek.

Reba grabbed her mother's arm, and held her: 'Listen,' she said. 'This is the way it is: I'm going away with Lisette. You can shout and scream all you want but you can't change that.'

Donna didn't shout and scream. Reba was still holding her arm, but now it looked as if she were supporting her. She even said, when the silence became prolonged, 'Are you all right?'

Donna nodded in reply. It wasn't that she couldn't but that she didn't want to speak. There was nothing to say: she saw it was hopeless; she had been through this before, with Si.

She told Reba: 'Go and swim. Do what you want.' When she saw Reba hesitate – as Si had hesitated – she added, 'I'm okay. Go on. I'll join you.'

'It's just at the end of the wood, you can't miss it.' Reba waited no longer. She was gone in an instant – running to Lisette.

Si had fled in the same way, afraid to look back. That had been almost two years ago, when he had first moved out. He had come in unexpectedly early while she had some friends in for lunch. They were having a Tarot reading, so she was embarrassed by his arrival because he always laughed at her for believing in the cards. Well, he could laugh – but there *was* something: why else should the Knight of Wands have turned up reversed three times for Wally Roth, before she had even had a suspicion what her then husband was up to? Si had gone straight into the bedroom, and Donna was having such an interesting time – she was getting the most brilliant reading that afternoon – that she was reluctant to leave her friends and follow him. When she did, she found him with two suitcases open on the bed, packing his clothes. She sat down next to the suitcases.

She didn't know what it was about. Of course she had been aware he was playing around, but that was nothing new. He had never moved out before: why should he now? Although she was silent, sitting with her pounding heart beside the suitcases, he said: 'Don't try to stop me. You can't.' He went on packing and she went on sitting. When he had finished, he shut the suitcases and put them on the floor. They were heavy to lift, and his face grew red with the effort. She still hadn't spoken one word. He said, 'I'll call you. I'll be at the Pierre if you need me.'

She nodded; they both looked at his suitcases; she said, 'You want help with those? I'll call someone from downstairs, if you like.'

But he was getting his strength together to pick them up himself. Before he could do so, she threw herself against him; she clung to him. At first his body was hard and unyielding against hers; he said again, 'You can't stop me.' But she wasn't even trying to do that; she was only sobbing helplessly, unable to believe what was happening. Suddenly he too clung to her as she did to him – as though he were parting from her not of his own volition but compelled to do so by some outward agency such as fate.

After Si's departure, she had gone back to her friends and they had finished their reading. No one suspected anything; and for the rest of the day Donna had remained calm. It was the same now in Reba's cabin: Donna was quiet and accepting. She ran a comb carefully up her dome of golden hair; she ate one of the pastries she had brought. Then she went to find the girls, stepping out of the cabin straight into the wood. Ancient layers of mould crackled under her high heels. The summer was just past its height, with the leaves too heavy for the branches that had to bear them, and also dusty and unfresh. She could hear the girls plashing around in their swimming hole. When she approached, she didn't step into the clearing but stood watching them through the shrubbery. They were naked, and Reba was splashing water against Lisette, who had her eyes shut and her arms crossed in front of her. Like a couple of mermaids, Donna thought without pleasure. A stone had lodged in her sandal and she lowered herself on to a mossy patch to take it out. Something pricked through her silk dress where she sat, and something else was creeping up her stockinged thigh. The one thing she regretted at that moment was that she hadn't asked the chauffeur to come earlier to take her home.

# TWO MUSES

Now that my grandfather, Max Nord, is so famous – many years after his death, a whole new generation has taken him up – I suppose every bit of information about him is of interest to his readers. But my view of him is so familiar, so familial that it might be taken as unwelcome domestic gossip. Certainly, I grew up hearing him gossiped about – by my parents, and everyone else who knew about him and his household set-up. At that time no one believed that his fame would last; and it is true that it did not revive to its present pitch till much later – in fact, till everyone had gone: he himself and his two widows, Lilo and Netta, and my parents too, so that I'm the only family member left to reap the fruits of what now turns out to be, after all, his genius.

Max, Lilo, and Netta had come to England as refugees in the thirties. I was born after the war, so I knew nothing of those earlier years in London when they were struggling with a new language and a new anonymity; for it was not only his work that was in eclipse, they themselves were too – their personalities, which could not be placed or recognized in this alien society. At home, in the Germany of the twenties and early thirties, they had each one of them had a brilliant role: Max of course was the young genius, whose early novels had caused a sensation, and Lilo was his prize – the lovely young daughter of a banking family much grander than his own. Netta was dashing, dramatic, chic in short skirts and huge hats. She loved only artists – painters, opera singers – only geniuses, the more famous the better. She never found one more famous than Max, which was maybe why she loved and stayed with him for the rest of their lives. It always seemed to me that it was Netta, much more than his wife Lilo, who fussed over him, adored him, made excuses for him. Lilo sometimes got impatient with him, and I have heard her say to Netta, 'Why don't you take him home with you and make everyone happy, most of all me?' But the moment she had said this, she covered her face and laughed, and Netta also laughed, as at a big joke.

They always spoke in English to each other; it was a matter of principle with them, although they must have felt much more at home in their native German, its idiom packed with idiosyncratic meaning for them. But they had banished that language, too proud to use it now that they themselves had been banished from its precincts. Lilo had had an English governess as a child so that her accent was more authentic than that of the other two – though not quite: I myself, an English child growing up in England, never thought of my grandmother as anything but foreign. Max's accent was so impenetrable that it was sometimes impossible to understand what he was saying (*always* impossible for me, but then I didn't understand him anyway). Yet, although he did not speak it well, Max's grasp of the English language must have been profound; he continued to write in German but spent weeks and months with his English translator, wrestling over nuances of meaning.

Since Max's work is so well-known today, I need not say much about it. This is just as well, for his books are not the slender psychological novels I prefer but huge tomes with the characters embodying and expressing abstract thought. Today they are generally accepted as masterpieces, but during his last years – which are those that I remember – this estimate was confined to a small group of admirers. In his own household it was of course accepted without question – even by my grandmother Lilo, although I now suspect that she was not as devoted a reader of his works as she should have been. In fact, I wonder sometimes if she read them at all, especially the later, most difficult ones. But Lilo was not really a reader. She liked to go for long walks, to make odd purchases at antique stalls, and to play tennis. Yet as a girl she had read the classics – mostly German, and Russian in translation – and, with all her desirable suitors, she had chosen to marry a young writer of modest means and background. An only child, she lived – an enchanted princess – in her father's villa in the salubrious outskirts of the city. Max would bicycle from the less salubrious city center where he was a lodger in the flat of an army widow. He brought his latest manuscript and they sat under the trees in her father's garden – in their memories, as transmitted to me, it seems to have been always summer – and he read from his work to her till it got too dark to see. He was so engrossed in his own words that he noticed nothing – it was she who cried, 'Maxi! A bee!' She saved him from it with vigorous flaps of the napkin that had come out with the coffee-tray. This tray also bore, besides the voluminous, rose-budded coffee-pot, an apple or other fruit tart, so that Lilo was constantly on the alert with the same napkin; and in other ways too she was distracted – for instance, by a bird pecking away in the plum tree, or by Max himself and the way his hair curled on the nape of his strong round young neck where it was bent over his manuscript. Sometimes she could not refrain from tickling him there a little bit and then he looked up and found her smiling at him – and how could he not smile back? Perhaps it didn't even occur to him that she wasn't listening; or if it did, it wouldn't have mattered, because wasn't she herself the embodiment of everything he was trying to get into words?

After they were married, they lived in a house – it was her father's wedding present to them – not far from the one where she had grown up; it too had a garden, with fruit trees, bees, and flowers, where Lilo spent a lot of time while he was in his study, writing (it was taken for granted) masterpieces. As the years went by, Lilo became more and more of a home-bird – not that she was particularly domestic, she never was, not at all, but that she loved being there, in her own home where she was happy with her husband and child (my mother). During the summer months, and sometimes at Easter, the three of them went to the same big comfortable old hotel in the mountains where she had vacationed with her parents. During the rest of the year Max traveled by himself, to European conferences, or to see his foreign publishers; he also had business in the city at least once a week and would go there no longer by bicycle but in his new Mercedes sports car. And it was here, in their home city, which was also hers, that he encountered Netta – or she encountered him, for there is no doubt that, however their affair developed, it was she who first hunted him down: her last, her biggest lion.

She saw him in a restaurant – one of those big plush bright crowded expensive places she went to frequently with her artistic circle of friends, and he only very occasionally, and usually only with his publisher. He was with his publisher that time too, the two of them dining together. They were both dressed elegantly but also very correctly, so that it would have been difficult to distinguish between publisher and author, if it had not been for Max's looks, which were noble, handsome. 'Oh my God! Isn't that Max Nord? Catch me, quick, I'm fainting—' and Netta collapsed into the lap of the nearest friend (an art critic). Soon she and Max were introduced and soon they were lovers – that never took long with her, at that time; but for him it may have been his first adulterous affair and he suffered terribly and made her suffer terribly. He would only meet her when he traveled to other cities, preferably foreign ones, so that they were always in hotel rooms – he checked in first, and when his business was concluded, he allowed her to join him. She wrote him frenzied, burning letters, which have since been published, by herself – '. . . Don't you know that I sit here and wait and die again and again, longing for a sign from you, my most beloved, my most wonderful terrible lover, oh you of the arched eyebrows and the – I kiss you a thousand times there and there and there . . .' Years passed and the situation did not change for them: he would still only see her in other cities, stolen luxurious nights in luxurious hotel rooms; and she, who had always lived by love, now felt she was perishing by it. She had divorced her husband (her second), and though she still had many men friends, she no longer took them as her lovers; later there were rumors that she had sometimes turned to women friends, her tears and confession to them melting into acts of love. Her looks, always brilliant, became more so – her hats more enormous, her eyebrows plucked to the finest line; she wore fur stoles and cascades of jewels, she glistened in silk designer gowns slit up one side to show a length of splendid leg.

It has never been clear when Lilo first found out about the affair. There was always something vague about Lilo – also something secret, so that she may have known about it long before they realized she did. But whatever upheaval there may have been in their inner lives became vastly overwhelmed by what was happening in the streets, the cities, the countries around them. They, and everyone they knew, were preparing to leave; life had become a matter of visas and wherever possible secret foreign bank accounts. Even when he went abroad, to conferences where he was honored, Max had only to lean out of his hotel window – Netta was there beside him – to witness marching, slogans, street-fights, trucks packed with soldiers. Everyone emigrated where and when they could; farewells were mostly dispensed with – no one really expected to meet again, or if they did, it would be in countries so strange and foreign that they themselves would be as strangers to each other. Max, accepting asylum in England for himself and his family, left at what was almost the last moment. Only a week later his books were among those that were burned, an event that must have seared him even more than his parting from Netta. He was by nature a fatalist – he never thought he could actually do anything in the face of opposition, and indeed he couldn't – so he did not let himself hold out any hope of meeting Netta again. But she was the opposite: she *knew* she had her hand on the tiller of fate. She told him, 'I'll be there soon.' And so she was – she and even some of her furniture; all were installed in a flat in St John's Wood, within walking distance of where Max lived with his family in another flat, up a hill, in Hampstead.

I always assumed that the three of them – Max, Lilo, and Netta

– all lived in the Hampstead flat, and on the few occasions when Netta took me to St John's Wood, I would ask why we were coming to this place and who lived there. It was very different from my grandparents' home, which was in an ornate Edwardian apartment house buried among old trees, whereas Netta's block had been built ultra-smart on a Berlin model in the thirties and had portes and central heating. Her flat was light and sparse, with her tubular furniture and her white bear rug and the large expressionist painting she had brought of a café scene featuring herself among friends – chic women and nervously intellectual men, whom I thought of as the inhabitants of this place. For Netta herself really belonged in the other household where she appeared to be in complete charge of all domestic arrangements. Had Lilo ceded this place to her over the years, or had Netta usurped it? Probably it had fallen to her lot by virtue of temperament – especially during the early years of their exile when they were aliens, refugees, with thick accents and no social circle. Only Netta knew how to cope; and when war broke out, it was she who sewed the black-out curtains for their flat as well as her own and stuck tape over the windows so that they would not splinter during an air attack. She always managed to get something extra on their ration cards, and in the winter she unfroze the pipes with hot water bottles and managed to get a fire going with damp lumps of rationed coal. She found domestic help for them – another refugee, Mrs Lipchik from Aachen, who was still with them by the time I began to visit the household. Even so, Netta's greatest contribution was not practical but what she did for their morale, or for Max's morale: he was the pivot of everything that had meaning for them.

These must have been difficult years for Max – exiled not only from his country but also from his language, his readers, his reputation. Netta created the conditions that allowed him to write new books. She had furnished his study at the end of the passage; it was his own furniture that they had brought with them, his desk and glass-fronted bookcases and the little round smoking-table with leather armchair. Even I, when I was no more than three years old, knew that I could only tiptoe down the passage, preferably with my finger laid on my lips (Netta showed me how). No one was allowed to enter the study except herself twice a day, once with his morning coffee and digestive biscuits, and again in the afternoon with coffee and doughnut. When the telephone rang, it had to be answered swiftly and in hushed tones; if he himself stuck his head out to ask who was calling, she quickly assured him that it was nothing that need bother him. Lunch, starting with a good soup, was served exactly at one – only then was Mrs Lipchik permitted to ply her noisy vacuum cleaner – and if, hungry or frustrated, he appeared before that time, Netta sent him back again. All this would come to fruition in the evenings when they would gather in the sitting room. This too was full of their German furniture, of light-colored wood and, though modern, more solid and conventional than Netta's, with woodcuts (I particularly remember a medieval *danse macabre*) and Daumier cartoons on the walls. While Max read his day's work to them, Netta was totally rapt, though engaged in sewing, or darning his socks; sometimes she would make him repeat a phrase and then repeat it herself and become more rapt. Lilo didn't sew; she said her eyes weren't good enough. Sometimes, sated with Netta's comments, he might look for some response from Lilo, but she either gave none or said something irrelevant like 'Maxi, I think your hair's going.' At once his hand flew to his brow – it was true, it was getting more and more noble, nobly arched – and Netta said quickly, 'What nonsense, nothing of the sort.' 'All right, don't believe me,' said Lilo, shrugging, knowing better.

Slowly, over the years, he became if not famous at least known again. This is the period during which I remember him best, when new admirers and literary historians came to call on him. Besides his study and the passage leading up to it, the drawing room (known as the *salon*) also became a silent zone at certain hours of the evening. Appointments for his visitors were regulated by Netta, and she was also the only person who entered, to bring a tray of refreshments and to listen in and make sure he wasn't being tired out by his visitors. He never was – he was too appreciative of this new respect and so was Netta, to witness him again taking up his rightful place as a European man of letters. Lilo did not participate in these sessions; she sat in the kitchen enjoying a cup of coffee with Mrs Lipchik. The two of them spoke together in German – the only time I heard that language in the flat – and it must have been a funny, racy sort of German, for it made them both laugh. I think sometimes they were also laughing at the visitors – I've seen Lilo do a comic imitation of some scholar she had seen arrive with his umbrella and wet shoes – and also maybe even at Max himself. Lilo always enjoyed laughing at Max, which didn't undermine her pride, or her other feelings for him.

Also, at this time, with foreign royalty payments beginning to come in again, their financial position became more stable. During their first years in England, and especially during the war, they had been almost poor, which affected the three of them in different ways. For Max, having no money was something he had been born to fear: he had grown up with a widowed mother who lived on a shrinking pension and had had to pretend they didn't need the things they couldn't afford like a summer holiday. These long-buried memories came back to him and often drove him to a despair that he could only share with Netta. For Lilo, who knew nothing about not having money, blithely accepted that now, for the first time in her life, she was without it. Unable to afford new clothes, she was perfectly content to wear her old ones, even if they were sometimes torn. This characteristic remained with her, so that my memories of my grandmother included a Kashmir shawl that was falling apart and holes in the heels of her stockings. When they could no longer afford to pay Mrs Lipchik, Lilo told her so without embarrassment; and she gladly accepted Mrs Lipchik's offer to wait for her money and was grateful when Mrs Lipchik, to keep herself going, took a part-time job, enabling her sometimes to help them out with her earnings.

Netta too found a job around this time – probably in response to one of the scenes she had with Max, when he buried his head in her lap: 'What are we going to do, Netta? Without money, how can we live?' Although Netta too came from a family of modest means – her father had held a lifelong position as accountant to a shoe-manufacturer – she didn't share Max's fear of poverty: from her youngest days, she had managed brilliantly with her looks and personality, finding jobs in boutiques and as a model, and later, living with or marrying, twice, wealthy men. Now, a refugee in London, she took what she could get and became a receptionist to a dentist, another refugee, Dr Erdmund from Dortmund. It was a full day's work, but she continued all her previous chores in the Hampstead flat. Sometimes, when there was a difficult case and she was kept longer in the surgery, she would arrive from the rush-hour in the Underground with her coat flying open to get Max ready for an appointment she had scheduled for him. She didn't even have time to unpin her hat while she brushed him down, lapels and front and back, for, whatever else, he had to be perfect, and he always was. Nevertheless, he would be complaining about the difficult day he had had, the telephone ringing and no one to answer it, both Lilo and Mrs Lipchik off somewhere or pretending to be deaf. Netta clicked her tongue in sympathy, and having finished with his coat, she got to work on his hair with a soft baby brush for, as Lilo had predicted, he had gone almost bald. She even had time to flick quickly through his mail – he had extracted the fan letters himself, leaving the rest to her. If she found anything disturbing, like an electricity bill or a tax notice, she slipped it into her handbag to take home to her own flat, for Lilo too did not care to deal with such matters.

Lilo spent her days in her own way, devoting herself to her daughter (my mother), and afterward to me, her grand-daughter. I was often sent to stay with her and would sit in the kitchen eating plum cake while she and Mrs Lipchik talked German; or Lilo would make drawings for me, of fruits and flowers, or a whole menagerie of animals out of Plasticine. When Netta was not there, I played at trains up and down the corridor – till the study door opened and Max stood there, in despair: 'God in heaven, is there no one to keep the child quiet!' The sight of him – looming and hostile – made me burst into tears, and Lilo would have to lead me away, while throwing reproachful looks over her shoulder at Max. To comfort me, she would take me out on one of her shopping expeditions; these were never for anything dull like groceries – that was Netta's province – but to antique stalls, where she would pick out the sweetest objects for me, like a painted Victorian picture frame or a miniature bouquet in enamel in a miniature vase. She liked to play tennis, and when they were both younger, she and Netta had played together; but Netta was too competitive, so that Lilo preferred to potter around with me on a court we booked for half an hour at a time in the public park.

When Max's reputation, and with it his royalties, had grown more substantial, Netta broached the subject of leaving her job. He said, 'Are you sure? Can we afford it?' She proved to him that they could, but he remained dubious: his inborn caution, as well as the experience of the previous years, made him reluctant to give up the assurance of a steady salary. 'What's wrong?' he said. 'What's got into you? You *like* your job.' Her eyes, still darkly magnificent in spite of lines around them, flashed: 'Who told you that?' But he couldn't go into it – he never could go into practical problems, especially those of a petty nature, it took too much out of him; and usually she was the first person to spare him, removing annoyances by shouldering them herself.

And now too, she did not burden him with facts of which she had never allowed him to be conscious – that it was tiring for her to do a full day's work and then look after his affairs as well as her own. She never mentioned anything of that, but what she did now decide to mention was something else that she had spared him. It had been all right, nothing to make a fuss about, during the days of Dr Erdmund of Dortmund – well, yes, he had had a crush on her, but he was after all a gentleman and never let it go beyond a squeeze of the hand or a stolen kiss behind her ear, which it hadn't cost her anything to permit. But Dr Erdmund had become old and had had to sell his practice – 'You never told me,' Max said, and she shrugged, 'Why should I?' The new boss was a younger man, though not very young – another refugee, from Czechoslovakia, with none of the cultured manners of an earlier generation of refugees. She didn't mind that – she had always been able to get on with all sorts – but unfortunately he had wandering hands and he could not keep them off Netta, which was really a bit thick. Max genuinely didn't understand, he had never heard of such a thing, and she had to explain to him how unpleasant it was to spend all day with someone and be on your guard constantly— 'You know, Max—' 'Know what, Netta, what?' 'Coming up behind me – he says he's a thigh man – oh, it's disgusting—' But Max was not disgusted; he laughed, he protested: 'You're imagining it.' 'Imagining it!' 'But Nettalein, how could it be? God in heaven, at your age.'

For a long time, no one – not even Lilo, who wasn't told the details – knew what had happened: why Netta suddenly withdrew from the household and told my parents and everyone else that she had had enough. She started a life of her own in her St John's Wood flat and entertained old friends with whom she had reestablished contact. She also had what she called her cavaliers – elderly gentlemen from Vienna or Berlin, who were very gallant and visited her with flowers and chocolates and always had a good joke for her they remembered from the old days. She kept herself trim with sports – her competitive games of tennis, and three times a week she went to an indoor swimming pool where she swam several lengths up and down, her arms pushing the water with the vigor of a much younger woman. In the afternoons she had her coffee in a restaurant in a hotel – the only equivalent of the sort of coffee-houses she had known in Germany, with deep armchairs and carpets and cigarette smoke and foreign waiters and foreign newspapers stuck on wooden poles. If there was no friend to join her, she went alone; she had adventures, for she was still very attractive with her flashing eyes, and her strong teeth intact, and always chic, the large hats of her youth replaced by little saucy ones over one eyebrow. Of course men of a certain age – incorrigible wolves, she called them – were always trying to pick her up and sometimes she let them, though insisting on respect. She knew how to deal with every situation – for years afterward, for the rest of her life, she told the story of the man who had taken, without permission, the empty chair at her table for two and had been bolder than she would permit: and she, without a word, had picked up her coffee cup and flung the contents in his face. 'You should have seen him! Dripping! And it was hot too! With hot coffee in your face, you forget all about being fresh with a woman.'

Around this time my parents, who were documentary film-makers specializing in aboriginal tribes, went away for almost a year, leaving me in the Hampstead flat with my grandparents. So I was witness to what might be called their second honey-moon – the time alone together that they had not had since Netta had become attached to them. Max, remote and selfish as he was, began to woo my grandmother all over again. With Netta gone, it was once more only to Lilo that he read his day's work in the evenings – even sitting on the floor the way he had done in the past, though now it was no longer so easy for him, with his increased weight and his custom-tailored suit he had to be careful not to crease. As before, Lilo did not listen too attentively; some of her attention was now bestowed on me, but Max didn't seem to mind when he looked up and saw her busy helping me pick out the right color crayon for an elephant's ear. They exchanged smiles then – maybe about me, more likely for each other – before Max went on reading; though he looked up again when, staring at his lowered head, she exclaimed, 'Oh Maxi, what a pity – it's really all gone now!' But when he ruefully passed his hand over his scalp – 'Really? All?' – she looked closer: 'There's still a little bit; so sweet.'

My grandmother's own hair was as long as it had been – she never cut it – but it had turned very grey. She continued to wear it the way she had done as a girl – loose and open down her back and around her shoulders. When people in the street turned to stare at her, I assumed that it was for her beauty. I thought she was beautiful, and I was never ashamed of her though she dressed shabbily – there was her frayed shawl and the holes in her stockings, one of which sometimes came loose and wrinkled around her ankle. Walking tall and erect, she was completely unselfconscious; if something interested her, maybe in a shop window or a flower growing in a hedge, she would stop and look at it for a long time. She was very fond of street markets and liked to talk to people selling pottery and costume jewelry and discuss their craft with them. She always bought something from them, but if on her way home, someone admired her purchase, she might simply give it to them and walk on. She remained my grandfather's muse for the rest of their lives: there were always reflections of her in his work, but not as she was in these later years, nothing of her gypsy quality, but the girl he had wooed in their youth. This girl – several theses have already been written about her influence – was wound into his work like filigree. She was the moonlit statue of a nymph in a deserted *allée* of poplars; she was the girl shining in white at her first communion and also the cold lilies adorning the altar. She was everything – every image – that was lyrical, nostalgic, breathlessly beautiful in his work, keeping it as fresh as on the day it was written.

Although at first they enjoyed their time together without Netta, they encountered difficulties. There was now no one to arrange appointments except Max himself – Lilo had tried, but she had several times given rival scholars identical hours and tended to get not only the days but the weeks mixed up. She also didn't like the telephone and Mrs Lipchik would answer, but she never understood what anyone was saying and that made her laugh so much that she had to put down the receiver (Lilo laughed with her). So then Max had to attend to phone calls himself, which disturbed him terribly in his work; several times he simply let it ring, but that disturbed him even more and he sat with his head between his hands. Also it was he now who had to deal with practical matters, which was very difficult for him, for though he was meticulous, he was very timid and would panic at anything with an official stamp on it like an income tax notice. In fact, these sort of communications had such a shattering effect on him that, like Netta had done, Lilo hid them from him, if she happened to see them; but unlike Netta, she did not deal with them and only stuffed them into a drawer and forgot about them till threatening notices arrived. Then they would search for them, and if they found them – occasionally they didn't – Max would blame Lilo for hiding them, and they would be angry with each other and miserable.

Once Lilo was so hurt and annoyed by Max – this was when my parents were home again – that she left the flat and came to us. She had often told us, as a joke, how she had several times run away from Max during their first years of marriage, packing up a suitcase and going straight back to her father's house. When she came to us, it was also with a suitcase; she didn't say anything and my parents didn't ask her any questions. It must have been the same when she had gone home to *her* parents – it would probably have been as useless then as it was now to expect any explanations or accusations from her. Unlike Netta, who had gone around complaining about Max to everyone who knew him and even to those who didn't, Lilo's pride expressed itself in silence. Stubborn and upright, completely oblivious of us tiptoeing tactfully around her, she sat on a chair in our house; but as the afternoon wore on, she moved her chair nearer to the window and looked out into the street, her elbow propped on the sill, her cheek on her hand. That was the way she must have waited in her parents' house – waited for the garden gate to open and Max to come up the path to take her home; without giving him time to ring the bell, she had jumped up and opened the door for him herself and said, 'Let's go,' not bothering about her suitcase, which her father's chauffeur had to bring after her. In the same way, my mother had to take her suitcase back to the Hampstead flat – because the moment Lilo saw Max from the window, she jumped up and went straight out to meet him: leaving us to gaze after the two of them walking down the street together, two elderly people with their arms around each other. They appeared to be an odd couple for romantic attachment – he like a banker in his fur-collared overcoat and Homburg hat, and she with her long loose grey hair, a gypsy or a poetess.

After that, my mother hired a part-time secretary to take care of his business affairs and professional obligations, ignoring his protests that he couldn't afford to pay a salary. The secretary was efficient and soon everything was as it had been with Netta: but when I say everything, I mean only the practical side because in other ways there was something – even I felt it – amiss, or missing. Of course this was Netta, her absence from their lives she had shared for so long. At that time, it never occurred to me that Max was anything but this disagreeable old man who disturbed my pleasant time with my grandmother; and even if I had been old enough to know him better, how could I have understood his need for Netta any more than did my parents, who thought it would be solved by someone else taking care of his practical problems. Emotionally he seemed – he was – completely fulfilled by Lilo, as was evident not only to his family but also to people who knew him simply through his work. Nevertheless – and this is being written about today – there was another element in that work, a hidden current coursing beneath the cool stream of his lyrical love. However, no one mentioned a second muse until Netta published his letters to her, after his death and Lilo's, which was less than a year later. In her introduction, Netta spilled every bean there was, giving time and place for all their secret meetings, all the hotel rooms in all the cities where they had met and the scenes they had had there – the tears they spilled, but also how she had always managed to make him laugh. In her account, their time together was fundamentally joyous and beautiful; and in his work too it was beautiful but also full of interior struggle and guilt, painful, often renounced yet inescapable, cut down only to grow again, a cancer of dark passion.

Lilo too must have missed Netta during the years of her absence. I accompanied her several times on visits she made to Netta in the St John's Wood flat – I went under protest, for it was much more interesting for me in the Hampstead flat, and familiar, with the comfortable furniture and all the amusing objects Lilo picked up at street fairs. At Netta's, there was always the danger of hurting myself on some sharp edge of her metal furniture; and I did not care for Netta's only picture – the café scene of herself and friends, who did not look like people at all but like geometrical masks. Worst of all was Netta herself – at home I was fond of her, she was always bringing me presents, and when I said anything that amused her, she shouted: 'Did you hear that? What a child, my God!' But here all she did was talk to Lilo, in a torrent of words, all of them complaints. When I plucked at Lilo's sleeve to ask to go home, Netta pleaded, 'One moment, darling, only one more little minute, my angel,' and not wanting to interrupt herself by kissing me, she kissed the air instead, with several absent-minded smacks of her pursed lips, and went right on talking. Although everything she said was directed against Max – how he had availed himself of her youth and strength only to throw her away like an orange he had sucked dry – Lilo did not protest or try to interrupt; the most she said was, 'No no,' which made Netta shout louder, 'Yes, an orange!' When at last I persuaded Lilo to go home, she got up reluctantly, lingering as if she wanted to say something more than only 'No no.' But she never managed to say much, and then only as we were leaving and Netta was kissing not the air but really me, kneeling down to do so and making me wet with her lips and with tears too, hot tears – Lilo, looking down at us, would say sadly, 'It was so nice when you were there.'

These words seemed to enrage Netta – not there and then but later, when she came to see my parents, as she did after each of Lilo's visits. 'Oh yes, so nice, so nice,' she cried, 'when I was there to do all their dirty work for them!' My parents tried to soothe her, they spoke eloquently, and after a while Netta sat quiet to listen to them: how much she meant to all of us, and whatever had been difficult in the past was now an indispensable part of the present so that she was missed terribly – 'Who misses me terribly?' she asked, eyes dangerously narrowed as though she were ready to leap on the answer and tear it to pieces. They said we all of us missed her, even I, though only a child, and of course most of all – her eyes narrowed more – Lilo and (yes?) Max. At that name, her eyes sprang wide open in all their dark beauty: 'Well, if he misses me so much, let him come crawling to me on his hands and knees and *beg* me to come back.'

With all the accusations she made, there was one thing she

never mentioned: the money from her salary that she had freely shared with Lilo and Max when they were in difficulties. Nor did she tell anyone that she was now herself running short of money and needed another job to keep going. We none of us knew that she was looking for work – she may even have been searching for some time and finally had to take what she could get: this was as manageress of a continental bakery and café. It wasn't called a café but a coffee-lounge; there were only half a dozen tables, usually occupied by elderly refugees who couldn't do without their afternoon coffee and cake. Nominally, Netta had an assistant, but none of them was reliable – 'Bone-lazy,' she called them – so that often she had to be both sales-lady and waitress. She seemed to like it, moving around the place with verve, and always with a personal word for her clientele. It was only a short walk from the Hampstead flat, so Lilo and I often dropped in and stayed for quite a while, with me eating more chocolate eclairs than I was normally allowed. There was usually at least one, and sometimes more, elderly gentlemen who seemed to be there as much to enjoy Netta's presence as the refreshments she served them. Their eyes followed her as she flew around the coffee-lounge, and the moment she approached their table they were ready with some gallant quip. If one of them tried to hold on to her hand longer than necessary while she was handing him his change, she good-naturedly let him, while giving us a wink. Lilo watched her in true admiration – the way she handled the business and the customers – and when we went home, she described the scene to Mrs Lipchik, saying, 'Netta is so wonderful.' She also praised her to Max, but he didn't like to hear about it at all: 'What's wonderful about being a waitress? And just around the corner to us. What an embarrassment.' Lilo reared up as if it were she who had been insulted. 'Oh, I didn't know you were so *grand*,' she said and swept out of the room, very grand herself.

One day Max surprised me by inviting me for a walk. 'Would you like to, little one?' he said with a smile that was as unnatural as the tone in which he spoke. I looked around at Lilo, but she had to nod several times and even frown at me a bit before I went reluctantly to put on my coat. Max continued to smile in a glassy way, but once out in the street, he forgot about me. He strode along, sunk in thought, with steps too large for me; when he realized I was lagging behind, he stopped to wait for me, but impatiently as though in a hurry to get to where we were going. Netta was at the counter, and when she saw us, she went right on chatting with her customer, her hands busy inserting a dozen pastries into their cardboard box. There was no table vacant, and we had to wait; Max's face had gone very red, but his head was raised loftily and he held me by the hand in an iron grip. Although I was his excuse for being there, when we were seated and Netta came for our order, he turned to me as if he didn't see me, asking: 'What do you want?' 'I know what *she* wants,' Netta said, 'but what do *you* want?' 'Netta, Netta,' he implored, his eyes downcast, in shame and pain.

And that was all he said, the entire time we were there: 'Netta, Netta.' He didn't address a word to me, and of course I didn't expect him to, he never did, and anyway I was there to eat my chocolate eclairs. He was like the other elderly gentlemen who came there and followed Netta with their eyes. Only with this difference, that she approached our table quite often – as often as she could – and lingered there to do something unnecessary, like exchanging the position of sugar bowl and milk jug. And we sat on, though there were others waiting for our table and glaring at us, so that Max felt constrained to order more pastry for me. He also tried to order another coffee for himself, but Netta said, 'Yes, and the indigestion?' for no one knew better than she what too much coffee did to him. Although totally engrossed in licking up the cream from my pastry, I was aware of the tension emanating from my grandfather. This became unbearable when Netta approached our table; and when she touched or maybe just accidentally brushed against him, he moaned: 'Netta, Netta.' Once she flicked at something on his shoulder – 'For heaven's sake, doesn't anybody ever take a clothes brush to you?' In stricken silence, he pointed at my plate, which was empty again; I looked up hopefully, but Netta said, 'I'm not having this child spoil her stomach, just to please you.' However, she brought each of us a glass of water, and ignoring the waiting customers pointing restively at our table, she still didn't give us our bill.

Over the following period of time – was it weeks, months, or even years? – I often accompanied Max on visits to the coffee-lounge. But although we were now steady companions, he never became anything other for me than the remote, gloomy figure he had always been. Holding me by the hand so that I wouldn't lag behind, he communed only with himself – shaking his head, uttering a half-stifled exclamation; and when we got to Netta's place of work, he concentrated entirely on her, vibrating to each movement as she passed, now close to, now far from, our table. And there was another burden on his spirit, of which I heard him complain to Lilo: 'But don't you understand! They're sitting there looking at her as if she were – oh my God in heaven – a—' 'The child,' warned Lilo. Who was there sitting looking at her? Next time in the coffee-lounge, I followed his burning eyes and saw what he saw: it was only another elderly gentleman like himself, dressed as he was very correctly, with spats for the cold weather. One of them I knew – it was Dr Erdmund from Dortmund, retired and in the habit of taking his afternoon coffee there. Sometimes he stopped at our table, to pinch my cheek and address a word to Max, very respectfully as was befitting with a famous author. Max never answered or even looked at him, and it was not only his hands but his whole body that seemed to clench up into a fist. And afterward he would mutter to Netta, darkly, awesomely – except that she was not awed, she tossed her head and moved around on her duties with even greater verve.

My days in the Hampstead flat were no longer as light-hearted as they had been. This was because of the change in my grandmother – *she* was no longer light-hearted: as with Max, there was a burden on her spirit, and in her case, *he* was the burden. When he was in his study, oppressive waves seemed to seep from under the door, so that, wanting to get as far away from him as possible, I gave up playing anywhere except in Lilo's sitting room at the other end of the flat. I also refused to accompany him to the coffee-lounge: since Netta regularly denied me my third round of pastries and we just sat on and on with nothing but glasses of water in front of us, I preferred to stay home with my grandmother. The first time I refused him he looked in such anguish at Lilo that she persuaded me to change my mind; but after that even she could no longer coax me – he of course never tried: it was not in his nature to coax anyone, he only knew to stand stricken till the other person's heart would melt of its own accord. But mine never melted toward him, not even when I watched him from the window – Lilo stood behind me, her hand on my shoulder – as he made his way with heavy steps toward the coffee-lounge, his proud head sunk low.

Ever since I had known them, my grandparents had slept in separate bedrooms. Max's was next to his study and Lilo's, which I shared when I stayed with them, adjoined her sitting room. But he had always come to say goodnight and stayed so long that I was usually asleep before he left. I had no interest in their conversation, which in any case was interspersed with long silences. These had once been soothing enough for me to fall asleep, with clear streams winding through the meadows of my dreams. But now all that changed, and though he still came to our room in his night-shirt and sat on the edge of the bed, there was a different silence between them; and when she took his hand, she did not tickle it as she used to but grasped it tight, either to comfort or hold on to him. Now I could not fall asleep, though I pretended to, while listening for anything they might say. This was often about Netta and her job – 'She says she can't afford to give it up,' Max told Lilo. 'She says she has no money.' 'But that's ridiculous,' Lilo said, to which he replied, 'Money is never ridiculous to those who don't have it.' 'But *we* have it,' Lilo said. 'Don't we? Enough for three?' 'I don't know,' he moaned, in despair. 'You know I know nothing about money.'

'Listen,' Netta said to Lilo. 'If you offered me a million pounds, I wouldn't do it.'

Lilo and I had come to visit Netta in the St John's Wood flat. It was not until I saw her sitting side by side with Netta that I noticed how much my grandmother had changed. She had lately had to have many of her own teeth extracted and the new ones hurt her, so that she was mostly without them; and she continued to wear her beloved Kashmir shawl, though the fabric had split with age in several places. I'm sorry to say that she now looked not so much like a gypsy but like some old beggar woman – especially in comparison with Netta, who was in a silk blouse and tight velvet pants, her nails and hair both red. And it wasn't only Lilo's appearance: she seemed really to be begging for something that she wanted very much from Netta; and though Netta kept refusing her, it wasn't Lilo but Netta herself who burst into tears – loud sobs interspersed with broken sentences that made Lilo say, 'Careful: the child.'

But I was busy exploring the flat, which had changed. It seemed somehow to have filled out, or rounded its contours, an impression that may have been due to additional items of furniture. Besides the tubular chairs Netta had brought from Germany, there were now low round upholstered little armchairs that people could actually sit in. And apparently people *had* been sitting in them; and they had stubbed out their cigarettes in the ashtrays that were scattered around on new little tables, and these also held glasses out of which guests had drunk wine. When I went into the kitchen and opened the refrigerator – which had always been depressingly empty – I found it stuffed with food like potato salad and roast chickens. There was also a tray of delicious little canapes, which I took back into the living room. 'Can I have one?' I asked, but just then Netta was shouting, 'A life! A whole lifetime I've given him!' so I had to say it again. 'Of course you can, my darling,' Netta said, 'you can have anything from me you want—' 'Oh thank you, Netta,' I said and retreated politely back into the kitchen, so that they could say whatever they wanted without having to warn each other of my presence. Anyway, Netta was shouting loudly enough to be heard throughout the flat – 'That's what I'm here for, to give, always to give, but now I tell you it's my turn to take!'

Lilo's voice was low, conciliatory, which only made Netta's rise more: 'Yes, I have my friends, that's not a crime I hope,

to try and get a little bit of a life going of my own?' And again
Lilo murmured, mild, protesting, and again Netta cried out,
'So who asked him to come and sit there and disturb me in
my work? He's welcome to come here to my home, I'd be glad
to entertain him in my own place for a change, because I've
had enough, up to here enough, of the dog's life he's made
me lead in his.'

Whereas Netta's flat was now comfortable and lively, the
Hampstead flat had changed in the opposite direction. It was
as if not Lilo and Max were living there but the original
Edwardian families for whom this ponderous structure had
been built. It had become gloomy and oppressive – although
the one person who had had this effect on me was usually
absent. I no longer had to fear that Max's forbidding figure
would appear in the door of his study, for he was now mostly
with Netta, and not only in the coffee-lounge. Now I feared –
not Lilo (I never feared *her*) but *for* Lilo: that, however cute
I tried to be for her sake, I could hardly make her smile. We
still went on our usual outings, no longer because she enjoyed
them but because she thought I would: but how could I, when
she didn't? Mrs Lipchik heaved heavy sighs as she cleaned,
and while she and Lilo still had their long coffee sessions in
the kitchen, these were no longer full of German jokes but
of secrets, problems. It was even worse when Max was there
with us: Mrs Lipchik's sighs were nothing compared with his,
especially those he uttered like groans when he came to Lilo's
bedroom at night. Sitting as before on the side of her bed,
with me curled up beside her, he spoke to her in whispers:
only to get up and pace around and then return and seize
her hands and implore: 'What shall I do? What *shall* I do?'
And she withdrew her hands and didn't answer him.

My dreams ceased to feature pellucid streams in meadows;
instead – if they were dreams – they resounded with the echo
of his voice, through which the word fate struck repeatedly
like hammer blows. Fate! It was the great theme of his later
books. Here Fate is the main character and human beings are
depicted as struggling helplessly in the grip of its iron claw. But

although he witnessed the upheaval of his whole continent and the destruction of his generation, he goes beyond the epoch in which he happened to be living to embrace the entire epoch of Man: Man in the abstract, from birth to death. And this is what astonished him and made him suffer – the suffering of Man, and all he has to endure in the course of a lifetime of inevitable decline; and also the swiftness of that decline, the inexorable swiftness with which a young man becomes an old one. It is no doubt a great theme, but how could I take it seriously when I identified its author with my grandfather whom I saw suffer because I made a noise playing outside his study door, or because his girl friend flirted with her dentist. In his last book there is a sort of dance of death in a landscape of night and barren rock where men and women join hands and revolve in a circle, their faces raised to the moon so that its craters appear to be reflected in the hollow sockets of their eyes. This might for others be a powerful metaphor for the macabre dance of our lives; but for me it is only a reminder of a birthday party we attended.

It was Max's birthday – his last, as it turned out – and, like all our celebrations during this year, the party was held in Netta's flat. For by then Max was spending all his days in St John's Wood – even his desk had been moved there – though he still showed up in the Hampstead flat for the sort of nocturnal visits I have described. Netta also came quite often, not with him but alone. I witnessed several scenes between her and my grandmother, only now it was always Netta who was pleading while Lilo remained stubborn and silent. This made Netta desperate and she stopped pleading and was angry, or pretended to be: 'My God, think of me all these years, in *your* house, and putting up with it – yes, gladly! Laughing and pretending to be happy, so that everyone could be happy! And you can't come even once, for *one* afternoon, for his sake?' For a long time my grandmother remained impervious, so that Netta might as well have been addressing someone blind and deaf. But gradually, over the years – for no particular reason, or perhaps because it didn't matter any longer, or that other things mattered more – anyway, we did go to Netta's flat, to her more important parties like when it was her birthday, or Max's, or even Lilo's: everything was celebrated there.

It was always the same guests who had been invited, and they were all Netta's friends, from the social circle she had formed around herself. They included people we vaguely knew, like Dr Erdmund from Dortmund and some of the other elderly gentlemen whom I remembered from the coffee-lounge. They were mostly German refugees who, like Max and Lilo and Netta, had had their youthful heyday during the time of the Weimar Republic. In fact, they might have been the embodiment of the big painting in Netta's flat of the German café scene, with geometrically shaped faces crowding each other around a café table. Now those triangles and cones had been realigned into the masks of old age, and the expression of nervous restlessness had frozen into the smile of the tenacious survivor. Their clothes were elegant – Netta insisted on glamorous attire for her parties – and they still held a wine-glass in one hand and a cigarette in the other, some with a long silver or ivory holder; and they were still animated by a kind of frenetic energy, a consumptive eagerness. There was dancing too – Netta rolled up her bear-rug and put on some of her old dance-records, and when the music started, she stretched herself up by her clenched arms and said, 'Oh my God,' and laughed at whatever it was that she remembered. They were all pretty good dancers – mostly fox-trots, with some very intricate footwork. Netta's favorite was the tango, and it suited her – inside her tight silk metallic dress she made movements as sinuous as those of a young siren; and the expression on her face no doubt reflected the sensations in her heart, which were those of her siren years. Her partners did their best to keep up with her, pretending they were not out of breath; but she discarded them one by one when they began to fail, and imperiously snatched up a fresh old gentleman.

The only person who refused her was Max: he would not dance, he could not, never had done, which was why Lilo had given it up too, long ago. So the two of them were always onlookers – except on that last birthday party when everyone had drunk a lot of champagne and excitement burned through the air like holes made by a forgotten cigarette. In fact, Netta was scattering dangerous sparks from the cigarette held between her fingers; and her eyes too sent out glints of fire and so did her red hair and her metallic dress. Discarding her last breathless partner, she turned to Max: he shook his head, he smiled, no, he would not. But for once she insisted and she grasped his hand and pulled him up; and at last, to please her, he let himself be dragged on to the dance floor and tried to imitate her steps. But he could not, and to help him, she pressed herself as close to him as possible to lead him and make his hips rotate along with hers. But still he stumbled and could not; at first he laughed at his own ineptitude, but when others too began to laugh, he tried to extricate himself from Netta's close embrace. She would not let him go, and perhaps to drown his angry words, she called to someone to turn up the record; and then, when it was really loud, she called out, 'Come on, everybody, what are you waiting for – New Year?' and soon they were all jigging up and down, with Max and Netta in their center. The more he struggled the tighter she held on to him, so that he appeared to be entangled in the embrace of an octopus or some other creature with long tentacles. His situation made them all laugh – even I did, till I saw how Lilo had hidden her face in her hands, and not because she was laughing. Suddenly she snatched at me in the same way as Netta had done to Max and made me get up with her. Although neither of us knew how, we tried to join the dance – and that made all of them turn from Max and look and laugh at us, at grandmother and granddaughter hopping and slipping on the polished floor. Although Lilo was getting out of breath, we stuck it out till the music stopped, and then she and I thanked Netta for the party and went home.

If it were not for the famous *danse macabre* in Max's last book, I might have forgotten all about that birthday party. I prefer to remember our walk home from it, Lilo's and mine, through empty streets on a cool autumn night. There was the smell of fallen leaves, and layers of clouds shifted and floated across the sky; the moon was dim, so that even when it came sliding out from between these veils, it didn't light up anything. Nevertheless, it seemed to me that it did illumine my grandmother's face when she raised it to try and identify some of the stars for me. She pointed at what she said was the Great Bear – or was it the Plough – I think she wasn't sure, and anyway her eyesight was not good enough to see that far. I don't know why I expected her to look unhappy – after all, we had just left a party with music and champagne and special birthday cake ordered from Netta's bakery; but anyway she didn't, not at all, on the contrary her face appeared as radiant as was possible by the light of that dim moon.

## Now you can order superb titles directly from Abacus

| | | |
|---|---|---|
| ☐ Every Man For Himself | Beryl Bainbridge | £6.99 |
| ☐ The Smell of Apples | Mark Behr | £6.99 |
| ☐ Breath, Eyes, Memory | Edwidge Danticat | £6.99 |
| ☐ Kalimantaan | C.S. Godshalk | £7.99 |
| ☐ The Page Turner | David Leavitt | £6.99 |

Please allow for postage and packing: **Free UK delivery**.
Europe; add 25% of retail price; Rest of World; 45% of retail price.

To order any of the above or any other Abacus titles, please call our credit card orderline or fill in this coupon and send/fax it to:

**Abacus, 250 Western Avenue, London, W3 6XZ, UK.**
Fax 0181 324 5678    Telephone 0181 324 5517

☐ I enclose a UK bank cheque made payable to Abacus for £...........

☐ Please charge £........... to my Access, Visa, Delta, Switch Card No.

☐☐☐☐☐☐☐☐☐☐☐☐☐☐☐☐

Expiry date ☐☐☐☐   Switch Issue No. ☐☐

Name (Block Letters please) _____

Address _____

_____

_____

Post/zip code: _____   Telephone _____

Signature _____

Please allow 28 days for delivery within the UK. Offer subject to price and availability.
Please do not send any further mailings from companies carefully selected by Abacus  ☐